TELESĀ

The Covenant Keeper

When Water Burns

The Bone Bearer

I am Daniel Tahi

TELESĀ WORLD

Ocean's Kiss

Fire's Caress

Published by OneTree House Ltd, New Zealand, 2021

© Lani Wendt Young, 2021

978-0-9951175-0-1

All rights reserved. No part of this publication may be reproduced, stored in a retrieval system or transmitted in any form or by any means, electronic, mechanical, photocopying, recording or otherwise, without the prior permission of the publisher.

All characters and events in this publication, other than those clearly in the public domain, are fictitious and any resemblance to real persons, living or dead, is purely coincidental.

Editor: Pip Desmond

Printed: Your Books, Wellington

10 9 8 7 6 5 4 3 2 1   1 2 3 / 2

TELESĀ

Fire's Caress

A TELESĀ WORLD NOVEL

LANI WENDT YOUNG

OneTree HOUSE

TELESA

Fire's Caress

A TELESĀ WORLD NOVEL

LANI WENDT YOUNG

CHAPTER ONE

Marc Gold was hiking up a mountain on an island in the Pacific. The heat was a blanket of humidity choking him as he pushed a pathway through the thick greenery, stopping every so often to check his GPS. His clothes were soaked through with sweat. If it weren't for the constant hum of mosquitoes he would have stripped off his shirt a long time ago. He paused to drink from the canteen in his backpack. The tepid water did nothing for his thirst but he gulped it down anyway. Then he turned to look back over the vast expanse of land spread out behind him.

Magnificent.

At least the view was worth the hike.

The guide he'd hired had refused to accompany him past the last ridge, muttering some garbled story about curses and spirits. But it took a lot more than superstition to stop Marc, and he'd brushed aside the vehement warnings and left the man behind. Three hours later Marc had succeeded in covering most of the territory set out in the land description, making note of all the significant landmarks and features that could be utilised in the final resort design.

The deal to lease the mountain had finally been signed a week ago and as Marc gazed across forest and hills, he was exhilarated. The plans were all drawn up and work on the project could start. In twelve months the resort would be nearly ready to open for business – the first in the Gold Resort global chain that would be entirely his brainchild from initial concept to finish. Designed for a post-pandemic world, it would have the highest level of biohazard security anywhere. It would start with its own airstrip so his clients could come in on their private jets, before passing through state-of-the-art body scanners. His team of scientists were constantly working on identifying the latest mutations of the virus and incorporating their markers into his screening sensors. Not even an asymptomatic carrier would be able to evade them.

The compound would be sealed tighter than any fortress, with a twelve-foot-high perimeter wall skirted with heat sensors. A five-mile radius of grass enclosure would remove any risk of airborne agents ever reaching his clientele. And nobody would get in without clearance. All staff would be hired in the US, cleared for all known viruses and then contracted to live onsite for twelve-month rotations. Guaranteeing not only virus-free safety but also unprecedented privacy for his clientele. The project would be its own self-contained town with stores, restaurants, high ball casinos, a lake and even beachfront property. Where else in the world could a person go on vacation with absolute peace of mind in this new age of Covid?

And yes, it would be beautiful, with nature on offer for those who sought it. Clients could have luxurious penthouses in the city block, but also spend weekends feeling at one with nature. He could see it now. The tree-house villas, winding pathways, canopied walkways high up in the massive trees, and conference rooms that hugged the cliffside, looking out over the spectacular ocean far below. There would be birdwatching bungalows, white-water rafting on the busy river he'd mapped, fishing on the lake, and mountain-bike trails for both cyclists and extreme-sport runners.

There was still some opposition to his project, from a local conservation group that was making noise about the usual environmental rubbish mixed in with chatter about preserving historical archaeological sites. They had protestors outside his town office and outside the project gate, but Marc wasn't worried. They were a minor nuisance only. He had dealt with their kind in other countries and knew their enthusiasm would fizzle out. Some would be successfully bought off and the remaining few wouldn't have any money to fund their passion. Usually a well-placed donation to local law enforcement was enough to get any lingering opposition stamped out. So no, Marc wasn't worried.

He was smiling at the vision of his project as he checked his watch. He would need to hurry if he wanted to get back to town before dark.

Marc was focused on the trail and retracing his footsteps so he almost didn't hear the woman's voice. He ignored it at first, mistaking it for a distant bird's cry. But then it came again, wafting and winding through the trees, curling around him like a soft, sensuous embrace.

He stopped in his descent, paused, listened.

It came again. The unmistakable sound of laughter. Lilting, light and playful.

"Hello?" he called out. "Is someone there?"

Abrupt silence. Even the forest creatures seemed to still and there was a halt to the rustling of the afternoon breeze through the multilayered greenery. He shook his head. Must have been a mistake. Once more, just to be certain, he raised his voice and called, "Hello?"

This time there was an answer. The clear, vibrant tones of a woman's voice, strong and assured. "Hello?"

There was a crackling of twigs and branches as someone made their way through the undergrowth. They were coming towards him. For one ridiculous moment, Marc felt a shiver of apprehension down his spine. Then just as quickly, he shook it off. There were no predators in Samoa – nothing beyond centipedes and the odd stray mongrel dog. That was a key factor in his choosing to situate the resort here. He had nothing to fear.

He gave himself a mental shake and laughed under his breath. Too much listening to the natives' rubbish about demons! He squared his shoulders and made his way towards the approaching sound.

He'd only taken two steps when a woman appeared out of the trees about ten metres ahead of him. Even at that distance, her beauty took his breath away. Long, lustrous hair framed her face and fell to her waist in rippling waves, sunlight catching on strands of light amid the dark brown. There was a flower tucked behind one ear, a deep wine-red hibiscus mirrored in the red of her lips. She wore a magnificent necklace, made of what looked to be boar tusks, jutting bold points of gleaming white, and a simple shift dress cut short. It skimmed her thighs, revealing the traditional tattoo he'd seen on other women. None wore it as proudly or as boldly as she did, though. But it was her eyes that caught him and held him captive. Deep pools of dark water, they seemed to slice through his very soul. He was drowning, swirling in a chaotic rush of feeling – husky desire, impending doom, the bite of a sweet mango, the sinuous curl of a centipede creeping up his spine, a hazy cloud of barbed pleasure.

As he stared, unable to look away, she cocked her head to one side as if considering him. Then she smiled, a half-smile that was both knowing and curious all at once. She raised one hand and beckoned to him. "Come!" she said and this time the smile she offered him was dazzling in its welcome. His breath caught in his chest and his knees seemed to liquefy.

She was the most beautiful – and fearsome – thing he'd ever seen.

His every sense screamed to him to turn and run. To shout for help. To refuse her. Why couldn't he move? He steeled his resolve, cut through the stupor that seemed to have cemented him in place, shook his head. No. Took a step backwards.

Must get outta here.

She raised a single eyebrow. Surprised. A single flick of her fingers, and wind from nowhere yet everywhere danced through the trees, threaded through her hair, tugged playfully at her shift dress and then continued towards Marc, enfolding him in its sinuous, perfumed embrace.

The perfume was strong, almost overpoweringly so. He was familiar with the golden-green blossoms of the ylang-ylang tree that many of the locals used to scent their coconut body oils. But it was mingled with something else now. A much deeper, thick aroma. It drenched him, suffused his being, seeped inside the fabric of his clothing, mingled with the beads of sweat that trickled down his back. It was heady and intoxicating. It seemed that the very pores of his skin opened up to soak it in, luxuriate in it. He breathed it in deeply, gloried in its pungent richness, exulted in all its daggered promise. The wind spoke of her. The very air spoke of her. Who was he to refuse?

Marc was lost.

He obeyed, walked towards her slowly and with each step closer, his pulse quickened and the excitement – threaded through with fear – intensified. He drew level with her and his gaze feasted on her hungrily. Up close, her beauty was even more arresting. She was tall, almost his height at six foot two, so she did not need to angle her head to look into his eyes. There was nothing sparse about her. Wild tangle of hair, lush red lips, heavy black lashes, richly oiled brown skin, a thick armband of deep-purple leaves tied in a knot. Generous curves barely contained by the cream shift. Strong muscled thighs stamped with bold black patterns. And everywhere the layered fragrance of mystery and allure.

"What is your name?" she asked in that husky voice redolent of coconut rum and smoke-filled rooms.

From far away, he heard himself answer.

His answer seemed to please her. "Marc? I have waited a long time for you to come."

It shouldn't have made sense but in that moment – lost in the nearness of her, the cloying fragrance of her – it made perfect sense. Of course. She'd been waiting for him. Just as he had been searching and waiting for her.

He wanted to taste her. Touch her. Hold her. It seemed his entire life had been holding its breath, waiting, anticipating this very moment. He reached for her and it was as if he moved and breathed in a river of rich, sweetened coconut cream, everything seemed to be liquid, his fingers dragging through a dazed haze. He cupped her face in his hands and the touch of her skin against his sent a jolt of lightning ricocheting through him. Then slowly, slowly, still swimming through syrup and sunshine, he kissed her. The barest, faintest meeting of lips. Marc kissed this enigmatic woman of the forest and drowned in the luxuriant delight of her. She tasted of the sweetest spiced liqueur, intoxicating.

Marc — billionaire hotel magnate, accustomed to being the master of all he surveyed — was enthralled. He — the man who had everything — knew in that moment he had nothing, was nothing. He was merely an empty shell of questions and desolate space, and she held the answers, the perfect key to all that was missing within him.

He thought he would die if he could not have her. He would do whatever she asked, give whatever she requested, obey her every command, just to be with her. When he considered leaving her, a storm of panic raged inside him and anxiety was an army of fire ants marching across his skin.

Marc sank to his knees before her, oblivious to the thorns and sharp stones at his feet. Carefully, hesitantly, he slid his arms around her abundant hips, barely containing his excitement at her closeness, at being able to hold her, that she permitted this embrace. This most arcane embodiment of all that was woman. He pressed his face against the time-softened siapo fabric of her skirt and breathed in deeply. Green earth, black soil, vivid scarlet berries of the palm tree, musky tang of the flying fox — all overlaid with aromatic sandalwood. He felt like weeping at the joy of it, the pulsing, throbbing promise of life.

He looked up at her and sunlight framed her, danced on her supple curves and the fire of her eyes. She lightly ran her fingers through his gold-blond hair, a sound of approval deep and low in her throat.

"I think I've searched for you my whole life," he said. Ridiculous words that made total sense in that heady moment.

She smiled. Pleased. Took his face in her hands, raised him up to stand and linked her fingers through his. "Come with me!" she said. "I have much to show you. We will start with my river."

Marc would have walked through fire and followed her to the ends of the earth. He was an ensorcelled man as he followed the woman of the forest like an obedient child. They walked hand in hand towards the sound of running water and the gleam of wet, black rocks glistening through the trees.

CHAPTER TWO

When Marc Gold failed to return from his hike, his guide Timona shook his head knowingly. "O le aitu," he said to his wife when he got home that night. "I warned him he was entering the land of the Teinc Sā but he didn't listen."

Makerita shushed him and covered their daughter's ears with her hands. "Don't speak of her! Not here. Not around the children."

Timona nodded soberly. Their daughter was beautiful. Even at only eleven years old, people already remarked on her light-brown hair and skin the colour of a young coconut – a softer-paler-brown than that of her parents. They made sure to always keep her close to them, slapping her whenever she laughed too loudly or played too boisterously with the other children in the village. It would not do for her to attract the attention of the aitu. To provoke her jealousy.

Makerita went to perform her nightly ritual of covering the

mirrors in their house, shrouding them with sheets, while Timona called the police to report the American missing.

"What did they say?" Makerita asked in a whisper so as not to wake the children.

"It's too dark for a search. They will go out tomorrow to look for him."

"Let's hope he pleases her," said Makerita. "That's the only way he will be found again."

The search commenced early the next day. The American was an important man and it would not do for such a rich and powerful foreigner to go missing in the Samoa mountains. The police sent twenty officers out into the hills, and other volunteers joined in. Timona pointed out where he'd last seen the man and the surrounding area was thoroughly searched. Nothing. Several of the volunteers who knew Timona reprimanded him for taking the American to the forbidden lands.

"I told him not to go there," he insisted. "The man was proud. He didn't listen."

"What did he look like?" they asked.

"A big, tall man. Very white. His eyes were blue-grey, like the sky."

The others nodded knowingly. It was as they suspected. A palagi man wandering in the forest of the aitu was just asking for trouble. He would not be found until she released him, they whispered among themselves. And she would only release him if he pleased her.

Another night, another day and still nothing. It was as if Marc Gold had disappeared from the face of the earth.

After three days, the police chief decided he had better inform his overseas counterparts. It was time to raise a wider alarm and alert the American's family. He had put it off long enough.

But before he made that call, Marc Gold walked down off the mountainside. Rumpled, disoriented but otherwise unhurt. With great relief, the police chief went to the hospital to see him. To ensure the American was all right and would not be causing a fuss in the media about how terrible Samoa was.

The chief's name was Rex Stevens and he had been a policeman for thirty years. He'd seen more than his fair share of the bloody, cruel, sadistic and sad – yes, even a small island nation like Samoa had its evil and oppressed. So when he walked into the ward and disturbed a cluster of his police officers muttering darkly in the hall, he was unimpressed.

"What's going on here?" he barked at the nearest officer. "Where's the American? Sergeant Tofi?"

"He's in there, Sir," she replied. "The doctor is checking him over."

"Everything all right?" Chief Stevens asked.

Tofi hesitated, darted several sidelong glances at the others. "Yes, Chief. Sort of."

The chief could tell when his people had been spooked and he didn't like it. "What's that supposed to mean? Is he injured? What did he say? Where's he been for the last three days?"

The officer stared straight ahead. "Physically he seems to be fine. It's just that – well, he has a certain smell ..." Her voice trailed away at the sight of the chief's incredulous expression.

"The man smells?!" He looked around at the circle of officers with disgust. "The man was wandering in the bush for three days. Of course he smells."

The group did that thing again where they exchanged glances loaded with meaning. But it was Tofi who dared speak in the face of their chief's displeasure.

"Sir, that's not the kind of smell we're talking about." She lowered her voice. "Sandalwood and mosoo'i. He smells like ... you know, Teine Sā. Aitu."

Immediately two of the others shushed her quiet and shifted on their feet nervously. Another laughed. A quiet, shamefaced kind of sound.

Chief Stevens didn't know whether to laugh or rage. He looked around at the group, all officers with several years under their belts, some with peacekeeping experience in foreign war zones. He would never have guessed any of them to be superstitious. He gritted his teeth. "Your work here is done. Stop wasting your time and mine. Get out. Now!"

He didn't wait to watch them disperse. Just continued on to the cubicle and wrenched aside the curtain.

"Mr Gold?" he said to the man sitting on the side of the bed as a doctor took his blood pressure. He was younger than Stevens had expected, in his late twenties, maybe thirty? Blond, broad, densely muscular and toned with the physique of an athlete, he emanated a powerful vibe of confident control.

Football player in college? Still keeps in good shape. Stevens' automatic assessment stemmed from tired envy as he contemplated his own balding state and the extra twenty pounds he kept meaning to get rid of.

"Chief Stevens of the Samoa Police," he said with a businesslike air. "You had us worried there."

The man gave him a tired grin. "I didn't plan on getting lost in the mountains. Sure is good to be back in civilisation."

"Had twenty officers out there searching for you," said the chief. He wanted there to be no doubts cast on the efficiency of his department. "Had a lot of terrain to cover and we don't have a chopper so we had to do the best we could with the manpower we have."

"I appreciate it, Chief," said Marc. "I was thinking of a way to show my appreciation and you've just given me the answer. How'd you like a helicopter for your search and rescue team?"

Chief Stevens was taken aback. "Doc, did he hit his head out there in the bush?" he jokingly asked the doctor packing up her gear at the bedside.

"Not that we can tell," she smiled. Then to Marc, "Clean bill of health, Mr Gold. You're lucky. Getting lost in the Samoa wilderness is a lot less risky than say – going missing in the Himalayas. Or the Amazon jungle. Some bruising, a few scrapes, mild dehydration. Nothing serious. A good night's sleep and you'll be fine."

She ducked out of the room and Marc stood, came over to shake Steven's hand.

That's when it hit him. The distinct wood notes of spiced aroma — sandalwood. Asi manogi. The man was drenched in it. Chief Stevens felt a sudden chill in the heat of the afternoon. The hair on the back of his neck stood up and he had the irrational urge to run. For the first time in his many years in the force, his fingers literally itched for a gun as every alert system in his body screamed a warning.

Danger. Run. Hide.

He fought for control. Wrinkled his nose. "That's a strong perfume," he said lightly.

Marc looked discomfited. "Yeah, I need a shower. Bad."

"No, I mean that's sandalwood. Asi manogi we call it in Samoan. An unusual thing to be smelling on a man who's just walked out after a three-day disappearance in the bush." There was a warning hidden under the polite commentary, and Marc heard it. Bristled at it.

His grin faded and there was a flinty hardness in his eyes. "I was stumbling around out there in the bushes for quite a while. Probably pushed my way through some sandalwood trees. Makes sense I would reek of it."

"It would," agreed Chief Stevens, "if native sandalwood trees weren't extinct. They think the last one got chopped down back in 1989."

The words hung suspended in the tense air between them as the two men locked eyes.

Marc looked away first. An almost derisive laugh. "In that case, I really scored a jackpot when I bought that mountain. I could add a sandalwood forest to my portfolio. Now, if you'll excuse me, Chief, I want to get outta here. You heard the lovely doctor prescribe me a good night's sleep. Are we done?"

Stevens sidestepped the challenge in the American's voice. "Sure. Glad my team could be of assistance." But he couldn't resist asking a question. "What were you doing out there all that time?"

"What do you mean?" said the American.

The chief shrugged. "Just wondering what you got up to out there in the forest."

For the first time Marc's cool composure seemed to slip. There was a look of confusion in his eyes, and was that a hint of fear? "I'm not sure. It's all a bit hazy. How long was I gone for again?"

"Three days," replied the chief, on alert now because he could sense that something was not quite right.

Marc shook his head as if trying to clear it of cobwebs. "It seems so much longer." He swayed a little and the chief moved to steady him with a hand on his shoulder.

"Hey, you okay? I can get the doctor back in here."

But as quickly as it had come, the moment of vulnerability passed. Marc shook off the chief's hand and straightened, assuming again that same mask of easy assurance. "I'm fine."

Marc pulled back the curtain and then stopped, turned back. "Oh, and Chief? I meant it about the chopper. I have selfish reasons." A cold smile. "We break ground on the Gold Mountain Project this week. When it's done, there will be hundreds of elite guests, VIPs coming to Samoa to experience the adventure of a lifetime. I'll feel better knowing your team is fully equipped."

With that last rejoinder, Marc Gold walked out of the hospital. Chief Stevens watched him go and hoped he would never have to see the man again. But there was a sick pit in his stomach that told him otherwise.

Marc caught a cab back to his hotel where he showered and then collapsed into bed. Within minutes, he was fast asleep. He dreamed.

A glistening pool nestled in the trees dappled with sunlight. The shock of cold as he dived and surfaced. The sound of her laughter beside him in the water, the feel of her warmth as she pressed against him, all soft curves and ripe mystery. The nip of her teeth on his bottom lip as she kissed him, playful and dangerous. Diamond droplets on her skin as he fisted handfuls of her wiry hair, tugged her head back, laved the line of her throat with his tongue.

Lying on a bed of springy fern, bodies still wet from their swim, looking up at the generous wonders of her as she knelt above him. Gripping her hips firmly, anchoring her as she threw her head back to the sky and exulted.

The majestic night sky above them. Firelight dancing on the valleys and contours of her lush ripeness as she fed him taro, hot baked from the coals – dipped in miti, salted coconut cream.

"You need your strength," she whispered against his skin.

Waking with the dawn to her whisper, "Another day together." His rush of happiness at the realisation that the dream wasn't over. She hadn't left him. The days blurred into nights and the time passed. She told him he could call her Masina but he knew that wasn't really her name. She gave him very little of herself. Whenever he asked questions, she brushed them aside like a buzzing mosquito. With annoyance. If he persisted, she silenced him with a glare. The laughing, sensual woman disappeared and in her place was one who reeked of danger, a bone blade to the throat. He learned quickly not to provoke that side of her.

It was a hazy dream, filled with a swirling rush of images and emotions. The rush of heady fragrance that filled her house, a spiced aroma. Teeth sinking into the juicy white flesh of freshly caught and cooked pigeon, the slippery feel of a river eel – its velvet-black skin in his hands, the pungent odour of fruit bat fat from its feasting on orange papaya. The guttural chant of a long-ago age, the beat of a wood drum, the slap of paddles in the water as an ancient vessel knifed through it.

Lying with her, tangled legs and arms, unsure where one ended and the other began. Tracing the markings of her malu, curious and questioning. Listening to her tell the story of her sisters Taema and Tilafaiga, bringers of the sacred art of tattooing. Her scathing indictment of the contemporary practice. "Men have stolen it from us. As they try to take everything from Fanua, she who gives them life." The sky darkening overhead as she bristled and raged so much that a wild wind whipped the trees around the house into a frenzy and he felt the knife-edge of fear as she unsheathed the fierceness within. Then just as quickly, she laughed, brushing aside such concerns as unimportant. "Right here, right now, this is all that matters," she purred as her hands moved to caress him.

He met her sisters. Some of them, anyway. They appeared from the tree shadows when he least expected them. Tall, majestic women with tattooed skin and clothed in siapo. Some greeted him with smiles and laughter, easy friendliness. They asked his name, shared their food with him, told him stories of their ancestors. Others ignored him. As if he were a pet that belonged to Masina, harmless but a nuisance to be endured. One wore feathers, but when he stole another look, he realised it wasn't a cloak. The feathers were hers. She caught his gaze and her dark eyes flashed a warning as she snapped her teeth at him and hissed. He didn't look at her again.

Later as he lay with Masina under the stars, she told him to keep his distance from the feathered one. "My sister Lefaga is a hunter of men," she said. "She brings retribution. She sees much darkness and it makes her hungry. My sisters know you are mine, but it's best not to test Lefaga's will." Marc knew he should have been worried about sisters who are hunters of men, but instead he felt light with the exhilaration of knowing that Masina had claimed him as hers.

Walking with her through green vines and the hushed call of birds, standing back in wonder as she revealed an opening in what seemed at first to be a cluster of rocks in the ground. An invitation. "Come, see our home." She took him down into caves. Through winding passages, rock walls marked with intricate patterns, their path lit by luminescent bulbs. "A substance found deep in the earth," she explained. "It gives light where there is none. And without need of any power source."

They came to a vast cavern, with walls that reached endlessly upwards. Numerous passages led to other places, Marc knew not where.

"Our ancestors first found refuge here millennia ago. It was used during times of great storms. They stored supplies here and when danger threatened, our people would take to the mountains and stay here until it passed. The Teine Sā were revered then, not feared. Not only were we the healers, we were also the creators and scientists." She took him through another passageway that opened out into a chamber that Marc could only describe as some kind of workshop. Or laboratory. The walls were covered in design drawings carved into the stone. Everything from irrigation systems to defence machines. Many of them Marc couldn't understand.

"This is amazing," he said as he studied the drawings.

"Yes," said Masina. "The people no longer follow us. But here we retain the records of our collective knowledge. Perhaps one day, they will again turn to Fanua and her guardians. For wisdom. For survival. Before it's too late." There was a well of dark sadness in her eyes, the first time she had revealed this much vulnerability in front of him, and Marc almost reached out to touch her. Comfort her? Soothe her? But the moment passed quickly and they continued on their tour of the complex.

"Here we have a library, if you will, of our ancestral knowledge." And into another vast cavern that opened up to the sky. Unlike the others, it was filled with trees, a mini-forest of greenery and colourful flowers. "This holds the bones of our ancestors. My grandmother and many of my sisters are buried here. Their spirits sometimes visit us in this space. It is sacred." She turned to Marc. "The project you are building, it will put all of this at risk. I have seen your plans. You will flood this valley for your lake. The waters will cover these caves. I wanted to show you personally so you could understand what will be lost if you go ahead."

Marc nodded. "I understand. I could have my people change the design plans somewhat. We could set aside this area so it's not included."

There was the hint of fire in her face. "Or you could stop your building completely. Go back to where you came from and leave our land in peace. Surely you could find somewhere in your own country to build a sanctuary from the disease that your kind keeps spreading. For you to carry out your project would be to desecrate the aitu. I'm asking you to reconsider. Be a friend to Fanua."

In that moment, he saw what it cost her to ask him. Fiery pride warred with pleading in her eyes. It pained him to see her in distress. He would do anything, give anything to ease her worry.

Marc woke to the cool, dark room, covered in sweat in spite of the airconditioning. There was a cloying perfume in the air. Choking him. Nauseating him.

He cursed. Would it never leave him? He stumbled from the bed, disoriented, to get water from the bathroom. Only then, as he confronted his reflection in the harsh artificial lighting, did his dream come back to him. A cold realisation stabbed him like a knife to the heart. He remembered he had said yes to the woman. He had told her he would stop all work on the project and gift the land to a conservation trust. Why would he have said such a thing? Even in a dream? Rational thought screamed at him.

Surely his lust-hazed dream couldn't have happened. She couldn't be real. He would never have made such a promise to anyone. Not even in a dream.

He tried to remember where he'd been for the last three days – and failed. There was only a hazy cloud in his head whenever he fought to recall what he'd done, who he'd been with. He felt a growing unease inside him, a rising panic. He needed answers. Marc threw on some clothes, called for a car and went to see Timona. The man who, in his opinion, had been a terrible guide, who had let him wander the mountain alone.

Timona and his wife weren't happy when the American showed up on their doorstep. Makerita chased the children out of the house, telling them to go and play at the far reaches of the banana patch.

"It's good to see you back safe, Mr Gold," Timona said, his eyes searching for any sign of her.

"When you told me not to hike any further," said Marc, "you said something about Tei-ne Sa?" He stumbled over the unfamiliar word. "What did you mean?"

The couple exchanged glances and then the wife nodded. Tell him. Then he will leave our house and we can be done with this business.

Timona talked. Of spirit women. Guardians of forest, ocean and freshwater rivers and pools. Beautiful women who wielded supernatural powers. They were vengeful and capricious. Quick to take offence and mete out their version of justice. Their weakness? Fair-skinned men come from afar. They took you and you were only ever seen again if you pleased them.

Marc listened with incredulity. Foolish imaginings and primitive folk tales! But more than disgust at Timona's ridiculous stories, he was angry. At the knowing sideways glances the couple gave him. Their supercilious grins. These ignorant natives really believed he had been taken hostage by some kind of twisted woman of the forest? And worse, that he had been her submissive plaything?

Don't these fools know who I am?!

By the time Marc left Timona's home, he was gripped in a tense rage and he had one purpose only. He made some phone calls and within the hour, heavy-duty trucks and bulldozers were brutally carving their way up the mountain. It was easy enough to find the pool and the rippling river that fed it. He couldn't remember how to find the entrance to the caves but it didn't matter. He would take this from her first.

Marc's orders were clear and the men obeyed. He ignored their dark muttering as they cast furtive looks around them into the forest. Their petty superstitions meant nothing to him. Money talks and makes things happen. And Marc had an endless amount of it.

They worked all day, clearing forest and carving up the earth. Finally, the last truck deposited its load of soil and rock, and the pool was completely filled in. All that remained was a heaped pile of dirt, surrounded by butchered carcasses of the forest. Only then did Marc feel some semblance of peace. Only then did his pulsating anger abate somewhat.

"Clear out!" he ordered.

Within minutes, only he was left in the fast-approaching twilight. He surveyed the scene and laughed. Called out, "Are you there? Come on out!"

How do you like me now, bitch?

There was no play of water rippling over gleaming black rocks, no birdcall, not even the rustle of a breeze. Whatever remained of the spirit woman was well and truly gone. Marc Gold was happy as he drove back to his hotel. He'd exorcised his demons, rid himself of any lingering taste of her, destroyed her hiding place. He was free of her. She would haunt his dreams no more. It was over.

It was on the quiet side of midnight when Marc jerked awake to the sudden knowledge that he was not alone in the room. His eyes flew open and he tried to sit up, but something had him pinned to the bed. The achingly familiar fragrance curled around him.

"What?" He could see no ropes or chains but still something had him restrained. He struggled and fought the invisible bindings in vain. A muttered curse.

That's when he heard her. The low husky laugh. "The master of the universe awakes," she said, a mocking edge to her voice.

He turned his head. She sat in the armchair across from the bed. Tonight she wore a feathered shift and a single boar tusk on a braided necklace of sinnet hung around her neck. She flicked the lamp switch and the light danced on the vibrant colours of her shift. Turquoise ocean, mottled eel green and whispers of mulberry red.

"It is beautiful, is it not?" she asked idly.

When he didn't answer, she continued. "Made with feathers of birds once found everywhere in our forests but now they are no more. Logging and pollution have destroyed their homes. But not just that. The very air and oceans have changed. The ocean rises and the air grows hotter with every year. When the storms come, the winds are a stranger." She ran her hands lightly over the feathers and there was an ancient sadness in her eyes. "The land, it hurts, bleeds. It cries. But no one is listening. Man no longer cares."

"What are you?" he demanded.

She stood and slowly walked towards the bed. "Timona and his wife told you. I am Teine Sā. You haven't earned the right to know my true name. Call me Aitu." Her eyes flashed dangerously. "You trespassed on my land and yet I welcomed you. I treated you well." A cold, knowing smile. "You enjoyed my hospitality many times over."

"You tricked me!" he said with venom. "Drugged me with some kind of aphrodisiac. I had no choice in it." Even as he spat the words at her, he knew them to be a lie as he was assailed by an unwanted memory. Her telling him after the first day that she would send him back to his life, that she only kept a man with her for a day and a night. Then him asking – no, pleading – to stay. Just a little longer. Just another day. The days blending into weeks. The memory of his weakness sickened him.

She flicked her wrist at him carelessly. "When it comes to pleasures of the flesh, you chose as any other man would have. As all men would. I may have beguiled your mind but your body was amply rewarded." Her sneer conveyed the depth of her disdain. "Men are all the same. Driven by lust and a thirst to possess. To control everyone and everything."

He struggled to break free, to fight, to leap from the bed, but it was no use. "You forced me, took advantage of me," he snarled.

Laughter. Dismissive and defiant. "I gave you the best nights of your life. You undeserving worm." With one light movement she was on top of him, legs astride his waist, gazing down at him with frightening intensity. "You made me a promise. To leave my home alone. To keep our archive safe. But you lied. You destroyed my home. Cut down my forest. You're going to flood my valley." She slipped her necklace up over her head, gripped the tusk in her right hand as she braced herself against his chest with the other. "It never ends. Time and again my home is desecrated. How many times must I retreat to the inland sanctuaries? How far must I go before I can be free of you? Man keeps advancing. He rapes the land. I am Fanua, spirit of earth and I am tired. I am angry. You will not go unpunished. You bring death everywhere you go. Nothing that breathes is safe from you!" She drew back her hand. The tusk gleamed whitely in the night, a bone blade in her hands.

Marc knew in that moment she was going to kill him. He opened his mouth to call for help, but she gave another careless flick of her wrist – and he couldn't open his mouth, couldn't move his head, couldn't scream. Terror choked him.

"Oh no, I'm not going to kill you. Not yet. Not now. Death is too good for you. Too quick. Too easy. Instead, a curse." The smile left her face and what was left chilled his soul. "You want to bring death everywhere you go? You want everything to wither at your touch? Then so be it." She brought her hands together to clasp the tusk and raised it up above her head, chanting something he couldn't understand.

She stabbed into his chest in one fierce stroke, then wrenched a line downwards.

Pain. Excruciating and endless. Blood. Black and roiling.

And over it all, the aitu laughed.

Darkness seethed with blood. Night laced with terror. Moon ridged with bone shards.

Marc awoke from the most vivid nightmare he'd ever had.

An urgent knocking at the door. "Sir? Are you all right?"

His shouts had been heard by hotel staff. Marc was disoriented and there was a throbbing ache in his chest. It took him a few minutes to reply. "I'm fine," he snapped. Then added, "Thank you."

Silence from outside the door, then hesitant footsteps as the night staff member walked away. Marc looked around him, dazed.

The sheets were drenched. At first he thought it was sweat, but when he flicked on the bedside lamp, horror gripped him. It was blood. Thick and coagulating. Dark and dirty on the white sheets and all over his upper body.

Frantically, his hands searched all over, feeling, where was he wounded? Where had the blood come from? Finding nothing, he stood and stumbled to the en suite, sickened by the sight that greeted him in the mirror. Blood-splattered and pale, he looked like a serial killer after a particularly hard day at work. Yet still he could find no sign of a source for all the blood. Grimacing, he showered, sluicing away sticky redness in the hot water until he was clean.

A deep sigh of relief as he dried himself off under the harsh glare of the fluorescent lighting. That's when he saw it.

What the hell?!

On the contoured rise of his chest, right over the racing thrum of his heartbeat – there was a scar where there hadn't been one before. Not a fresh raw wound with red pinched skin. No. A line of long-healed, rippled skin that spoke of a very deep, very incisive cut, almost like a surgeon's scalpel. And around it, issuing from it, black tendrils, as if his capillaries and veins were filled with pulsing black ink. Dark and virulent, the vine-like pattern splayed out from the scar like a black flower about the size of his hand that stood out against the gold tan of his chest. He brought his hand up to feel the markings. There was no pain and the scar felt smooth and cool to the touch. But the black tendrils were slightly raised so one could trace them clearly with their fingers. They pulsed and emanated blackness. He didn't know what they were or where they'd come from.

A muttered curse under his breath as he exited the en suite. He'd need to see a doctor and he wasn't happy about it. It would be time taken away from his work and would mean subjecting his body to the scrutiny of local medical staff that he didn't have much faith in.

He'd forgotten about the blood-soaked bed, and the sight stopped him in his tracks. Need to get rid of that.

He stripped the bed with quick efficiency. The blood hadn't gone through the mattress protector so that was something. He stuffed the incriminating evidence into a large duffel bag. He would dispose of it later, and the missing sheets would be added to his bill. He didn't care. He had other things on his mind. Namely, what were the markings on his chest? And how did they get there?

Dimly, he recalled the hazy details of his startling dream. The woman with her leering taunts, the way she had bound him with some unseen force, her attack with the boar tusk. Something about blood in the wind.

No, it made no sense. Marc's rational, logical assertion over time, space and order had no room for such wildly illogical and fanciful imaginings. For that was all they were.

He'd been through a lot in the last few days. The stress of it all was getting to him. He needed rest. He would shake off such nonsense. He took another look at the markings on his chest. It was probably a skin infection of some kind. A tropical bacteria. Easily cleared up with antibiotics. And quickly too, because he didn't want to be infected with some nasty bug.

He put on a shirt and buttoned it up, covering the markings. He would see a doctor first thing in the morning.

Nothing would stop him from proceeding with this resort. Nothing would get in the way of this dream project.

Nothing.

Marc was driven, ambitious, and ruthless when he needed to be. His wealthy family legacy, enhanced by a Harvard business degree, made him a powerful addition to the Gold Resort chain. His disappearance in the island bush was an embarrassing temporary glitch in the plan, one he would rather forget.

Over the next few days, he threw himself into his work, setting up a base to facilitate the swift development of the newest gem in the Gold holdings. His capable assistant got him a course of antibiotics and he told himself that would be enough. The scar on his chest, laced with its filigree of black, was an anomaly that he didn't need to explain to anybody. That he could successfully block from his mind. That he could ignore.

Until he couldn't.

Until it started spreading.

And then the Hunger started.

CHAPTER THREE

"Teuila!" The shout from the next room startled her, making her smudge the lip liner she was trying so carefully to apply.

"Rats!" she muttered under her breath as she grabbed a tissue to wipe away the mess. She raised her voice, "What, Bree?"

"She's in here somewhere, I know it. We're not leaving until we find her and kill her! Y'hear me?"

The double doors burst open and a woman in hot pink entered, brandishing a can of bug spray in one manicured hand and a high-heeled shoe in the other. Abundant chest heaving with righteous indignation. "I bet you she came in here."

Teuila sighed, turning away from the mirror. "That centipede is miles away from here by now. I'm telling you, it's way more scared of you than you are of it. Let the poor thing go, already."

It wasn't the right thing to say. Bree narrowed her eyes and redirected her anger. "Poor thing? How can you say that about the bitch? You saw what she did to me." And in case there had been some memory loss, Bree strode over to shove her arm in Teuila's face. Red swelling with two distinct fang print marks in the centre.

Teuila was immediately contrite. This was Bree's first visit to Samoa and the humidity was killing her. A centipede bite in the middle of the night had only made her suffering worse. "I'm sorry. You're right. Shall I get you some more ice?"

Somewhat mollified, Bree shook her head. "No. I want to do a search in this room. I've already had the housekeeping staff look through mine."

Teuila tried not to smile. 'Look through' was too tame a term to describe what Bree had put the hotel through, starting at four a.m. After the shrieking and curses, after a doctor had been called, Bree had demanded her room be turned upside down in an attempt to locate her attacker. After a fruitless hour, she'd then insisted on all new mattresses, bedding and furniture for her suite. She wanted to get a new room but the hotel only had one premium double suite and the thought of exchanging it for a downgrade budget room had Bree shuddering with horror. Neither of them had slept much as a result, and now Teuila was vainly trying to cover up her tiredness with make-up. Which was tricky considering she wasn't very skilled at make-up anyway. She noted wryly that Bree still looked like a supermodel, in spite of her 'horrific experience', and her make-up was impeccable.

"I'm sure that centipede has been scared off by now." A sudden brainwave. "Besides, centipedes are like bees. They can only sting once. So even if your centipede is hiding in here somewhere, it wouldn't be able to bite you. It's probably curled up dead in a dark corner."

Bree's eyes lit up. "Really? They can only sting once? Are you sure? Why didn't the doctor tell me that?" A hint of suspicion.

Teuila silently asked the universe to forgive her lies. *It's for her peace of mind.*

"Because that doctor was a palagi. New to Samoa. She doesn't know about centipedes. Not like people who've lived here with centipedes since forever." Changing the subject. "But if it makes you feel better, let's spray in here again. Give me that." Teuila took the can and commenced spraying under chairs and tables. Again. Cringing inwardly as she contemplated all the chemicals they had ingested in the last twelve hours as Bree had gone on a bug spray rampage. "Why are you calling it a she anyway?"

"Because it's a she. Sucker-attack in the dead of night when your opponent's sleeping? Sign of a bitch. So if it's dead, I want to find the body. I want to see the creature that did this to me."

It was time for a distraction. Or they would never get out of there. Teuila adopted a look of regret. "We should cancel. You can't go to the auction like this."

Bree whirled around. "What? You can't cancel. Don't be stupid!" Immediately she was all businesslike and the centipede was forgotten. "I've worked way too hard on this for you to bail now." She checked her slim, gold watch. "We need to get a move on. Let me look at you." She walked over to study Teuila's emerald sheath with a critical eye. "Hmm, not bad. That colour is good on you and it will complement the Ocean Spirit piece you'll be standing next to."

"Everything isn't about my sculptures, Bree," Teuila laughed.

"Well, it should be," was Bree's response. "This is the worst possible time to be out of the art scene. You should be in New York right now with this collection, maximising your award buzz. Instead of – "

"Instead of here in Samoa, the creative furnace that inspired all my work?" said Teuila, still teasing. She knew better than to take Bree's muttering too seriously. Before Bree became her agent, she had been her best friend at art school. Bree had taken the business route in the industry while Teuila had spent the last six years setting the art world on fire with her sculptures and installation pieces. Bree's antsy mood didn't scare her in the slightest. "You should be happy. Being back here is going to kick-start a creative frenzy and I'm going to churn out pieces like a factory line of awesomeness. Any minute now." She frowned back into the mirror and patted at her wild mane of hair. "Are you sure about this?"

Bree rolled her eyes. "Yes, I'm sure. It looks great when you leave it natural."

"I don't know. My jungle-Samoan-girl hair gets even wilder with the crazy humidity here. Ugh. Maybe I'll straighten it. We've got time."

"No we don't. I'm calling for the car in five minutes. That's not enough time for you to straighten all that. We can't be late. Leave it wild! It suits the image I'm building," was Bree's unsympathetic response as she click-clacked back to her suite.

Teuila made a face at her retreating back.

"I see you!" said Bree over her shoulder.

"Love ya," Teuila sang out in return as she went to the bathroom in search of hairpins. In time to surprise a foot-long centipede making a dash for it across the shower floor. "Ah, there you are." Quick and quiet, she killed it with an expert stamp and grind of her shoe before Bree could see the wriggly evidence of her lie. "Gotcha. Now stay there till we get back so I can show Bree that it's safe for her to sleep tonight."

A short while later, the two women were in a sleek limousine on their way to the gala event. The auction was being held at the Robert Louis Stevenson Museum, a stunning restored colonial house which had been the author's home. The guest list was a veritable who's who of Samoa. Teuila's Sacred Earth collection would be auctioned including the centrepiece, Ocean Spirit, winner of the recent Pinnacle Award. All proceeds would go to the Nafanua Women's Centre, a local women's refuge and school.

It was the reason Teuila had returned to Samoa after so long. And why Bree had agreed to come with her. Why she'd put her ruthless agent agenda on hold and wasn't really giving Teuila a hard time about everything. When it came down to the wire, Bree knew how important this was to her best friend.

The car pulled up to the front entrance and Bree reached across to squeeze Teuila's hand. "Hey, you know I think you're magic, right?" She smiled in the dim light. "In spite of all my bitching and hating on this trip, you know I'm proud of you, yeah?"

"I know. Thank you. I couldn't have done this without you." The two shared a smile.

"Now, let's do this," said Bree.

They exited the vehicle and paused for a moment to gaze up at the house. It was a clear night with a full moon and the ornate frontage loomed before them, imposing and grand. To the right was lush forest and everywhere else were vivid tropical gardens. Light from bamboo lanterns streamed from the open terrace where crowds of beautifully dressed people laughed and socialised. The buzz of conversation and the chink of glasses. A band played from some unseen corner and the air was fragrant with jasmine – and something else. Meat? Teuila looked around. At the far side of the gardens, bare-chested men in traditional lava-lava dress were cooking a whole cow and several pigs on the spit.

Teuila walked halfway up the steps to the entrance, then stopped abruptly. Bree bumped into her. "What's wrong?"

"There's too many people in there." There was a hint of panic in her voice. "I changed my mind. Let's go back to the hotel. They can do the auction without us."

"Whatever!" Bree kicked into agent gear, proving yet again why *NY Art Critic* magazine had named her 'The One to Watch' in their latest issue. "You are going to get in there and smile and schmooze and sell yourself and your artwork with charm and passion, you hear me? Because you're Teuila Mataloa, winner of three different art awards in the last year. Your first show was completely sold out in forty-eight hours and you've been commissioned by the Tate for their new foyer piece. Not only that, we spent three hundred dollars on that dress. And you look amazing in it. You got it?"

Teuila nodded. Because that's what you did when Bree gave you a kick-in-the-butt pep talk. She let go of Bree's arm and forced her face into a smile. "Got it."

"Good. Now, remember what I said about the key people you need to woo, okay?"

They walked in together and Teuila's nervousness was drowned out by the noise, bustle and colour of the crowd. She was obedient. She smiled, nodded, made small talk and laughed at the right moments as Bree worked the room like the pro that she was. Every now and then she gave Teuila that look. The one that checked her temperature, asking 'You okay?' Bree knew her so well and Teuila was weak with relief that she was with her, that she had agreed to come on this trip. Returning to Samoa and trying to support the women's centre with her art was her dream – but she couldn't have done it without Bree.

A week before their trip, Bree had been beyond thrilled to get a call from Nightline, wanting to do a story on the auction and a two-part documentary series on the Nafanua Centre. Teuila's insides curdled at the thought of being on camera, but she was going to grit her teeth, smile and bear it. Bree had set everything up – arranged for the pieces to be transported to Samoa and the necessary media focus to attract international bidding. Across the far wall of the room, a line of tables with phones and computers was set up where operators would take the international bids. The auction would be live-streamed online as well. Teuila gazed at the cameras and her skin crawled at the exposure but she forced herself to remember Bree's words. "Don't be stupid, Teuila! The more interest you can drum up, the more focus there will be on the charitable institution you're donating the proceeds to."

This is all for the centre. Keep focused on that and everything will be okay. If it weren't for Mrs Amani and the Nafanua Centre, you'd be dead. And you certainly wouldn't be here with a collection valued at seven figures.

As if in answer to her thoughts, Mrs Amani appeared through the crowd. She took Teuila in a warm embrace. "You look beautiful."

Teuila smiled and hugged the older woman tight. "Mrs Amani, I'm so glad to see you. I need all the friends I can get tonight. All these people, strangers. Making me nervous."

Mrs Amani patted her arm in reassurance. "Of course I'm here. I wouldn't have missed this for anything." A half-frown then. "And I've told you to call me Beth. You're no longer a student of mine."

Teuila smiled at the older woman's gentle chiding. "Sorry. Old habit." She didn't think she would ever feel comfortable calling her former principal by her first name, though.

Beth Amani continued, "You shouldn't be worried. This is your night. All these people are here for you. To celebrate your achievements, and all hoping for the chance to meet you."

That didn't help. Teuila felt a lurch of sick panic low in her gut.

Bree grabbed her arm just then. "Excuse us please, Mrs Amani. I need Teuila to meet someone." Without waiting for a reply, she dragged Teuila away, muttering firm instructions half under her breath. "Come on. This one is important. You need to be on your best behaviour. Be sex on a stick with him."

"Huh, what? Excuse me, Mrs ... I mean, excuse me, Beth." Before Teuila could get anything else out, Bree was moving them towards a palagi man with his back to them. A light tap on his arm.

"Mr Gold?"

He turned. "Yes?" Tall and broad, he emanated an assured power cloaked in an air of reserved elegance as if he might say, 'Bond, James Bond ... ' Blond hair, granite features. But his cool reserve gave way to an appreciative smile as his gaze took in the two women. He greeted Bree politely, but his flinty blue-grey eyes were locked on Teuila with an intensity that was almost uncomfortable. He reached to shake her hand and when their fingers made contact, Teuila felt the restrained strength in his grip. As if this man was battling the urge to hold her and never let her go. It was disconcerting.

"I'd like you to meet Teuila Mataloa," Bree continued, unaware of the undercurrent. "This is Marc Gold, hotel financier and – "

He interrupted her. "And a great admirer of your work. Please, call me Marc." Without asking, he smoothly took a glass of sparkling champagne from the tray of a passing waiter and gave it to her. "It's an honour to meet you, Teuila." A wide gesture at the displayed artwork. "I've been musing upon the collection, trying to decide which pieces to acquire for our new resort."

"It's lovely to meet you, too." Teuila sipped at her drink and fought not to take a step back, away from this man who exuded an almost overwhelming assurance and power.

"Your art overwhelms me. It's breathtaking. Incomparable."

"It is?" She felt stupid. Clueless. Dammit, she wasn't good at this. At the inane small talk and pretending to be fascinated by everyone and everything.

Marc leaned in and his voice sank to an almost sensual lower register. "Yes. I was in awe of the collection but I must say, now that I've met you, I find its creator even more compelling."

This man's confidence was too much for her. He reminded her of her ex, Kennedy, and that wasn't a good thing. Teuila wanted to get away. She looked around for a convenient excuse to escape. But Bree read her mind. She nudged her sharply and laughed. "Marc, tell us about your new resort. You're building in the mountains somewhere, yes?"

He acknowledged her research with a salute of his glass. "That's correct. It's in the early stages of construction but we'll be opening soon."

"It's amazing how fast the resort is going up," another man

jumped in eagerly. "We've never seen construction move so quickly. Mr Gold's company brought in all their own team and equipment. It's impressive."

The man accepted the praise with a distracted air, his gaze still fixed on Teuila. "We're very committed to the project," he said smoothly. "And I don't believe in taking things slow. If it's right, then why wait? What do you think, Teuila?"

Did he just imply what I think he implied? He did not just say that ... He did!

Teuila was sure she must resemble a bubbling blowfish as her every thought sputtered out before the full force of this man's directness.

Beside her Bree smothered a giggle and then, aware of Teuila's flailing composure, she covered for her. "I'm sure she would agree, Marc," she said. "Teuila's dedication to her art is without rival, and the speed at which she completes a project is mind-boggling. The art world hasn't seen anything like it. Why, her larger installation pieces that would take any other artist months on end, even years, she finishes within a matter of days."

Teuila was uncomfortable with any reference to how fast she created her pieces. It always sparked the same stealthy creep of fear and panic. That someone someday would guess at her Gift. That she would be accused of being a freak and a fraud. She blanched and her hands shook as she gulped another mouthful of the unpleasant burning liquid.

Unaware of her discomfort, Bree continued full speed in agent mode. "Teuila is like no other artist. Did you read Franklin's review in the New York Times? He said, 'She gives life to whatever she touches.'"

There was a sudden flash of something in Marc's eyes, Teuila wasn't sure what. But it made her uneasy. "Hands that give life?" he repeated. "What a fascinating descriptor. One day I will see you at work, Teuila."

It came out more like a command than a request and Teuila's insides clenched convulsively. A centipede of fear crept up her spine and she fought with everything she had not to shrink from him, not to turn and run from the room.

Stop it! This is a PR event and fundraiser for the Nafanua Centre. Talking to strangers and selling yourself and your work is part of the job, remember? You can do this.

Teuila took a deep breath and arranged her features into an icy smile. "Impossible, Mr Gold. Some artists require complete solitude to unleash their creativity. It's such an intimate process to create each art piece. I could never allow anyone to watch me work. You understand."

An arched eyebrow as he raised his glass to her. "I will make it my goal then to attain that level of intimacy with you."

WTF! Just who does this man think he is?

Bree stepped in. "So which pieces in particular are you interested in, Marc?"

"The focal piece of the collection will be ideal for the main lobby of the resort." He nodded his head at the massive installation in the centre of the room that was covered in red velvet elei cloth and would be unveiled later in the auction.

"Oh, I don't know about that, Marc," said Bree, with all her agent's guns blazing. "That's the winner of the Pinnacle Award, as you know, and there are quite a few international bidders looking to buy it tonight. Be prepared for a price war. It could get pretty fierce."

Marc's gaze was locked on Teuila as he replied, "There's something you should know about me. When I see something I want, I pursue it with everything I've got. And I always get what I want."

Teuila flushed under his searching gaze. Bree's knowing smile was triumphant. "In that case, we wish you the best of luck tonight, don't we, Teuila?"

Relax! He's only flirting with you. It means nothing. It's all for a good cause. Think of the centre. Think of the centre.

She was able to manage a smile at the confident man before her. "Yes, of course. If you tell me a bit about the setting of your new hotel, maybe I could suggest some other pieces that would be suitable, too."

Marc offered her his arm. "I would like that. Very much. Perhaps you would do me the honour of a guided tour, a breakdown of Teuila's work for art dummies?" He flashed her a boyish grin that put Teuila more at ease. He looked a lot less like a brutally confident Kennedy then, and a lot more like a teasing, pleasantly handsome man.

"I'd be happy to," she lied.

Bree had a smile of satisfaction as she watched them stroll away. Acquiring an insanely wealthy patron for Teuila's work had not been on the agenda for this trip to Samoa but she certainly would not pass up this opportunity to maximise her client's opportunities.

And such a handsome opportunity too! Teuila hadn't dated anyone since the jerk in art school who had smashed her heart to smithereens. Marc Gold could be exactly what she needed.

In more ways than one.

CHAPTER FOUR

The car pulled up to the front of the museum and the driver glanced in the rear-view mirror. "Are you sure about this?"

Keahi's expression was inscrutable. "Leave it, Reuben." He got out without waiting for his door to be opened, hesitated as he scoped his surroundings and then barked, "Go park. I'll meet you inside."

Reuben didn't bother reminding his employer that the point of having a twenty-four-hour security presence was so that his bodyguard would have him in his sight every minute. Keahi made up his own rules. Always had. So Reuben kept his thoughts and misgivings to himself and went to park the car.

Keahi took advantage of the arrival of a party of five to slip unnoticed past the official greeters and ushers at the entrance. The longer he could keep his identity a secret – the better. He moved along the outskirts of the party, keeping his face slightly averted while at the same time searching the room. For her.

"Drink, Sir?" An earnest waiter presented a tray of Vailima. "There's wine if you prefer."

As always, the mere mention of alcohol sent a wired tingle through him. Even now, after two years on the wagon. Would it ever go away? "Got any juice?"

"Be right back," the man replied. He reappeared a few minutes later with a glass of chilled tropical nectar and Keahi tried not to grimace at the tart sweetness. Or compare it with the way Jack Daniel's would burn his throat. Liquid fire that brought with it blessed numbness. He cursed under his breath. He was letting this get to him, when it shouldn't. Just a meeting of two old friends was all. Who the hell knows if she even remembers you? Or wants to see you? So what if she does? Or doesn't? Just do this, then get back on that plane and fly outta here.

Yes, Keahi had demons he needed to put to rest. He agreed with his therapist on that front. It was the method for dealing with those demons that they disagreed on.

"You know this isn't healthy, right?" Jake asked the question without recrimination. Simply stating an indisputable fact. "The surveillance you have on this woman, the long-distance stalking, the anonymous financial support – these are not the signs of a balanced individual, a man who has made incredible progress in therapy. You've come so far, Keahi. You know it, I don't have to point it out to you. But this? It's the last crutch holding you back."

Keahi paced the length of the gym. It was a strange place for a therapy session but he and Jake had figured out long ago that a couch in a corporate office setting wasn't helpful for a man who was more comfortable in the ring than anywhere else. When Keahi was on tour, they Skyped. And when he was in town, Jake came to him and conducted their sessions in Keahi's state-of-the-art private gym, sometimes with Keahi beating a fight bag when things got particularly intense. It had been two years and yes, they had come a long way. In the beginning, Keahi would have bloodied the sparring post and his fists by now. All while Jake sat in his armchair, calmly studying his client and waiting for his rages to subside. They were more than client and therapist now. Jake was the closest thing Keahi had to a friend and the only person who could talk to him this way. Besides Reuben.

"She's not the only one my foundations support," argued Keahi. "So what, it's a crime to do charity work now?"

"It is when it's accompanied by twenty-four-hour surveillance and heaven only knows what else. You're not completely honest with me about your involvement in this woman's life. When are you going to let her go? What are you afraid of? How do you feel when you think about letting her go, cutting all the security?"

Keahi jammed his hands into his pockets in an attempt to conceal how tightly clenched his fists were, battling for control of his raging emotions as Jake's questions got him thinking – against his will – of letting Teuila go. No more cameras. No more bodyguards. No more updates. No more knowing where she was, who she was with, what she was doing, if she was all right ...

He swore. Kicked a chair and sent it hurtling across the room. Jake sipped at his green tea and adjusted his glasses. Alerted by the noise, Reuben knocked discreetly and entered without waiting for a response. "Everything okay?" His expert eye assessed the environment, read the situation – and then he left without waiting for a response.

"You didn't see the footage," Keahi argued. "If my guy hadn't been on her, she would have been mugged, or worse, that first year of college. And then that apartment she was in was a pit. A health hazard. The landlord was in violation of twelve different building codes. She couldn't stay there in those conditions. I'm looking out for an old friend."

"Is that what you call buying the whole building so you could get her apartment renovated? Oh, and installing a gym and planting a martial arts trainer in the building in the hope she would take up classes? All that comes under looking out for an old friend?"

Keahi's shoulders slumped. "I'm not hurting her. You make me sound like some psycho sicko creep. I would never hurt her."

"She's not the one I'm worried about," replied Jake. "This obsession hurts you. Your fixation is preventing you from moving forwards."

Keahi turned away, thinking on the words he had no argument against.

Jake broke the silence. "She's not your sister. Nothing you do can bring Mailani back or make up for what happened twenty years ago. You know that, right?"

Keahi didn't bother answering. He commenced hitting the bag. Controlled strikes and spin kicks, the sound reverberating through the gym as Jake sipped on his tea.

At that moment, there was a shift in the crowd and he saw her. He'd known she wouldn't be the kid he'd left behind, but he wasn't prepared for this. For her. In the flesh. Grainy photographs and hazy video footage were a poor replacement for the real thing. She was listening to some man who was standing way too close to her. She smiled up at him and Keahi had a surge of anger. Why is she smiling at him? Followed by confusion. Why does it matter? He downed the rest of the glass of juice. Studied her.

She hadn't got much taller since the last time he'd seen her here in Samoa. He felt the ghost of a smile as he remembered how he used to tease her about her height – or lack of it. 'Tic Tac' had been his nickname for her, the spicy 'Red Hots' kind – which always made her grimace. Perfect for the forever-angry, always-ready-to-scrap, tiny girl that she was. She had hated it. Which made him use it more, just to irritate her. Because what most people didn't know was that Teuila's anger was a shield for the fear that lived inside her. And when she was scrapping with him about something as paltry as a nickname, it helped her forget for a little while that she was afraid.

But tonight nothing about her was reminiscent of that long-ago nickname. Tonight she had none of the hostility of her teen years, and if fear was still her constant companion, she was hiding it well. Instead she stood straight and poised, carrying herself with the grace and coiled strength of a person in tune with her body. Even if Keahi hadn't known about her Muay Thai training, he would have guessed it from the way she moved, the contoured lines of lean muscle in her arms and back, apparent even from here. Unlike most of the other women present, she wore no jewellery or flowers as adornment. Her deep emerald sheath gown was a stunning complement to her dark skin. Her hair was a mass of riotous curls framing her face. Wildness and mystery. He muttered a curse under his breath. What kind of dress is that, anyway?! It clung to her body in fascinating ways. The man beside her leaned forwards to whisper something in her ear and she laughed. When she laughed, her eyes lit up and she looked happy. Another difference. The Teuila he knew had rarely been happy.

A slice of fury cut him deep. This was a mistake. He shouldn't have come. Should have just phoned in his auction bid from the hotel. Better yet, he should have stayed in Los Angeles and had his agent deal with it. He didn't need to be here. He didn't need to see her, talk to her. What did they have to say to each other, after all?

A crowd buzzed around her, wanting to congratulate her. She greeted them all with a quiet confidence and surety, thanking them, flushing a little at their compliments. A warm heat built in him then, not from the mugginess of the tropical evening. He smiled in the darkness and acknowledged it for what it was.

He was proud of her. His gaze swept the room, lingering on the art pieces that bore her name on the placards. She had done all this. She had worked hard, come so far. He remembered the darkness that used to live inside her, a darkness he understood all too well – and he was happy. No, he had done the right thing coming here tonight. He was going to celebrate her journey, toast her achievements, add his congratulations to the others. And then he was going to turn around, walk right out of here and go straight to the airport where a private jet waited for him. Once he got back home, he would halt all the surveillance, stop tracking Teuila's career, stop worrying about her path, and report the success of his mission to Jake. He'd come here tonight with a plan and he was going to stick to it.

Until the man beside Teuila brought his hand up behind her to dance his fingers along the bare skin of her spine. A confident caress of possession. Which immediately caused her to stiffen and shift away. No one else noticed, only Keahi. That look in her eyes made him clench his fists. The fear that she tried to clamp down and replace with lightness. It was only a fleeting glimpse but it was enough to take him back to a day long ago when a sullen, fourteen-year-old girl had asked him if he could teach her how to fight back …

"What do you want, kid?" His words were harsh but his tone wasn't. Keahi had spent enough years as a beat-up little kid to recognise another.

"Can you teach me?" The request took supreme effort. She didn't like asking for anything, especially not from a boy.

He stopped his rhythmic blows to the workout bag. "Teach you what?" He looked at her. A slight figure of a girl, wiry hair pulled back into a thick braid and dark eyes that hinted at hurt. He'd noticed her in his classes here at the centre. Always hovering on the edges of the lessons, pretending not to pay too much attention but every nerve attuned to his instructions, her eyes greedily memorising his every strategic throw and twist. And now here she was. Still cautious. Still poised for flight at the first sign of threat.

He took his time unstrapping his gloves, not making any sudden movements. It came instinctively to him because he had lived a lifetime in her shoes. She waited till he was done. Until he had tossed the gloves to the side and she had his complete attention.

"Teach me how to kill someone."

If she thought to shock him, she was disappointed. Keahi gave her a casual shrug. "Sure. Be here tomorrow afternoon. I'll give you lessons three times a week."

Then he got his bag and left. He didn't see the way she looked at him, the almost-reverential awe. He never did. He wouldn't have recognised it even if he had.

Here, on this glittering, colourful night of celebration, Keahi didn't like seeing that relic of the past in Teuila's eyes. It made him grit his teeth, a muscle tensed in his jawline. His eyes were locked on the scene before him. Teuila shifted ever so slightly away from her male companion but the man was oblivious to her discomfort because he only moved closer. He reached again for her, this time to take her hand in his, bring her fingers to his lips.

Keahi didn't breathe. Just ground his frustrations into the glass he was holding. The sound of glass shattering had heads turn his way. A passing waiter leapt to assist him. "Sir, your hand. Let me clean that up for you."

Keahi knelt beside the waiter. "Sorry about the mess."

The conversation in the room resumed and everyone turned back to their party chatter. Everyone that is, except Teuila. She looked and their eyes met. A flash of recognition and all emotion drained from her face. She was no longer listening to the crowd around her. Her gaze was locked on the man across the room, half on his knees, picking up broken pieces of glass. Keahi was caught. For a moment he couldn't move, couldn't breathe. A rush of memories assailed him. Memories of a young girl who had lived through far more in her fourteen years than most people endured in a lifetime. A girl who didn't exist any more because there she stood now, a grown woman.

An achingly beautiful woman in an emerald green dress.

And then the moment was gone. The waiter handed Keahi a napkin for the blood on his hands. A svelte woman in sky-high heels and a shocking pink dress nudged Teuila, diverting her attention. Teuila turned away, back to the conversation around her, but her eyes lingered on Keahi.

"Can't put it off any longer. Here goes ..." Keahi muttered under his breath. He rose to his feet and strode towards the centre of the room. He was oblivious to the admiring glances from the women in the crowd and the murmur of questions. Samoa was a small place and strangers always stood out. Especially strangers who looked like Keahi.

He wasn't particularly tall, he didn't tower over people, but he moved with a compact power and strength that simmered with restrained fury. Tonight he wore dark slacks and a red-patterned elei shirt. The scarlet blaze emphasised his black skin and close-cropped, dark hair.

Eyes lingered on the muscled symmetry of his arms and neck covered in Pasifika tattoo markings. If you looked closer, you could make out the faint scar tissue underneath. Even here in these opulent surroundings, even now dressed in casual island elegance – no one could mistake Keahi for anything but a man of wrath. One who had fought, bled and hurt others. He smiled as he drew closer to his target, but it was a smile that didn't reach his eyes. It was a smile of calculating confidence as he made his way towards the man who had touched Teuila.

But before he could reach him, a woman exclaimed, "It's him! I don't believe it. It's Keahi Meredith!" An excited buzz as others joined in her admiring chatter. Keahi's path was blocked as a cluster of women surrounded him.

A woman grabbed at his arm with sweaty fingers. "I told my friend it was you but she didn't believe me. 'What would he be doing here in Samoa?' she said. But it is you. Oh, I love your movies."

The tight smile on Keahi's face was automatic as he shifted into celebrity mode. Polite chatter and ready grins were what these women wanted. It's what they always wanted. That and more. Sometimes he gave it to them. But not tonight. Not here. He wasn't interested. He smiled, answered questions, signed autographs and obligingly posed for photographs – when all the while his every nerve was alert to the woman halfway across the room.

"How long are you here for?" a woman in red asked. She leaned in closer to breathe throatily, "What hotel are you staying at?"

Keahi allowed himself to be distracted from his target but Teuila was the sun that he orbited, always keeping his set distance but never straying too far, always in perfect alignment with the centre of his gravity. He was a pro, after all. He smiled, made light conversation with the excited crowd around him. He was engaging and charming. Anyone who studied him would have been unable to detect the tension just underneath the surface of his smooth, cocktail-party demeanour.

The band started playing and the Master of Ceremonies invited the party to make the most of the music. A luscious woman in purple, hanging on Keahi's every word, squealed, "Oooh, I love this song. Don't you?"

Before she could press him into dancing with her, Keahi gave her a practised smile. "Excuse me."

He walked away without waiting for a response, leaving her chastened and agog with curiosity. The crowd, the scene, the noise, the music – everything melted away for Keahi as he walked towards his reason for breathing on this night. The closer he got to her, the more frantically his pulse raced – and strangely, the calmer he felt. Yes, this was right. Him being here, him approaching her. It was right.

She looked and saw him. Her friends were talking to her but she was no longer listening. Her eyes were trained on him and she paled. He drew level with her and everyone around her was staring.

Now that he was here in front of her – words escaped him. It seemed they eluded her, too. So they just stood there and stared at each other.

The fair woman beside her broke their connection. An exclamation of surprise. "I thought you looked familiar. You're –"

Keahi gave her what he hoped was a dazzling smile. "Keahi Meredith."

She shook his hand with a firm grip. "Brianna Grayson." She turned to Teuila. "And this is –"

"The reason why I flew all night to get here. And endured several Covid scans along the way. Good to see you again, Teuila." He took her hand in his, and her touch sent a sudden wire of electricity through him.

Teuila's face went white while Bree exclaimed, "You're friends!"

"No," Teuila blurted. She tugged her hand away from his.

An uncomfortable chill as everyone picked up on her antagonism.

"It was a long time ago." Keahi smoothed over the jagged edges of the conversation.

Teuila raised her chin defiantly. "Yes. A very long time ago." She took a step back as if to flee, and bumped into the sleek American.

He steadied her with a casual touch of his hand, a smile. "Careful!"

"Oh, sorry," said Teuila, flustered.

"My pleasure," he said with a slow smile that made Keahi grit his teeth, the sudden knife-edge of hate taking him by surprise with its ferocity. The man kept his arm at Teuila's back as he gave Keahi an appraising glance. The two men locked eyes. Assessing. Evaluating. The noise of the party around them died away to a distant hum in Keahi's mind. It seemed he was locked in a tunnel of rage as his every sense screamed for him to tear this man away from Teuila and rip his throat out. In clearly defined slow motion, he saw it happen.

Right hand to the back of his head, bring his face to meet my left knee. Nose into the brain. Pull his bleeding face back, hold him steady. Reach, grip the sweet spot of the throat. Rip. Let him drop in a heap. Take Teuila's hand. Walk with her to the door, outside, away from here.

Keahi forced his breathing to slow, settled the bloodthirsty urge within. This was not the time or the place. The agent, Bree, was introducing them and Keahi nodded politely at the other man.

Always the diplomat, Bree skilfully navigated. "You've come a long way for this auction, Mr Meredith. You're a collector?"

"Keahi, please," he gently corrected with a smile. "Not a collector.

A big supporter. Of the Nafanua Centre. I used to be a volunteer there and we have a history. I heard what Teuila was doing and wanted to stop by. Maybe see if I could buy something. Anything to help the centre."

"Of course," said Bree. "That's what we all want, right, Teuila? To make sure this auction is a wild success so we can do our best for the Nafanua Centre."

Before she could answer, the auctioneer announced the start of the night's main event. "You're up, Teuila," laughed Bree. "Go get 'em!"

"Allow me to escort you," said the smooth American.

"Thank you," said Teuila. A cool glance back at Keahi before she gave Marc a dazzling smile and took his hand. "Having you close will help with my nervousness."

The two walked towards the podium. Their easy familiarity was a knife to the gut for Keahi. He wasn't sure why. She owed him nothing. This was the first time they'd seen each other in over a decade. Of course she would have friends. A lover. A partner. Admirers.

But why hadn't he been told about this man? He barely paid attention to Teuila's speech as he searched the room for Reuben, only to have him magically appear at his side. "You need me, Sir?" he said quietly. Unobtrusive.

"Why hasn't there been anything about that man in the reports?" Keahi snapped.

"She must have only met him on this trip," Reuben replied. Without being asked, he quickly gave Keahi a brief rundown on Teuila's escort. What he had managed to find out in the twenty minutes since arriving at the function. Who he was and what he was doing in Samoa.

Keahi looked back at Teuila and the hotel magnate where they stood laughing and exchanging pleasantries as the auction kicked off. They didn't look like strangers. And there was something about the way Marc looked at Teuila, the way he touched her, the almost feral hunger in his eyes. Keahi didn't like it.

"I need more. Get me everything on Gold," he said. "Tonight. Get the LA office on it. I want a full report by morning."

Reuben nodded and walked away. Keahi stopped him. "Reuben."

"Yes, Sir?"

"Shadow her. I want to know who she leaves with and where she goes."

Reuben didn't like it. Against the security expert's recommendations, the two men had come alone to Samoa with only the pilot and the flight crew on the private jet. If he tailed Teuila, Keahi would be left without a detail. But one look at his employer's face and he knew better than to try and argue. A nod and then he disappeared into the crowd.

Keahi knew he was being irrational. Seeing threats where there probably were none. But he didn't care. When it came to Teuila, rationality went out the window. Always.

He went back to staring at the beautiful couple across the room as he rejoined the party. So intent on the spectacle that he didn't notice Bree move from where she'd been standing on the other side of a carved screen divider, a thoughtful expression on her face.

The auction was as excruciating as Teuila had expected. She hated seeing her artwork sold, and it was always slightly traumatic to see her creations being divvied up by strangers. She knew it was silly and she knew she would have to get over this reluctance one day. Especially if she wanted to have a successful career as an artist. Bree found her repugnance frustrating, and they were always at odds about when a piece was ready to be sold, to be displayed. If it were up to Teuila, she would never let any of them go.

Tonight's auction was breaking records for her art. Marc Gold proved to be a dedicated buyer who purchased four pieces in a row. "For my new resort," he explained with a smile. Teuila's cheeks were hurting from so much smiling as each final bid was read out and applauded. It wouldn't do for her to look tired or pained. Not when every dollar was going to the Nafanua Centre. Her anxiety eased somewhat when Beth came to stand with her, took her hand in hers, "Oh, Teuila, I can't believe how successful this is! Are you sure you won't keep some of the proceeds from tonight's sale? This is too much money. What about you and what you need for your career?"

Teuila squeezed her hand with a reassuring smile. "It's all right. I told you, I'm fine. These pieces – all of them – are for the centre."

Beth smiled fondly at her. The older woman knew her like a

mother. Knew she would rather be anywhere but here, the focus of this glittering spectacle. "You look stunning," she said. "I'm so proud of you."

The two exchanged a look that spoke volumes – of a relationship that had begun as rescuer and abuse survivor, then changed to refuge director and unwilling, resentful student, and finally blossomed into that of trusted friend.

Teuila blinked away the tears that threatened. "Nothing I do could ever repay you or the centre for what you've done for me. I wouldn't be here, have all this – if not for you."

Beth waved away her emotion with an embarrassed laugh. "Don't be foolish, child. Your gift is yours. Your hard work made this happen."

All the pieces were sold in quick succession. Teuila breathed a sigh of relief that now the night would come to a close.

"We have one more piece – this one from the artist's private collection," the auctioneer announced.

Teuila was puzzled. What piece? Her gaze swung to Bree. She had supervised the packing and loading of the collection while Teuila had been at an art festival in Paris.

Bree gave her a reassuring wave and moved to stand beside her. "I found this at the back of the studio. That painting you did a long time ago, the one you told me that you didn't like? I had an assessor take a look at it and they loved it. This is the perfect place to test the waters for your branch into painting, intro you as more than just a sculptor. Even if it is just a simple piece. Figured someone would buy it, especially as it's for a good cause and when the amazing artist is standing in their midst. Auction fever, you know."

"No, I don't know," protested Teuila. "Bree, I'm not branching into painting. What are you talking about?"

Her eyes widened as the auction assistants carried in a covered painting. A knot of worry built inside her. Suspicion and dread, confirmed when they unveiled the piece.

"No!" Teuila moaned softly and bit her lip.

Off to the side, Keahi saw her distress and trained his eyes on the source.

It seemed but a small thing. A painting of a girl standing in a field, surrounded by butterflies, vivid brushes of colour so real, so lifelike, it seemed as if they would flutter from the canvas. But it was the figure holding hands with that girl who gutted Keahi. A boy, every inch of him marked with tattoos. The couple stood hand in hand, cocooned in wonder, as if butterflies provided them a sweet sanctuary from all the harshness of the outside world. It was a joyous painting, piercing in its simplicity and abundance of colour.

Keahi was rooted to the spot, a roar in his head as he stared at this memory plucked straight from his shared past with the girl who it seemed had done everything she possibly could to become someone different. To leave the past behind and step into the light.

Teuila fidgeted with her hands and whispered fiercely to her friend. The pair seemed to be arguing as Teuila insisted the piece be removed from the auction and Bree told her it was too late to back out.

The auctioneer went to the mike. "It's titled Butterfly. What am I bid for this final piece in the collection? Who would like to start the bidding?"

Teuila was furious. Not because the painting was precious to her. She was rigid with worry and anger because Keahi was looking right at her and then back again at the painting. What if he was remembering that day long ago when he had stood with a scrawny, frightened girl and she had called to her Gift with the stirrings of joy within her, joy in the boy who had stood with her and guided her, believed in her? The boy who had saved her from the excruciating shame of a beating in the market at the hands of her mother and her mother's boyfriend, the man who had abused her. Her nails bit into the palms of her hands as she fought to stay calm.

It was a long time ago. You're not that girl any more.

Then a voice rang out clear and assured. "Add a dinner date with the artist and I'll bid fifty thousand dollars!" It was Marc.

A ripple of laughter and knowing chatter rippled through the crowd. The man gave Teuila a frank smile from across the room and turned back to the auctioneer. "Fifty thousand for the painting and the honour of the artist's company over dinner, and since it's for a good cause, I'll throw in another fifty thousand." A dramatic pause. "I bid one hundred thousand dollars."

The buzz intensified. Everyone turned to look at Teuila and she flushed under their expectant gaze. The man had made no secret of his interest in her from the very start of the night and it flustered her. She wasn't used to this kind of attention. Men didn't approach her at parties, flirt with her over champagne, or make such public bids for her company. She was mortified, speechless.

But Bree wasn't. "Done." She gave Marc a mock severe wave of her finger. "Just dinner, mind you. No funny business." Laughter from the crowd. Unseen by the others, she slipped her hand into Teuila's. A whisper. "Don't worry. I'll go with you. You wanted mega bucks for the Nafanua Centre? You got it."

The auctioneer picked up the gavel. "All in the name of a good cause, one hundred thousand for this last piece in the collection, and dinner with the artist herself, to the very generous Mr –"

Before he could finish, before he could tap his gavel, a voice rang out through the room. "One million dollars."

Shocked silence, and then a rustling sound and hum of conversation as everyone turned to source the crazy person who'd just made the bid.

Keahi.

He stood with his hands in his pockets, casually leaning against an ornately carved post at the rear of the room. A sardonic smile that didn't reach his eyes.

"What was that, Sir?" asked the auctioneer. Flabbergasted.

"I bid a million," said Keahi as he strolled towards the front of the room. "For the painting. And for a date with the artist." The crowd parted before him, all talking about this new development. Curiosity, rumour and insinuation rippled like the gauzy tendrils of the lion fish. Beautiful but barbed.

Movie star ... MMA world champion ... Oscar winner ... dangerous ... look at his scars ...

The auctioneer didn't wait to give him a chance to back out. "Sold!" he exclaimed with an enthusiastic rap of the gavel. "Sold, sold, sold."

Bree gave a shriek of excitement and the crowd erupted into frenetic applause.

But the look on Teuila's face was anything but happy. A cluster of fawning women pressed on Keahi on all sides, tittering and fluttering their eyelashes as they congratulated him on his purchase. A man who could bid a million dollars for a date with a woman – was a man they wanted to know. A man they wanted to be with.

Keahi fended off silky hugs and breathless air kisses with detached politeness as he struggled to search through the crowd for Teuila. Where was she? He wanted to see her face, look into her eyes.

Then he saw her across the room, leaving the party with the blond American. The man had an arm possessively at her back as he escorted her out, accompanied by the agent. A fleeting glimpse of emerald green and then she was gone. Keahi was left to deal with the adoring press of people.

And make arrangements to pay for his painting.

"One million dollars!" Bree shrieked as she followed Teuila into her suite. "You didn't tell me you knew Keahi Meredith."

"I don't," Teuila snapped as she took off her shoes. "Ugh, feels so good to get these off."

Bree ignored her attempt to detour the interrogation. "So how come he wants to tear your clothes off and lick you all over?"

"Don't be stupid."

Bree wasn't deterred. She followed Teuila into the bathroom and stood behind her as she started taking her make-up off in front of the mirror. "I know what it looks like when a man wants to get in your pants."

Teuila grimaced at her crudeness. "What do you know about men? You're a lesbian."

Bree brushed away her argument with an impatient flick of her fingers. "Desire looks the same. Men or women, it makes no difference. Besides" – a flash of her cheeky grin – "nothing makes a man hotter than girl-on-girl."

"Ugh, stop it!" Teuila turned and started pushing her out of the bathroom. "Enough, already. I don't want to talk about sex. Lesbian or any other kind. Now get out before I call Frances and tell her how many servings of pineapple pie you had at the party." She slammed the door and locked it with extra emphasis.

"You wouldn't dare!" Bree yelled through the door. "Those pieces were tiny. Minuscule. Three of them equal one decent piece."

"Whatever!" Teuila yelled back, glad her pie distraction was working. "You had lots of those coconut caramel dumplings as well, the fa'ausi. Loaded with sugar and carbs."

Bree was diabetic and Frances, her girlfriend back in New York, had roped Teuila into a promise she would help monitor Bree's diet.

Bree narrowed her eyes and banged on the barrier with one fist. "You're not getting out of it that easy, Teuila, y'hear me? This isn't about pie or dumplings. A Hollywood star shows up at your auction on this dinky island in the middle of nowhere and has a bidding war with a hotel chain millionaire for the chance to sex you up. A million dollars. Can you believe it?!"

The door swung open. "They did not pay to have sex with me. A million dollars for the painting, Bree." Teuila's face was murderous and Bree backed away, still smiling, because her hook had worked. "A painting that wasn't supposed to even be in the auction."

Bree didn't care about the painting. "How do you know him?" Hands on her hips. Confronting. "I'm not gonna leave you alone until you tell me."

Teuila knew only too well that she meant it. A groan. "It was a long time ago. I was a kid."

The nonchalance didn't fool Bree. Not for a minute. "And?"

"And he was volunteering at the centre. Teaching a self-defence class. That's all."

Bree waggled her perfect eyebrows. "Oooh, an illicit teacher-student relationship? I'm scandalised. I didn't know you had it in you."

Teuila made a sound of disgust as she walked to sit on the bed. "It wasn't like that. I was fourteen, new at the shelter. He was a good instructor," she said unwillingly. "And he knew some other people I was friends with, like Leila and Daniel."

"Leila, the millionaire CEO and lawyer who heads up the trust that oversees the Nafanua Centre?" Bree hadn't yet met the power couple that Teuila had spoken of infrequently over the years, but she knew Teuila had a lot of respect for them, almost awe, and that they kept in touch.

"Yeah, so I guess you could say, me and Keahi, we were friends too," said Teuila. All the fight had gone out of her, and there was an air of quiet sadness about her. Vulnerability.

Bree felt guilty about teasing her. "I guess that explains his generous donation to the Nafanua Centre then." But she still couldn't let it go. "So what happened with you two? When's the last time you saw him?"

"He'd come here from Hawaii and he didn't stay long. A year and a half maybe? He was older than me. Nineteen. Left and went back to Hawaii for some MMA thing and that was it."

"Did you two stay in touch?" Bree watched her like a hawk, reading beyond words and into body language.

"No," said Teuila. "I never heard from him again. Until tonight."

"Hmm, so he never called, never wrote, never Facebook friend requested you, even?"

Teuila rolled her eyes. "Bree, would you stop? No. Nothing. The man's been busy, hello! MMA then UFC world champion, working the fight circuit through Europe and Asia for two years before getting into movies, surprise nomination for Best Actor for his first film and then winning the Oscar for his second …" Her voice trailed away at the sight of Bree's grin. "What?"

"I thought you said, you didn't know anything about where he'd been or what he's been up to for the last twelve years?"

"I don't," blustered Teuila. "I watch the news just like anyone else, that's all."

"Sure you do," intoned Bree sagely. "Well it looks like he's been watching you a little bit too. Flying all the way over here for your auction when he could have phoned in his bid and his donation. Y'know, seeing as how he's such a famous busy man after all. He even told his bodyguard to find out where you're staying and to dig up info on Marc Gold. The man is nuts about you. He couldn't keep his eyes off you tonight."

"Yeah? Well I'm not interested," said Teuila with a renewed sense of disdain. "Marc Gold is way more appealing."

Bree frowned. "Really? He doesn't seem like your type at all."

"And an overly tattooed and scarred cage fighter is?" exclaimed Teuila. "Marc is handsome, intelligent, powerful, he knows art. And he's rich."

Bree slumped back on the bed, pensive, biting at her bottom lip. "I don't know. There's something off about him." All semblance of teasing fled as she sat back up. "Something that makes me uneasy. I can't explain it."

Teuila wanted to argue with her, but she couldn't. She'd felt the same thing. A prickling, simmering undercurrent of something unknown. Like looking into the still waters of a black lake, searching for the ominous ripple revealing the monolithic, fearsome beast you knew was lying in wait below.

Bree continued. "Well, take his money and his patronage for your art because your career needs it, but if I were you, I'd keep my emotional distance from Marc. Don't let him anywhere near your vajayjay."

"WTF, who talks like that?" exclaimed Teuila as she leapt up to pace the room. "Of course I'm not going to have sex with him, which I'm assuming you meant by that reference to my vagina." A groan. "Why do you say stuff like that?"

Innocent incomprehension as Bree studied her nails. "What? Would you rather I said, 'Don't let him near your pussy'?"

"Aargh, I'm not listening," said Teuila as she covered her ears with her hands.

"You can't talk. Who says 'WTF' in a real conversation outside of text-speak, huh? Or 'fudge'? What are you? Twelve? In a convent? A Mormon housewife? It's 'What the fuck!' Teuila. Repeat after me. What the F ... U ... C ... K!"

This was not a new conversation, and it always ended with Bree in fits of laughter and Teuila chucking missiles at her in an effort to shut her up.

"That's it," Teuila said wearily. "I'm going to bed. Leave me alone. Go and call Frances."

"But we're having so much fun figuring out the mysteries of insanely rich handsome men who want you badly enough to pay lots of money for a dinner date with you." Bree checked her watch. "Besides, time difference. Frances is at work and can't play."

"I'm tired," protested Teuila. "And the only one having fun here — is you. Fudge you!"

"Ooh, is that what you're going to say when Keahi Meredith tears your clothes off with his teeth? 'Oh please, Keahi, fudge me!'" Bree mimed an orgasmic motion with lots of accompanying sound effects until Teuila threw a pillow at her.

"Out. Now." Teuila suddenly pointed at a spot on the wall behind her panting, moaning friend. "Look out, centipede!"

A shriek as Bree bolted to the door while Teuila gave in to hysterics of laughter. "I'm kidding," she amended. "No centipede. I'm kidding!"

Bree was unamused as she poked her head back around the connecting door. "You're a bitch, you know that? Don't come to me for advice when you're trying to figure out how to take on Marc and Keahi at the same time."

"You love me, ha." Teuila got serious. "Hey, Bree?"

"What?"

"You did a great job with the auction. I could never have done it without you. We raised a lot of money tonight and you made it happen. Thank you."

Bree's scowl eased. "You're welcome." A pause as she chewed at her inside cheek. "I'm sorry about the painting. I didn't know how much it meant to you. I should have asked first."

Teuila smiled. "It's okay."

The two women said goodnight, and soon Teuila was alone in the darkness. Her words of reassurance had been automatic, but as she lay there musing over the evening's events, she knew them to be true. Keahi seeing that painting, owning that painting – really was okay. It was right. Because no matter what had happened since then, Butterfly was a joyous moment that had only been possible because of him.

CHAPTER FIVE

Marc fought to contain his wild rush of excitement as he placed a call to his Los Angeles office. "I want a file on Samoan artist Teuila Mataloa, based in New York. Everything there is to know about her."

He told the driver to go faster as they drove up to the elegant house he'd leased in the Vailima hills. The ache was building again. The same insistent clawing Hunger that had become his steady companion ever since that night. It started at the mark on his chest and razor-scraped its way through his torso and through his arms and legs. As if he were being eaten from the inside by an army of ants. It kept him up at night, restless and fitful as the gut-wrenching ache filtered into his dreams. No matter what he ate, how hard he worked out in the personal gym attached to the house, no matter how much alcohol he drank or how many pills he took – it was still there.

At the house, he sent his people away with a curt dismissal and once he was sure he was alone, he tore his shirt open and went to stand before a massive mirror.

Even though he knew what he'd see, it was still an unpleasant surprise. Because there was always the whisper of hope that maybe, just maybe – the black patterning would be gone. As quickly and as unexpectedly as it had come. That the whole thing was just a bad dream.

But there it was. Covering the entirety of his upper torso, a filigree of black lines, slightly raised from the skin, as if someone had injected his veins with dark ink. Foreboding yet darkly beautiful against the chiselled expanse of white skin. It pulsed with life and as he studied it with horrified fascination, there was another roiling surge of pain followed by the prickling sensation of thousands of tiny needles. Or the gnawing of teeth? He'd long given up scratching at it, he knew that did nothing. Creams, lotions and skin treatments. They gave him no rest, no peace. Like some parasitic alien thing growing inside him. It wanted something, only he knew not what. The Hunger was constantly biting, always pulsing and pulling at his skin as if longing to get out, to burst free.

Except for tonight. When he met that artist and held her hand in his, the constant irritant had suddenly stilled, as if soothed by some unknown force. The longer he'd spent in her company, the more the hungry pain had eased to a quiet, dull ache, enough to make him forget its presence entirely. There was something about her, an aura she radiated, that seemed to negate the dark foreboding that threatened to erupt from deep within him. He felt the same thing from her artwork. It, too, emanated a kind of healing, throbbing energy. It seemed inconceivable that no one else could feel it. And then when her agent described her as having hands that give life – it made total sense to him. Of course!

He had hoped her effect on him would last beyond being in her presence. But as soon as he had escorted the two women to their car and bid them farewell, the familiar pain had returned, with an even more vicious bite because he had remembered for a few hours what it felt like to live free of it. Now it seemed unbearable.

He swore as he gripped the table edges tightly and gazed down at himself with loathing. He couldn't live like this. He wouldn't. Not any longer.

Who knew if it was desperation or rage which drove him to get a knife from the expansive silver kitchen and then back to the hall mirrors for a better view of the task at hand? A deep breath, a mutter under his breath, "Screw you, Aitu!" as he braced himself. He intended to dig the blade into the side of his midriff, just an inch, carving away a section of the top layer of his skin. But his hands were shaking and the blade was sharper than he expected. It slipped and sliced his careless fingers. He flinched.

"Aargh!"

Blood.

But unlike any blood he'd ever seen. A purple so deep it seemed black. It dripped from his hands, eager and quick, a thick fluid that seemed to have a life of its own. Marc stood by a cluster of decorative ferns, growing in enamel pots. Drops fell onto the lush greenery and instead of congealing on the leaves, the blood continued to flow, sinuous and sure, expanding until it coated every leaf and stalk. Marc stared, stunned, the pain of the cut forgotten at the sight of his blood – if that's what it was – moving and acting as if it was an agent unto itself. A living, breathing thing.

What happened next made him stagger back in horror. The lush greenery wilted to a withered brown, sucked dry of life, the brittle remnants disintegrating until nothing but a pile of dust remained.

"What the hell?"

The blood was no longer dark. Instead it pulsed gold, as if brimming with light. Then, as Marc stood frozen in disbelief, the blood returned to him, seeking and finding its point of exit, even as he vainly tried to brush it away. It fed back into the blade mark and Marc was no longer resisting because he was flooded with the most exhilarating sensation, better than sex, more intense than any artificially induced high. He sank to his knees, cradling one hand in the other, as fierce joyous pleasure raced through him. The bleeding stopped and the violated skin sealed over smoothly as if it had never been cut. But Marc didn't notice because he was lost in the pulsing wondrousness of life.

How sweet it tasted. How richly textured and redolent. Who knew a simple collection of ferns could contain so much essence and texture? Before they had been harvested by a landscaper and transplanted into pots for sale to the house owner, the plants had flourished in a tropical rainforest. They were rich in memory. The overwhelming bouquet of sweet nectar infused with sunshine. A hint of dark earth, teeming with life. Wind-kissed leaves tasting of faraway places. Roots strong and sure that anchored them to that which gave them foundation. The rustle of birds far above in the trees. A distant splash of water, wet rocks, the leap of fish and the ponderous movement of fat, lazy eels. Mystery and sunlight. The quiet peace of hidden places in the forest floor, the glorious tangle of bush undergrowth.

Marc drank it all in. Life flooded his senses and he was drunk on it. He wanted to feast forever on this unparalleled deliciousness.

He came to sometime later. Dazed and disoriented. He was lying spreadeagled on the floor, surrounded by brittle twigs and a light film of dust. Not a leaf of greenery anywhere. The cut was gone and in its place, the faintest spiderweb of a scar. He pulled himself to stand and confronted his reflection. Astounded. The black web on his torso was gone — no, not true. It was there but now it lit up his chest as if painted on with a brush dipped in white gold.

It was beautiful.

And it no longer pained him or ate at his skin like some breeding, parasitic thing. Rather, it shimmered and breathed with a quiet kind of joy, in utter harmony with his breathing and the pulse of his heart.

"Unbelievable," he whispered. He felt like a man reborn and he couldn't stop tracing the vibrant patterns all over his upper body, marvelling at their beauty.

For the first time in weeks, he slept that night without pain, without waking, without blood-laced dreams, and awoke refreshed and revitalised. His staff were pleasantly surprised at the change in their boss. They had come to expect the surly brusqueness and violent rages that the hungry pain had sparked in him.

Later that day, his assistant brought him the hastily prepared file on Teuila. He read it quickly.

Interesting ... He'd known from the promotion for last night's auction that she was a former student at the Nafanua Centre, had guessed she had a dismal past, but there were some unusual details about her background story.

She had first come to the centre when her mother was taken to hospital. The police report showed the mother had suffered horrific injuries from an abusive partner. The mother had promptly returned to her partner as soon as she was discharged from hospital. Teuila went home with her. A few months later, she came to stay at the centre again when her mother was taken to hospital after another beating. Again the mother refused to file charges against her partner, and again she took her daughter home with her. Not long after, Teuila ran away and went back to the centre. Not hard to guess why. But that's where things got interesting. Police records showed the mother came to report her daughter had been kidnapped or – more probable – she didn't want to go home and the Nafanua Centre refused to force her. Police had been sympathetic to the child's plight but as Teuila was underage and the laws so dismal at protecting children, they hadn't been able to give the centre director legal grounds to keep the young girl.

Then without warning the mother withdrew her complaint against the centre, and Teuila remained there permanently. Regular payments started going into the mother's account from the patron and trustee of the Nafanua Foundation, established by a very wealthy woman named Leila Folger. A tidy sum that continued until Teuila's twenty-first birthday, many years of blood money to keep a woman from the child she didn't deserve. Teuila remained a full-time resident at the centre before winning an art scholarship at eighteen to the academy in New York where she'd excelled. But what stood out for Marc was the note that the mother's partner had died in a car crash. On the same week that the payments started going into Teuila's mother's account.

Marc's eyes narrowed. It was all too neat. Mother gets paid to stay away and the violent partner conveniently dies? He kept reading the report.

A brief affair with an older student at the academy, not much evidence of a social life, and no other hobbies or interests beyond her art. A behemoth of a studio loft was another anomaly. She had leased it even before she won the Tate award, presumably before she had started making any money from her art. How could she have afforded such prime real estate?

More frowns as Marc searched through the paperwork, reading between the lines, picking up on what was missing. Perhaps Teuila had another generous benefactor or patron. Even her apartment raised questions. The complex had been purchased several years ago and undergone extensive renovations. He scanned through her bank records and barked out a question to his assistant.

"Lindsey, her rent never increased. Why not?"

"Excuse me, Sir?" The assistant was baffled.

"The building had an entire floor outfitted with a gym, pool and Muay Thai club, state-of-the-art security installed – and yet her lease payment never went up. Makes no sense. Who bought the building?"

The woman was happy to be able to point it out. "It's right there on page six. A subsidiary company called Fire Holdings. They own real estate all over New York and in Los Angeles, as well as in Hawaii …"

He brushed aside her input with impatience. "I saw that. I mean who owns the subsidiary company? Who's the major shareholder?" At her baffled shrug, he stood up from the desk. "Find out. Follow the paper trail. When I said I wanted everything on this woman, I meant it."

The assistant scuttled to the door. "Yes, Sir."

"See what everyone else in that building is paying for rent. Got it?"

A nod and she exited, closing the door behind her with an outward sigh of relief to be escaping his presence.

He paced the room as he read through a file on Keahi Meredith. A much thicker pile of papers. He skimmed it impatiently, seeking the connection between him and the artist. There it was. Keahi Meredith had come to Samoa with a team to compete in a Pacific outrigger canoeing competition when he was a teenager and stayed on for another eighteen months once the team had left. He'd attended the local university and volunteered at the centre, teaching self-defence. There was no mention of him knowing Teuila but remembering the look on her face when she'd first caught sight of him the night before, Marc was confident the two had been friends. Or enemies. Or something meaningful enough to provoke such a strong reaction. He had to double-check.

"Lindsey!"

She opened the door almost immediately. Harassed and anxious. "Yes?"

"There's no mention of Keahi Meredith ever meeting Teuila Mataloa again after he left Samoa?"

"No, nothing."

"You're sure?"

"Oh yes. He's an international celebrity, Mr Gold. His movements are fairly well documented, even when he doesn't want them to be. The press has a love-hate relationship with him." A dreamy light in her eyes told Marc all he needed about how his assistant felt about the man voted *People* magazine's 'Sexiest Man Alive'. That rankled. And it disturbed him that he even cared.

"I'm not interested in the info from fluff pieces, Lindsey. This report is unacceptable. Get me the dirt, the truth on this man."

Unfortunately, the effects of consuming a few plants didn't last long and by the afternoon, Marc's chest throbbed with the familiar hungry pain. He wanted – no, needed – to see the artist again. And until he could? He would make do.

Marc left work early, driving home with single-minded intensity. Once there, he stalked into the kitchen, ripping buttons as he tore his shirt off, scrabbling with shaking hands for a knife. Now that he knew what to do, it seemed as if the Hunger had multiplied. He could already taste the golden life on his tongue as he strode out into the backyard, eyes searching for the best spot. In the deepest recesses of his mind, a voice of reason niggled at him. "Stop. What are you even doing? This is crazy. You need to get help. See a doctor. Go back to the States and get a specialist to figure this out."

But he shut it down. The Hunger was too overwhelming. Even stronger was the anticipation of what would come. There was no stopping him. He had to have it. He needed it.

Marc came to a halt beside a cluster of bushes. Red and green spangled leaves swaying softly in the afternoon breeze. He gripped the knife and without hesitation, slashed at his midriff. A different spot from the one he'd cut before, but still where the skin pulsed with raised lines of black. The pain was brief, quickly eaten up by the rush of release as black liquid gushed and pooled at his feet, breathing and living. Searching. He was captivated by it, watching as it made a beeline for the nearest living thing. Grass growing at the base of the bushes. Within a heartbeat, it had consumed the plant, leaving only a smattering of dry deadness that fragmented in the wind. It wasn't enough. The Hunger still resonated with darkness. The grass had barely made a dent in it.

"More," he said, without even knowing he spoke aloud. The Hunger moved with lightning speed to the bushes. Racing up a trunk and out along every branch, covering each leaf. Absorbing its every molecule. The bush was as tall as Marc and only once it was covered in Hunger, did the blood seem to sigh with contentment before returning to earth and then the few steps to Marc. He sank to his knees, eager for the feeding. A flash of doubt. What if it didn't work this time? What if yesterday had been a one-off? What if he never tasted that joy again?

He needn't have worried. The Hunger returned to the cut, seeking its home, filling him with an incredible lightness of being. It was unlike any feeling he'd ever experienced. He fell back on the ground, lost in golden exhilaration as the sweet taste of life filled him. He could have wept with the joy of it. The utter contentment. This was truly being alive. This was what he would crave forever and always.

Marc didn't know how long he lay there surrounded by sky and forest. When the high faded and he woke to himself again, the sun was sinking beneath the horizon and the prickle of ants crawling on his skin made him sit up with a start. His chest was a spangled tapestry of shimmering gold thread patterns, a quiet pulse of contentment. He stumbled inside the house and never once looked back at the circular patch of deadness amid the lush greenery.

Wasn't that what the earth was there for? To feed man's hunger?

CHAPTER SIX

The morning after the auction was a mad rush to get sorted for the first day of filming with the documentary crew. Bree had arranged for a make-up artist and hairdresser to work their magic on Teuila, against all her protests. "You will do as you're told," said Bree. "This doco airs in prime time."

"But it's only half-an-hour long. Nobody will notice me."

"It airs in prime time," Bree said again, as if that was the only counterargument she needed to offer.

"But I won't look like myself."

Bree ignored her like a whiny child and Teuila resigned herself to the transformative efforts of the skilled team. When they were done, Bree assessed her with a critical eye before pronouncing her TV-ready. The drive to the centre was a short one. Teuila took in the scenery while Bree was glued to her phone, sending emails and rapping out curt messages to her online assistant.

The tension within Teuila coiled even tighter as they drove up the long drive to the centre gates. It had been years since she was last here and although she'd loved it as the home she'd never had, it was still a place she associated with the girl she used to be. Frightened, angry, lost and confused.

Bree paused in her work to shoot her an astute glance. "Hey, you all right?"

Teuila nodded. A quick smile. "Sure. Just nervous about the interview."

She was glad when Bree seemed satisfied with her reply. Her friend knew that she'd spent her teen years in a refuge for survivors of domestic violence but Teuila had been sparing with the rest of the details of her life before New York. Bree believed she was an orphan before her reinvention, an abandoned child who had found a home at the centre under the care of Beth Amani. Bree didn't know Teuila had a mother out there somewhere. She didn't know about the years of sporadic abuse Teuila had lived through. Or the greatest secret of all – how Teuila produced her awe-inspiring art pieces. How true the statement, 'She gives life to whatever she touches' really was.

Bree was her closest friend and she trusted her like no other. But only one person knew all her secrets.

And he'd walked out of her life those many years ago without even a backward glance.

A welcoming party waited for them at the centre. Senior students carrying freshly made ula of golden moso'oi and frangipani. Shy smiles as they draped the fragranced necklaces over their visitors. Several of the film crew shiny with the harassed sweat of new visitors to the island bustled over to give them terse instructions. They were taking still shots and setting up and they would be ready for the interview in another half hour. Mrs Amani ushered them into an expansive conference room and Bree collapsed into a chair with a grateful sigh at the air-conditioned comfort.

Teuila excused herself. There was somewhere she wanted — no, needed — to visit. The centre had grown since she was last there, new classroom blocks and a beautiful new library. But the grove of trees at the far end of the property was still there. It had been much easier for her fourteen-year-old self to squeeze through the gap in the fence, but after one panicked moment when her hair caught on the chain-link wire, Teuila was through the barrier and into the trees.

It had been too long. She closed her eyes and raised her face to the breeze, breathing in deeply the scents of the forest. Lush green, woven with a hint of frangipani, the underlying richness of black earth, the cloying taste of fresh-cut green grass, and a hint of salt from the not-too-distant ocean. Branches rustled a greeting and leaves trembled as Fanua greeted her daughter. This had been her retreat all those years ago. Where she had come to escape the crowded confines of the centre and get lost in the solitude. Teuila sank to her knees and carefully dug her fingers into the soil as the grove of frangipani trees rejoiced in her return with a shower of blossoms dancing in the breeze. Pink-tinged petals, wine-red, scarlet and pearl-white.

It was like music. The gently pulsing sound of life, of earth, breathing in harmony with her, soothing her ragged heartbeat. Dozing flower buds awakened and turned their faces towards the woman kneeling in the grass. Vines unfurled from the trees above and leaned to encircle her. The feather-light breeze danced its way through her hair, whispered against her cheek. A nearby stream picked up speed and added its refrain. Everything that breathed radiated its message of welcome. Nature spoke and Teuila listened. She listened and she knew she was not alone. People had always let her down. Failed her. Hurt her. Disappointed her. Betrayed her. But Fanua never had and never would.

A rush of indefinable joy as familiar life welcomed her home. A hint of reproach. *It has been too long*, the voices said. *Why have you stayed away from the land which loves you? Which nurtures and soothes your soul?*

She nodded silently, unable to stop the happy tears streaming down her face. *I'm here now*. A gossamer cloud of butterflies fluttered into view, enveloped her in an intricate embrace, their red and blue velvet wings a caress against her skin in the dappled sunlight.

A voice startled her reverie. "You've still got it."

She leapt to her feet with a muffled sound of surprise, butterflies scattering in her panic as she turned to face the interloper. "You!"

Keahi raised an eyebrow at her disapproval. "Yeah, me. Problem?" Without waiting for a reply, he walked forwards and bent to trail his fingers through the thick blanket of blossoms. A smile. "I forgot just how amazing your Gift really is."

"I'm not surprised. It's been twelve years." With that curt response, she spun on her heel and started walking back to the centre, wiping the evidence of her tears from her face and hoping he hadn't seen her crying. Never show weakness in front of your enemies.

"Hey, wait up." Keahi strode after her.

Teuila turned back. Calm, poised and professional. "I have to go. There's a TV crew waiting for me." She liked the way that sounded. Yes, I have television appointments too, so there.

"They're still setting up. They won't need us for a while yet."

"What?"

"I just came from them. Still working on camera angles and stuff. They'll come get us when it's time."

"Us? What do you mean us?"

Again the raised eyebrow as he grinned slightly. "I'm in the doco too, didn't you know?"

"No, I didn't. Why would you be in it?" demanded Teuila, hands on hips. She knew she was being rude, but she didn't care. Not when she was trying – and failing – not to notice how striking he looked in the daylight. How much he'd changed over the years and yet stayed the same. The tattoos and ridged burn scars, the close-cropped dark hair and chiselled features she knew well. His lingering, haunting face often appeared at the edge of her dreams. The knowing smile with its mocking edge. The lean, rangy, muscled frame that moved with restrained grace and agility. They were all familiar and aroused a prickling wave of heat inside her – even as she tried to stamp down on it and shut it down. There was a difference, though. An easy certainty that hadn't been there before. Born of confidence? From success and celebrity perhaps? The Keahi she had known had burned with restlessness, an edge of anger always simmering just beneath the surface.

"Because it's trying to raise the centre's profile," replied Keahi.

"So they're featuring a movie star just because he – what? – volunteered here for a few hours a lifetime ago?"

"Pathetic, I know." A shrug and an easy smile. "But clever marketing."

"In that case, they don't need me. May as well do the whole series on you. The camera loves you," spat Teuila. Women the world over love you. Ugh. Stop it, Teuila.

"Don't be stupid. They've already got the whole thing scripted," said Keahi. "Having us both is good television. And that means it's good for the centre."

She gritted her teeth at the logic of his argument. Knowing she couldn't back out no matter how much she wanted to, because raising the centre's profile and increasing its capacity to help other children like her was supposed to be the purpose of this whole trip. And having a mega-famous film star like Keahi would guarantee that.

"Why'd you do it?" she demanded. Arms folded across her chest. Wishing there was a wall between them. Make that an ocean. That would be safer. Less likely she would betray herself.

"Do what?"

"If you wanted to give the Nafanua Centre a million dollars, you could have just donated it directly."

A slow smile. "But where's the fun in that?" he drawled.

His glee was an irritation. Especially remembering her unsettled sleep the night before, plagued with memories and questions, and all of them with his name on them. "Is that what this is to you? Is that what I am to you? A joke? You made a spectacle of me last night. Everybody was laughing at me because of what you did."

The raised eyebrow. The one she'd always been thrilled to see when they were teenagers all those years ago. And then she'd decided she hated it, after the world had 'discovered it' and raved about his 'rakish charm' in the tabloids.

"That's not what I saw," he said. "You owned that crowd."

"Bidding for a date cheapened what was supposed to be an art auction. How can I hope to have the art world take me seriously when you made me a piece of merchandise?"

His grin disappeared, replaced by something else. Something cold and predatory. "That wasn't me. Your boyfriend did that."

She stopped herself from the quick denial. It was none of his business who she was dating. Or not dating. She owed this man nothing. He was nothing to her. And she needed to cling fast to that.

A defiant rise of her chin. "So we can agree then that it was only a donation to the centre. We don't actually have to go on a date."

Confidence replaced the coldness. "What? You don't want to have dinner with an old friend?"

"But we're not friends, are we?" she replied.

If her words cut him, he didn't show it. Only another easy grin. "I thought we were. It's what I'm going to say in the interview. Would you rather I call you my lifelong blood enemy? Say the word, and I'll follow your lead."

Teuila was trapped. She knew it wouldn't help anyone to have any animosity between them show up in the documentary. And it certainly wouldn't help the centre.

"Aren't you in a rush to get back to Hollywood? Why waste time on dinner?" she said.

"Hawaii."

"Excuse me?"

"I live in Hawaii, when I'm not working," explained Keahi.

A shrug to show she didn't care where the hell he lived. So long as it was far away from her. "I won't keep you. This documentary should only need you for today. Forget the dinner." She started to walk away, back to the school.

"I don't think so." His words stopped her in her tracks. "I paid a million dollars for the privilege of having dinner with you. And I intend to collect on that."

She wanted to argue that he'd paid money for a painting, but she didn't want that memory – or its traitorous memento – brought into the conversation. An exasperated sigh. "But what's the point? You don't want to go out with me."

"You don't know what I want with you, Teuila," he said. "But I paid, and you're going to deliver."

A sharp wind rustled through the trees. It sent frangipani blossoms spinning in a cloud around them. Their soft perfume soothed Teuila. Calmed her somewhat. This man was trying to get under her skin and she wasn't going to let him.

"It's a very generous donation," she said stiffly. "It will do a lot of good for the children at the centre."

"I didn't do it for the centre," said Keahi, the look in his eyes dark and unreadable, his voice no longer confrontational. There was emotion there, yes, but it was something tender and gentle. A glimpse into the boy he'd once been when it was just the two of them. When they were friends.

There was a shivering sigh as boughs rustled and creaked. A hovering splash of red as a sega mo'o seemed to stop mid-flight. Taken aback. Surprise. Shock. The day caught its breath as she did.

And then a voice called, "Teuila where are you?" Irritation and the sound of approaching footsteps. Bree came into view on the path. "There you are," she said. "Beth said you might be here. I had to get a student to find the key to the gate so I could get through, and now I'm all sweaty and there's dirt stuck on my heels. What on earth are you doing out here?" A sly grin replaced her annoyance as she caught sight of Keahi. "With the Sexiest Man Alive. Why am I not surprised? Hello, Keahi. The crew is ready for you both. That is, unless you two are busy? I can come back later ..." Her voice trailed away suggestively.

Teuila's face burned as if she'd been caught doing something illicit. She looked flustered. "We're coming."

"Mmm, without even touching ..." Bree's blue eyes sparkled with mischief. "You must be good, Keahi!"

He laughed easily while Teuila flushed even more. "No, I didn't mean ... Ugh. Whatever." The thought made her even more annoyed with Keahi. She stalked off back in the direction of the centre.

The filming of the documentary wasn't as painful as Teuila had thought it would be. She had to admit that was because of Keahi. He joked with the crew and immediately put everyone at ease with skilled confidence. There was a moment in the tour of the school when the interviewer asked Teuila why she had been at the centre as a child. She'd known they would ask about her abuse and she'd practised what she would say. But in that moment, with the cameras trained on her and the room full of curious crew members, she froze and felt the prickle of tears. The last thing she wanted to do was cry in front of this crowd of strangers. On camera. She felt the overwhelming urge to run from the room and never come back.

Before she could move, Keahi stepped between her and the camera. "The centre provided a lot of youth with the education they needed and couldn't get anywhere else. It was how we first met, wasn't it, Teuila?" He threw her a golden smile and her cold panic dissipated a little. "I was teaching my kickboxing class and she was the most serious and feisty kid I'd ever seen. A fast learner. It didn't take her long to start kicking the teacher's ass!"

Everyone laughed at that, and the director called, "Cut," so they could do a retake.

"Oops, sorry for the cussing," said Keahi. It was impossible for anyone to be angry with him, though, as he flashed a contrite smile and looked so earnest that even Teuila half-believed him.

She watched him from the other side of the room as he moved among the crew, asking questions, learning everyone's names, and cracking light jokes. From there he went to sit with the students who had come to watch the filming. He obliged their requests for selfies, and signed their shirts and notebooks. One young boy who didn't have a notebook took off his seevae kosokoso and asked Keahi to sign them – which he did – amid much laughter and teasing from the other children. Teuila had to admit she was surprised by him. This wasn't the Keahi she remembered. That boy had been surly and often churlish, lashing out at the slightest opportunity. Only when it had been just them, and she had been vulnerable, had she seen his gentle kindness, the wry humour. Whenever others were around, he'd become the bitter, sardonic Keahi who stirred up trouble everywhere he went and said offensive things as second nature. There was a world of difference now. This man emanated a friendly warmth that others responded to easily.

"He's an actor, he's faking it," Teuila muttered to herself. But if she were completely honest, she would have to admit that she felt a stab of jealousy to see him so relaxed and at home with a room full of veritable strangers.

By midday, Teuila had to admit she was glad that Keahi was there. He took the pressure off her and made the experience much less anxiety-inducing than it would have been otherwise. The producer had them take the camera crew on a tour of the school, and Keahi had funny anecdotes to share about different spots along the way. Listening to him talk, Teuila was surprised. He had always projected a world-weary air when he came to teach classes at the centre, as if he hated the people and the place. Now she realised that had been one of his acts. Pretend you don't care and it hurts less when people reject you. Pretend you don't care and others will have fewer expectations of you.

When they got to the gym where Teuila had taken self-defence classes with Keahi as the instructor, the producer asked if they could get some footage of the two of them in the ring, maybe sparring. But the last thing Teuila wanted was to be on camera in gym gear, or to do anything that would bring her into close proximity with Keahi. She made up an excuse and they took a break. The school had prepared a generous lunch and once she had finished her plate of sandwiches and fruit, Teuila went over to Keahi.

"Thank you," she said, trying not to sound begrudging. She had to give credit where it was due, she told herself.

He raised that familiar eyebrow. "For what?"

"For that." She gestured expansively at the crew setting up for the next shot. "You made it bearable. You're good at it. I don't know if I could have got through it without you there." The words were dragged over rocks of unwillingness but she had to say them. Just as she anticipated, the compliment lit up that familiar, crooked grin of self-assurance.

"We always made a good team," he said.

For a moment she was taken back in time to when they were teenagers united against a world determined to break them, over and over again. The rush of familiarity made her angry. It reminded her what it had been like before he had left. Suddenly. Abandoning her. Without any goodbyes or further word.

Unaware of her turmoil of emotions, Keahi added, "And sometimes a movie star comes in handy, eh?" His easy smile did strange things to her insides. Slow-burning, not unpleasant things which inexplicably irritated her.

She frowned and said, "I wouldn't know. Thankfully I lead a low-key life with no movie stars in it."

He was unfazed by her sudden hostility. Which she should have expected because this was Keahi after all. He'd had a lifetime of shrugging off antagonism, rolling with sucker punches, and lashing out when he felt like it. He gave a lazy roll of his shoulders. "Oh, I don't know, life with me can be pretty exciting. You might like it."

"No, I wouldn't," she said. "All I want is to be left in peace so I can make my art."

"Really? You didn't seem to mind that creep's attention last night. He wasn't exactly leaving you in peace, was he?" He spoke lightly but Teuila saw the tell-tale twitch of his jaw which told her he was gritting his teeth. It was something he used to do when they were kids, and seeing it after all these years gave her a rush of confidence. It was a reminder that he was still Keahi. And while he might be an Oscar-winning actor, he couldn't conceal everything from her. Seeing her with Marc last night had bothered him. That knowledge gave her a buzz. It shouldn't have, but it did!

"He's a fan of my art," she said primly.

At that moment Bree interrupted them, her face alight with excitement. "I just got off the phone with that fan. Teuila, he wants to commission you to do a series of feature pieces for the new resort. He's willing to pay whatever you ask. This is it! I've set up a meeting for you two. He says he wants you to work closely on the project together."

Teuila should have been excited. But all she felt was a cold pit of dread. She couldn't explain it, but Marc Gold made her uncomfortable. A sense of disquiet. But the look on Keahi's face surprised her. He was angry. No, more than that. He looked murderous.

"Don't do it," he said.

"Excuse me?" said Teuila, with ice in her voice.

"You don't need him. He's not safe. You shouldn't work with him."

"Don't tell me what to do," said Teuila. "I'm capable of making my own decisions, thank you."

"I didn't say you weren't," said Keahi. "But you need to be smart and keep away from that man. I can read him a mile off. He's dangerous."

"And you're not?" Teuila hit back with daggered sweetness. A sudden thought. She turned to the film crew, called out to the producer. "Actually, I've changed my mind. Can we do a sparring session after all? Give you some more footage to choose from? The kickboxing classes are why Keahi got involved in the centre in the first place."

The producer nodded eagerly. "Of course. Let's do it. I'll have the team set up over here."

"A sparring session?" said Keahi. Puzzled. "Really?"

"What's the matter, Keahi?" said Teuila. "Scared to get in the ring with your old student?" She bunched her thick hair into a bun, tying it out of the way as she kicked off her shoes.

She didn't wait for an answer, just went to change into workout gear. By the time she returned, the film crew was in position. Keahi was across the room talking to the crew when she walked in. She didn't notice his face. She didn't realise that when he saw her, it was as if the world stopped. She had stripped down to her tank top and a loose pair of shorts borrowed from one of the older students. She was all sparse strength and muscle. Gone was the skinny, bruised kid of so many years ago. His eyes ran appreciatively along the curve and contour of her arms, the lean cut of her torso and then to her legs. Corded muscle and bulk. She walked to the centre of the ring, dancing lightly on the balls of her feet as she shook her arms loosely with a little smile on her face as if welcoming the freedom of being out of her formal clothes and back where she belonged. Where she felt alive. Awake. Free and ready.

A long, low whistle from the camera guy beside Keahi broke through his haze. A muffled exclamation. "Would you check that out!" Keahi turned, wanting to rip out the man's throat.

But before he could react, Bree stepped in. A hand placed on his arm. A teasing laugh. "So, Keahi, are you sure you want to take on my friend in the ring? She looks impressive. So much so that I'm afraid for you! Does your agent know that you're jumping into fights with people when you travel? Don't they forbid that kind of thing? In case of injuries. Y'know, to the merchandise?" Bree waved airily to encompass his whole body. "You're a lucrative product."

Keahi laughed as if he knew she wanted him to. But not before giving the camera man a last glare so loaded with menace that the man instinctively moved several feet back. "My agent trusts me. Besides, this is only a sparring session. Between old friends."

Bree looked over to Teuila warming up at the bag with single-minded focus. She'd already worked up a light sweat and the sheen glistened on her skin. Bree dropped her voice, "Are you sure about that, Keahi? She looks scary. I'm not sure she thinks the same way about this sparring session as you do. Let me go talk to her."

Keahi tugged his shirt up and over his head, throwing it lightly to the side before walking to the square. The gathered audience of students cheered loudly as he took up position in the ring. He waved at them with a casual grin. "This is only a demo. Remember kids, don't try this at home, okay?"

He walked to face Teuila, trying hard not to stare at her body, keeping his eyes firmly trained on her face. "So, where shall we start?"

Before he could finish his sentence, Teuila hit him with a sharp kick to his abdomen. He auto-flexed and the kick glanced off him harmlessly, but he was caught off guard. "Hey, hey, easy there, girl. I thought we were going to work out the rules of engagement first."

"You talk too much," said Teuila. Her voice was low and deadly. She kicked again. This time he blocked and then crouched into a fighting stance. She smiled. But it wasn't a kind smile. "That's more like it. No talking. Just fight."

She followed up her words with a spinning round kick and then a combination of punches to his face and torso. Keahi countered and feinted, swayed and blocked but it wasn't easy to evade her. Teuila was lightning fast and fuelled with a fierceness that was unnerving.

"Why are you holding back?" she asked.

"Why are you so angry?" Keahi replied. "I thought we were f–"

Teuila punched him in the face. So fast and hard that he didn't see it coming. Her fist caught him and it hurt. Ouch. But it was the look of satisfaction in her eyes which cut him more.

"I'm not going to hurt you," he said through gritted teeth.

"Why?" asked Teuila as they circled each other, wary eyes, measuring and anticipating. Her voice was mocking. "Because I'm a woman? Because we're friends?"

With her eyes still on him, Teuila called out to her agent. "Bree, call Marc. Tell him I'd love to meet with him. To discuss him becoming a patron of my art. Over dinner. A date."

She was baiting him. And it worked. Keahi spun, kicked, dipped and swayed. One minute he stood in front of Teuila and the next he had her in a chokehold. He could smell clean sweat and a hint of citrus as she struggled in his arms. He spoke over his shoulder at Bree. "Wait! Don't make that call."

Bree, already on the phone, gave him a helpless shrug as if to say, 'Sorry, already doing it.'

Keahi's jaw clenched as he fake-smiled for the rapt audience. Light teasing with a razor undertone. "You shouldn't make important business decisions while you're in the ring."

"Why not? I'm good at multitasking."

He tightened his grip, "First throw and pin wins. Agreed?" Another wide-open smile for the crowd who cheered them on. Then he whispered against her ear so the film crew couldn't pick it up. "And when I win, you cancel that meeting. And stay away from that man."

Because she was facing away from him, Keahi didn't see the effect his words had on her. The flash of dangerous fire in her eyes, the brief moment of meditative contemplation as she took a deep breath. Followed by the smile. The one that Bree could have told him meant only one thing. Keahi, you are so screwed.

All he felt was her body soft against his as she stopped resisting and relaxed, her back against him. One minute she was all fight and rage, the next she was pliable and supple. The transformation was abrupt and so extreme that Keahi was taken by surprise. He was no longer grappling an opponent but embracing a fiercely beautiful woman whose body melded into his as if they belonged together. He breathed her scent in deeply, eyes half-closed, as he was swept away in a rush of longing. The crowd melted away. Everyone and everything that wasn't Teuila disappeared. Didn't matter. He wanted to look into her eyes, see her face. See if the longing and aching need that growled deep within him was echoed in her. He wanted their lips to touch. He wanted her kiss. His grip loosened, ever so slightly.

All it took was a heartbeat of letting down his guard, and in that moment she slipped free of his grasp and caught his legs in a sweep kick so he fell backwards. It all happened so fast that he didn't have time to brace himself. He hit the ground hard. It forced all the air out of him, leaving him gasping and stunned. Teuila pinned him, both her legs firmly hooked on either side of him, her elbow at his throat. She was breathing heavily and sweat dripped from her face onto his. He could see her face. Her eyes. And no, there was no longing or aching need in them. Only triumphant fury as she leaned in to say, "Don't ever tell me what to do. I see who I want to see."

Then she stood and walked away, leaving him in a dishevelled heap on the ground and the crowd cheering for the victor.

But Keahi wasn't going to let her get away that easily. He leapt up and ran after her. Caught her outside the door. Just the two of them. "Wait." He grabbed at her arm, spun her around. "What's your problem? That was supposed to be a friendly spar. What was that? Ever since I got here you've been wanting to kick the shit out of me. Why?"

Teuila was breathing heavily. "Let go of me."

"No. We need to talk."

"We have nothing to talk about." Her voice was nearly a shout now. "Let go of me or else I'm going to break your arm. And you know I know how."

Keahi dropped his hand. Ran his fingers through his hair in frustration. "What is your problem?"

That was when Teuila's tight rein of control broke. "You left," she said, shaking with rage. "You were supposed to be my friend. And you left."

"What are you talking about?" said Keahi, puzzled.

"Twelve years ago. You're here one day, gone the next. No goodbyes. No message. Nothing. I have to hear it from Leila that you've gone back to the States. You couldn't even tell me yourself? I thought we were friends." She crumpled, leaned back against the wall, her eyes shut tight against the tears, fists clenched, hating herself for baring her soul like this and allowing him in. "You left and didn't say goodbye. Why?"

It was Keahi's turn to be at a loss for words. To struggle with truth and lies, the unravelling of the shroud of secrecy. "Things happened. I needed to get back."

"Things?" demanded Teuila. "The day before you left, we talked about everything. You told me about your sister. I told you what I'd never told anybody. I trusted you. But you disappeared without trusting me enough to say why."

"I can't tell you."

"You can't tell me?" Teuila was incredulous. "Even now? When it doesn't matter any more?"

"You wouldn't understand."

"Try me," said Teuila with pleading in her voice.

"I'm sorry. I can't."

"Why? Because I'm too young? Because I'm just an abused kid that you feel sorry for?" Teuila spat the words, every one heavy with pain. "In case you haven't noticed, we're not kids any more, Keahi. And you don't get to show up here, throwing your money around, thinking you can buy me and make everything okay. Not even with a million fudging dollars. You may have forgotten everything about the past. But I haven't."

And with that, Teuila left, slamming the door behind her.

"Ouch." It was Bree in the hall. An unreadable expression on her face. "Teuila doesn't cuss. But I do. In case you need a translation, she meant, a million fucking dollars." And now there was nothing but ice in her eyes. "I don't know what's going on here, but it's clear you two have history. Teuila's more than my client. She's my friend. I've never seen her this mad before. You hurt my friend. What are you going to do to fix it?"

110

"Want to talk about it?" asked Bree as they drove back to the hotel.

"Not really," bit out Teuila.

"Okay. But can I say that you were kickass amazing out there?" said Bree. "I didn't know you could do that. I mean, I knew you went to the gym and worked out but I didn't realise you were doing stuff like that. And when you knocked down the world's sexiest, most badass man and trapped him in that chokehold?" Bree's awe turned into an exultant shriek. "That was the best thing ever!"

Teuila couldn't stay impervious to her buzz. A small smile cracked the haunted frown. "It wasn't bad. Do you think they'll put that into the documentary? I hope not."

"Who cares if they do? I got the whole thing on my phone and it's going up on my Instagram as we speak." Bree's laughter filled the car and the driver gave both women a quizzical look in the rear-view mirror.

"I feel silly for holding this grudge for so long. It's childish, I know," confessed Teuila. "But I can't seem to help it."

"If you were hurt and never resolved it, then of course you're allowed to feel whatever you want to. Don't beat yourself up."

They continued the rest of the drive in silence, with Teuila staring out at the scenery, deep in thought. It wasn't until much later, after they'd both showered and ordered room service, that Teuila spoke again. This time in the air-conditioned privacy of their suite.

"He was my friend, y'know? I didn't have many. Well, I didn't have any! Until I met Leila and Daniel and the others. They made me part of their group and I felt for the first time like I belonged. But Keahi was different from the others."

Bree nodded emphatically as she sipped from her glass of wine. "Oh yes, I'm sure he was. All that delicious bad-boy wickedness!" She was trying to make Teuila smile and it worked.

"No, not like that. I mean, Keahi was the only one who had lived a life like mine. Who knew what I was going through. He understood. And he didn't judge me for any of it." A thoughtful pause. "Not that Leila and Daniel would have been judgy. They were always kind to me and never made me feel looked down upon. But their lives were so perfect compared to mine that I knew I could never fully explain what I was dealing with. Keahi knew."

Bree said gently, "Stuff you've never told me, right? It's okay. I know there's a lot about your childhood that you haven't shared with me. But you know you can if you ever want to talk, right? I'm here for you."

Bree reached out to take Teuila's hand in hers, squeezed it. For a moment the two were united in a moment of understanding that went beyond words.

"I know," said Teuila.

"But back to Keahi, the wicked sex god," reminded Bree with a sly grin.

Teuila laughed and the mood turned light again. "Yes, I had a crush on him. A schoolgirl crush. But I knew nothing would ever come of it. He was older than me. And so into Leila back then that everyone could see it." An eye roll. "So I had my crush but it wasn't a big deal. It was his friendship that meant the world to me. I could talk to him, confide in him and know that he understood. There was one time when he stood up for me, actually stood up to my mother's boyfriend." A deep breath. "The man who was abusing me. Nobody had ever fought for me before. Not even my mother. Keahi took him on, this man who terrified me. My fear ruled my life then. Even after I went to live at the centre, I was always afraid of him. Scared he could see me, no matter where I went. Hear me. That he would know every time I told someone about the abuse. That he would punish me. It sounds so silly in the light of day to talk about it. But I truly believed he was some all-powerful being that could reach out and get me, no matter where I was." She shuddered and Bree came over to hug her.

"I'm sorry, Teuila. I hate that you went through that. I'm sorry you weren't protected and loved the way you should have been."

There were a few tears, but Teuila smiled through them at her friend. "You should have seen Keahi that day. He was a skinny eighteen-year-old. Not the built man he is now. And he was shorter than Toma." A grimace of distaste at the mention of her abuser's name. "But he fought him, knocked him down. And I realised for the first time that Toma wasn't invincible. He was only a person. A horrible, evil person. But still only a man. Who could be stopped. Silenced. Knocked down. Keahi did that and it set me free in a sense."

"And then?" prompted Bree.

"And then he disappeared. Got on a plane and left. Never looked back." A wry grimace. "Oh, but he told Leila he was leaving. She's the one who let me know finally where he'd gone. Turns out she drove him to the airport, even."

Bree heard the long-ago hurt in Teuila's voice and hugged her friend again. "I'm sorry. You didn't deserve that."

Teuila tried false cheer. "It was a long time ago. I should be over it."

"Fourteen-year-old you deserved better than that from your friends. And now twenty-six-year-old Teuila certainly deserves better than for a movie star to snap his fingers and have her come running. Screw that! You make him work for it, girl."

"I tried asking him today. He said he couldn't tell me why he left so suddenly. Even now, he can't even give me that." She punched the pillow viciously. "Aargh, I wish I'd punched him several times more!"

"Oh, girl, you hit him enough. Besides, we can't afford to get sued for permanent damage to that million-dollar face. Nah, there's other ways to make him suffer. Delicious ways even."

A peal of laughter then. Bree turned serious. "Did you mean it about meeting Marc? You don't actually want him for a patron, do you?"

"I thought you liked him. Money and connections, things we need, right?"

Bree shook her head. "I'm not sure any more."

"It's only a meeting. It'll be fine." Teuila spoke with a certainty she didn't feel.

CHAPTER SEVEN

When Teuila came down to reception for her meeting with Marc, there was a stranger, a white woman, waiting instead. Impeccably dressed in a cream linen suit, she greeted Teuila with a smile which didn't reach her eyes.

"I'm Lindsey Atkins, Mr Gold's personal assistant. He's asked me to please escort you to the Sanctuary property. Come, the car is this way."

Teuila was glad she had refused Bree's offer to accompany her to the meeting because for sure Bree would be making all kinds of snide comments right now about men who thought they were too rich and too important to come in person to meet a woman they had invited to lunch.

The drive was uneventful. Her escort snapped orders at the driver and then worked on an iPad the entire way, leaving Teuila free to observe her surroundings as the car took them to an area of the island that she was unfamiliar with. They drove for over half an hour into the mountains and deeper into the forest. There were few houses here but unlike most isolated spots of Samoa, the road was perfect. No potholes or unevenness anywhere.

Teuila couldn't help herself. "This road. It's beautiful. It looks brand new."

Lindsey didn't even look up from her computer. "Yes. Mr Gold had it made. Construction couldn't begin on the project until there was an adequate roadway." She may as well have added, 'You simpleton'.

Teuila gritted her teeth and resolved not to ask any more questions.

On arrival at the site, she heard the chanting first. Loud, urgent sounds.

"What's going on?" she asked as the car neared the crowd that had gathered outside the massive ornate steel gates. Security guards and barriers lined the road, keeping the protestors at bay. They were a diverse group, all ages, a mixture of palagi and Samoans. Several of them held signs aloft, with written slogans about saving the earth and protecting the environment.

Lindsey's reply was a derisive wave of her hand and a sneer. "Ignore them. A bunch of troublemakers and short-sighted fools. This land has been underutilised for centuries. Only now that Mr Gold is pouring millions into it, do they suddenly care."

The crowd shouted louder at the sight of the car.

"They think Mr Gold is in here," said Lindsey. "Don't worry. We will drive right through unimpeded." She went back to her iPad, with a frown of concentration, leaving Teuila to observe the action outside.

But the car came to a stop before it reached the gates. Lindsey barked an order at the driver. "What are you waiting for? Drive on!"

The driver turned to give them both an apologetic look. "I'm sorry, Ms Atkins. They're not moving out of the way. They're blocking the road this time."

Another sound of impatience from Lindsey. Teuila had to bite down on her smile. She knew it was rude, but it felt good to see this flawless model of efficiency get flustered. She turned to look out her window again, this time studying the apparent leaders of the protest who now stood in front of the car. One of them looked vaguely familiar. A young man with close-cropped dark hair, wearing a red shirt with his ie faitaga. An unusual choice of attire for a forest protest, mused Teuila. Half to herself, she said, "Hey, I think I know that guy. The one in the front? We went to school together. Right from kindergarten to high school." She put the window down so she could get a better look.

Lindsey ignored her, intent on issuing curt orders on her cell phone to the compound security.

Then the man looked right at her and his face lit up in recognition.

"Teuila? Is that you, sis?" he called out.

Teuila broke into a huge smile as she leaned out and waved. "Sione! Yes, it's me."

Teuila opened the door and exited the vehicle, ignoring Lindsey's order to get back in the car! She pushed her way through the noisy crowd. They were focused on the car and wanting to see the billionaire owner of the project, so they paid little attention to her.

Both laughing, Sione and Teuila embraced in a warm hug. She felt a rush of homesickness for the old days. Flooded with the memories of the good times growing up here, because yes, there had been some good times. She'd spent the last twelve years trying to put her abusive past behind her and move on, but it had meant she also purposely blocked out all the good things. The friendships she had made at school. Like Sione.

"Look at you!" he exclaimed as he held her at arm's length to look her up and down. "All grown up and beautiful, and a famous artist, too."

Teuila tried to shrug off his admiration. It always embarrassed her when she was praised for her work. "No, I'm none of that. A trying artist," she corrected him. "Trying hard."

Sione shook his head and his smile was wide and open. "No. Definitely famous. I saw you on the TV the other night. At your art auction. Your work is amazing. I told all my cousins – that's my friend on the TV. We go ways back! They didn't believe me."

The driver appeared at her side, a hand on her elbow. "Miss, the boss wants you to get back in the car. Please. She said it's not safe out here."

Teuila knew he was only doing his job, so she didn't get mad at him. Instead she gave him a smile. "I'm fine. I can walk to the gates from here. Don't worry."

He was reluctant to leave her. Probably more afraid of facing Lindsey than he was of offending her, so Teuila reassured him. "I'm with my friend here. He'll make sure I'm all right. Won't you, Sione?"

"Of course," said Sione. He added in Samoan, "Aua te popole uso." He waited until the driver was out of hearing and then turned back to Teuila, this time with questions in his face. "What are you doing here with them?"

Quickly Teuila explained she was there to check out display sites for a possible commission job. Sione frowned when she got to the part about meeting Marc. "You should be careful with that one," he said. "I don't trust that man."

Teuila nudged him as she gestured at the protest. "I think I can tell. So what's this all about, anyway?"

The crowd was singing now, a beautiful Samoan song about the toloa bird and its forever love for its home, the river that always calls for it to return. It was a familiar song for most Samoans and Teuila felt a lightness in her chest to hear it. *I'm like that toloa bird. Tried to stay away for so long, but home always called to me. And here I am …*

"The short answer is that this project is being built on an archaeological site, an early settlement that dates back over a thousand years. LiDAR technology shows there's a structure even bigger than the Pulemelei Mound. It's covered with forest vegetation, but it's there."

The Pulemelei was a pyramid-like structure in the Palauli district of Savaii, the largest ancient building in Polynesia. It stood as a testament to the engineering skill and ingenuity of their ancestors. To find another even bigger than the Pulemelei was an amazing discovery.

"It was only recently detected, and then Gold bought the lease," continued Sione. "We don't know how much of the ancient remains he's already ruined with his buildings. And we'll never have access to it now that he's put his Sanctuary, Gold Mountain Project there. But we know he's removing most of the native trees and plants so that he can replace them with flora and fauna that's more familiar to his clientele."

Teuila frowned. "Destroying all that history is an awful thing. And why would tourists come all this way and want to see trees that look exactly like what they have at home? What's the point?"

Sione shook his head, a look of weary resignation on his face. "Who knows how the mind of the coloniser works? I better let you go in. Don't want you to be late for your meeting."

Teuila was unwilling to let this link to her childhood slip away so easily. "Can we meet up again sometime? Talk more? Catch up?"

Her worries that her old friend might be angry with her because of her connection to this man who was responsible for the imminent destruction of Samoan history and heritage were somewhat allayed by the warmth of his smile. "Sure. I'd like that."

The driver appeared at her side again, and this time Teuila allowed herself to be escorted back to the vehicle. Security personnel at the gates gave her hard stares of disapproval which she ignored.

In the car, Lindsey was even icier than she'd been before. "Mr Gold expects punctuality. And he won't like it that we stopped so you could fraternise with the protestors."

Teuila gave Lindsey a sweet smile. "Unlike you, I don't work for Mr Gold. It's not my job to worry about his happiness." Her storm-filled eyes dared the other woman to bite back. Wisely Lindsey said nothing.

The gates opened at the touch of a button. As the car idled, waiting to drive in, Lindsey stowed away her iPad and turned to Teuila. "Can I have your cell phone, please?" It wasn't a request. At Teuila's surprised look, she added, "Company policy. No unsanctioned photographs or communications from within the Sanctuary are allowed. For security reasons. You understand."

No, Teuila didn't understand. But she'd come this far and wasn't about to back out now. She quickly sent a message to Bree telling her about the phone embargo and a breezy, 'Send the army if you don't hear from me by nightfall! Haha!' Then handed the phone over.

The gate shut behind them with a click of finality which made Teuila even more uneasy.

It was as if they had entered a different world. It didn't even look like Samoa anymore. The paved road was lined with sweeping trees that Teuila knew immediately weren't local. It took them to a second security perimeter and once they entered that gate, the full majesty of the Sanctuary was on display. Teuila was reminded of the one time Bree had taken her home to visit her parents. Bree had grown up in an exclusive suburb outside Washington DC, huge homes spaced out over rolling fields and carefully tended flower beds, interspersed with golf courses and country clubs. That's what the Sanctuary looked like. A luxurious estate that screamed of wealth and privilege.

Lindsey pointed towards a cluster of structures far in the distance. "The Sanctuary town is there. We have a shopping mall, cinemas, cafes and restaurants. Our clients will bring all they need with them, but we will ensure they want for nothing while they stay with us."

There was a shine of blue off to the right. "What's that?" asked Teuila.

"The lake," explained Lindsey, warming up just a little in her role as tour guide. It's clear that she felt much more at ease here in the Sanctuary, behind the safety of the looming guard walls and rows of security personnel. Rather than out there 'with the unruly natives', guessed Teuila.

"You can't see it from here, but if you keep driving past the lake, you eventually get to the ocean. We have a beautiful golden sand beach with villas where you can fall asleep to the sound of the waves, wake up and walk right out into the sea. And all private of course. The perimeter is fully secure even to the ocean."

"Of course it is," said Teuila with a grimace of a smile. She was beginning to understand why Sione and the others were protesting outside the Sanctuary.

The car drew up to a grand house, several storeys high, that looked like a colonial mansion. White columns holding up the sky. Marc came down the steps to greet them, opening the car door for Teuila. There was an artfulness about the whole thing. As if it was staged. Or at the very least, all the elements chosen for their maximum effect. And the one controlling all the elements, Marc Gold.

"Teuila, welcome to the Sanctuary. It's a pleasure to have you join us." Everything about him was smooth and practised. "Come in."

Once again, Teuila felt that undefinable tingle when his hand touched hers. It wasn't unpleasant, but it wasn't exciting either. He always held her hand for a fraction longer than necessary, the kind of touch that made her question its meaning. And while he was the picture of courtesy and manners, he always stood a little too close, prompting Teuila to edge back a bit or find a reason to move away. She couldn't explain why. It was simply a feeling.

She followed Marc into the house as Lindsey disappeared with the skill of well-trained employees who know exactly what their boss wants without them saying a word. Teuila didn't notice her going, though, because she was too busy admiring the stunning sculptures and art that adorned the foyer. "You have a Maretti?" she breathed in awe as she gazed up at the white marbled figure of an Amazon warrior that had pride of place in the room. "I've only seen her work in pictures, never up close."

Marc had a satisfied smile on his face as he watched her reactions. "Yes, I'm a collector of her work. I own more back in my New York apartment, but I only had this one brought here. One day you can tour my collection."

It wasn't a question. Or even an invitation. It was a statement of fact. As usual, he spoke with an easy certainty that rankled her. Did everyone who had unimaginable wealth see the world that way? Talk to everyone that way? As if they never had to ask because they already knew what you would do because they decreed it? It left Teuila with a sour taste in her mouth and almost ruined her enjoyment of the Maretti. Almost.

"This is the first space I have in mind for one of the commissioned pieces you will make for me," said Marc pointing to the opposite side of the room. "I want a Samoan warrior sculpture that will complement the Maretti. With these high ceilings, it should be a big bold piece that stands quite tall –"

"The first space?" interrupted Teuila. "You want to commission two pieces?"

There was a flash of annoyance on his face. Irritation at being interrupted? He quickly hid it, though, with that same practised smile. "Oh, wasn't I clear? The Sanctuary is a big resort. A world unto itself almost. I want several pieces commissioned specifically to complement what I'm creating here. What I want from you will require your full-time attention for quite a while. At least a year."

He said it as if she would be thrilled and honoured to be chosen. As if of course she would drop everything and devote a year of her life to making art pieces for his resort. His arrogance grated on her. "I can't take on that kind of commitment. I have a lot on my plate right now."

He continued as if she hadn't said anything. As if what she wanted and what she thought meant nothing to him. "It's important you see what I have built here and truly understand the vision for the Sanctuary. Then you can decide."

Teuila changed the subject. Because she wanted to shake his composure, she asked a question that she knew he wouldn't like.

"Who are the protestors outside?" Feigned ignorance. "What are they here for?"

Again the glimpse of dark in his face. Anger. It came and went so quickly that she could almost have imagined it. This man was good at pretending. A smile and airy wave of his hand. "A few disgruntled locals with concerns about the environmental impact of our project. Some rubbish about local legends and this being sacred land. Which is due to ignorance on their part because this is an entirely self-sustaining, renewable energy development which will truly be a remarkable achievement once it's open. A role model for others in the region. Come, let me give you a tour."

Teuila winced inwardly at his brusque dismissal of Samoan legends. Marc must have forgotten she was Samoan. Was she going to remind him? The burden of being a brown woman was having to decide every day whether you wanted to waste energy and time countering racism and ignorance. "I am not your educator or your racism instructor," she muttered to herself. So she bit her tongue and followed him as he led the way to a shuttle cart parked outside. She told herself that she had committed to meeting with this man and listening to his offer. It wouldn't be professional or polite to leave before he'd had a chance to explain what it was.

The tour went by quickly. The estate was vast but all the houses had been built the same so they had the vibe of 'if you've seen one, you've seen them all'. Marc gave her a running commentary on the project. The Sanctuary had its own airstrip for private jets to bring in their rich and famous owners. "That way ensuring peak convenience for them, and also privacy," he explained. The compound had its own stores, a medical clinic, everything that anyone from a privileged background would want. "So they don't ever feel like they're deprived, even though they're vacationing in a third world country, you know?"

Teuila nodded. Yes, she knew. Oh, the suffering a privileged palagi had to endure when they vacationed overseas …

From the shelter of the shuttle cart, Marc pointed out the private beach. Golden sand, lacy white surf, and coconut palms swaying in the breeze.

And not a brown person in sight to detract from the white fantasy.

Teuila absolutely had to query that part of Marc's tour. "You're not hiring any Samoans?"

"No," he said matter-of-factly, as if he was surprised she would even ask. "We want to ensure the staff have the skills and experience to cater for this kind of clientele. We're bringing in everyone we need and they will live in the staff quarters provided." He waved a hand off into the distance, beyond some trees.

"So how is the resort going to benefit the country?" she asked. Even as she kicked herself for the question. Did she really want to get into it?

"Oh, don't worry!" said Marc. "I'm paying a hefty price for this land. Samoa is getting a great deal." He continued with his tour, indifferent to the impact of his words on Teuila. "We have solar power, our own farms and cattle ranch, gardens for our fresh fruit and vegetables, and regular cargo plane flights from the US. We won't need to source anything from the locals, which will cut down on interaction."

This far inside the compound, they could no longer hear even a hint of sound from the protestors. It was as if they were in an entirely different world, removed from the Samoa that bustled and breathed outside its walls. "But that's the aim, isn't it?" said Teuila. "You don't want your guests to know that they're in Samoa."

Marc was delighted that she got it. "Yes. That's right. I want them to feel at home, as safe as they do when they're at home. With state-of-the-art trace sensors to check for any hint of the virus, people can be assured that this is a destination which guarantees them no exposure or risk. That's another reason why all our staff will be on strict contracts from the States and never leave the compound until it's time for their annual leave back home. Since Covid and its mutations, international travel hasn't been safe like it used to be. The

Sanctuary changes that. It reduces the infection risk and guarantees full viral safety for our clients."

The tour continued as Marc pointed out all the places where he wanted a sculpture. In the town square, at the entrance to the arts centre, at the front gate to the airfield. It was overwhelming. Finally Marc was done. "So, you've seen the Sanctuary. What do you think?"

She had to consider her words carefully. She could sense that her opinion mattered to him, but she was also mindful that she was alone in a gated compound with a man who was used to getting his way. In all things. A slight edge of warning tiptoed up her spine, and in that moment, Teuila wanted to be outside the Sanctuary walls. Away from there.

"It's very beautiful here," said Teuila. "And I can see why a place like this would be attractive to people."

It was a diplomatic and deliberately neutral answer, and Bree would have seen it immediately for what it was. Fake as hell! But Marc nodded his head with a smile. Pleased. Because he couldn't imagine anyone having a dissenting view so it was easy to accept her platitudes.

"We will go back to the house, have some refreshments," he said.

Teuila was relieved. But riding in the shuttle cart with a man you were trying very hard not to touch was exhausting. Every bump and jolt along the way had her jarring in her seat and jostling against his shoulder. And every time, she felt that same crawling sensation of wrongness. As if something inside her recognised something in Marc that shouldn't be there. Only that made no sense ...

Back at the grand house, Marc rang a crystal bell and the tinkling sound summoned two servers dressed in white who set up refreshments on a side table. They served Teuila a glass of chilled lemon water over ice, and a dainty plate of tiny cakes and sandwiches. The kind of food you took polite small bites of. Everything was delicious but unsubstantial. Teuila knew she would have to go to Sula's Bakery the minute she got back to the hotel and get herself several keke pua'a and a few coconut buns. Real food. Mac watched her as she ate, and the look in his eyes was indefinable. It was as if he was searching for something, trying to puzzle her out, as though she was a mystery that needed to be solved.

"Is anything wrong?" she asked. Direct and to the point. "You keep staring at me."

Marc smiled. It was meant to be reassuring. "I apologise. I don't mean to be rude. I feel like I know you from somewhere. Not that I've seen you before, no. More that I know you. Has anyone ever told you that you have an aura about you?"

"No," laughed Teuila. Marc sounded a bit silly, now, and that put her at ease.

He leaned forwards in his seat. The arrogance was gone and in its place was an earnestness that made him seem less predatory. More like a regular person. "I don't know how to explain it. When I shook your hand that first night at the auction, I felt something." Seeing her knowing expression, he rushed to clarify. "No, I don't mean in a sexual way. I mean that every time I'm with you, I get a boost in energy. It sounds strange, I know. I don't understand it myself. It's in your artwork, too. It makes me feel ... alive? Exhilarated?"

"Well, I've never had anyone give me that sort of feedback about my work before," said Teuila as she tried to choose her words to meet this puzzling new side of the man. "Thank you. I think."

Marc leaned back with a shamefaced smile. In that moment he looked younger and vulnerable. Less the hardened, practised billionaire. "I apologise again if this is all making you uncomfortable. That's not my intention. You see, I've been ill. Nothing serious," he hastened to add. "Some sort of tropical malaise that has put me under the weather. Not myself. But when I met you the other night, for the first time in a long time it was like that malaise lifted. I was myself again. Alive. I feel it every time I see you. Perhaps it's the gift in you."

"Gift? What do you mean?" said Teuila, her voice cold, as a thud of warning pounded in her chest. What did Marc know about her Gift?

"You know, your artist's gift. Your amazing talent that gives the world your sculptures and paintings."

Teuila's panic seeped from her. "Oh, that gift."

"Why, what other gift did you think I was talking about?" said Marc and now there was a hint of dark curiosity in his gaze. Like when an apex predator gets a whiff of the scent of its prey.

Teuila laughed nervously and waved away his question. "Nothing. You have me flustered, that's all. I'm not used to accepting compliments for my art. Bree is always telling me that I have to stop being such a mess when that happens."

Teuila needed a distraction. "Can we go outside?" she asked, walking to the nearest set of sliding doors that looked out over the shimmering silver lake.

"Of course," said Marc. He opened the doors and motioned her to go first. "This is my favourite view."

They walked out onto the deck that stretched out over the water. It was glorious. The magnitude of the lake took her breath away, with water stretching as far as the eye could see.

"It's magnificent," breathed Teuila. "I had no idea there was a lake this size up here. I thought only Lake Lanuto'o was on this island."

"Oh, this isn't a crater lake like Lanuto'o," explained Marc. "This lake is man-made. All this used to be forest."

"Really?" said Teuila. "You cleared all this area for a lake?"

"We didn't need to clear it. Simply flooded the valley. The forest didn't go anywhere. It's all underwater now." He carried on describing all the activities that the lake would cater for. "It's filled with several species of fish flown in specially. So our clients can enjoy a wide range of sport and relaxation activities while they stay here."

The talk of fishing, jet-skiing, hydro-boating – all of it faded to a blur as Teuila thought back to her conversation with Sione. "But what about the archaeological remains? Sione said something about an ancient city that's in this area." A gut punch of dread as she asked, "Did you flood all that, too?"

"Some of it, but not all," said Marc, seemingly unaware of her emotions. He pointed off to the right. "See those mountains? There are rock formations out there. It's not much. Whoever the early settlers were, they didn't build with metal, only wood and stone. So it's only the foundations of whatever the structures used to be. There is one large structure, though. A type of star pyramid, made from rocks. It's massive. They say it's even bigger than the one found on the other island." A casual shrug. "I'm not sure."

"I'm surprised they let you lease that land then, the section with the city on it." said Teuila.

"Oh, I agreed not to build over it. We're going to have it preserved and restored. Turned into a historical site with a nature trail. So the guests can explore and hike there. It's going to be a beautiful destination. Good for mountain biking, too." A frown then. In that moment he was nothing like the personable man who skilfully put Teuila at ease with charm and wit. It was as if the curtain slid back a little, allowing a glimpse of what stood behind it. "The majority of the group outside is being misled by a few profiteers with a hidden agenda. Before our project came along, the ruins were just pieces of stone overgrown by trees, decaying further each year, unseen and uncared for by anyone. My company is spending millions of dollars to safeguard this land and everything on it. Including key parts of this country's history. Who knows what damage the elements and further time would have wrought on those crumbling artefacts."

"But if this place is going to be sealed off from the rest of the country, doesn't that mean no Samoans will get access to the historical site? Only foreign tourists?"

He didn't like her question. "Yes, that is true. But there's always trade-offs for everything, don't you agree? We are taking excellent videography of the restoration process and there will be plenty of archaeological information made available for public access online and in other places. The Samoan people can rest assured that a vital piece of their history has been restored and preserved with the highest degree of security. We will take very good care of it. Come, let us go inside."

It was a decisive end to the conversation. Teuila cast one last look over her shoulder to the distant mountain before turning to follow Marc into the building. There was something out there. Calling to her. Something familiar and welcoming. Only she didn't know what it was.

Finally it was time for her to leave. Marc summoned the car and accompanied her to the hotel, dismissing the driver and taking over the wheel himself. There was a moment when she worried he would try to kiss her goodbye, but it was only a fleeting concern. He was too clever for that. He walked her to the hotel entrance and shook her hand. "Thank you for coming to the Sanctuary. I hope you have a better sense now of the kind of sculptures that will suit its special beauty and uniqueness."

It was only when Teuila was in the elevator and heading to her room that it occurred to her she hadn't even said she would take on his commission. Not once had he asked her. He just assumed she was going to do it.

Marc was in agony. He was a man who prized his self-control above all else. It was discipline that had got him where he was in life. But today had been the biggest challenge to that control. Being in close proximity to Teuila for even a few minutes was a test of everything he possessed. He was drawn to her. The very sight of her, the scent of her, the sound of her voice, the delicate dance of her laughter, made him hungry. So very hungry. The darkness had been gnawing away at his insides from the moment she arrived at the Sanctuary, all through the tour, during the drive back to her hotel. When she sat next to him, it was as if she had flipped a switch, one that unleashed a dam of feelings.

He didn't understand why, where it came from. Only that being next to her awakened the Hunger in him like nothing else. It made no sense because he felt both replete and empty when he was with her. He hadn't been lying earlier when he told her that she gave him new life, that his malaise was erased by her presence. What he didn't say was that at the same time, her nearness drove him mad with Hunger. He puzzled over it as he walked back to his car. The sun had set and the parking lot was deserted.

"Hello, Mister. You buy some ula?"

Marc turned with a start. He'd been so lost in thought that he hadn't heard the young boy approach. It was a flower seller. One of the many youngsters often seen around Apia selling assorted sundries. This one had an arm looped with flower necklaces. A light breeze carried the sweet fragrance of moso'oi and frangipani.

Marc waved him away. "No," he said abruptly. "Thank you."

"Please? You buy some ula and then I can go home," said the boy, hopeful and eager as he held the leis out closer to Marc.

Again the fragrance enveloped Marc, and this time he tasted something else too. Life. Marc snapped. Later he would tell himself that he'd only wanted to consume the flowers. That's all. That he'd only meant to feed on the blossoms and the greenery. The boy hadn't been in the plan. The boy was an accident.

It only took a moment's decision, and Marc's Hunger burst forth. He didn't even need to cut his skin any more. A mere thought and the Hunger poured out with determined force, gushing from every pore of his body, everywhere that the raised filigree of ancient patterns pulsed on his skin. It came dark and brooding, a coil of viscous blackness that moved with whip-like speed. The boy only saw what looked like a serpent. A giant eel of myth and legend. He stumbled backwards, cried out. Surely he thought of running? But it was too late. The Hunger enveloped him.

It was long after midnight when the torchlight of a security guard tapping on the car window woke Marc. He was lying on the back seat of the car, dazed and weak. He had stumbled there after the unfortunate incident with the flower boy. The guard probably thought he was drunk and sleeping it off. Marc waved at him in an appeasing fashion before getting into the driver's seat and revving the engine. He gave the man a hundred-dollar bill and a tired smile. The guard lit up with thanks at the unexpected gift and waved him on.

On the winding drive home Marc reflected on what had happened. The feeling of satiety after the golden Hunger had returned to him was greater than that from devouring a few plants. A high more powerful than any drug, a joy more potent than any happiness, a feeling he would never forget. Did he feel bad about the boy's death? Of course he did. But it was a guilt that he quickly clamped down on. It had been an accident, he reasoned. It was never going to happen again. He brushed aside the memory of the boy's face, the muffled cry before the coiled Hunger silenced him forever. No, that memory was better buried deep and dark. Right now all that mattered was the utter peace and contentment that enveloped him. Tonight for the first time in months he would sleep well.

CHAPTER EIGHT

Teuila was sketching at the table when there was a knock at the door. "Delivery. For Miss Teuila."

Bree poked her head in from the other room. "You expecting something?"

"No," said Teuila. Puzzled.

She opened the door to a young man from the reception desk. "These were left at the front desk for you, Ma'am."

He handed her three packages. "Careful," he warned. "He said the other one is fragile."

"Who said? Who brought these?" asked Teuila. But the man shrugged a careless I-don't-know and left.

"Ooh, a mysterious delivery. Gifts!" said Bree. "Maybe they're from Marc, to apologise for being a jerk-face yesterday." Ever since Teuila had returned from the Sanctuary and told Bree about her visit, the agent had been ranting non-stop about the arrogance and creepiness of white male billionaires. As far as Bree was concerned, no amount of money would be worth Teuila taking on Marc's commissions. "Keahi was right about him," she'd snapped. Teuila, used to Bree's temper, had stayed quiet through most of her tirade, but deep inside she agreed. Which then made her annoyed because she hated admitting, even to herself, that Keahi had been right.

There was a card with the gifts and Teuila opened that first, much to Bree's irritation. There was no name. Only three words.

I remember everything.

"Well? What does it say?" demanded Bree. "Who's it from?"

"I don't know," said Teuila. Quiet and contemplative as she moved to open the first package. The seed of a suspicion planted. Could it be?

"What? No name? So what's in the card?" Bree grabbed it and read it for herself. Frowned. "What does this mean?"

Teuila's breath caught in her chest at the sight of the bracelet nestled on a bed of black satin. A thread of delicate butterflies, each a different colour, exquisite in their fiery perfection. Red, scarlet, crimson, orange, forest green, violet sunset and sunburst gold.

"That's beautiful," breathed Bree. Her face furrowed in concentration as she reached to take a closer look. An exclamation of surprise. "These are real, Teuila!"

"What do you mean?"

"I mean that these aren't just pretty sparkles. See the designer? This is a Bianca Palermo. An Italian brand. They make couture jewellery.

For royalty and the extremely rich. No paste or plastic for them."

Teuila shook her head in disbelief. "No. That can't be right. That means —"

Bree nodded as she picked out different butterflies on the bracelet. "That this is a real emerald? Yes. And this one is a ruby. A topaz. An opal. A diamond — that has to be the biggest diamond I've seen up close."

Teuila dropped the bracelet back into its box as if it was made of acid. "It must be worth a fortune. I can't accept that." She folded her arms across her chest, a stubborn set to her jaw, a look that Bree knew well. "He'll have to take it back."

"Who?" demanded Bree. "You still haven't told me, who's the mystery gift giver? It must be Marc, the kazillionaire. Right?"

But Teuila knew she was wrong. The contents of the second package confirmed her suspicions.

"What the heck?" exclaimed Bree. "Soda? Who sends priceless jewellery and a six-pack of soda?"

This time there was a grin on Teuila's face. "Grape soda specifically. I can't believe he remembered!"

"Who?"

"Keahi," explained Teuila. She couldn't contain the happiness bubbling up as she opened a can of the long-ago taste of her childhood and took a sip. Eyes closed at the burst of artificial flavour.

Bree shook her head as she looked at her friend. "Girl, you're strange, y'know that? A man gives you priceless jewellery and you look at it like it's a dead rat dragged in by the hotel cat. He gives you cheap off-brand soda and you're lit up like a Christmas tree. And having a fit of joy."

Teuila laughed at her friend's bemusement. "It's a memory. There was a day, a long time ago. I'd run away from the shelter, because, well, just because. Keahi found me. He gave me a can of grape soda and we talked. He convinced me it would be safe to go back. But what I remember clearly from that conversation was the soda. It was my first time trying it and when I told him, he said he would bring me a can every time he came to the shelter. Which he did a couple of times. Until …"

"Until?" Bree prompted.

Teuila frowned, the delight in the soda fading. "Until he left and I never saw him again."

"So that's what the note means," said Bree. She wisely made no reference to the butterflies. She'd already seen how both Teuila and Keahi had reacted to the sight of the butterfly painting at the auction. The man had spent a million dollars on it. If that wasn't a sign of something, Bree didn't know what was. "What's in the other box?"

Both women looked at the final package sitting on the table. It didn't seem possible such small items could trigger so much emotion but Bree could sense the tangle of emotions in the room. Teuila was struggling. She could feel it.

"Go on. Open it," said Bree as she nudged Teuila. Bree was excited. Keahi was turning out to be a man of surprises with an unexpected flair for creative gift giving.

"A knife?! What kind of present is that?" said Bree. Horrified.

But there was only awed wonder on Teuila's face as she reverently tugged the blade from its sheath. "It's a Cold Steel Tai Pan 3V. I don't believe it!"

"A what?" said Bree.

"One of the best combat knives you can buy. It's seven point five inches of CPM 3V steel, resistant to breaking or shattering. It's got a bit of chromium in it so it's great at withstanding corrosion and wear, but it's also got a diamond-like coating over the blade to increase its wear resistance. And look, it even comes with a strap holster so I can wear it under my clothes!" Like a child with a new toy, Teuila immediately started fitting the holster to her right thigh, adjusting the straps, a huge smile on her face.

"Why would he give you a knife?" demanded Bree, hands on her hips. "And more important, why are you not freaking out about it?"

"I've been taking combat classes that include fighting with a knife. I was saving up to buy a quality blade, but nothing like this. It's so beautiful. And lightweight. So sharp …"

Teuila was lost again in the excitement of her new gift and Bree rolled her eyes. But before she could say anything snappy, the phone rang. When Bree answered it, she had a sly smile on her face. Loudly she said, "Why, hello, Keahi! Fancy getting a call from you right now! What was that? You're in the neighborhood and you want to drop by to see Teuila? Is she available?" A pause as she looked over to where Teuila stood, frozen, with a panicked look on her face. "Of course she is. And she would love to talk to you. Come on over!" Bree turned her back on Teuila who was now making frantic 'No' gestures. She hung up, then announced with a wicked smile, "Right. Get ready. Keahi is meeting you in the garden courtyard."

"But I don't want to see him," said Teuila. Flustered. Hands going up to check her hair, a frown as she realised how messy it was. She made a beeline for the bathroom to grab a brush, even as she continued to berate Bree over her shoulder. "It's bad enough I have to go on a date with him on Saturday night. What am I supposed to say to him right now? Why is he by our hotel anyway?"

Bree had flopped onto the sofa and was flicking through a magazine. "Oh, I don't know. I'm not sure he was driving by the hotel. I may have misheard him. He could have been at his place."

"You trickster!" said Teuila through the clean T-shirt she was dragging over her head. "I don't believe you. Actually, no, I do believe you. You're evil. You always have been."

Bree was unshaken by her tirade. "I'm a doer and a pursuer. I see something. I want it. I go get it. I work like hell to make it happen. That's why I'm your agent."

Teuila chucked a throw cushion at her from across the room. "And that's also why you're going to get fired soon as my best friend." A deep breath to calm herself. "So, how do I look?"

Bree heard the nervousness in her friend's voice and relented. "Gorgeous. As always. And Teuila?"

"Yeah?"

"It's obvious from the gifts that he's trying to make amends for the other day. And maybe amends for other things, too. If you're honest with yourself, then you'll admit you do want to see him again. And you do want to talk to him. About your shared past. And how he was your friend and he hurt you. I hope you get to have that conversation. Maybe not today. But sometime soon."

Teuila gave Bree a grateful smile. Her friend always knew when to ease up on the teasing and the toughness, and give her the encouragement and perspective she needed. "Thanks. Now give me the bracelet. I'm going to return it." She pulled a face. "I know you're just trying to distract me so you can keep it!"

Both women laughed as Teuila walked out the door, her step a little lighter.

As she made her way to the meeting spot, she worried about what she would say and how she would react to whatever he had to tell her. She was so distracted that she bumped into Keahi in the garden walkway. Literally. Walked right into him with a suddenness that knocked the breath out of her.

"Hey, I got you." His voice was low and honeyed in her ear as his hands came up to steady her. "You okay?"

His touch sent chills up her spine, like a rush of wintry airconditioning had caught her off guard in the Samoan heat. Which, she reminded herself, made no sense considering what Keahi was. Inside. It had been many years, but Teuila would never forget what it felt like to stand beside him as he burst into flame. The rush of heat that made her eyes water and singed the tips of her eyelashes. How beautiful he was with his muscled, lithe form transformed into rippling currents of fire. Jewelled red, starburst gold and hibiscus orange. The sounds he made, the sizzling crackle as his feet met the ground, leaving burnt patches in the grass. His whoop of joy every time he lit up. And how happy it had always made her to be the source of that spark when she drew down fire from the sky and set him alight. In those moments, she had felt truly close to him, a kinship that none other shared because she alone knew the darkness he struggled with inside, the sadness that forever threatened to drown him and kept his fire stifled.

Teuila wasn't sure how long she stood there in his steadying arms, lost in memories, but she felt a rush of embarrassment when she realised he was speaking to her. Concerned.

"Teuila? Are you all right?"

Brought back to her surroundings, she leapt away from him as if he had literally burnt her. Tripping on loose gravel and almost falling into a gardenia bush. A muffled shriek as he helped her recover her balance. Again.

"I got you."

Teuila had to laugh now. It was getting too silly. She drew in a big breath. "I'm sorry. Not sure what's come over me. Falling all over the place here." Even as the words left her mouth she groaned inwardly, knowing she'd given him the perfect set-up. And he didn't disappoint.

A casual shrug of his shoulders, teasing laughter in his dark eyes as he drawled, "I tend to have that effect on women. I would apologise, but what would be the point? I'm not doing it on purpose. It's just naturally me. I can't help it."

Teuila rolled her eyes at him, faking irritation. But secretly she was relieved. His teasing dispelled the charged electricity of the moment before when she'd been in his arms. She didn't know why Keahi's nearness sparked that reaction in her. She'd got over her teenage crush on him long ago, laid it to rest along with the memories of their friendship. So why was she behaving like a flustered schoolgirl now? She gave herself a mental shake. Stop it, Teuila!

"Thank you for coming by," she said. Polite and formal. Trying to create distance between them, concerned he would sense her turbulent emotions.

Keahi shrugged, a grin as he pointed at the box she held in her hand. "You got the delivery."

"Yes. They're beautiful."

He interrupted. Teasing. "Cans of grape soda are beautiful?"

Teuila had to laugh. Again. She seemed to do that a lot around Keahi. When she wasn't angry at him, seething, raging mad, he had her laughing, light and happy. "No, they're not. But they were definitely a surprise. I haven't had grape soda for years, I don't know how long … Probably not since I left Samoa."

"And what did you think? Did it taste as good as you remembered?"

"Actually, it did," said Teuila.

"Don't lie," said Keahi, still with that same teasing grin. "That stuff is all chemicals. Nasty."

"Yes," conceded Teuila, "but it tasted great. Because of all the memories."

For a moment the two were united in a shared smile and a cocoon of the past.

"I can't believe you remembered it was my favourite," said Teuila.

"Like I said, I remember everything," said Keahi. There was a sadness in his eyes, one that spoke of shared dark times.

"I wasn't expecting it. You didn't need to buy me a present," she said.

"I wanted to show you that I'm sorry," said Keahi. The words were tugged out of him like a hook buried in a fish that didn't want to let it go but would choke to death if it didn't.

"Sorry? For what?"

"The other day. I had no right to tell you what to do. You can meet with and have lunch with whoever you like. And do commissions for whatever clients you choose to. I was outta line. I apologise."

"Thank you," said Teuila.

"I hope I haven't screwed it all up."

"What do you mean?" said Teuila.

Keahi jammed his hands in his pockets and seemed to be searching for the right words. "You and me. Us. This."

Teuila wanted to say, There is no us. Because that's what logic and independent-woman thinking dictated she should say. But she didn't. Deep inside, there was a small, still voice that whispered, Yeah, there may be no 'us', but you know you want there to be!

"Sure," she said. "We're good. Friends."

He didn't look disappointed at her choice of words. Just gave her a smile. "Friends. I'm glad."

She jumped back to the script, the things she'd planned on saying before she'd walked down to the garden. She reached out to Keahi with the box. "But I can't accept this."

He looked at it and then back at her face. "The bracelet? Why not? You don't like it? I can flick it back to the store and have them change it."

His dismissiveness made Teuila doubt her resolve. And suddenly feel very embarrassed. What if Bree was wrong? What if this wasn't some deliriously expensive piece of couture jewellery? And that was why he seemed so casual about it?

"All of it together. It's too much. Too expensive. I can't accept it all," said Teuila. Again she tried to hand him the box.

He shrugged and took it. Didn't even look inside to check it was all there. Just slipped it into his pocket. There was a sly grin on his face. One that was knowing and teasing. He smiled as if he knew something she didn't.

"What? What is it?" she demanded. Knowing she sounded rude but saying it anyway. Sometimes Keahi had that effect on people.

"You're not giving back the knife, I see."

"No ... because it's functional. A practical, useful gift. Something I need for my work and that I can use to do many useful things ... unlike jewellery that's only for looks. For show. And not useful at all. The soda didn't cost much and I know I can pay you back anytime for that. But the bracelet, I can't afford it, and it wouldn't be right, and what if I lost it, I would feel horribly guilty forever." Teuila was rambling. She knew she wasn't making sense, and she knew that he knew she knew it too. With every nonsensical word coming out of her mouth, the grin on Keahi's face grew.

Finally he put a stop to her blithering with a rise of his scarred eyebrow. "So let me see if I have this straight. The soda is fine as a gift because it's cheap. And it's memories. So you're keeping that. The bracelet cost a lot of money and you're uncomfortable about wearing something that expensive from me. Because it means you owe me and you don't think you can ever pay me back. But the knife? Ahh, you'll accept that because it's useful. No matter what it cost. Because, unlike the bracelet, you can cut someone's throat with it. So that makes it okay." Suddenly he wasn't teasing any more. There was serious intent in his eyes. "Because you can use it to defend yourself. Even to kill someone if needed. And that makes you feel safe."

He spoke the deadly words into the afternoon sun and they sliced the frangipani-fragranced air with precision. Neither of them had moved but suddenly they were only a breath apart, bound by something that went beyond time and distance. Outside a makeshift gym, a scarred weary boy with a forever chip on his shoulder, and a girl with forever fear and wariness in her eyes. A girl who asked a boy to teach her how to kill. And he said, 'Yes, I will.' Because he understood her fear and knew her pain as his own. And that forged a bond that would never break.

So Teuila nodded, all attempts at concealment gone. "Yes. I'm keeping the knife. I love it. Thank you."

The smile he gave her then was uncensored and free. "I'm glad. I thought it was the perfect fit for you. Are you wearing it?" His gaze moved down, searching.

Teuila instinctively reached for the reassuring feel of the harnessed blade in its holster strap at her thigh. Even as she lied. "No."

"Liar. I know you couldn't resist putting it on. Go on, show me."

And because she was excited to share her weapon with someone who appreciated it, Teuila parted the floral fabric of her skirt at the split seam so she could slide the blade from its sheath. There was reverence in her words as she admired the way the sun caught on the steel. "Isn't it beautiful!"

"Yes, beautiful," said Keahi. But he wasn't looking at the knife. There was danger and risk in the air, hot and heavy, as his gaze moved from her bare thigh upwards to linger on her face. Teuila's chatter died away as Keahi brought up a hand to gently brush loose strands of her hair from her eyes. It was the briefest of caresses, but even that whisper of a touch was enough to set her whole body aflame. There didn't seem to be enough air for her to breathe. The day turned from pleasantly sunny to scorching hot. Teuila wanted to step away from him. Move. Get as far away as possible. Yet she also longed to lean a little closer. Bridge that gap between them that ached of desire. She was confused. What's happening to me? This is a childhood friend I haven't seen for years. We barely know each other as adults. We have nothing in common any more. Total opposites. This is stupid.

She should move away. She had every intention of creating distance between them. It was the sensible thing to do. She was stern with herself. Step away, Teuila! Now.

Instead, she took a trembling breath and stepped closer. So close she could see the pulse beat in the line of his throat. He was going to kiss her. She knew it. And welcomed it with every fibre of her being.

But, with a muttering under his breath that sounded suspiciously like a swear word, Keahi stepped back, breaking the web that had moments ago seemed as binding as eternity. "I have to go. Just wanted to check you got my delivery. And apologise in person. I'll see you on Saturday."

With those terse words, Keahi turned and left, leaving Teuila shaken. Disappointment quickly turned to anger. He was playing with her. As if she was still that broken child he'd known so many years ago. A child he could lavish attention on one minute and dismiss the next, without ever looking back. He had made her think that he cared, that they did have a shared 'something', even if it was only a childhood friendship. And she had been too quick to believe him. He's an actor, remember? That's what he does. He pretends to be and feel things that he's not. Don't fall for any of it! Rage burned white-hot inside her, at war with the exhilaration that still remained. She stalked back to her room, determined that when they next met, she wouldn't let her defences down so easily.

CHAPTER NINE

There were more surprises in store for Teuila. She had barely walked into the room when reception called. "There's a woman here to see you. She says she's your mother."

The phone slipped from Teuila's fingers and she had to grab hold of the table as the room swayed around her.

Bree came to her side, concerned. "Teuila? What's wrong? Are you sick?"

"No, I'm fine. Thanks. A bit dehydrated, that's all."

"Who was that on the phone? Is everything okay?"

Teuila nodded as she grabbed her purse and headed for the door. "I have to go out. Get some fresh air. I'll be back soon." She left Bree with a hundred questions written on her face.

The elevator ride downstairs seemed to take an eternity. The words pounded inside her head and chest. Your mother. Your mother. Your mother.

Teuila knew that there had been a very real possibility she would see her mother on this trip. Samoa was a small place. She'd told herself that she was ready. She could handle it. 'I'm a grown woman now. With a successful career and a life all my own. She doesn't have any power over me any more.' But now that her mother was here in the hotel? Teuila wasn't so sure. And what would she tell Bree? How was she going to explain to her best friend that, Oh, by the way, I'm not actually an orphan. My mother is very much alive and ta-da, she's right here! Teuila wasn't looking forward to that conversation. Bree was going to be hurt. Possibly angry. No matter, I'll deal with that when I have to. First things first ...

She saw Siela as soon as she walked into the lobby. She wore her hair differently and her make-up was more subdued than Teuila remembered, but in every way that mattered, she was still Teuila's mother.

Unfortunately.

Teuila allowed a hug, but held herself stiffly as her mother exclaimed, "Oh, Teuila, it's so good to see my daughter again!"

They sat across from each other and Teuila was grateful for the coffee table between them. It acted as a kind of security for her, guaranteeing distance. No matter how flimsy.

The waiter asked if they wanted any refreshments, and politeness made Teuila nod, invite her mother to order. Siela asked for vai tipolo instead of alcohol and Teuila allowed herself the faintest leap of hope. But she waited until the waiter was out of hearing before she spoke. It had begun raining outside, and Teuila had to raise her voice over the sound.

"How did you know where to find me?"

Siela sipped at her drink with an appreciative smack of her lips before waving her hand nonchalantly. "This is Samoa. When I saw in the newspaper that you were here, I had to come see my baby. I missed you so much. It's been such a long time."

You mean when you heard about my art auction, you had to come and see if you could get some money off me, is what Teuila wanted to say. But didn't. What would be the point?

"So how are you?" she asked. Still an alcoholic? Still staying at the clubs till they close? Going home with the man who bought you the most drinks? Still sleeping off your hangover all day while your boyfriend of the month molests your child?

A surge of anger ripped through her, so thick and hot that it surprised her. She thought she had buried her feelings about her mother and her childhood trauma. Buried them deep enough and for long enough that they could never hurt her again. I guess I was wrong. Outside, a strike of lightning razored the sky, the sharp crack making people in the café jump in their seats.

Calm down. Breathe. You're going to lose it.

Another roll of thunder boomed, followed by a jagged light that struck so close to the hotel that the power pole lines sizzled and crackled.

"Oka! So loud," said Siela, casting a fearful glance towards the nearby window. "A big storm outside."

For a wild moment Teuila thought about how easy it would be to twist a lightning bolt their way. It could come right through that window and strike her where she sits. It would blast us both. I wonder what that would feel like. How much would it hurt her? Hurt me? Hurt us? Would it kill us both?

She knew she was walking dangerously close to that point of no return. The line she had drawn for herself all those years ago when Pele the fire goddess had rained death and destruction from the heavens, threatening to erase them all from the earth. Teuila allowed herself a moment to remember that day, the final battle where she had been the conduit and channelled the different gifts of Tangaloa into one, making it possible for Daniel Tahi to stop the woman who would eventually become his wife. It had been the most terrifying day of her life, coming so close to death. But greater than the near-death experience was the realisation that she, Teuila, could wield that same kind of power. If she chose to. She had promised herself then, covenanting with the earth, ocean and sky, that she would never use the Telesā powers to hurt anyone or anything. Ever. And she had held to that promise. Even when Kennedy had hurt her in college, betraying her with her room-mate. She'd been tempted for only the briefest of moments to call for fire and sear his skin off, wipe that sneer off his face … Instead, she had walked out and never returned. And knew she'd made the right decision.

She'd stumbled upon using her Gift to create beauty when she started sculpting at art school. Instead of laboriously chipping away at a lump of rock, she had summoned water to help reveal the masterpiece that she knew lay within it. When fashioning pieces from clay, she loved to first speak to the earth, asking for Fanua's permission, and once that was granted, asking her for inspiration. Letting Fanua guide her hands as she fashioned exquisite pieces that entranced audiences and art critics alike. Using her Gift to create works of beauty that brought awe and joy to people – and which she could sell to give much-needed money to the centre which had saved her life – felt to Teuila what Fanua wanted her to do. It had frightened her to be used as a conduit in the battle against Pele. Yes, it had been necessary and yes, she had chosen to do it. And would do it again. But afterwards, surveying the destruction around them, the bodies of those killed by either Pele or the renegade Covenant sisters, Teuila had asked herself what if others with less noble purposes than Daniel found out about her gift for channelling and concentrating Telesā collective powers? For jump-starting latent gifts? As she could do for Keahi? They could force her to do things she didn't want to do. Use her to bring about the same kind of damage that Pele had wrought. The thought of it made her breath seize in her chest.

No. Teuila stared at the woman sitting before her who was gulping down a second glass of lemonade. No. She would not break her earth covenant for this woman. You're not worth it.

Outside the storm eased as Teuila forced a smile. "Sorry, I didn't hear you. What did you say again?"

Siela smiled. "I said I have a job. I'm a manager at one of the local restaurants. It's an important job. I've been there for a year now."

She was trying so hard to impress Teuila that she felt a pang of guilt. Would it be difficult to be nice to this woman? Just this once? She would be leaving soon and would never have to see her again.

"That's great. I'm happy for you."

Siela prattled on and Teuila only half-listened. She had spent so many years putting up an emotional wall to protect the child she'd been that she could barely rustle up any connection to this woman who had birthed her. Siela was a stranger to her.

"It's been nice to see you but I have to get going," said Teuila. "I have work to do."

"Oh, of course," said Siela. She hesitated, and the veneer of confidence fell away. She looked anxious and afraid.

Okay, here it comes. She's going to ask me for money. I knew it.

"Before you go. There's something I want to ask you," said Siela.

Teuila stood, and a mask of coldness slid into place. "I'm sure you do. But I don't have the time ..." *And there's no way you're ever getting any money from me.*

"Please. Wait!" said Siela leaping to her feet and coming around the table to reach out with a trembling hand to grab Teuila's arm.

Before Teuila could shake her off, Siela spoke in a rush of words. Pleading. "I've wanted to see you for a long time. So I could tell you that I'm sorry. For what I did to you. I'm sorry I wasn't a good mother to you. I didn't protect you. I should have listened to you and believed you. Can you forgive me?"

They were words Teuila had longed for a lifetime to hear. Words she had given up hope her mother would ever speak. The hurt and longing for those unspoken words she had poured into her art over many years. Anger had fuelled her strong, sure hands as she summoned water to carve the massive statues which stood guard at the entrance to the finest galleries in New York. Tears had mingled with the clay of the figurines which the toughest critics had hailed as 'ground-breaking and mind-blowing' for their portrayal of the mother-child bond. And rage had lit the fire of the kiln that baked the coil pots and plates to fierce perfection. Every time she saw them in a magazine, gracing the tables of the world's rich and powerful, she felt a sense of pride and satisfaction. I did that. I made those. I fought for everything I have and I've succeeded against the odds.

Siela was waiting anxiously for her response. Teuila knew she should be glad that her mother was saying the things she'd wanted to hear her say. But were they too little, too late? And how much of Siela's appeal was genuine and how much was inspired by the news of her daughter's success? The hope of money?

Teuila took a deep breath and steeled herself as she spoke. "Thank you," she said in a stiff, formal tone. "I appreciate your apology. I need time. To think about everything. And I really do have to go."

Siela's hopeful smile faded as she stepped back, shoulders slumped.

"Of course. I understand. Can I see you again? How long are you in Samoa for?"

Thankfully Teuila was spared having to answer as she caught sight of the familiar figure of a man striding into the reception area. Marc. She didn't know why he was here at her hotel, but he was a gift right now. An escape.

"Oh, one of my clients is here, I have to go," she said. "Please excuse me."

Teuila tried to move fast. The last thing she wanted was for Marc to meet her mother. The less her old life and her new one converged – the better. But she was too late. Marc saw her in the café and immediately approached them with long, sure strides. Doesn't this man do anything in half-measures? Doesn't this man ever move slowly?

He smiled as he drew near. "Teuila! There you are. I was going to have reception call up for you. How convenient that you're waiting for me."

She wanted to shout that she hadn't been waiting for him but gritted her teeth. She angled her body to try and conceal Siela behind her but Marc was too observant.

"And who is this?" He reached out his hand to Siela who had followed Teuila eagerly. "Hello. I'm Marc Gold."

Siela was delighted. She lit up, visibly preening in Marc's gaze. "I'm Siela." Defiantly she added, "Teuila's mother."

If Marc was surprised, he was too polite to show it. He gave her a warm smile of greeting. "This is an honour. I had no idea Teuila's mother would be here."

You and me both. Teuila was inwardly rolling her eyes at Siela's simpering. Her mother had always been a lightweight when it came to charming men, easily swayed, easily impressed.

Siela reached out to shake Marc's hand. As she did so, the happiness on her face slid away, leaving her looking blank and panicked. Only Teuila noticed because Marc had moved on to more important matters, turning to her with a brusque voice. "Teuila, I came to discuss a business proposition with you. Let's talk."

As usual, it wasn't a question. His assumptions rankled her. Again she wondered, Why am I meeting this man? Why am I spending time with him when he has my every nerve on the defensive offensive? Immediately she shoved that thought away. She couldn't go through life automatically mistrustful of every man she met. Just because of some long-ago trauma. She put on a bright smile. "Yes, of course." She turned to Siela. "Thank you for coming to see me. We will talk again. Another time."

But Siela's delight at meeting Marc had disappeared. She was edgy and anxious. Fearful even.

She ran after Teuila, grabbed at her arm. A hushed plea. "Please, can I tell you something? One more thing." A dark look at Marc. "Alone."

If Marc was annoyed at the delay, he hid it well. He mimed a hands-off motion and stepped away. "Of course. Teuila, I'll be waiting for you outside."

Siela waited until he was out of sight before she spoke. "Teuila, there's something not right with him. That man, he is dangerous. But more than that, he is ..." She paused, struggling to find the words. "Broken. Twisted."

Teuila sighed. "You just met him. Not even two minutes." And let's face it, you're not exactly the best judge of character when it comes to men, are you?

"I can feel it, he is cursed," announced Siela.

"Cursed? What are you talking about?"

"He has been cursed by an aitu and now he is like death. Don't you see it in his eyes? Can't you feel it when he touches you?" Siela rubbed at her hand in distaste. "The minute he touched my hand, I felt the darkness. It made me want to pua'i!"

Teuila was impatient as she remembered all the vomit-worthy men her mother had brought to their house and left her daughter alone with. *Where was your distaste then?* "Look, I don't know what you think you felt, but Marc is a client who has spent a great deal of money on my art. I have to go. He's waiting."

"Please!" said Siela. And this time emotion choked her throat and tears glistened in her dark eyes. "I'm afraid for you. That man is going to hurt you. Don't go with him. You must stay far away from him. He is cursed by an aitu. He needs a taulasea. Please!"

Teuila had never seen her mother like this before. So much raw caring and concern for her well-being. It made her angry. *Where was this motherly instinct when I was a child? I could have sure used it back then.* That anger made it easy for her to break free of

Siela's grip, and respond with polite detachment. "I will keep that in mind. Thank you. I must go."

She walked away without looking back. But she could feel Siela's eyes on her.

Marc led her to a table in the reception area, asked her with light concern, "What was that all about? Your mother, she seemed upset. Worried about something?"

And because she still seethed with anger, Teuila told him. With a laugh so he would know that she didn't take Siela's words seriously.

She expected Marc to laugh along with her but his reaction surprised her.

"She said what? I'm possessed? By an a-ee-too? What's that?"

The intentness on his face made her embarrassed. She wished she hadn't been honest. "Oh, nothing. Aitu is the Samoan word for demon, or spirit. It's silly. Forget I said anything."

"What would make her say something like that?" The question was phrased lightly, but Teuila could feel that his whole body had tensed. Was it anger? Hurt? Pride? Fear?

She tried to find a way to defuse the situation.

"There's something you should know about Siela. She and I, we don't have a regular mother-daughter relationship. In fact, that's the first time I've seen her or talked to her in twelve years. She's not a person that I have wanted in my life. So please, I wouldn't pay any attention to anything she has to say to you." Teuila hadn't planned to bare any sliver of her soul to this man, and the unexpectedness of it had emotions threatening to spill out. Without meaning to, without wanting it at all, Teuila's voice caught on a hiccupped sob as tears came to her eyes. "I'm sorry. I didn't mean to load any of my personal issues on you like this. Please forget I said anything. Forget you even met that woman. Just give me a moment and I'll be fine."

She fumbled in her purse for a tissue, a handkerchief, anything to dry her tears. She was aghast at her loss of control, especially in front of this man she didn't trust or feel at ease with.

"Here," said Marc. His voice had a softness she hadn't heard before. He handed her an immaculate white handkerchief, neatly folded and pressed.

"Thank you. I'm sorry about this."

"No, please. I apologise for upsetting you. That wasn't my intention. Seeing you cry, it cuts me up inside." Marc reached across and took her hand in his. "It was unforgivable of me to upset you."

"You?" protested Teuila. "It's not your fault. You didn't do anything to upset me. It's Siela. We have so much history that even a brief meeting can trigger a lot. It's stupid. I should be stronger. I should be over all that by now." She grimaced as she blotted at her tears that showed no sign of slowing. "I'm embarrassed to fall apart like this in front of a client. It's unprofessional of me."

Marc clasped her hand in both of his. There was an intensity in his eyes as he spoke. "Teuila, I hope you can look at me as more than just an art buyer. I know it hasn't been long, but I want us to go beyond a business relationship. To one where you can share your feelings with me, and know you can trust me. I would like to be that kind of friend for you."

Teuila relaxed when he said 'friend'. A friendship with this enigmatic man she could handle. Especially when he was like this. Maybe the other facets of him – the arrogant and cold man who held his wealth to himself tightly like a suit of armour, the darkly brooding man who stood a little too close for comfort and who breathed in her scent as though he was starving and she was the giver of the only thing that would satisfy his hunger – maybe all those were simply covers for this Marc who listened without judgement, gave her a handkerchief and dried her tears. Maybe this was the real Marc Gold.

"Look, the reason I came by the hotel," said Marc, "is because I have a proposition for you. For work."

Marc proceeded to explain his offer. And it was a generous one, a job that Teuila could only describe as a dream position. A five year, full-time art residency. "Accommodation, travel, a vehicle, a stipend, art supplies, whatever you need." He named a salary that made Teuila's head reel. "After our meeting yesterday, I realised I want you to do so much work that it makes sense to offer you a job. But you will retain creative licence. Every piece you make during your residency, you will own and can do what you like with. I will offer to purchase pieces for the Sanctuary and for my other hotels around the world, but it will be up to you whether you sell them to me. Otherwise, you can carry on doing your exhibition and gallery showings in New York or anywhere else."

Teuila was incredulous. "And all I would do is make art?"

"Yes," said Marc. "And live in the Sanctuary."

"Which means, I wouldn't be able to leave," said Teuila with slow realisation. "Like the rest of your employees, I wouldn't be able to cross the Sanctuary borders."

"You would be at the corporate level, which means you would be able to use our private air service to the US. And you would have greater leave entitlements. But no, you wouldn't be able to move freely about in Samoa. Sanctuary rules."

Teuila already knew she was going to say no to the job offer, but his next sentence affirmed her refusal.

"If it helps with your decision-making, I will be making the Sanctuary my world base. So I will spend the bulk of my time here. We would see a great deal of each other."

He really thinks I would love the idea of being locked in his Sanctuary, with him for company? Save me from the confidence of privileged rich white men ...

Teuila took a deep breath as she tried to think how best to politely decline his offer. He had caught her at a vulnerable moment and she was mindful of Bree's warning that it was never smart to have a billionaire for an enemy. So even though she would have liked nothing more than to turn him down flat, and to leave no room for any misunderstanding about where she stood in relation to the Sanctuary and to him – Teuila held back. Weighing her words. Before she could reply, another visitor interrupted.

Sione.

"Teuila! I was asking the receptionist to call up to your room, but here you are," said Sione. His smile was warm and open, his gaze taking in everything in one astute glance. Marc and Teuila sitting together at a table. She felt a stab of guilt. As if she was betraying something, or someone. But she didn't know who. Or how! She leapt to her feet, tugging her fingers from Marc's.

"Sione, hi." She turned to introduce the two men, noting that while Sione was relaxed and chill, the American had lost his smile and warmth.

"I know you," said Marc to the newcomer. "You're one of the leaders outside my development every day."

"And you're the billionaire who's cutting off access to our heritage and history. Not to forget, also the man who plunged a hundred acres of native bush under water. Nice to meet you in person. Only ever seen the shadowy outline of you going by in the flash car." His words were light but the undertone was tense, and Teuila felt the animosity.

Marc spoke only a few more curt words and then excused himself, citing work commitments. "Let me know soon about the job, Teuila," he said. "It's a limited time offer."

Sione and Teuila watched him stalk away. She breathed a sigh of relief, glad to be free of the tension.

"A job, eh?" said Sione lightly. "You going to work for the billionaire?"

Teuila grimaced. "I don't think so."

"He is not happy with me," joked Sione with a grin.

"Can you blame him?" said Teuila. "You two are on opposite sides of a pretty steep cliff."

"And where are you on that cliff?" asked Sione, his eyes still teasing. Teuila immediately felt at ease, knowing this was her friend. "Hey, I'm not attacking you. Believe me, I know we all gotta eat. I don't judge you for doing your job."

Teuila shook her head. "I'm not sure, Sione. There's so much I don't know about. It's been a long time since I was last here. Do you have time to catch me up? Let's sit."

The two found comfortable seats at a corner table, ordered refreshments and proceeded to talk. There was seriousness as Sione explained their conservation and environmental reasons for the protest, but there was also lots of light laughter as the two reminisced about their schooldays.

"I can't believe you're an environmental lawyer now!" said Teuila as she sipped at her tea.

"You thought I would play rugby and Xbox forever?" laughed Sione.

"No, that's not what I mean," protested Teuila. "You were so into cars back then. I remember that's all you could talk about. Your dream truck and the race car you were going to drive when you got old enough."

"Ah yes, I remember," said Sione. "I still love cars. I run a business with my two brothers, importing electric cars. The conservation work doesn't put food on the table. The car business feeds us."

He became serious again as the subject turned back to the billionaire developer. "I know it's none of my business. But I wouldn't feel right if I didn't warn you, tell you what I'm feeling. And please take this in the spirit that it's offered." Sione was hesitant and Teuila could tell he hated having to broach the topic.

"You want me to be careful of Marc," she said helpfully. "You think he's not to be trusted and he's got shady motives for doing what he's doing."

Sione seized on her words with relief. "Yes! Be careful. That's all I want to say. You're all grown up and as your old friend, I'm proud of you and everything you're doing. But that man? All he cares about is money. And himself. He's a cold-hearted machine who looks at our land, our water, our air, even our people – and all he sees is money. How he can make more. And he doesn't care who he steps on to get it. You don't have any brothers, so I'm gonna be the brother and watch out for you. If you need me, need help of any kind while you're doing work for him, you call me. I'll be there. Okay?"

Teuila felt the concern in his words and she was grateful. "Sure. I'm pretty tough now and have learned a lot about how to take care of myself. But I won't say no to a brother and his offer of help. Thank you, Sione."

The time slipped by so fast that it was a shock to Teuila when her phone beeped with a message from Bree, reminding her that she would be leaving for the airport soon. "Oh, wow, I didn't realise it was getting late," she said as she called for the waiter to bring their bill. "I have to go. I'm sorry, Sione. My agent is flying out tonight, back to the States. Back to her office and hounding people to hire me! Honestly, she's the only reason I have a career."

"But you're staying on to do that work for Marc?"

"No, not for that. I already had my reservations about him, and after everything you've told me about the Sanctuary, it's not something I want to be associated with. I'm staying on for a couple of weeks. To spend time with Mrs Amani. At the centre. I'd like to get reacquainted with home. Maybe get inspired and make some pieces, I don't know. The opportunities are endless."

The two exchanged a warm hug, promising to meet up again soon.

CHAPTER TEN

It was late by the time Sione finally left the office. Several of the protestors had been arrested by police that day, and working on their release paperwork had delayed his regular caseload. His shoulders ached from sitting hunched over at a desk, and his stomach protested loudly as he walked to his car, reminding him that he hadn't eaten since breakfast. He was glad there was nobody around to hear it.

He had almost reached his car, one of only two left in the dimly lit lot, when his phone pinged with a message from his wife. 'Are you nearly done? I got us dinner from Pinati's. Hurry home! I'm hungry.'

Sione smiled to himself as he quickened his steps. Eager to get home. To see the woman whose patient support for his conservation work made all the difference to him.

He was putting a carton of files into the back seat when he felt a prickle of unease, a lurch of fear that caught him off guard. It reminded him of childhood. Being sent out to the umukuka to get something for his mother, and the way panic at the shadows would have him scurrying back to the light. It made no sense and it always made him laugh once he was back in the safety of the house and the familiar hum of the TV in the front room.

Sione turned around and had to catch himself so as not to jump, startled. A man had come up behind him in the parking lot. So quietly that Sione hadn't heard his footsteps. He stood there a few feet away, his face in shadow.

"Whoa," exclaimed Sione. "I didn't hear you." He peered into the shadows and recognised the stranger.

"Mr Gold," he said. Surprised. "What are you doing here?"

The visitor didn't answer at first. His silence was unnerving.

"If this is about the group that was arrested today and charged with trespassing" – a nod at the case box in the car – "I've got the files right here and we'll be disputing the charges. First thing in the morning." A thought suddenly occurred to him. It made him grin. "Unless maybe you're here to tell me you've had a change of heart? You're going to drop the charges?"

It was an olive branch Sione offered. A light quip designed to ease the tension in the still sweat-laden night. But Marc didn't take it. He shook his head and there was no answering smile on his face.

"What do you know about the historical settlement on my land?" Marc asked. Abrupt and demanding.

"Your land? You mean, our Samoan people's land," Sione corrected. "I'm not an archaeologist. Or a historian. I only know what the researchers have told us."

"Which is?" said Marc.

Sione's code of politeness was fast being exhausted. "Is that what you came all this way to talk about? At this time of night? Can it wait till tomorrow?"

"No, it can't," said Marc. And this time there was restrained rage in his voice. Sione took an inadvertent step back. An instinctive shift in response to the menace that seemed to emanate from this man.

"She sent you, didn't she?" snarled Marc as he moved closer towards Sione. "She's your leader. She's driving all of you. She's behind all of it."

Sione was confused. "Who? What are you talking about?"

"That demon bitch. Saumaeafe." Marc's pronunciation of the Samoan name was awkward, but it was enough for Sione to recognise it. Marc saw the light of recognition in his eyes and he leapt at it. "You do know her!" Two steps forwards and he had Sione in a chokehold, slammed up against the side of the vehicle. "Tell me where she is."

Sione was angry now. Who did this palagi think he was? Putting his hands on him? Raging and threatening like this? Sione pushed Marc's hands away and shoved back at the American. A hard, decisive push that had Marc stumbling. "Get your hands off me! I don't know where she is."

"You're lying," said Marc. "You're protecting her. You're working for her."

"That's impossible," said Sione. "Saumaeafe isn't real. She's just a myth. A ghost story told to scare children and make them behave themselves."

Sione spoke matter-of-factly, somewhat relieved to find that his visitor was only upset about a mythical figure from the stories of his childhood. But his calm logic enraged Marc further.

"She's real, I tell you," he shouted, his words disturbing a flock of flying fox in a nearby esi tree. They chittered and squeaked as they flew away with a flurry of wings. "I've seen her. Talked to her."

Reacting to the frantic panic in the other man's voice, Sione raised his hands in what he hoped was a calming gesture. "Look, I don't know who you think you met. Or what she pretended to be. But Saumaeafe is only a legend. An aitu, a type of demon. Sure, there's lots of stories about her, and you'll come across folks who say they met her or got cursed by her. But there's always some practical explanation for whatever they tell you. I can assure you, Marc, Saumaeafe isn't a real person. And she's definitely not the leader of our conservation group."

Marc threw back his head and laughed. It was a sound that chilled Sione's blood. "She's got you under her control and you don't even know it. All the things you're doing? The marching and demonstrations? The endless injunctions you keep filing in court against us? All of it, she's making you do them. She's pulling the strings. It's all part of her plan against me. To stop me. Shut me down. But it won't work. I won't let her win. I won't let you get in my way."

It was clear to Sione that the American was clinging to his sanity by a thread.

"All right man, whatever you say," said Sione. "Look, you need to get some help. Is there somebody I can call for you? Because you sound like you're locked in some kinda paranoia here. I got to go, my wife is waiting for me. But I don't like to leave you like this."

Another time, another place, another person may have seen the genuine concern in Sione's offer. But tonight it only served to push Marc further to breaking point. "She's probably watching us right now," said the American as he glanced around, eyes searching every shadow. He raised his voice again. Shouting into the void as he stalked back and forth. "Show yourself! Come on. I know you're there. But I can face you now. Take you on. Yeah, that's right. Thanks to your curse, I have what it takes to end you. And all your followers." He threw his head back and laughed again, a strange fire in his grey eyes.

For the first time in what was turning out to be a very strange night, Sione was afraid of his visitor.

"I have to go," said Sione. Quietly, more to himself than to the man who shouted at ghosts in the night. Sione moved towards the driver's seat where the open car door beckoned. Safety and escape a few metres away. Hoping that he could get out of there without having to get physical with this man.

But Marc had other plans for him.

"Stop! You're not going anywhere."

Sione braced himself for a fight, assessing the other man's height and weight, calculating the risk involved in using a rugby-style tackle on him. The American wasn't as big as Sione so he was confident he could take him down.

Which would have been true if Marc had been a regular man. Not a person who carried an aitu's curse. Sione was prepared for a punch, a push, even a tackle. But Marc just smiled as he ripped open his shirt, stripping off and baring his torso to the night. Sione recoiled at the sight. At first glance, it looked like Marc's body was tattooed, every inch of skin criss-crossed with patterns. But the longer he looked, the clearer it became. The man's chest, no, his entire body was covered in pulsing threads that writhed and squirmed just under his skin. Or were they on top? Sione couldn't be sure. It wasn't a static tattoo. It was as if something living was attached to his body, a filigree of parasitic life. It moved like worms. Thread worms. Sione felt sick to his stomach.

Marc flung his arms out wide. "What's wrong?" he asked with eerie delight. "You going somewhere? We were just getting to know each other."

"What is that? All over your skin?" asked Sione. Fascination and revulsion combined. "Man, are you sick?"

"This is how I know you're lying. Saumaeafe is real. She exists. She thinks she hurt me. Cursed me so I would quit the project. But she won't beat me. I've made this power work for me. I've made it mine. See?" Marc flexed his arms.

The creature on Marc's skin — for surely that's what it must be, an organism feeding off him — began to pulse and flow, rippling across his body like a wave building to a crescendo, towards his arms and then down to his hands. From there, it poured out to the ground, liquid darkness, a foul ink that pooled at his feet. Then it moved towards a nearby tree. The creature — that was the only way Sione could describe it — slithered like a snake, lightning fast. When it reached the tamaligi tree, it coiled itself around the trunk, moving higher and higher until the entire tree was covered with its pulsing energy.

And then, faster than Sione could react, the tree withered and died right before his eyes. A shrunken husk surrounded by a cloud of dust twirling lightly in the evening breeze. The once dark creature was now a shimmering golden colour. It hung in the air for a brief moment, a column of glowing, ephemeral bliss that vibrated and swayed in the night. It had a terrible beauty that Sione couldn't look away from.

"What is that?" he said. Disbelief. Shock.

Marc ignored him, intent on his creation. Another laugh and a clap of his hands. "Now, come to me!"

The golden coils listened. Sinuous and supple, the creature melted down into itself, back into a pool on the ground and then slithered towards its host. Sione wasn't sure if it was obedient to Marc's voice or acting as a sentient being on its own volition. What he was sure of was what he witnessed when the creature reached Marc. It started at his feet, encircling him in its viscous hunger until he was completely encircled in its coils. But, rather than being afraid, Marc rejoiced, hands outstretched and an exultant shout. "Yes! Feed me."

The next instant the creature had become one with Marc's body again, melded into the fibre of his being and dispersed into a writhing pattern all over his skin. Only this time it pulsed with a golden light.

Marc turned back to Sione. "Do you see what I can do? Unimaginable power coursing through my veins. It's like nothing I've ever felt before."

"The tree? I don't understand," said Sione. "What have you done? What's wrong with you?"

"There's nothing wrong with me," said Marc. "That's the key. She thought she was destroying me. That I would fall to this force, this power. But I have mastered it and made it mine. Just like I've done with the land. And when she dares show her face to me again, I will make her suffer. She will submit to me."

Again Sione tried reasoning with Marc. "You need help. A doctor. Or a taulasea that can handle this kind of sickness. There's traditional healers who specialise in healing curses. There's one in my village. She's very old, very wise. She will know how to fix you. I can take you to her. Probably not tonight because it's too late, but in the morning." Sione moved towards the open door of the driver's seat, trying not to show how urgently he wanted to get away, trying to project calm reassurance. "Get some sleep tonight and I'll take you to the taulasea tomorrow. I have to go." No sudden movements. Stay cool. Keep him distracted and happy. Get in the car and get the hell away from here, now.

"You're not going anywhere," said Marc. There was a dark look of hunger on his face. "You think I'm going to let you spread the word about my power? You won't shut me down. You and your master, you can't stop me." There was no doubting the intent in his eyes. Sione turned to run, but he only got a few steps away before the creature reached him. The coils wrapped around his legs, tripping him so he fell on the hard concrete. The creature was surprisingly cold for something that glowed with so much light. It wrapped like a vice around his body, twisting tighter and tighter.

"Get off me!" shouted Sione as he struggled, trying to free himself from the bindings. But it was no use. He tried calling for help, but the lot was deserted, in an industrial area where there was nobody nearby to hear him. He was yanked off his feet and held aloft as Marc looked up at him. The vice grip around his waist and chest was painful, squeezing the air from his lungs as he tried to kick free.

"Let me out of here!" said Sione. Anger at war with fear. "Put me down!"

But Marc kept talking. Rambling on about demon women of the night, curses and all he planned to do to Saumaeafe when he saw her again. Sione took advantage of Marc's distractedness, reached into his pocket for his cell phone. Holding it behind his back so Marc couldn't see it, Sione awkwardly pressed the redial button. It went straight to Rita who picked up immediately.

"Sione? Where are you? I'm waiting for you ..."

Sione shouted as loud as he could, praying that Rita would decode his words. "You can't hold me prisoner. Release me now! Do you hear me, Marc Gold? I'm going to call the police. When they find out what you've done, you'll be locked up and your resort project shut down. Did you hear me? Call the police to come to my office, now."

"Shut up!" snapped Marc. The creature shook Sione violently, like a mad dog shaking a bedraggled kitten in its jaws. It felt as if every bone in his body was being jolted out of place, and the whiplash to his head was even worse. In the melee, the phone slipped from his fingers and fell with a clatter to the ground.

Rita's worry was loud and clear in the night air. "Sione? What's happening? Are you okay? Sione? Talk to me, please!"

Marc put a stop to her voice with a grinding smash of his foot. "Trying to call for help, Sione?" He looked up at his captive whose face was flushed red as he gasped for air, his kicks and struggling growing weaker by the second. "You don't get it, do you? There's nothing or no one who can help you. Because I didn't come here to chat. Oh, no. I came here to kill you."

Right up until the moment he died in a searing rip tide of pain and brilliant light, Sione didn't quite believe that his life was in danger. That all of this wasn't some terrible dream. The disbelief was a cushion that ushered him from life to death. The dust that had been conservation lawyer Sione Wilson scattered in the wind.

Marc stood for a few minutes with his eyes closed in exhilaration as he revelled in the new life that coursed through his veins.

"Aah," he breathed. "So much more satisfying than a tree."

CHAPTER ELEVEN

"Do you really have to go?" asked Teuila as she hugged her friend close.

Bree laughed lightly as she hugged her back. "You know I do. I'd stay longer if I could. But somebody has to keep the offers coming for you while you're burying yourself on this rock for a while." She became serious. "You be careful, okay? I'll be worrying about you."

"I'll be fine," reassured Teuila.

"I'm a lot less worried than I was because I know you'll be staying with Beth," said Bree.

"Exactly, no reason for you to worry about me at all," said Teuila. "I'm looking forward to spending some time with her. It's been ages."

Bree waved a stern finger at her. "You're also going to be doing some creative work, too, don't forget. You've got that exhibition coming up in a few months and I'll expect to see some sketches of what you're working on. You're not just staying behind to lounge about and live a life of hedonistic pleasure, non-stop partying."

Teuila rolled her eyes. "Oh, please, there's only one partygoer in this duo, and it's not me."

"Have you made a decision about Marc's commission work?" asked Bree. There was no more teasing in her eyes now, only concern. "Because you know I fully support you turning it down. I don't like the thought of you working up at that Sanctuary place alone."

"I wouldn't be alone," said Teuila wryly. "It would be me and a few hundred other staff."

"Yes, and somewhere there would be Marc Gold, hovering around, plotting how he can persuade you to jump into bed with him," said Bree with tart directness.

"Nobody's jumping into bed with anybody," said Teuila. A frown. "I can't work for him. I'll give Marc my answer and be done with it."

"Good decision. Now, you have to promise me that you'll update me about everything you get up to here. No secrets." Bree was stern and Teuila pushed away the twinge of guilt that reminded her she still hadn't told her best friend about her #notDead mother.

She gave Bree a bright smile. "No secrets. Daily updates. Got it. Now get going. The taxi driver is going to leave without you soon. And take all your hundreds of bags with him."

The friends embraced once more before Bree finally got into the cab. The car was halfway down the driveway when Bree leaned out the window to yell a parting shot at Teuila.

"You have my permission to jump into bed with the movie star, though!"

Heads turned to look at the palagi woman shouting out of a taxi, and Teuila wished the ground would open up and swallow her. Even as she burst out laughing and waved one more time at her wild friend. Trust Bree to have the last loud word. And trust that word to be something do with sex.

Teuila watched her drive away before going back inside. She was alone now. Well, somewhat alone. Her bag was packed to move to Beth's house at the centre, and she had her mother's phone number burning a hole in her pocket from the day before. So no, she wasn't alone. But for the past two years Bree had micromanaged her schedule and shepherded her every public move, guided her every career decision. At the time it was what Teuila had wanted, and needed. That kind of agent management allowed her the freedom to focus entirely on her art. All she'd ever had to do was put on the dress Bree bought for her and show up to the gallery or art world fundraiser. Knowing how Teuila hated surface socialising, Bree always made sure she didn't have to endure a cocktail party for too long, or smile at strangers for a minute more than needed. The next month in Samoa without Bree would be a new experience. And the first of those experiences on the horizon was her date-but-not-a-date with Keahi. Teuila couldn't stop the little grin on her face as she went to her taxi. A smile tinged with anxiety about the unknown, the possibilities …

Keahi had that effect on her, even when he wasn't anywhere near her.

That night Teuila cooked dinner for herself and Beth. The older woman had come home late from a busy day at the centre and her face lit up when she saw the table set with Teuila's best attempt at lasagne and salad, followed by dessert.

"That was delicious, Teuila!" said Beth as she finished the last bite of mango pie.

"You don't have to sound so surprised," teased Teuila. "I can cook, you know."

The older woman laughed. "I never doubted that you could. It's just that I didn't expect a good pie to be on your repertoire."

"Oh, we artists can be multitalented," said Teuila as she stood to clear the plates from the table. "To be honest, I pretty much lived on noodles and toast when I was at art school. Even when I moved into my own apartment, I was still only opening cans and ordering cheap takeout. It's Bree who taught me how to cook halfway decent meals."

"So I have her to thank for that lasagne. And the pie, oh, what a pie!" Beth had a soft smile on her face as she watched Teuila at work in the kitchen. "She has been a blessing in your life. I'm so glad you have that kind of friendship. I worry about you in America. So far away from home. So dangerous."

"I've told you, Mrs Amani, I live in a very safe building. And our neighbourhood is great. Really friendly. We look out for each other. You don't have to worry about me."

"You know you don't have to keep calling me Mrs Amani," chided the older woman gently. "I've told you before that Beth will do."

"Sorry, I keep forgetting," said Teuila. "Old habits die hard."

"And I certainly don't expect you to cook for us every night," added Beth. "You're my guest."

"I like to," said Teuila. "I enjoy cooking. And I don't have crazy busy days dealing with a hundred and one different people and their issues like you do at the centre. I don't know how you do it. And in all these years, I don't think I've ever seen you angry. Or lose your temper with anyone."

"Oh, I have my moments, trust me," said Beth with a knowing smile. "I'm no angel."

Teuila finished doing the dishes and the two women went to sit on the veranda with a pot of koko. The aroma of rich chocolate filled the air and the buzz of night bugs was a steady hum of activity in the moonlit garden. A cool breeze rustled through the nearby mango tree where a clutch of chickens was settling in for the night, scrabbling for spots in the branches.

"It's beautiful out here," said Teuila.

"It is," agreed Beth. "I don't come out when it's just me. So I miss out on it." She leaned back in her chair, cradling her mug in her hands as she put her feet up on a nearby stool, breathing a sigh of contentment. "This is lovely."

Teuila threw her a sideways glance, trying to gauge the other woman's mood and energy level. She'd been wanting to ask Beth about Siela ever since her mother had shown up at the hotel the other day. But perhaps she was too tired.

"Are you going to tell me?" asked Beth, sipping her koko, gazing out at the stars overhead.

"Tell you what?" said Teuila.

"What's been on your mind. Something's troubling you. Is it your date with Keahi tomorrow?"

"What? That? No, of course not," said Teuila as she tried (and failed) to sound casual and nonchalant. "It's no big deal. It's Keahi. Just an old acquaintance from my childhood, that's all."

Beth didn't argue with her. She smiled to herself and kept on drinking her koko. And waited.

There was a long pause, broken finally by Teuila. "Siela came to see me."

Beth sat up straight and there was concern in her voice. "Are you all right?"

Teuila waved away her fears. "Yes. She wasn't looking for a fight or any drama."

"What did she want?"

Teuila summed up for Beth her conversation with the woman who had given birth to her. She didn't like the tremor in her voice as she did so. She preferred to keep her emotions in check when it came to her mother.

Beth listened as she always did – with a non-judgemental air and a peaceful aura. The kind that invited you to confide in her. It reminded Teuila of the times she had met with the director when she was an angry little girl who had first come to the centre so many years ago, and Beth had been able to get her to trust her and open up. When she finished telling Beth about her mother's visit, she felt a weight lift from her shoulders. She knew she'd made the right choice to tell her. She took a deep breath and drank a big gulp of koko. The hit of sugar helped lift her spirits as she waited for Beth to reply.

"I'm proud of you, Teuila," said Beth with quiet certainty. "You conducted yourself with grace and strength in what must have been a difficult meeting. All the more so because it was sprung on you out of the blue."

Remembering the strike of lightning outside and the wind battering at the windows of the hotel, Teuila winced. "I'm not so sure that I was as calm and gracious as you're thinking I was."

"You didn't hit her. Or try to kill her. I'd call that grace and calmness. I'm not sure I could have been that restrained."

Teuila gave her a surprised look. "What happened to 'violence is never the solution'?"

The two women shared a smile as Beth shrugged, "Never say never. Sometimes violence helps you feel better!" The mood lightened, and then Beth asked, "All joking aside, Teuila, how are you feeling about what your mother asked of you?"

It was the question she had been struggling with, and she tried to put that struggle into words. "I used to dream about her saying exactly those words to me, y'know? Acknowledging what wrong she did, how she hurt me. Asking for my forgiveness."

"But?" prompted Beth.

"But while I'm glad she's finally said them, I don't think forgiveness necessarily means you have to let someone into your life. I can forgive her and let go of my anger towards her, but I don't want her in my life. That's okay, isn't it?"

Beth nodded. She reached over and took one of Teuila's hands in hers. "It's more than okay. Besides, what matters here are your feelings, and you have every right to decide on your path forwards and whether you want her to be part of it. I support any decision you make. What matters is your happiness, Teuila, your healing. I've always said to every child who comes through the centre gates, forgiveness of your abuser is not a requirement for your recovery. Forgiveness for yourself, greater love and acceptance for yourself – yes. But for your abuser? No. Now, if that's something you choose to do, then yes, make that part of your journey, and my prayer and hope for you is that you can forge a new and healthy relationship. Otherwise, you know, I don't hold with that rubbish about Christianity supposedly teaching you that you must forgive your abuser and let them back in your life." Beth made a sound of disgust and Teuila had to grin.

"I don't understand, though," said Teuila. "Why now? All those years I was still living here, I never heard from her once. Nothing.

Not a message, not a visit, not a call. Which I was glad of because she'd already proven that any contact was harmful. That entire first year? I used to be terrified every day that she would show up at the centre."

"I remember," said Beth. "You bit your nails down to the skin. And you never slept a full night. Always waking up to check the windows and doors."

"You knew about that?" asked Teuila, surprised.

"I know everything that happens inside our centre."

Teuila nodded, chewing at her lip as she confronted painful memories. "By the second year and then the third, though, it was like a dark cloud lifting from me. Whatever kept her from bothering me again, I'm grateful. I don't know if I could have moved on. And while, yes, I'm ready to forgive her, I don't want to let her into my life again."

Beth gave her a shrewd look. "There's something you should know, Teuila. And I hope it adds clarity to your decision-making."

"What is it?"

"That final time your mother's partner tried to hurt you? When he broke into the centre? Remember that?"

"How could I forget it?" said Teuila with a grimace. "It was also the last time I saw Keahi before he left. A lot of reasons to remember that night …"

"Leila visited the centre earlier that day. She had just come back from her honeymoon. We met and she asked me how you were doing. I told her I was concerned about you because your mother had taken a renewed interest in you. I believed it was because she knew of Leila's friendship with you." There was compassion in Beth's eyes as she reached out again to take Teuila's hand in hers. "Your mother had financial gain on the brain, she knew of Leila's inheritance and that's why she was trying to get back into your life. I'm sorry if that hurts to hear, Teuila."

Teuila shook her head. "Don't be sorry! It's true. I have no illusions about the woman."

"What you don't know is that Leila went to see your mother. She offered to pay her to stay away from you. A generous weekly amount that would stop the minute Siela tried to contact you again. Siela took the deal. It was a confidential arrangement. The only reason Leila told me about it is because it was my job to let her know if Siela ever came near you. As you know, Leila and Daniel have travelled, lived overseas for some years for schooling and for work, but the payments have never stopped."

For Teuila, the sultry air suddenly seemed too thick to breathe, choking her. She stumbled to her feet and walked to stand at the deck, holding tightly to the railings as she struggled to calm her racing pulse. Overhead, the full moon in the spangled sky looked down, impassive and unfeeling as Teuila battled with a maelstrom of emotions.

"You're angry," said Beth, a quiet statement of fact. She stood and walked to stand beside Teuila, concern heavy in her voice.

It was that worry which calmed Teuila, which she clung to gratefully. All her life Beth had been the one certainty. The person who knew what darkness she had come from and had never spurned her, disappointed her or let her down. It was Mrs Amani who had made sure she had further art lessons when Teuila first fell under the spell of her creativity. Teuila realised she had never thought to ask where the money had come from to pay for those lessons, only that they were the bright spot in her days. And it was Beth who had first encouraged her to apply for the prestigious scholarship in New York, even when Teuila refused because she didn't think she could ever qualify. As the flood of memories rolled over her, Teuila turned to look at the diminutive woman beside her. She saw what she hadn't noticed before. That here was a woman who had devoted her life to advocating for children who had their voices taken from them. She had never married and never had any children of her own. She lived alone, still spending the bulk of her days hard at work at the centre. Threads of grey in her hair, lines of worry and laughter in her face that hadn't been there when Teuila was last in Samoa.

Beth spoke with sincerity. "Teuila, sometimes you find it difficult to let people in, to believe that others care about you and your happiness. Leila didn't do this from some saviour complex, or even out of charity. She did it because you're her friend and she cares about you. Daniel, Keahi, Simone and the rest of your group, I know you all went through great adversity. You've always kept the details to yourself, out of wanting to protect me, I think. You never wanted me to worry about you. But I know you endured much together and so you must believe me when I say Leila and Daniel are your friends and this was done out of alofa for you."

Mrs Amani had been her guardian and the only mother she'd known from the time she was fourteen. And so Teuila was able to anchor herself in this certainty and find her way through the mess of her emotions. She smiled at the older woman. "I'm not angry. I understand why Leila did that and why you supported it." A deep breath and a wry grimace. "It's embarrassing, though, kinda humiliating to think that my waste-of-space mother has been a parasite sponging off those who care about me. I'm sorry for that."

"I'm not," said Beth, brisk and no-nonsense again like the woman Teuila was used to seeing. "My job at the centre is to protect our children no matter what and using whatever means necessary. Paying off that woman may have been Leila's idea but it's one that worked successfully and I have since used a similar model in a few other cases that warranted it."

Teuila raised an eyebrow. To which Beth replied, "I'm not going to share details of other students. But you're not the only child who came through our doors with an abusive parent who insisted on hounding their every step. I did what I had to do for them. I got sponsors to privately fund them to stay away. And I would do it again."

Teuila had to smile at the ferocious intensity on the other woman's face. It was a familiar expression, one that Teuila had seen any time one of the students had been threatened or put at risk. It felt good to see it now. "Well, surely Leila has long since stopped those payments. I'm all grown up and Siela no longer has any kind of hold on me."

"We wanted to tell you everything when you turned eighteen, but you got that scholarship and everything was so crazy here while we rushed around to get you ready to start at the academy, remember? You left before your birthday and I didn't want to risk Siela finding out about your scholarship and trying to stop you. Leila kept the payments going until you turned twenty-one, just to be certain."

"So Siela hasn't been freeloading off my existence for four years," said Teuila. "Perhaps she thinks I'm going to be a good daughter and support her."

"Or maybe she's sincere and really does want your forgiveness and nothing more."

Teuila agreed. Reluctantly, but it was a possibility she couldn't deny. "Thank you for telling me. I needed to know. You've given me a lot to think about."

"I'm going to head in to sleep now. Leave you to your thoughts." She turned to go back into the house and then paused. "Teuila, in case you don't know, I'm so very proud of you and the woman you have become."

"Thank you."

The two women shared a look that spoke a thousand words. All of them redolent with alofa.

Teuila went back to musing on the stars. There were things she needed to do, people she had to talk to. Like Leila. She would have to contact her, thank her for the inestimable gift she'd given her – a life free of her mother's interference. Teuila shuddered as she tried to imagine how differently her life would have turned out if Siela had been free to assert her parental rights over her. A stab of nausea as she contemplated those possibilities. No, she wasn't going to let her pride blind her to the value of what Leila and Daniel had done for her. She would thank her childhood allies and hold her head high. She would even offer to pay the money back to Leila. It would take her some time to do it, her savings wouldn't be enough. But she would get there eventually. The decision made Teuila feel better. Resolute. With that issue resolved, she moved on to other much more tangled questions.

What would she do about her mother now? And what had Siela meant about Marc being cursed, possessed by an aitu?

But most pressing of all, what about Keahi?

CHAPTER TWELVE

"Where are we going?" Teuila knew she sounded ungracious but she couldn't help it. Being alone in a car with Keahi – even a car as expansive and spacious as this one – was making her hot and flustered. There's not enough air in here ... "Can we put the window down?" she asked Reuben, injecting more warmth into her voice than with Keahi. It wasn't the driver's fault she was stuck in close-proximity meltdown with *People* magazine's Sexiest Man of the Year.

"Is it too hot for you?" Keahi asked. Without waiting for a reply, he used the remote to turn the airconditioning up a notch. Which caused chill bumps down her back. Skin that would have been covered up if Bree hadn't bullied her into wearing this damn backless shift. Even when the woman was a floating head on a camera a thousand miles away, she still had the power to make Teuila change her dress.

"No, that's not it," she said tersely. "I get carsick." Lies. But she couldn't very well tell him that being in a car with him made her hot, flushed and dizzy – could she?

The window slid down immediately, soundless and silky smooth. Which made the space seem less enclosed. But admitted a wild rush of wind that demolished her carefully arranged hair. At first she tried to obtrusively hold it in place, but then she gave up. Sullenly. Fine. I'll just be a wild bush woman on this date and it'll be all your fault, so stuff you, Keahi.

Finally the car stopped and Teuila got out. She looked around in surprise. "We're at an airstrip?"

"Yes," replied Keahi. "I hope you're okay with helicopters."

"I don't know. I've never been in one." Again she winced inside at the abruptness of her tone. *What's wrong with you? There's no need to be rude to him!*

Reuben stayed by the limousine as Keahi took her arm and ushered her towards a black chopper on the grass airstrip.

"Isn't Reuben coming with us?" she asked. Nervous.

"No. I don't usually take Reuben on dates with me." There was laughter in his voice and she bit back on a cutting retort.

"But who's going to fly the helicopter?" she asked. Puzzled. Looking around.

In answer, Keahi took two helmets from the panelling and handed her one. Within a few minutes she was strapped in, and he was in the pilot's seat, flipping levers and pressing buttons. The blades started whirring. Slowly, then building in momentum until the sound was deafening. Teuila gripped the sides of the seat but was determined not to let him see her anxiety.

"You're the pilot?" she shouted over the blades. "You really know how to fly this thing?"

He grinned, his eyes trained on the field ahead. "Licensed to fly for five years now."

He made it sound dark and dangerous, as if he was 'licensed to kill', and Teuila felt another stab of resentment towards him. Did he have to be good at everything? More importantly, did she have to be so susceptible to his every move and action? Why couldn't she be immune to them? Even now as she fumed, she was painfully aware of his nearness, the hint of his scent as he leaned across to flip several switches. Decadent chocolate and a bite of red chilli. He smelled the same as he had twelve years ago, and that familiarity reassured her, eased her anxiety. This is Keahi. Your friend. You know each other. You can do this. It's just a friendly dinner between friends. Yeah, right.

She snuck another glance at him in the pilot's seat, drawn to his hands on the controls. Strong, sure and capable. What would it feel like to be touched by them? He wore a long-sleeved shirt with the cuffs rolled up to his elbows so she couldn't see his shoulders or arms. But she remembered their sparring session at the centre, him shirtless, the way the cables in his shoulders tensed and flexed when he was warming up at the bag. Nothing but muscle and sheer power. She knew he could lift her with those arms, raise her up, hold her, brace her against him. With ease. There was a twisting in the pit of her stomach at the thought. She was lightheaded and not because they were in a chopper.

Focus, Teuila!

Keahi glanced her way. "Don't worry. I promise this will be painless. I got you."

She gave him a forced smile. I'm not scared. Lies. It seemed she was constantly lying when she was around this man. Concealing her true feelings, trying to rein in her body's instinctive reaction to him.

She felt a clutch of fear when they first took off, swiftly replaced by a rush of adrenaline and wonder. All her panic faded away. "Woohoo! This is amazing."

"You like it?" he yelled over the roar of the blades.

She nodded, looking out over the landscape beneath them. The sun was setting as they made their way over the island, heading towards the Aleipata coast. The sky caught fire in a magnificent array of colour, as if they were flying through a silken tapestry of wonder.

Keahi was focused on his flying, which gave her a chance to study him. He was relaxed, with a half-smile playing on his face. Obviously at home in the sky. At ease in his skin and with himself. He was the Keahi she remembered, and yet he wasn't. What was she doing here with him? What did he want from her?

He interrupted her reverie, pointing into the distance. "There. That's where we're going."

Twilight had cast its shadows on the terrain below. They were hovering on the edge of the coastline, and far to the left she could see cliffs and the crashing surf. And directly beneath them, an opening in the green carpet, ringed with lights. Keahi brought them closer and she could see it was a chasm that dropped to the gleam of water.

"To Sua Trench!" she exclaimed.

"You've been here before?"

"No. Just seen it in the tourist brochures. We didn't have money to go to places like that …" Her voice trailed away, she was embarrassed at revealing too much. Then shook herself because it wasn't as if Keahi didn't already know all the sordid details of her childhood.

But that was the old Keahi. The one who was my friend. The one I thought I knew. The Keahi who wouldn't have left me.

The memory made her throw up her defences again. *Be careful, Teuila. You don't know what he wants. Don't let him back in. Don't let him hurt you all over again.*

With that stern reminder, she looked back to the trench below them. It was ringed with a circle of flares, and the water itself was sprinkled with lights.

"Floating coconut candles," Keahi said in answer to her unspoken question.

"Hang on!" And they started descending.

Keahi landed the chopper on the gravel parking lot and helped her exit. The touch of his hand on hers set her on edge and she endured it only for as long as she had to, moving a safe distance away from him as soon as she was on the ground. She looked around at the admin office and caretaker's home in the distance. Everything was deserted.

"Where is everyone? Are we even allowed to be here after hours?"

A laugh as he grabbed a couple of backpacks from the chopper and handed her one. "I booked the whole place. Nobody's gonna chase us out. Come on."

Still she wasn't convinced. "Wait, what? They let you have the whole trench to yourself? Without even security to make sure you don't trash it? How do they know you're not going to throw a drunken bash with idiots falling off the edge? Ruining the landscape? How did you get them to give us access to the whole place like this?" Then she remembered. "Oh, right. An obscene amount of money." She frowned.

Keahi gave her that arched eyebrow. The one that did unsettling things to her insides. To the insides of millions of women across the globe. Remembering that made her arch an eyebrow back in determined disdain.

Still he wasn't shaken. "Money. Sometimes it comes in handy."

"Obviously."

"Hey, it's how I got you to come on a date with me," he teased over his shoulder as he walked towards the entrance.

"This isn't a date," muttered Teuila. She followed after him, muttering under her breath about rich Americans who thought they could throw money around and make everybody jump to do their bidding. *Which is exactly what I'm doing. Leaping to do what he wants. Dammit!*

"It's not a date," she snapped, louder this time. "I'm doing a service project for the centre."

"Sure. Whatever you tell yourself so you can sleep at night."

The sound of his laughter danced in the twilight as he continued along the pathway, and she quickened her pace to keep up with him.

"Here we go," he said.

And then she had no words because they were at the top of the trench and it literally took her breath away. Just reached inside her and yanked it right out, completely.

A wooden ladder descended to the silver water. The moon had slipped out from her hiding place while they landed and cast black diamonds on the lilting surface that was spangled with floating coconut candles. It was like standing on the very edge of the Milky Way and knowing if you took a step, you would float in a hazy burst of night sky.

"I did have to make some guarantees before they would let me book out the place," said Keahi. "I had to promise that nobody would get injured. That I would take very good care of whoever I brought here."

His voice beside her in the moonlight was a caress. Sending shivers down her spine.

"You cold?" Concern.

"No. I'm fine. Just in awe. It's beautiful." Teuila gave a frustrated laugh. "Beautiful is such an inadequate word."

"Yes it is," he said. He wasn't looking down into the trench though.

He was staring at her. It was a look that punched all the air out of her chest and had her reeling. She didn't know what she would have done if he hadn't looked away and walked to the top of the ladder entrance.

"Let's go. If I promise not to look up your dress, are you okay for me to go first? Just in case."

He started down the ladder without waiting for a reply. He moved with graceful ease, every step sure and unhurried. She thought again how much he reminded her of a predator, a panther? Sleek and irresistible. Yet every ripple of muscle screaming a warning. Danger!

Which makes me an idiot for not listening to the warnings ... Keahi's never pretended to be anything other than what he is.

He was waiting for her at the bottom on the wood platform, and when she stumbled coming off the last rung, he was ready to catch her in his arms.

"Got you."

Teuila froze. Even through their combined layers of clothing, she could feel the hard contours of his chest, the ridges of his abs. This close, there were more layers to his scent. He smelled like earth, green forest and ocean spray. Still that hint of koko. Rich, dark lushness. Sweet and hot. It was ridiculous but in that moment she wanted to lean against that chest and kiss the underside of his jaw. What would he taste like? Salty with an edge of chilli? Sweet koko with the bite of crushed almonds? Would his kiss burn? She felt herself lean a little into him, relishing the feel of him against her. Just a taste ...

Thankfully he released her before she could do anything about her absurd desires, and went to unpack the bags. Teuila was oddly disappointed that he'd let her go so fast.

Within minutes there was a dinner picnic laid out at their feet. A cloth, crystal glasses, and a meal for two. He'd thought of everything. There was even a cushion for her to sit on. But the finishing touch – he knelt and fished out two of the floating candles for their centrepiece.

"So what do you think?" he asked with an expansive spread of his arms to encompass the platform beneath them, the silver shimmering water, the night sky far above, the picnic spread. "A dinner fit for a genius world-famous artist?"

She flushed. Always uneasy with praise. "No genius artist here. Just me. And yes, it's perfect."

"Hungry?"

To her surprise, Teuila found that she was. The individually packed boxes were mini surprise packages.

"Poke?" She had a piece. "This tastes like my favourite from –"

"Amanaki?" Keahi said. "Yes, it is."

"How did you know?" she asked.

"I'd like to say that it was a lucky guess, but Mrs Amani might betray me."

"She told you where to get my favourite poke?"

"I asked."

The rest of the dishes were more of her favourites. Oka and

fried breadfruit. Octopus baked in coconut cream. Slices of roast pork with taro still warm from the umu. An assortment of fresh fruit, golden pineapple, luscious bites of watermelon, sunset-orange squares of papaya, misiluki bananas – all sprinkled with toasted coconut. And for dessert, sticky, sweet, caramel faausi.

"I see you didn't waste any picnic space on vegetables," teased Teuila as she ate.

He laughed. "Of course not. A dislike for greens is something we'll always have in common!"

Keahi's smile was the boyish one she remembered from her youth. It put her at ease, and for the remainder of the dinner, she was able to almost forget who he was now. Who she was now. Who they both were. They laughed, talked about safe, light topics.

"That was delicious," said Teuila. "All of it. Thank you, Keahi."

He smiled. An open grin without any dark possibility to it. "You're welcome. I may have twisted your arm into coming to dinner with me, but it doesn't mean I didn't want you to enjoy it. It hasn't been too awful for you, has it?"

"No, of course not," she said. "It's been perfect." Too late she realised she'd forgotten to censor her reaction to him, tone it down. The triumphant light in his eyes shook her, a reminder that this man was used to being fawned over and adored the world over. She certainly didn't need to add to it. She had to change the subject, and fast. She grabbed the first thing that came to mind. "So, why don't you have a Mrs Keahi yet?" Even as the words left her mouth, she was kicking herself. No! Why would you ask him about other women? You idiot! Too late. She ignored the teasing grin on Keahi's face and pushed on in the pretence that this was an innocent question. "I mean, a movie star like you has lots of options."

"I haven't found the right one yet," said Keahi.

"How about you?" he asked.

"What about me?"

"You must have a boyfriend back in New York. Someone special." Supreme acting skills were at play now. Casual. At ease.

"There was someone," said Teuila. "I thought he was special. But, he wasn't."

"What happened?"

She gave him an arch look. Like I'm going to tell you!

He appealed to her with wide-spaced arms. "What? Come on, put a brother outta his misery. You have the upper hand here. My life is an open book, thanks to parasite reporters. You know everything about me, probably even stuff about me that I don't know. While I know nothing about you."

Teuila laughed in disbelief. "Excuse me? So I get to read about you and your every encounter with Hollywood sex symbols and groupies, and that makes you the one who needs sympathy here?"

A careless shrug and the cocky grin she remembered so well. "What can I say – I got woman skills."

"Woman skills?! What are those?"

"A gentleman doesn't talk." He faked zipping his lips. "I don't divulge the secrets of my skills with the ladies. Respect, y'know."

Teuila counted off on her fingers. "Are those the skills that scored you a Playboy cover model, an Oscar nominee, a Riverdale actress, and a yoga instructor? Oh, and let's not forget the waitress you met in Cabo." Too late she realised what she was revealing.

"Aha, you really are informed!" Keahi was triumphant. "You've been keeping up on me all these years."

"It's kind of hard not to," argued Teuila. "You're all over social media whether I'm looking for you or not."

"Oh, come on, admit it, you were looking for me."

Teuila ignored his preening. "So tell me, if these skills are so legendary, how come none of those relationships lasted more than a month? How come none of those talented, stunning and seemingly intelligent women wanted to stick it out with you? Hey, one of them even went into rehab after she broke up with you. What a recommendation for your skills," she added drily.

Keahi's grin faded. There was a bleak sadness in his eyes. "I made a lot of mistakes. The biggest one was trying to be with someone when you're screwed up inside. I hurt some people. And got hurt by others. I like to think I've grown from all of it. But sometimes I'm not so sure."

His honesty made him vulnerable, and she suddenly regretted her attack. Which made her more open than she had planned to be. "It was at the academy. He was my art tutor."

She paused, caught in a memory that still had the power to razor her insides. Keahi said nothing. Just waited.

"I was a fool. I see that now." A self-conscious laugh. "Why did I think we had anything in common? He was everything I wasn't."

"Which was?" Keahi gently prodded.

"White. Rich. The golden boy of his family. Old money. They went skiing in Aspen and his sister name-dropped Paris Hilton a lot. Whatever." She knew she sounded wistful and she hated it. Hated the self-doubt. So she smiled triumphantly. "A shitty artist."

Keahi laughed with her. "Yeah?"

She nodded. "Not a single original bone of creativity in his body. Art school was his idea of being rebellious, I think. He went back into his family's company afterwards."

"So no award-winning exhibitions at the Tate for him, then?" teased Keahi.

"No," said Teuila and they shared a grin of mocking solidarity before she got that haunted look in her eyes again. "I loved him. I thought he was the one, y'know?" A bitter laugh. "So stupid! He was my first. Well, as much as someone with a history like mine can have 'a first'."

She didn't need to expand, and there was comfort in that. Keahi was part of her journey to recovery. Had always been part of it. He knew exactly what she was talking about.

She was struggling. Hurt at war with anger. Fear trampling on strength. Any other man would have reached out a hand of comfort, but Keahi knew better. He slid down to sit lower, with his back against the rock wall. Slowly. Keeping his distance. Giving her the space she needed to feel safe enough to get the words out.

She was so agitated she barely noticed. "I was a fool. Thought I could have sex and it would be different because I loved him. But it wasn't. It was a disaster. I froze up. He asked about my freak-out and I made the mistake of telling him everything. Every sordid detail." A wild rustling of leaves and the crackling of branches betrayed her inner turmoil. Keahi shot a wary glance upwards at the cluster of trees spanning the edge of the trench as they seemed to sway and lean towards the young woman whose voice spoke to them. "The look in his eyes. It was disgust. I sickened him." Teuila stared down at her clenched fists. "I should have known then it was over. But I was weak, y'know? Hopeful. I ignored the warning signs. We tried a couple more times after that but it wasn't any good. He didn't have the courage to break up with me. I caught him with my room-mate. She clearly didn't have a problem with sex." A grimace at the flashback. "So yeah, that was the end. I never saw him again after that. I think he transferred. That's the sum total of my romantic history. Nothing as exciting as yours. Kinda pathetic actually." Again with the self-conscious laugh. "I should thank him, though. Because of him, I've been spared lots of other rejections. There aren't many men who can accept a woman as damaged as me." She raised her head then, in proud defiance. "I figure, screw it. I'm better off without them. My art gets the best of me now."

She was trembling, shocked by her own honesty, unsure why she had chosen to spill everything out to this man she had barely reconnected with only a week ago. But glad. Speaking out loud was freeing, and her eyes told him that while she hoped he would handle her truths with care, she didn't need him to. She would climb back up that ladder and walk away from him without looking back because she was a warrior well-used to walking alone.

When Keahi did speak, his words were a surprise.

"Thou art fearfully and wonderfully made."

The darkness in her eyes dimmed at his words, and a smile chased away the shadows. "That's my favourite scripture and the inspiration for my key work —"

"In your Ragged Soul exhibition at the end of your final year at the academy. Yes, I know."

"But how?"

"I went to see it on one of my trips to New York." He shrugged at her look of incredulity. "I was doing some movie promo there round about the same time, so I stopped by." He could see that she still didn't believe him. "Fine. My therapist is an art freak, goes to all the shows. He knew about my connection to Samoa so he told me about this crazy, brilliant new sculptor that everybody was raving about, from a dinky little island in the South Pacific."

Teuila's wonder was slowly turning to something else. "You came to see my exhibition?"

"I didn't want to get in the way. You had all that press around you and a bunch of stuck-up art crowd, so I just hung back and watched you do your thing."

She gaped. "You saw me? You were there that day?" She was

fighting against a tidal wave of rage, a gut feeling of betrayal. She didn't know what was worse, thinking that Keahi had ignored her all these years, forgotten her very existence – or finding out that he'd known about her art and had actually come to her exhibit, seen her and didn't talk to her! "I don't understand why you wouldn't say hi to an old friend."

"I planned to," he said. "But I was late to catch a flight and my agent rushed me out of there before you finished your interviews with the critics."

He said it as if it made total sense, and Teuila had to concede that it did. Why would he put himself out simply to say hello to a runaway kid he'd known once, a long time ago? She choked down her anger, knowing it would only expose the depth of her feelings for him. And that was something she definitely did not want to do. Keahi must never know about her ridiculous crush. Because that's all it was, she told herself fiercely. A silly leftover well of emotions from when she was a teenager. She only needed to exorcise them and she would be fine. A deep breath and a fake bright smile at Keahi. "So you saw my exhibition."

"Yeah. I looked at all your stuff and I gotta admit I didn't understand it all," said Keahi with a sheepish laugh. "But the bits I did get? Blew me away."

She was suddenly shy. "Yeah?"

"Some of it scares me."

"Why?" she asked.

"It's so honest. That takes courage I don't have. Maybe that's why I like being an actor. I don't have to be me." Keahi moved to change the subject. "I'm sorry about what happened with your loser ex. Senator's spoilt brat son wasn't good enough for you. He wasn't worthy of you. And Teuila, there is nothing broken about you. It takes strength and courage to make it through the crap that life has thrown at us. You make beauty and meaning out of bits of old trees and chunks of rock. When I came to see your exhibit, I was going through a rough time. In therapy, which can put you through hell before it helps you fix the mess, and seeing your work? It helped. I may not understand all your art, but it raises me up. Shows me a piece of the divine. Makes me think that, hey, maybe there's some of it in all of us. Even me."

Teuila flushed with a combination of embarrassment and happiness at his words, unused to compliments. Especially from him. She gave him a grateful smile which turned to confusion. "How did you know his father was a senator?" Suspicion. "I don't think I mentioned that."

"You said he was old money," said Keahi easily. "I took a guess. Your boyfriend was a fool. If you were mine, I would never let you go."

Teuila couldn't breathe for a moment. Stunned. Her mind a swirling mess of confusion. Why did he say that? He's only trying to be nice. Because he feels sorry for you. He doesn't mean it the way you think. She looked at him and Keahi met her gaze with unflinching directness. There was no teasing or uncertainty. Only open declaration. If you were mine, I would never let you go.

It was too much for her to handle. She frowned and looked away, dangled her hand in the silken, black water.

"Want to swim?" he asked from behind her.

She looked back at him, doubtful. "Are there sharks?"

A grin. "I don't think so. Tourists wouldn't pay twenty dollars to come here and swim with sharks."

Still she wasn't convinced. She'd always wanted to swim at To Sua, but night-time seemed to bring an element of danger to the ocean.

"Why don't you talk to it and find out?" asked Keahi.

She stiffened and yanked her hand out of the water. Threw him an angry glare, as if he had slapped her. How dare he bring that up?

"Hey, it's me," he said. "Your secret is safe. Just like I know mine is safe with you."

She looked at him in the moonlight and he didn't flinch. Instead he met her gaze, open and honest. No mockery or sarcasm. Just Keahi. She felt her instinctive barriers relax. In that moment she knew the truth of his words. She doubted everything else when it came to Keahi, but of that she was certain. Her Gift was safe with him. It always had been.

He sensed her walls coming down. "Do you use it much?"

"Do you?" she evaded.

"You know I can't. Not without a trigger." A resigned shrug as he looked out over the water. "Haven't been many of those where

I've been. Which is probably for the best. It's not like it ever did me much good. A genetic anomaly, a freak, having a male Telesā anyway. Remember?"

The space between them was filled with a rush of memory.

"You don't really believe that," she said. "You loved your Gift."

"Did I?"

She raised her chin in defiance. "Yes, you did. I felt it."

The invisible link that tied them became a little more tangible. A delicate gossamer thread.

"I didn't use it for a long time. After." After you left. "Then we had a volunteer art teacher do some classes at the centre. She had us work with clay and even though I wasn't listening, wasn't searching for it – it spoke to me. I felt it come alive under my hands. My first sculpture almost made itself. I moved on to working with stone, wood. And every time, it felt right. Y'know? It felt like – "

"Home. It felt like home," said Keahi.

The gossamer thread strengthened into a silver cord, binding them as if they belonged together. It was a relief. A homecoming.

"Yes," said Teuila. "Home. And it didn't matter that I had no friends, or that everyone had left me. It was okay that everyone had moved on. Because I had my Gift. I had Fanua and she never turned away from me."

She hadn't spoken of her Gift to anyone since she had left Samoa. And not since Keahi had she shared her feelings about her Gift with so much vulnerability. It felt so good to be able to open up now, to speak her secret into the open air. Like a waterfall finally unbound. The rush of a storm long barricaded.

"I'll never have Leila's fire power. Or Daniel's ocean force. I can't wield the storm as fiercely as those Ariki from Rarotonga could. It's like I only have whispers of everyone's Gifts. 'Fire'." Teuila snapped her fingers and a flame flickered in the palm of her right hand. "Water." With the other hand she cupped a handful of water and tossed it lightly into the air, where it spun a sinuous dance of silver, twirling a delicate pattern around the flame. "Earth." A thought, a summons, and the frangipani tree poised at the edge of the trench heaved a sigh in the wind and leant forwards with a shuddering rustle of branches, dispelling a handful of white blossoms far above them. "And Air." A delicate breeze picked up just a fraction, barely enough to notice, but more than enough to pillow the flowers and divert them from their path towards the water. They slowly twirled in a lazy circle above the couple, as if buoyed by invisible threads. "Only party tricks, really."

"No," disagreed Keahi as he looked in awe at the elements in action around them and at the woman who spoke to them all. "Your control is amazing. I never saw any of the others capable of anything like this. It's breathtaking." He reached out to softly cup her face in his hands. "You take my breath away."

And then he kissed her.

Teuila had often wondered, daydreamed, what it would be like to be held by Keahi. Kissed by him. Now she realised that her teenage imagination had been woefully inadequate. Kissing Keahi was like walking into fire, melding with it and becoming one. Both terrifying and wildly exhilarating at the same time. He was familiar, her childhood friend, the only one who had ever understood her pain – and all her defences gave way to that safety and belonging. But he was also danger and risk, the thrill of the unknown and unchainable. All the contradictions rolled into one overwhelming force that left her breathless. For a brief instant she thought about resisting, pulling away. The sensible choice! But then she said no to sensible. She was tired of sensible. She wanted desire. Joy.

She wanted Keahi.

Fire raged through Teuila, burning her from the inside out. Keahi's mouth on hers was hibiscus-red desire and searing golden need. His hands cradled her face gently, as if she were a fragile flower, but his kiss was unbridled and overwhelming. He kissed her like the world was ending and her touch was the last thing he wanted to savour as he met death. He kissed her like she was the sun and he was the forest unfurling to meet the dawn, like he would not and could not make it through the day without her. Teuila knew that as long as she lived, his kiss would be forever seared into her memory. All of it. The velvet embrace of the star-spangled night sky above them, pink petals of frangipani lilting on the sea breeze, sweet fragrance, the rough scrape of the wood platform on her bare feet as she stood on tiptoes meeting his hunger with her own. Speaking to his need with hers. His hands tangled in her thick hair, tugging her head back, exposing her throat to the moonlight as he kissed a path of fire down the curve of her neck, moving aside the straps of her shift so he could nip, kiss and bite the arch of her shoulder. He murmured her name under the stars as he kissed her mouth, face and the line of her throat. She felt as if she was drowning, no, as if she was burning up in a wildfire, no, as if she was caught up in a tempest, all at once, and he was both the cause and the anchor that would save her. She clung to him, a soft whimper of protest in her throat when he broke their kiss so he could look into her eyes. His gaze promised magic and wonder, danger and desire, all in one.

"Don't stop," she breathed.

"I don't want to," he said, his voice a harsh growl in his chest. He kissed her again, this time slow and sensual, taking his time, savouring the taste of her, the feel of her pressed against him. No walls, no mockery or sarcasm, no pretence. Just two people giving of themselves freely and completely. Teuila felt as if she would cry from the perfection of it. This moment in time. This perfect closeness.

There was a rustling, fluttering sound and Keahi broke away again, this time to point out something behind them.

"Look!" Awed wonder. Keahi turned her gently. "Where did they come from?"

The starlit night was filled with hundreds of butterflies. A tapestry of luxuriant colour, vibrant and perpetually in motion, dancing on the light breeze that played on their skin.

"I don't know whether to be amazed or afraid," said Keahi with a grin, one arm holding her close against his chest, the other outstretched towards the fluttering cloud of colour. "Are they here to attack me because they're worried for you?" He faked a serious tone. "Do you come in peace, flying soldiers?"

Teuila laughed. With her head cradled against the broad strength of his chest, secure in the warmth and safety of his embrace, she realised, this is what happiness feels like …

"I'm sorry. I didn't call them. Sometimes Fanua just does things. She feels what I do and then she reacts. It's often a surprise to me." She reached out and an array of butterflies softly lowered themselves to perch lightly on her arm, delicate and ethereal. "They mean no harm. They come when I'm …" She snuck a glance up at Keahi, suddenly unsure whether to say it. The look in his eyes encouraged her. As if she was the only person on earth who mattered. A little voice in her head warned, He's an actor. He practises that look all the time and probably uses it on every woman he meets. You can't trust him. But she shook off the warning. "Happy. The butterflies come when I'm happy. It hasn't happened a lot."

Keahi smiled as he turned her to face him again, cradling her face in his hands. "It's my personal mission then to make sure we see butterflies every damn day that we're together."

The perched butterflies took off into the air but Teuila didn't notice. She was too busy getting lost in the magic that was Keahi. She could have stood there on the water platform and kissed him forever, but the booking for To Sua only lasted until midnight.

Neither of them wanted to breach the rules, especially Teuila who didn't want to deal with an angry caretaker who would have no patience with a kissing couple. It wouldn't be too bad for Keahi as a foreigner. There were different rules for a tourist. But for a Samoan woman? There would be much berating and complaining about Teuila being 'kaukalaikiki' and probably a few mutterings of 'paumuku' thrown in for good measure.

They packed up what was left of their dinner and climbed back to the surface. It wasn't until they were at the chopper again, though, that Teuila finally broached the topic that had been simmering ever since she and Keahi had sparred earlier in the week.

"So, is it safe to bring up the question again?" Even as she spoke the words, she was second-guessing herself. Did she really want to do this? Here? Now? It had been the perfect night – so far. Why ruin it? But she knew if she didn't, it would bother her always. She turned to face him head-on, reminding herself that she wasn't that scared little girl any more. She was a grown woman, a successful artist, an equal to this man. And she was strong enough to know the truth.

"What question?"

"Are you ever going to tell me why you left Samoa so suddenly? One minute we're hanging out in the tree house, drinking purple soda, swapping pain stories, and the next you're gone. And I have to hear it from someone else. You didn't tell me you were leaving. You didn't say goodbye."

Her voice broke a little on the last word and she half-turned away as she struggled to keep her composure. Don't fall apart in front of him. Be strong. Don't let him see how badly he hurt you.

She clenched her fists tightly, and the cut of her nails into her palms helped steel her. She looked up at the man who stood beside her in the silver moonlight. "Why?"

"I couldn't stay. I had stuff going on that I couldn't tell you about. I had to leave the country. Fast. It wasn't safe. It wouldn't be safe to tell you now, either."

She looked up into his eyes and found only truth there. Truth and a flash of pain. Whatever it was, Keahi still hurt from it, and that knowledge made her more willing to accept his answer. Or lack of an answer.

"I see. But you told Leila and Daniel. They drove you to the airport." She couldn't stop the accusatory tone in her voice.

"I didn't want their help," said Keahi and now there was tense anger in the air. "I didn't want anyone's help. But I didn't have the money to fly out. They loaned it to me. I paid them back as soon as I could."

He was angry because he was proud. She knew what it was like to have to accept charity and so she eased up on her interrogation. "I understand. It's hard to accept help sometimes. But it's been fifteen years. Surely the big secret, whatever it was, can't be a big deal any more?"

She didn't want to sound whiny or vulnerable so she stopped herself from adding the words of her heart ...You were my friend, my only friend, and you left me.

He reached out to take her hand in his. Reassuring. "I'm sorry. I was a selfish kid back then. I should have said goodbye. I wish that I could have. Can you forgive me?"

It wasn't an explanation, but it was an apology all the same. Somewhat mollified, Teuila squeezed his hand and gave Keahi a half-hearted smile. "Sure."

"I promise, no more disappearing." He leaned over to claim her mouth with his. A kiss that left her reeling and sent all doubts flying. For now.

Back at the airstrip, there was a car waiting for them. But no driver.

"I'm driving you home," explained Keahi. "Reuben left it for us. Gives me a bit more time alone with you. And I want every minute that I can get because who knows if you'll give me another date?"

He paused to send a text. "Reuben always wants me to check in with my whereabouts. It's annoying but bitter experience tells me that if I don't, he gets antsy and stalks me. Popping up where I don't want him to."

There was an easy affection underneath the feigned irritation, and it made Teuila grin. "How long has he worked for you?" she asked.

"Ten years," said Keahi. "He's the best in his field, used to shadow presidents and sheikhs. Now he just drives me insane with how security-paranoid he is. He doesn't get it that we're in Samoa and there's no danger here. Not like back on the mainland. I told him he needs to chill and take a holiday. Can you believe it, he expected to fly us tonight? And when I said, 'Hell no!' he said, all right, he would be waiting at the airstrip to escort you home. How am I supposed to continue charming you with him breathing down my neck?"

"Oh, you were pretty confident about your charm working on me tonight, were you?" laughed Teuila.

In answer he tugged her to him so he could enfold her in his embrace. Again she drowned in his kiss. This time he half-groaned as he released her, carefully stepping away as if he needed the space. "If we don't go now, I may never return you home." His tone was light and teasing but the hunger in his eyes filled her with excitement.

"Don't make promises you can't keep," she teased back, half-wishing he would sweep her away.

Outside Mrs Amani's house, the kiss he gave her was soft and lingering, filled with want and need. When he released her finally, she felt bereft. Incomplete. Being in his arms felt good. It felt right. It left her weak and on fire at the same time. Which pretty much described her tumultuous feelings for this man.

"Now see, I couldn't kiss you like this if Reuben were here, could I?" he said with a crooked grin. "Thank you for tonight."

"Ah, but was it worth the hefty price tag?"

He pretended to consider it and his drawn-out pondering made her laugh. "I don't know," he said. "My findings were inconclusive."

"What does that mean?" she spluttered in mock outrage.

He tugged her back into his arms and she melted into his embrace willingly. She whispered against his ear, "Tell me I'm not worth it … I dare you."

A low rumble of a laugh deep in his throat as he replied, "Are you kidding me? I know what you'll do if I say something you don't like. You'll kick my ass."

"Yes, but it will be oh so delicious for you," she teased. "The most enjoyable defeat ever."

His eyes turned serious as he gazed down at her in the moonlight. "You're exquisite."

"You're not so bad yourself," said Teuila, trying to be light and casual when all she wanted to do was pull him into her room and keep him there all night. Forget all night, how about forever? The depth of her feelings for this man scared her, shook her to her core. How was it possible the boy from her childhood could have transformed into this man she both knew deeply and yet remained a mystery? She reminded herself that any woman with half a brain would know not to take whatever was happening between them seriously. He's a movie star, the sexiest man alive. He could have any woman he wanted. He probably has. She would only be one of many who felt this same fire and magnetism from him. There was a reason he was world-famous after all. He knew how to sweep you off your feet and take you captive in his magic spell. She needed to put the brakes on her feelings. On her hormones. On her expectations and hopes for this. Whatever it was.

As if sensing her reservations, Keahi released her. A fleeting grin as he bade her goodnight. "Sleep well."

She watched him walk away, and then before she went inside, he stopped and turned, that familiar crooked smile on his face.

"Teuila?"

"Yes?"

"Tonight wasn't worth the million dollars," he said. "It was priceless. Inestimable."

And with those final words, he left her, adrift in a swirling vortex of emotions.

CHAPTER THIRTEEN

Keahi was jubilant as he drove away from the centre compound. The date had gone even better than he had hoped. He smiled as he remembered the kiss. The closeness. The fire. The magic of Teuila's Gift she had shared with him. It always left him awed and humbled. Seeing Fanua's majesty and grace reminded him how small and insignificant man truly was. And how reliant on Fanua in every way. You got a sense of that from every piece of art that Teuila made. To be in her presence when she called on her Gift was to experience Fanua's wonder on an entirely different level. But more than her Gift, Keahi was entranced by the woman Teuila had become. She was beautiful and talented, yes, but beyond that, she was strong and determined. Resolute in her path and what she wanted from life. None of his distant surveillance and monitoring of her activities had adequately captured the person she was now. He wished he had reached out to her long ago.

He was so caught up in his thoughts that at first he didn't notice he was being followed. A monstrous jeep, sleek black, hurtling through the night and gaining on him. By the time he realised he was being tracked, it was too late. The jeep surged ahead of him on the narrow road. He swore as the jeep swerved in front of him, forcing him to jerk the steering wheel to the left to avoid a collision. He brought the car to a sudden halt. The driver of the jeep opened the door and exited. Keahi was fuming as he leapt out.

"What the hell was that?" he demanded as he stalked towards the jeep. "You nearly hit me!"

His words died away as he saw who the other driver was. Marc Gold. "It's you." Keahi's eyes narrowed as he stopped a few metres away. "You ran me off the road. Why?"

Marc shrugged as he folded his arms and leaned against the black jeep. "We need to talk."

"That's what the phone is for," said Keahi. There was restrained threat in his voice and fire in his eyes. Anyone else would have felt it and stepped back.

But not Marc. "You had your million dollar date with Teuila tonight."

Keahi raised an eyebrow but said nothing. Marc continued.

"With her financial obligation to you paid, I suggest you stay away from her now."

"Oh, really," said Keahi. "You suggest?" He threw his head back and laughed. The burst of sound pierced the night. "Oh, I get it now." There was a look of disdain on his face as he turned away from Marc to walk back to his car. "I'm not doing this."

"Where are you going?" demanded Marc.

"Home," said Keahi, his hand on the car door. "I've got nothing to say to you. Only this, you run my car off the road again and I'll hurt you."

Keahi was angry but nowhere near losing control. He was used to being challenged in the streets. Any celebrity who made a career around action films had more than their fair share of run-ins with people – usually men – who were out to make a name for themselves by getting into a fight with an action star. It was why people in Keahi's position never went anywhere in public without a bodyguard. Not because they couldn't fight back, but because it would be bad for their profile if they did. In the early days, Keahi would leap to react whenever he was challenged by brash, drunk anti-fans. He got into altercations that always ended with the wannabe opponent in hospital and Keahi's manager having to smooth things over with a pay-out and a confidentiality agreement. Over the years Keahi had learned it was much cheaper and less hassle to exercise discipline and walk away from the aggressor. That was his plan tonight. But Marc had other ideas.

"I saw you with her," snapped Marc. "You put your hands on her."

Keahi turned back, fury in his voice. "You followed us?"

"I saw enough," said Marc. He flushed and spat out his words, "Think you're special, don't you? Because of your movie star status and those magazine-cover looks, you think you can get every woman you want? That all you have to do is snap your fingers and they come running?"

Keahi laughed. He had to. "Magazine-cover looks? Oh, you haven't looked close enough, have you? All the Photoshop in the world, all the airbrushing, can't hide these scars. Pretty boy? That's a title I'll leave for your kind." And then all humour fled. His voice cold and hard as stone. "It wasn't my idea to buy a date with an artist. I outbid you so Teuila wouldn't have to endure a night with you. This island isn't here for your pleasure, rich boy. You're no better than the first colonisers who came to take whatever they could, with no regard for who they hurt along the way. Now, you don't get to say Teuila's name to me. Our relationship is none of your business and you will not, you cannot, commodify it. I'm warning you. Stay away from her."

Keahi turned and walked away, done with the conversation. It was the dismissiveness which rankled Marc more than anything else, though. That Keahi could turn his back on him and see him as someone trifling and small. It enraged him as nothing else could. He reacted. A thought, an unleashing of the darkness within. It was fast this time. Not like with Sione. No, this man would die quickly.

The Hunger ripped from Marc in a rushing wave. One minute his body was a patterned tapestry of markings, the next it was leached clean as the Hunger poured forth. It raced along the pavement and the low hum of its craving alerted Keahi to its advance. Too late, though. He half turned and the Hunger was upon him. It ensnared his feet, tripping him to his knees, and then swathed him in its coils. Keahi didn't even have time to shout before the Hunger shrouded his entire body, lifting him up off the ground.

"Yes!" exulted Marc, his eyes alight with excitement and anticipation, hands outstretched. "Consume him!"

Keahi kicked and struggled. His world was dark, the breath was being crushed from his chest, panic choked him. What was happening? He couldn't breathe. Couldn't see. Couldn't move. Couldn't cry out. The pressure built in his lungs, the overwhelming need for air, for release. Time dragged and Keahi's struggling slowed. He knew with sudden clarity that he was going to die.

The Hunger started to glow, a shimmering in the night that echoed the distant draping of stars overhead. But before it could carry out its familiar devastation, there was the roar of an engine as a fast-approaching vehicle accelerated, the blaring of a car horn.

Marc barely had time to turn before the car hit him, throwing him several feet across the dark road. A thud and a sickening crunch of impact. The Hunger immediately released its grip on Keahi. He fell to the ground in a wash of light. Dazed and gasping for air, he tried to get to his feet, stumbled a few steps as he coughed and gasped, trying to pull air into his starved lungs. A screech of tyres, a door opening, and Reuben's command. "Get in! Quick." Keahi half-fell into the front passenger seat. He hadn't even shut the door when already Reuben had accelerated away, racing him to safety.

"Talk to me," said Reuben, eyes on the rear-view mirror, checking for any pursuit. "Are you all right? Do you need the hospital?"

Keahi's throat felt like burning coals as he choked out an answer. "No. I'm fine."

Reuben's snort of disgust conveyed what he thought of Keahi's lie. "Buckle up. We're getting out of here."

"Wait," said Keahi. "We have to go back. Find out what that thing was."

Reuben's face was impassive granite. "We're going to the airport. I've radioed for the jet to be ready. Emergency evac protocol activated."

Keahi swore. "No. We're not leaving. You just hit a man at full throttle. You killed somebody."

"No, I didn't," said Reuben. "And no, we are not going back there."

"Reuben!" Keahi's tone left no room for dissent as he shifted into employer mode. "That man needs medical attention. Once he gets that, then we can turn him in to the police. Turn around."

"No," said Reuben. "He doesn't."

"What does that mean?"

"You didn't see what I saw," said Reuben. "After I hit him. Reversed to come pick you up. That thing. That creature? A snake or whatever it is. It went back to him where he was lying on the ground. Went inside him. And he sat up again. Looked all right to me."

"That's impossible. You hit him. I heard the impact. Nobody could survive that."

"I saw what I saw, boss," said Reuben. "I don't know what we're dealing with here. But that thing? It isn't human."

Keahi winced as he ran a hand along his ribcage, checking for breaks. There was nothing but resolve on his face, though, when he snapped an order at his head of security. "Cancel the plane, Reuben. I'm not leaving."

"But, Sir," protested Reuben.

"You can patch me up back at the house. Get a full security team on a jet over here right away. I want enough for a twenty-four-hour detail, seven days a week."

"Good plan, Sir," said Reuben. Surprised but approving. "I'd feel much better knowing you have a complete team on you."

"Not for me," said Keahi. "For Teuila. That freak has a fixation on her, and until we figure out what he is and how to eliminate him, we're not leaving her unprotected anywhere."

CHAPTER FOURTEEN

Marc was back there. In that place. With her. Only this time he wasn't an honoured guest but a prisoner of torture. Bound with ropes made from tree vines, on his knees in the dirt, his arms spreadeagled between two posts. A circle of women stood around him. Women unlike any he'd ever seen before. With faces that rippled and twisted from human to something else. A bird of prey. The feline, unblinking stare of a cat. The gleaming tusks of a boar. The darting tongue of a lizard. And the leader of them all, Saumaeafe. She was the one who brandished the bone blade, so sharp it drew blood even when she traced it lightly against his skin.

"Marc Gold, what are we going to do with you? Hmm..." she said.

That voice. He would know it anywhere. In the darkness. At the dying edge of madness. It tiptoed through his waking dreams and resounded in the echoing corridors of his mansion. He knew that no matter how high he built his walls, or how far away he travelled, that voice would follow him everywhere.

He tried to speak but his throat was parched dry and words felt like raw skin scraped on sharp coral.

She knew his need even as he could not speak it. She stepped back, motioned for one of the women to bring him water which he gulped eagerly.

"Please," he rasped. "Release me. Haven't you punished me enough?"

She laughed without humour. "Punishment enough?" She looked around at her sisters. "What think you? Has this creature suffered enough?"

Saumaeafe grabbed his hair and pulled. Hard. Forcing his head up and back so he had to look out over the valley that lay spread before them. The flickering lights of the Sanctuary town. "What do you see, Marc?" She didn't wait for him to answer. "You see riches. Progress. But that was our home. The forest, the water, the air, the earth. All of it is what gives us life. We have been here for longer than you can even comprehend. You think you've built a sanctuary for your people to retreat to, as long as they can pay? Somewhere they can hide from the pestilence and destruction that they themselves have caused in their own lands? But this land is ours. Our blood and breath. When will it stop? Your thirst for taking. Controlling. Owning what was never yours. Your kind always think you can buy with money what can never be yours."

"No," protested Marc, finally finding his voice, his resolve. "Our development will help the people of this country. Take it forwards."

"Help?" spat one of the sisters. She reached out with lightning-fast anger and raked her claws down his face. "You've destroyed our forest. Flooded our caves. We are homeless, now. Doomed wanderers. And without our trees, our aitu will weaken and die." She looked ready to rip him to shreds with her bare hands, and Marc shrank from her strength. He tasted blood in his mouth. Bitter red iron.

"Take the people forwards?" asked Saumaeafe with a knowing smile on her face. "Tell me, how many people has your Hunger consumed?" She turned to pace back and forth, counting off on her fingers. "Let me see, it began with that child. Yes, the flower seller. An innocent little boy. All he wanted was to get some money for his family to buy food. That was his only wrong. Asking the rich palagi to buy an ula pua. What did you give him in return? Death. That poor child. Then there was the woman. The one who approached your car at the traffic lights. Yes? It was late that night and she was obviously unwell. Intoxicated? High? What did she want from you?" Saumaeafe didn't wait for him to answer. "Ah, yes, money. She offered to sell her body to you. Perhaps to buy more drugs? Or food. Even a pair of shoes perhaps. She was barefoot, wasn't she? You noticed that detail because there was broken glass on the road and still she walked across it to your shiny, expensive car and you wondered if it hurt her. The glass surely didn't hurt her as much as your Hunger did. After her, you killed two construction workers. Police are still searching for them, but they'll never find their bodies, will they? Who else? Hmm … ah yes, that lawyer, the protest leader. Another unwary victim. So many. But you're still hungry, aren't you, Marc?"

As she recited a list of victims, it seemed to Marc that their hazy images appeared before him. Ethereal and ghostlike, but oh so very real and tangible to him. He gave a half-sob, a smothered groan. Of pain? Fear? Revulsion? He wasn't sure. He knew he wanted her to stop talking. Stop summoning their ghosts.

"This is all your fault," he said. "You did this to me."

"I?" The smile she gave him was filled with derision. "I merely unleashed the Hunger that has always lived inside you, Marc. I gave you a Gift. Of power. And what have you done with it? Exactly what I knew you would. Because it will never be enough for you." She motioned towards the vast valley below. "Even all this won't satisfy you. You come in search of a sanctuary from the hell your kind have caused out there in the world. But it won't last. You'll destroy this place eventually, too. As surely as you've consumed life after life with your Hunger."

There was a sadness in her eyes. One that spoke of generations of loss and longing. "Immortality's curse," she said – more a whisper to herself than to any other – "is that just as we stand as guardians, so too we must bear witness to your greed and foolishness as it ruins us all." A single tear glistened on her cheek as she stepped closer to Marc and reached to clasp his face in her hands. "This is your last chance. I can take the curse from you. If you end this now. Stop this project. Remove all trace that it ever existed. Take your people and your machines. Go back to America. Let this forest breathe again. Let us live."

Give in to this woman? Marc didn't hesitate. He spat in her face.

A tense silence in the night as all the women turned to stone in their dread. As one, they looked to Saumaeafe to see what she would do. A long pause as she met his gaze, as he felt himself get lost in the dark pools of her eyes, drown in them. Terror crawled up his spine, a spider moving with slow precision towards its prey. What would Saumaeafe do?

She wiped the spit from her face and rose to her feet. "So be it. You've made your choice." She turned to the sisters. "Let all witness, the man has chosen his path. He was given a way back. A way out. And he refused it. Let the curse be sealed."

A sister came forwards with a kava bowl filled with clear liquid. Water? Saumaeafe raised it to the moonlight and spoke a single word. "Vai."

Another came with a bone blade and slashed at Marc's shoulder. With total disinterest, though. He was no longer a matter of any concern or importance to them. She just cut at his flesh and smeared her hand in his blood and raised her palm to the sky. "Toto."

She then washed her hands in the kava bowl before melting back into the circle. Another woman came forwards, this time to kneel before Saumaeafe and clench her fists in the dirt which she sprinkled into the kava bowl. "Palapala," she intoned.

There was a rustling sound, of leaves? Of feathers. The women parted to make way for another. She was dark, tall and lean. Near naked, her body was clothed in feathers, tufted lines of black and speckled grey, and a glorious pair of wings trailed lightly behind her. Her hooded eyes seemed to pierce right through him. She tugged a single feather from the tufting at her throat and placed it in the kava bowl. That's when Marc saw the talons of her fingers. Razor sharp and fearsome. When she spoke her voice was a rasp, an unwilling use of words. "Manulele." But unlike the others, she didn't immediately walk away. No, she came to Marc and with a swift movement, grabbed his hair, pulling his head back and exposing his throat. She made a guttural sound, then a hiss, as she brought up her claws and drew a single line of redness along his neck. She stared down into his eyes and Marc saw only death there. Terror was a bat trapped in his chest, wings beating vainly at the confines of his ribs, pleading for escape. It choked him. The pain of the cut burned and he felt the droplets of blood congealing on his skin.

Saumaeafe spoke a warning. "No, Lefaga. Not now. His time will come."

The owl woman released him. Marc thought he heard her whisper so only he could hear, "The garden will be waiting for you." But it made little sense to him, so he wondered if he'd imagined it. He couldn't stop the half-sob of relief as she released him and walked away, back into the shadows. This woman wasn't human at all. She was feral, untamed and unbound. Wild night and birds of prey tearing into hot flesh and still-beating hearts. Marc knew the memory of her eyes would be seared into his brain for all time.

Still the ritual was not complete. Another came forwards. This time a woman with skin of bark and leaf tresses for hair. She seemed impatient to be done, to be gone. She barely gave Marc a second glance as she tossed a handful of moss into the kava bowl. "La'au."

When all had come forwards and added their piece to the kava bowl, it was done. Saumaeafe raised the bowl to the moon and chanted words Marc couldn't understand. He was afraid of what they would do to him once the chanting was finished, but at its close, she merely placed the kava bowl on the ground and walked to stand with her sisters, leaving him alone in the centre of the circle, the bowl beside him. None of the women had eyes for him, though. They all looked to the heavens. He was nothing. Time stretched on. What were they waiting for? And then it came. A single lightning strike, sudden and jagged in its ferocity. It razed the kava bowl and consumed it in white fire, leaving only a pile of ash that scattered in the night breeze. It was so close that Marc felt the burn of it on his face and he shrank from its heat.

"With this, the curse is sealed," said Saumaeafe, speaking to the women rather than Marc. They all nodded in agreement. In validation? "We will watch from afar. And wait. Yes?"

Again the women nodded. And then they melted into the shadows, leaving Marc alone. Relieved to be alive but bereft and confused. What had just happened? And what were they waiting for?

The dream ended. For surely it must have been only a dream?

He was alone in his bedroom, drenched in a cold sweat. He stumbled from his bed to carry out a frantic search of the premises, wanting – no, needing – to make sure there were no intruders. No women with talons and feathers lurking in the shadows. The sun was just coming up over the mountain but he felt bone weary, as if he hadn't slept at all. There was a twisting stab of pain inside him. Hungry. I need to eat. After the interruption to his feeding the night before, when that car had come out of nowhere and smashed into him, he had returned home, angry and empty. Gone to bed still raging. Without satisfying the Hunger. And now this morning, it had intensified.

Marc pushed a button, summoned his personal assistant, told her to meet him in his home office. So what if it was early morning? All his staff knew they were at his beck and call, twenty-four-seven. He dressed quickly, hands shaking as Hunger gouged at his insides. Impatient.

The intercom beeped. Lindsey. "I'm here now, Mr Gold."

It was a struggle for him to walk sedately to his office. Not run. He took deep breaths, trying to calm himself, steady his focus. It would be an annoyance to have to replace Lindsey. She was efficient and understood how he liked to work. But Hunger was stronger than his desire for convenience. And he could always get another assistant. He could have another one, or two or three, flown in on his private plane by tomorrow. What mattered was that nothing should stop him from completing the Sanctuary.

He opened the door, a smile on his face. "Good morning, Lindsey. Thank you for coming …"

CHAPTER FIFTEEN

The insistent ringing of the phone dragged Teuila from the depths of sleep. She was having a fabulous dream, one in which she and Keahi were walking along a moonlit beach, holding hands, stopping often to embrace. The sand was soft beneath her feet, the ocean breeze was a light caress on her skin, and Keahi's arms around her were strong and secure. He was whispering words in her ear that she wanted to hear. Things like, "I'm sorry I left you all those years ago. It was the biggest mistake of my life…" and "I've dreamed of this day always, having you here by my side, in my arms …" and "You're everything I've ever wanted in a woman. Those actresses and cover models? Pfft, they're nothing to me. So what if one is also a neuroscientist and the other has two Oscar awards. They pale in comparison to you and your brilliance … oh, Teuila, say you'll be mine." Teuila smiled in her slumber. There was no way she wanted to wake up just yet. She turned over and tugged the sheet over her head, trying to hold tight to the delicious dream.

But the damn phone wouldn't stop intruding.

"Oh, fine then." She sat upright, brushing a hand through her wild mane of hair as she reached for the phone that wouldn't leave her alone. "What?"

It was Bree. A faux whisper. "Is he there next to you?"

"What?" spluttered Teuila. "No, of course he's not next to me."

Bree sounded disappointed. "Oh, why not? Was the date a bust?"

"It was awesome."

"I hate to burst your bubble, Teuila," said Bree, "but if it really had been awesome he would be in the bed next to you. And you wouldn't be answering my call because you'd be too busy moaning in morning sex ecstasy."

Teuila had to laugh. "Girl, not every amazing date ends in bed." She teased, "Sometimes it means great conversation, a meeting of minds and a harmony of souls."

Bree made a vomit sound. "Oh please, not the poetic soul rubbish. A meeting of bodies is the only kind of union I'm interested in."

The two friends laughed together and then Bree got back to business. The million-dollar date. "So where did he take you?"

Teuila told her about the evening. Everything from the helicopter ride to the floating candles and dinner under the stars. She left out the Fanua Gift details, of course.

Bree sighed over the phone. "Okay, you've cracked through the walls of my steel heart. That's romantic. He even had your favourite foods? I'll give it to Keahi, he knows how to woo a girl."

"It was beautiful. I had a great time with him."

"Is he a good kisser?" Bree asked. "Does he know how to touch you the right way?"

"I'm not telling," said Teuila.

Bree groaned in disappointment. "We're best friends. I tell you everything about my dates. I told you all about Francis' amazing skills at —"

Teuila cut her off. "And I told you I wasn't interested in the details. That stuff is private."

Bree laughed again, a trill of light an ocean away. "I bet you're making a 'yuck' face at me right now. You're cringing as usual, because you can't handle it when the conversation gets dirty. Fine. Just give me a yes or no answer. Did he kiss you?"

Teuila went quiet and Bree pushed. "Come on, answer me and I promise I'll leave you alone and won't bug you for any more details."

"Fine. Yes, he did."

Bree was triumphant. "I knew it! And was it good? Did you melt? Just a yes or no."

"Yes," muttered Teuila. "That's it. I'm not saying any more about it. I mean it, Bree."

But Bree had got what she wanted and knew when to back off. Another laugh. "That's all I needed. He kissed you and you liked it. I give it a week and he'll have you in bed with him."

"What? No he won't."

A long-distance shrug. "That man is smooth. He's got skills. You two have history and it's obvious there's something between you. It only takes a spark! It's only a matter of time before it all ignites."

Teuila wanted to protest but knew it would be futile. Besides, she would be lying if she said there was no fire between her and Keahi. The question was, what did she want to have happen now?

Teuila's plans for the day included teaching an art class at the centre, but before she could head out, frantic barking from Beth's dogs alerted her to visitors. She looked out the window – a police truck?

There were two officers in the vehicle and they didn't look happy about the three dogs biting at their tyres and jumping up at the windows. Teuila called the dogs off and shooed them into the back yard. Only then did the officers feel safe enough to exit the car. A man and a woman in uniform.

"Can I help you?" asked Teuila. "Mrs Amani has already gone to work at the centre. I can show you where her office is."

"Are you Teuila? The artist?" asked the female officer. She was short and plump, with her dark hair pulled back into a low bun.

"That's me."

The male officer put out his hand and introduced himself. "I'm Sergeant Tofi. This is my partner, Sergeant Filo. We'd like to speak with you about a missing person's case. We believe you may have been one of the last people to see him. Sione Wilson?"

"Sione's missing? Since when? What happened?"

The police explained that Sione had last been seen three days ago. "His wife reported him missing to police when he never came home from the office."

Teuila quickly calculated. "Three days ago? That's when I saw him. He came by the hotel I was staying at and we had a coffee. A catch-up."

The two officers exchanged a look. A nod. Sergeant Filo said, "Yes, that's what his wife says. He told her he was meeting with you that afternoon. You're old school mates?"

"Yes, that's right. I went to a meeting at the Gold Mountain Resort Project and saw Sione in the protest outside. We talked and made plans to meet up somewhere less noisy."

"How long was your catch-up?" asked Sergeant Tofi.

"About an hour and a half?" said Teuila. "My agent was leaving that day, catching a flight back to the US and I had to go see her off."

The officers lost some of their detachment as again they exchanged a glance and checked their notes. "That checks out with what the hotel staff have said," said Sergeant Filo. "You two shared a drink and then Sione left in his white Hyundai. Alone. At no point did you two go upstairs to your room."

Teuila raised an eyebrow at the officers, hands on her hips. "Of course we didn't. He's an old friend I hadn't seen for almost fifteen years. I know he's maried and they have two children. He showed me pictures of his family. Wait, am I a suspect here?"

Sergeant Tofi rushed to calm the conversation. "No, of course not. We have CCTV footage from the hotel of you two meeting and then Sione leaving alone. We also have hotel staff who confirm your whereabouts for the rest of that day."

"So you already checked up on me," said Teuila drily. "I'm relieved I'm not under investigation, but why are you here, then?"

"What do you know about the American? Marc Gold?" asked Sergeant Filo.

How had the conversation gone from Sione to Marc? Teuila's eyes narrowed. "Why?"

"Sione's wife received two phone calls from her husband late that night. In the first, he told her he was leaving the office and would be home soon. A short while later he called her again. Only this time, he didn't speak to her."

"What do you mean?" asked Teuila.

"The wife claims that in the call, Sione was screaming," explained Sergeant Tofi. "He was being attacked by something. Someone. She says that Sione named Marc Gold as his attacker. We have the cellphone records showing two calls were made, but no way of verifying what was said on them."

"And it's been three days with no sign of Sione. His car was unlocked and his personal belongings scattered everywhere in the parking lot. Signs of a struggle." The sergeant's face was grim.

"You think he's hurt?" asked Teuila. "Or even ...dead?" Worry for her friend gnawed at her chest. "His poor family must be a wreck."

"Did Sione talk about Mr Gold at all? Tell you anything about their protest work at the Gold Mountain Project?" asked Sergeant Filo.

Teuila told them everything she knew, everything she could remember about her conversation with Sione. It wasn't much, and she could tell the police officers were disappointed when the interview was over.

"Is Marc a suspect?" she asked them as she walked the officers back to their car.

"We can't comment on an ongoing investigation," said Sergeant Filo.

"And who knows, maybe Sione wanted a break from his wife and kids," added Sergeant Tofi. "He could show up in a few days. Without a body – or any other physical evidence – we really don't have much to go on. It's only the wife's word that Marc was there with Sione that night. And she's pretty distraught, so not really the best witness right now."

With that, the police got into their car and drove away. Teuila was left to mull over the prickle of unease down her spine as she thought about Marc Gold and his possible involvement in Sione's disappearance. There was no disputing that Sione and his team of activists were a thorn in Marc's side, and Sione's legal efforts in particular were a challenge to the Sanctuary's future. She'd seen how passionate Marc was about his project, the look in his eyes when he talked about his vision for the future, and the hint of rage that had slipped through his defences when he talked about the protestors. She knew Marc would do almost anything to make his dream a reality.

But would he hurt someone for it? Make a man disappear? Would he kill for it?

There was only one way to find out.

CHAPTER SIXTEEN

"She's gone to his compound."

"What?" Keahi didn't have to ask who Reuben was talking about. Teuila was the only woman on his mind these days. "When?"

"She left about twenty minutes ago from the centre. Told them she had a meeting with Gold."

Keahi swore as he grabbed the keys to his bike on his way to the door.

"Sir, there's something else you should know. I met with the police commissioner this morning and they have a file on Gold, a few troubling things." With quick efficiency, Reuben gave Keahi a summary of his conversation with Chief Stevens. Everything from Marc's mystery disappearance in the forest to his possible involvement with the disappearance of a lead activist lawyer. "Police haven't connected it with Marc, but the chief is also dealing with several missing person cases, a child who worked as a street vendor, two construction labourers, and a female sex worker. He's keeping a lid on it so far because the police don't want to alarm the public, but off the record? We're looking at a possible serial killer here, a predator. And after what I saw Marc do last night I'd say he should be their lead suspect. We should get down to the station and file a report about his attack on you so they can bring Marc in for questioning at least."

"No time," snapped Keahi. "Teuila's up there with him and that means she's in danger." He broke into a run down the stairs and to the garage.

Reuben followed him, worry etched on his face. "Sir! We need a plan first."

"You wait for the team to get in. Then all of you come and me at Gold's compound."

"You shouldn't go alone …" Reuben's words trailed off as Keahi kick-started the bike and roared away down the drive. Reuben was left talking to himself, shaking his head at the futility of trying to tell his boss what to do. The man never listened.

Keahi was a fast rider. He loved speed and the feel of the earth flying beneath him, the world whipping past in a hazy rush. But today, he hated every minute of the drive to the mountain compound. Even with the bike screaming along the winding road, it felt sluggishly slow. Every second that ticked by was another eternity in which Marc could hurt Teuila. Keahi couldn't let that happen. He wouldn't let it happen. He remembered his helplessness that long-ago night when his sister Mailani had been attacked, and he urged the bike forwards even faster until it seemed the wheels barely touched the ground.

Finally the gates came into sight. Keahi brought the bike to a screeching halt, wheels spinning dust and gravel. This was the first time he'd been to Gold's compound and he was taken aback at the security. The place was like a fortress with more security measures in place than any prison Keahi had ever seen. The walls were sheer masonry and loomed above him, at least thirty feet high. At the top were lines of wiring, discreet, but Keahi knew they would be loaded with electric voltage. Another layer of protection. It was impenetrable. The question was, did they want to keep people out? Or keep people in?

There were two guards at the perimeter gate, sitting nonchalantly inside their air-conditioned guardhouse. They were both watching a movie on the TV screen. Keahi figured they must not get many security threats. He peered through the glass window and saw the film they were watching was one of his. Blade's Edge, the one that had won him his Oscar. Keahi hoped that would make this easier.

"Excuse me, I need to get in, please. To see Marc Gold."

The two men looked up, blasé and bored. "That your bike? Noisy. Why the rush?"

"I have to see Gold."

"Do you have an appointment?" asked one guard, his eyes flitting back to the movie.

Keahi gritted his teeth through what he hoped was a reassuring smile. "No, but we know each other. We go way back."

"No appointment, no entry." Both guards turned back to the television, oblivious to the fact that the lead star was standing right outside their guardhouse.

Keahi tried a different tactic. "Look, I need to reach my friend. Teuila Mataloa, the artist? She's in there right now, an appointment with Gold, but there's been an emergency and I must speak with her right away. I've been trying to call her cell phone but it's not going through."

One of the guards shrugged and pointed at a box on the table beside him. "It's over here. Policy. Nobody goes in with a cell phone."

Keahi battled a wave of fury. The man had her in his compound and she had no means of calling for help? His voice was loaded with threat. "You open this gate for me, now. I have to get my friend out of there."

The mood changed. The guards stood up and their hands instinctively went to their sides. Keahi knew what that meant. Guns might be illegal in Samoa but it was clear that these two were carrying.

"Look here, man," said the first guard. "This is private property and you don't have an appointment. Get back on your motorbike and ride on out of here."

The second man added his two cents worth. "We don't want any trouble, but if you're here to make some, then we will take the appropriate action."

Keahi wanted so badly to break the glass, grab them both and smash their heads together. But he took a deep breath and strove for a conciliatory air. "There's been a family emergency back home and I need to get my friend out of here and to the airport as quickly as possible. You understand, right?"

The first guard had a bemused look on his face. "Hey, hold up. You look familiar."

The second said, "Yeah, do I know you?"

That's when it clicked for both of them. "You're Keahi Meredith. No way! We were just watching you."

Keahi put on his best movie-star smile. "Yes, that's me. Nice to meet fans all the way out here."

The guards came out of the office, falling over themselves to shake Keahi's hand and ask for selfies. There was much handshaking and use of the 'uso' word as the men exchanged pleasantries. Keahi was about to explode with impatience as his mind raced with pictures of the hundred-and-one things Marc could possibly be doing to Teuila behind the walls. Finally, he said, "So how about it, guys? Can you let me in now? So I can get my friend?"

Immediately their grins fled. "No, sorry. We can't."

"That would get us in a lot of trouble with the boss," explained the second man. "Look, we can call in and leave a message with Mr Gold's assistant that you're here."

"No, don't do that," blurted Keahi. "I don't want him to know I'm here."

"Why not?" asked the first guard, suspicion bringing a frown to his face. "What's going on?"

Keahi didn't care any more about appeasing these men, all he wanted was to find Teuila and keep her safe.

"I didn't want to do this," he muttered as he swung at the guard in front of him, knocking the man to the ground. The crack as his fist met the man's face was sharp in the afternoon sun and so satisfying. It felt good to finally be letting out some of the pent-up worry and tension.

But before he could launch an attack on the second guard, the man had whipped out a taser and zapped him with a juddering hit. Keahi fell to the ground, a jerking mess of pain and confusion.

"What is wrong with you, man?" the first guard shouted as he stumbled to his feet, a hand up to his bleeding nose. He ran over and aimed a vicious kick at Keahi's ribs. "You sucker-punched me!"

"He thinks he's tough," said the second guard. "A badass. Just because he's a movie star he thinks he should be able to get in anywhere and do whatever he wants. Well, I got news for you, Mr Bigtime Badass. We don't take shit from anyone. Not even Hollywood stars."

"Yeah. And your movie sucked, anyway," added the first guard. He barked orders to the other man. "Get the cuffs! We'll lock him up and deliver him to the police station in town. Book him for assault and attempted breaking and entering."

Through a red haze of pain on the ground, Keahi could see the man approach with a pair of handcuffs. "No," he managed to spit out. "You don't understand. I have to help her. She's in danger." He staggered to his feet.

The men laughed. "Whatever. The only person in danger here is you. Turn around." More well-placed blows as they forced Keahi into a chokehold, restrained his hands behind his back and snapped on a pair of handcuffs.

"Take a photo of us now," leered the first guard with the still-bloody nose. He pretended to get into a fight pose, facing Keahi as his friend took pictures with his phone. Picture time done, he slammed his fist into Keahi. One punch to the face and another to his solar plexus. The guard was breathing heavily from exertion but still exultant. "Not such a badass now, are you?"

Keahi swayed on his feet but managed to hold his stance. He tasted blood in his mouth and the sharp stab of pain in his side told him one of his ribs was probably cracked. He took a shallow breath and fought for calmness. "Be reasonable," he said. "Let me go and I can make it worth your while. I have money. Name your price and get me out of these cuffs."

"Oh, so now you're trying to bribe us?" scoffed the guard. He shook his head. "Nah, I'm having too much fun kicking your ass and putting it on social media." He took another swing at Keahi but this time Keahi ducked and swayed easily out of his path. "Hey, stand still, movie boy. Trying to be Mr Tough Guy but you're nothing. Getting your ass kicked here."

The other guard agreed. "Yeah, everyone knows you pretty boys don't do your own stunts. You have someone else taking the punches for you and doing all the fight moves. You only step in for the cameras when it's time to smile, look pretty and kiss the girl."

Keahi gritted his teeth as he shook his head tiredly at the two men. "Y'all have got to stop calling me pretty boy," he muttered. "I've had enough of this."

Keahi shifted into fight mode. As a child of an abusive mother and then a broken foster system, he'd become a teenager who resorted easily to his fists when threatened. He carried a strongbox of pain and anger within him and it had always been the fuel he needed to get through tough times. Violence had been the easy and immediate answer to his problems. When he'd first been recruited into the world of mixed martial arts, he'd been a vicious fury in the ring. He approached every bout in a maelstrom of rage, often requiring attendants to pull him off his opponents long after he'd beaten them to a pulp on the ground. He would emerge from those fights like a man possessed, unaware of his actions and their repercussions. And then he'd met Bruce. A legendary trainer in the MMA, everyone wanted to be coached by him. Everyone wanted to be mentored by him. He'd selected Keahi, and it was only under his tutelage that Keahi had learned there was something better to fight from than rage. Something more powerful and far more deadly. Something that guaranteed a win every time.

Control.

Keahi turned to that discipline now. Locking away the panicked worry for Teuila. Cutting off the ache in his ribs and the throbbing pain in his face. Cauterising even his frustration at being met with obstacles in his path. None of it mattered. He shut it all down and focused. It took only the barest of milliseconds for him to assess the situation. Someone had once asked him what that process looked like and he'd tried to explain, and failed. It was something he couldn't put into words. Time slowed so that everything around him was a step away from being frozen, as if held in action frames. He could anticipate an array of possible moves – from him, from his opponents – and run through all the potential counteractions until he arrived at the one most likely to succeed. Based on factors that had become as familiar to him as breathing, thanks to his many years of training and fighting in the ring. It was rare to meet anyone who could surprise him tactically. It had only happened twice before, and each time his opponent had been a master of their art. One was the semi-finalist he fought, and almost lost to, in the world championship, a young man from Thailand who had been training in Muay Thai since he could walk. The other had been a silver-haired gentleman shuffling with a cane along a quiet street in Honolulu. Bruce, who even at the grand age of seventy-eight had managed to easily disarm Keahi and knock him to the ground. It was how the two had first met, and it was Bruce who had taken Keahi's raw rage and talent and made him into the razor-sharp blade that he was now.

These security guards were no match for him. Even with cuffs on.

With his centre calmed and in control, Keahi acted. A single kick to the face of the first guard and the man went down, a look of shock in his eyes as he fell. The second leapt to push a button, a call for help, and immediately lights started flashing and a siren screamed a breach alert. He was still fumbling with the taser trigger when Keahi headbutted him into oblivion. He dropped with a grunt.

Breathing heavily, Keahi looked around for the keys to the cuffs, wincing at the shriek of the sirens. "Where's the switch to turn that off?" he muttered under his breath. He entered the guardhouse, eyes searching for keys and off-switches.

The TV screen flickered, and a live feed took over from the film that had been playing. It was Marc from somewhere inside the compound.

"What's going on down there?" he said over the security system. Then he saw Keahi. "Ah, it's you." A slow-growing smile. "Let me guess, you've come for the girl. Well, you can't have her. You know why she's here, don't you? She's come because I've made her an offer she can't refuse. And if she does refuse, then I have other plans for her. As your friend so rudely interrupted our conversation last night, I didn't finish my meal. And I'm still hungry."

"Stay away from her," said Keahi. But Marc had switched off his camera and Keahi was left talking to an empty screen.

The thought of Marc hurting Teuila, that darkness coiling around her, consuming her, the thought of losing her – it was too much for Keahi. Something inside him broke. The trauma lashings that bound the coverings on a long-buried vessel finally withered and died, and fire clawed its way out. It was slow. Arduous. And it hurt.

He stumbled outside and fell to his knees at the immensity of it, trembling at the terrible beauty interwoven with destructive monstrosity. He couldn't stop it. He didn't want to, and yet he was filled with dread. What was happening to him? And then he was no longer wondering, because he knew.

Fanua Afi was here. So very, very strong. So very powerful.

Fire erupted from Keahi's hands, tearing through his veins and stampeding through every muscle and fibre. The steel cuffs melted in a fiery hiss. He threw his head back to scream in agony, and fire bled from his eyes and gushed from his mouth. He burned. Every part of him, it burned. It hurt. But also, it was good. Every part of him rejoiced that at last he was who he was meant to be. That finally, he was ready to embrace fire's caress.

Keahi had burned before, long ago. But it was nothing like this. Those explosions had been ignited by another, fire stolen and borrowed from others. This, this was different. From far away, Keahi felt rather than heard a woman's voice. A mother's voice. He'd never heard it before, but he knew it as intimately as he knew himself. It was Fanua. Or maybe it was Tangaloa-lagi? Whatever they were named didn't matter. What mattered is that they welcomed him. They were proud of him. They had missed him and waited so very long for him.

"My son, finally."

There was so much alofa in those three words. She could see all he had been, knew all he had done, the good, the bad and the ugly. And still she loved him. It was a homecoming. An embrace. It was the love of the mother he'd never had. A stark world of difference from she who had betrayed her children's trust time and again. Molten tears stained his cheeks as he slowly rose to his feet, hands outstretched as he gazed with awe at what he had become. No – he corrected himself as Fanua Afi whispered to him – at what he had always been. A snap of his fingers and golden sparks lit up the air. A twist of his hands and ropes of ruby red spun with crimson painted the air before him. He was fire and glory, lava and fury mingled in one. And he was here for the woman he loved.

Keahi ignored the blaring siren. He walked to the walls that towered before him, pulled his arm back and hit with all the power and furious intent he carried inside. The wall blew apart, brick and mortar crumbled, leaving a gaping section. The explosion was deafening, followed by the crackle of electricity as live wires were left dangling. The way was barred no more. Cars raced towards the gates, flashing lights identifying them as security reinforcements. Keahi set off at a run towards the buildings he saw in the distance.

"I'm coming, Teuila."

CHAPTER SEVENTEEN

She was in a part of the house that she hadn't been in on her first visit. A man in a dark suit and tie had said to her that "Mr Gold will see you in his private quarters," as he showed her to an opulent living room. Another attendant had brought refreshments. The tea was served in fine, bone china teacups. The dainty cakes were adorned with spun sugar. There was the soothing sound of a water feature somewhere in the background. It danced along to the classical music track that was playing softly from an unseen sound system. Glass doors opened out to a serene garden, carefully tended rows of flowers that Teuila had never seen in Samoa before. It was peaceful, beautiful and elegant. She should have felt at ease. Instead, Teuila was battling with the prickling sensation of warning. *I shouldn't have come ... I should have just called. I can still leave ...*

Too late. Marc strode in with arms outstretched in welcome.

"Ah, Teuila. It's lovely to see you here."

She smiled and allowed the usual courtesy hug and social kiss of greeting. As always, Marc's handshakes and hugs lingered a bit too long and left Teuila's skin with the crawl of insects. It added to her resolve, though, that she was making the right decision to turn down his job offer.

The pair sat on the luxurious sofas and Teuila leapt right into the first reason for her visit, concern for her friend making her bold. "Have you seen Sione?"

Marc raised an eyebrow in question. "Who?"

"My friend. The lawyer who came to see me at the hotel the other day. You two knew each other?"

A nod. "Ah, yes, the activist. Leader of the rabble that's always causing a disturbance outside. Except on Sundays and public holidays. Thankfully we get a reprieve sometimes."

"He's missing. His wife told police that he never came home the same day we met each other. She's very worried."

Marc gave her a practised look of bland politeness. One she felt sure was refined from years in boardrooms and negotiations. A look that said nothing. "Oh? I'm sure he'll turn up soon. Perhaps the man needed a break from his family."

"No. This is serious, Marc. His wife said she got a call from Sione late that night. A call for help. He was being attacked. Do you know anything about it?"

"Why would I?"

Teuila leapt to her feet, paced the room, agitated. "Because she says Sione was shouting your name. That you were there."

Marc looked affronted, drew himself up on the sofa. "I assure you, I know nothing about whatever happened to this man. His wife is mistaken."

Teuila studied him, wishing she were a mind reader. Marc met her gaze with unflinching intensity, and she could read only truth in his stormy eyes. She knew he was containing his anger. But Sione was her friend and he was missing. So she pushed on. "She was very insistent about the call. And I know you aren't happy about the protest outside and Sione's legal efforts to stop the Sanctuary from going ahead."

Marc laughed. Disbelief. "Therefore I must have done something to the man? Abducted him? Disappeared him? Killed him? This is nonsense, Teuila. Yes, the protestors are a nuisance to my project. And yes, taking their claims to a court of law is a further waste of my precious time. But that's all they have been to me and will be – an annoyance and a waste of time. Your friend and his associates are like pesky mosquitoes. All their rubbish claims have been thrown out of court, the Sanctuary has been given all the permits it needs to open, and nothing can stand in our way now." He paused and there was sadness in his eyes. "I'm hurt you would think this of me. I've been generous and open with you."

A stab of guilt made Teuila back-pedal. "I'm sorry. I have no right to accuse you of anything. I'm just worried for my friend and upset for his family. That's all."

"I accept your apology. Your compassion for those you care about is commendable. I have had some dealings with the local police, made donations. I will reach out to them and see what additional resources they need to help with their investigation into this matter."

Teuila was relieved. "Thank you. He has two small children. They need their dad." All she wanted was to leave. But he had other ideas.

"Now that you're here, we can discuss your new position with Gold Industries. I'm thrilled to welcome you to the Sanctuary team. I can't wait to get you all moved in."

"What?" said Teuila. "Oh, you mean the artist job." She shook her head. "No, I'm not taking it." Realising her abruptness sounded rude, she rushed to add, "I can't. Thank you anyway."

Marc's face darkened and she caught a glimpse of seething fury in his eyes. "I'm disappointed, my dear."

The 'my dear' made her skin crawl and in that moment she knew with a rush of relief that she was making the right decision.

"While I am honoured and flattered by your faith in me with this offer, it wouldn't be right for me to accept it."

"Because of the protestors." Marc's voice was grim.

Teuila corrected him. "No, because of the cultural legacy and spiritual importance of this land. My work draws its creative soul from the earth and champions an environmental protection message. It would be hypocritical of me to work for a man, a project, that stands in opposition to that. So, no, I can't take on your commissions or accept your job offer."

There was a heavy silence. Marc stood and walked slowly to stand at the window, looking out over the valley below. Without turning back to her, he spoke, almost idly. "Do you know why I bid on your artwork that night at the auction?"

"Because you appreciated my art?" said Teuila with a raised eyebrow, daring him to contradict her.

"Oh, you're very talented. There's no doubt about that. Your art is exquisite and I appreciate it very much," said Marc. "But that's not why I sought to acquire it. To acquire you."

Teuila raised her chin. Defiant. "Who said anything about acquiring me?"

Marc laughed. Low and dangerous. "Oh, it was always about acquiring you, Teuila." He turned and walked towards her as she instinctively backed away. "You see, there's something about you. A certain feeling that I get. You're not all that you seem to be."

"What do you mean?" said Teuila, her pulse racing. Her heart was pounding, a drumbeat chant that said, danger, danger, danger …

"I can't quite put my finger on it," said Marc as he studied her, his arms folded across his broad chest, his eyes narrowed. "It's not a scent or your physical attributes – though they are attractive, and in another place, another time, I might have been tempted by a dalliance."

Teuila was reeling now. A dalliance? What the hell! Who does this man think he is?

But Marc was gazing out the window again. "Something happened to me out there, you know."

"Yes, I heard. You went missing, you were lost for a few days in the forest," said Teuila, striving for a return to a normal, sane conversation. One where she didn't feel like a bird cornered in a trap while a hound circled for the kill. "It must have been quite an experience. Although our forests aren't really dangerous. Not like the wilderness in other countries, of course. We have no predators or poisonous creatures."

Marc ignored her attempt to lighten the conversation. "No. Samoa has much worse. Aitu. And I was their victim. Their prisoner. They tortured me. Put me through unutterable abominations. You can't even begin to imagine."

"What are you talking about?" said Teuila. Confused.

"They call themselves aitu. Demons. And what they did to me while they held me captive, it makes me sick to my stomach. But worst of all is the curse they placed on me. The Hunger I can never be rid of. No matter what I do, who I consume, it's always there. Burning me up inside."

Teuila flinched at the violence in his tone. "I don't understand. What happened to you? If you're sick, then you need to get help."

"There's only one thing that helps me," said Marc with quiet finality. He focused on her again and Teuila mentally kicked herself for drawing attention her way. "And today you're going to help me. Yes, I had plans for you, but if you're not interested, then no matter. It's not important. You can still be useful." He started telling Teuila what had happened to him in the forest. He told her of Saumaeafe.

Of nights spent in a haze of pleasure and days touring the intricate network of caves beneath the forest where she and her sisters lived. How he'd been surprised by the light airiness and beauty of the caves, the silken blue waters of their subterranean pools, some warm and soothing, perfect for luxuriating in after a long day. Others icy cold and a blast of refreshment on the skin.

"But it was all sorcery. Trickery. I wasn't in my right mind. They must have drugged me with their filthy potions. And then when they finally released me, a curse."

Teuila decided that Marc was mentally unbalanced. Delusional? She wasn't sure what he was rambling on about but she knew she should leave. "I'm sorry you had that experience. I hope you've sought help for dealing with it. But I have to go. I'm teaching an art class at the centre and I'm already late."

She walked to the door but before she reached it, Marc pushed a button on a remote control pad and the door sealed with a click of finality. She tried the handle and it was locked. Simmering anger burned alongside fear within her. She turned back to her host. "Please open this door."

"Oh, you're not going anywhere," said Marc. "Don't be so rude, Teuila. I haven't even kissed you yet."

Teuila grimaced. The thought of this man kissing her made her feel ill. Marc had pushed her too far and she was done being patient and polite. She quieted her fear and called on her years of Muay Thai training to give her strength. She had sparred with opponents far bigger and stronger than him, and was confident that she could get herself out of this situation. "This is going too far, Marc. I won't let you keep me here against my will. Open this door, now!"

Marc ignored her as he stripped off his shirt and tossed it to the side. Immediately she moved into a fighting stance. The sight of his stamped torso caught her in her tracks. The patterns on his body were unlike any she had ever seen. They pulsed with an eerie light and seemed to move and ripple on his skin. "What's wrong with your tattoos?"

"Oh, they're not tattoos," said Marc. "Meet my Hunger."

And then the patterns coalesced into one sinuous coiling thing. A kind of creature? It rushed from his body like a wave unleashed, and before she could move, before she could turn and run, it was upon her. Wrapping around her with thick tentacles that throbbed with life. They felt clammy and hot against her skin. She opened her mouth to scream but a coil pressed against her face, covering her mouth and nose, muffling her voice, cutting off her air supply. It happened so fast that Teuila barely had time to think. There was a rushing sound in her ears as she fought to breathe, as the constriction around her chest tightened further. From far away she heard Marc laugh, maniacally. "Now, consume her!"

The coils around her began to change colour, from swarming black to pale grey, and then melded into a light dusting of gold. The pressure around Teuila's face and chest eased and she took in a precious gulp of air with a half-sob of relief. The viscous substance seemed to be whispering. It was a low hum, barely discernible. She wasn't sure if it was directed at her. She strained to make sense of the words, and was hit by a rush of images, sensations.

Green grass, sweet and new, still warm from the heat of the sun. A hibiscus bush, scarlet flowers, petals tinged with pink, pollen stamen swaying with happiness in the breeze, reaching out towards a nimble honey bee. A tree. Tall and stately, ringed with ancient years, firmly rooted deep in the black earth. It had seen much come and go, bowing before hurricane winds and standing strong before shuddering earthquakes, a home to many insects and feathered beings. There was familiarity, belonging, comfort and refuge. And above all, there was pulsing, breathing life. In all its complexity and wonder. Teuila smiled at the joy of it. The oneness of it.

But then, as quickly as it had come, it was gone. All of it. Erased in a heartbeat, reduced to a scattering of dust in the wind. Emptiness, desolation. Death and finality. Teuila turned her head to look at the man who stood before her, laughing at her captivity. She knew he had killed them. And it filled her with sadness. But then it got worse. The images, the whispering, the sensations changed. As the Hunger melded with her life force, she could feel it. Talk to it. Listen to it. She knew its heart and the source of its appetite. The images shifted.

This time there was a boy. A small child holding a line of frangipani ula. Interwoven with the fragrant yellow-green of moso'oi. She could clearly see his face, hopeful, as he offered an ula to the rich palagi man. "Faakau sou ula? Please?" She could see the tiredness in his eyes. This was his last few ula and once he'd sold them he could go home – not to a beating and chastising from his aunty and uncle – but to a job well done, some koko and bread for dinner and then bed. But instead of money, instead of even a rude brush-off, the boy got something else. Teuila knew what was happening before the boy did. She saw the horror in his face, the way he tried to run, tripped and fell. She felt the coil of the Hunger as it wrapped around his little body, she saw it glow to gold as it consumed him. She felt him die because she felt the Hunger feed and be sated on his life. Teuila was sick with rage. But it wasn't over.

She saw a woman on the side of the road, walking with a drugged stagger, leering into the fancy limousine as she asked if the rich palagi was looking for a good time. Marc opening the door of the car, inviting the woman inside and driving her to an isolated spot in the bush. And then she, too, was a mere dusting of minute particles. Gone. Consumed. Teuila was assailed by another face, and another. She saw all of Marc's victims, what he had done, who he had killed.

And she saw Sione.

"No!" A muffled sob. She didn't want it to be true. She wanted this to be a terrible nightmare. A mistake. But she knew instinctively that the pulsating force, this Hunger or creature that lived symbiotically inside Marc, spoke true. Her Gift, that which entwined her soul with Fanua, that spoke to the trees, the earth, the water, the wind and rain – somehow it recognised this creature and knew it as one of its own. A friend? No, Teuila closed her eyes, breathing deeply, searching within for the voice that always spoke clearest to her when she was creating her art. It gently corrected her. No, the creature is not a friend. It is family. A manifestation of Fanua. Yes, a darker, more deadly side to her, but was that the fault of Fanua? Or of he who bore the Gift within him?

The Hunger released her. Gently. Lowered her to the ground and receded. She was weak and the room was spinning, but she was alive. She grabbed onto a chair for support, swaying and breathing hard as she looked at Marc. "You killed them. All those people. That little boy. My friend, Sione. You killed them all. How could you?"

Meanwhile Marc was confused. Yes, the Hunger had engulfed Teuila, almost completely, and yes, it was lighting up with that familiar, sated, golden luminescence, but she was still moving, struggling, still breathing. How could this be possible? "Why aren't you dead? What's going on?"

The Hunger returned to the host and Marc felt again the glorious rush of liquid power and joy as it shared with him its harvest. There was no doubting that it had fed on Teuila and indeed, he was surprised by how rich a life force she had. "For such a small woman, you pack a lot of power in you," he said with admiration as he relished the way his entire body lit up, his every cell flooding with a wave of lush, green life. He closed his eyes for a moment, lost in a high of swirling colours and sensations. "Amazing," he murmured. "Your energy has so many layers to it. So many colours and textures. Most people only have one or two, but this? Yours?

I taste the sunshine. I can feel the sand beneath my feet and smell the salt spray in the air. There are flowers, too. So many flowers, I've never seen so many. The jewelled colours. And is that a waterfall? Moonlight. Silver and gold. Birds flying overhead."

Teuila fought a wave of nausea. This man had violated her. He had literally absorbed her emotions and memories. Or was it rather that he'd fed on her Gift? That which nurtured her creativity and spoke to Fanua? She tried to stand tall, but reeled as another wave of dizziness hit her. Whatever he'd done, it had left her sapped. That knowledge fuelled her rage, though. And with that rage came a well of strength.

"You're a parasite," she said. "Feeding off people, off Fanua. And you don't care how you hurt and destroy. All that matters is you."

Marc didn't care about her feelings. He was still trying to make sense of what had happened. This new twist. He walked around in a circle, studying her, trying to untangle the puzzle, muttering to himself. "You're still alive. Unbelievable. We fed on you, we were filled, most assuredly we were filled – and you're still standing. Yes, a bit weak perhaps. But nothing that a few days of rest won't fix, I'm sure." A look of delight in his eyes then. "You are a gift, Teuila. The universe has sent me a most delicious present. The very best kind. The gift that keeps giving."

"What are you talking about?" spat Teuila. Her malaise was scaring her. She was afraid of this man, but more than her fear, she was angry and wanted to fight back. Only she was exhausted. She needed a little time. Delay him! Distract him! Buy herself just a little bit of time.

"I shall keep you," said Marc. A triumphant smile of glee.

"Keep me?" said Teuila. "I'm not your pet. Nobody's keeping me anywhere."

"Come now, I saw your revulsion about those so-called murders. Your distress at the thought of innocents dying. You can prevent more of that happening. You want to be noble and join the saviours of the earth? This is how you can do it."

"You're out of your mind," said Teuila. "I'm walking out of here and reporting you to the police."

Her mention of police didn't even put a dent in his mood. "Oh, you're not going anywhere. There's something special about you. I always sensed it, but this is beyond my wildest dreams. You have what seems to be an endless well of life force inside you. For some reason we can feed and be sated, and yet here you still are. Feisty and as annoying as ever. I will make you a personal addition to my household. And you will feed us regularly." Seeing her look of horror, Marc rushed to add, "Oh, don't worry! There won't be any sexual demands in this. I've decided you're too precious to waste on that sort of activity. You will be treated well. A guest of honour. Only the very best of everything. We can't have you getting sick or too tired to perform your function. And I'll see to it that you have all the art supplies you need so you can keep yourself occupied. You'll have a very nice life here."

And now it was Teuila's turn to laugh. Both at the utter ridiculousness of what Marc was saying, but also because her world wasn't spinning quite so much any more, and the ground had stopped heaving beneath her feet. She was regaining her balance and strength.

"I am no one's prisoner, pet or food source," said Teuila. Each word was spoken with quiet finality. "You won't be keeping me here. Or using me to fuel your insane hunger to possess everything and everyone."

Marc jeered. "And how are you going to stop me? You haven't seen all that I can do."

He threw back his head to laugh and Hunger poured forth, rich and vibrant from its feeding on Teuila. "Watch me now, Teuila."

Black life seamed with gold and red rivulets flowed from his tattoos, encasing first his face and head, then pouring down over his chest, arms and legs until he was armoured in it from head to toe. He reached out with an arm that stretched impossibly long and warped into claws, raking them along the granite floor, the full length of the room. As if a giant digger machine was ripping up the stone, leaving deep gouged marks. "See, Teuila? I'm so much more than you think I am. My power and strength are unstoppable."

"Is that it? I'm supposed to be impressed that you can mess up your fancy house?" It was her turn to laugh. "You have no idea what I've seen and what I've been through, Marc. When you've withstood a goddess, a man's petty tantrum doesn't scare you. There's something you don't know about me. I am so much more than you think."

Teuila walked with calm, slow steps across the room, sidestepping the gouge marks until she stood at the open doors to the veranda. She turned away from him, even though her every sense was screaming a warning not to turn her back on a predator. She gazed out over the valley and breathed in deeply the air that spoke of ageless trees, ancient earth, the burgeoning signs of new life as Fanua constantly sought to renew herself against the onslaughts of man.

"I am the Tangaloa Bone. The keeper of not one, but all three of Tangaloa's gifts. A gift to be used for good. To protect and preserve against all threats. And you, Marc Gold, are a pestilence that threatens Fanua."

Teuila went inside herself to what, as a little girl, she called her happy place. The place she spoke her hopes and wishes to. The place where fears went to die. It was the place that sent tree warriors to stop the rape of a small girl when she was lost and afraid. The place that moved mountains blocking the path of truth seekers. The place that wrapped her in alofa whenever she was sad and lonely. The place that inspired timeless works of art, pieces that spoke to her soul, reminding her of Tangaloa's sacred trust to watch over and keep Fanua well. The place that would not let anyone hurt her.

Teuila spoke to Fanua, and Fanua answered.

There was a low rumble from deep beneath the ground where Marc stood. It started as a distant roar and then grew. It was the churning of a machine, that swelled in sound as it rushed ever closer, up through the dirt, up towards the sunlight. There was a grinding of stone and a clattering of wooden rafters as the house began to shake. The ornate mirror on the wall dislodged from its mooring and fell to the floor with a smash. Shards of glass caught the light. Marc fought for his balance as the ground heaved. "What's happening?" he shouted.

Teuila just stood and watched the distant forest from the deck, her face impassive to what was happening behind her.

A giant fist of rock punched through the floor, upwards, right next to where Marc was standing. A massive crash as wood splintered and brick disintegrated. The rock column went through the ceiling. Then another surge of rock pushed up through the floor, and another and another, until Marc was surrounded by a circle of rock formations, caging him.

It was then that Teuila turned to face him, the man who thought he could contain a daughter of Fanua. Marc barely recognised her. Green vines adorned her like a warrior dress. Her eyes bled white with purpose, and a cloud of butterflies hovered around her, a cloak of moving, fervent colours. In that moment she was the human embodiment of Fanua. Green, gold, pulsing energy and lush life.

In the years since she had first tapped into the Gift within her, Teuila had gently nurtured it, watering it like a little seed that needed a gentle hand to grow. Every time she created a new artwork, she had nourished that seed. Her creations were not ripped from the earth, forced or powered into being against their will. Always she had carried on a conversation with Fanua, one between child and teacher in the early days. And what a teacher Fanua had been. When treated with respect and honour, she was generous and abundant. Unlocking mysteries that others could spend a lifetime researching and still come up short. Revealing to Teuila so many of the sacred intricacies that gave earth its richness and life. When she walked with crickets and bees, they told her their story. When she melded wet clay and water, they whispered to her of their mysteries, inspiring her designs. When she pondered immovable rock and seams of ore, they moved to her suggestion, forming ethereal creations that awed all who looked upon them. Years of being an artist who created in harmony with Fanua had honed and refined Teuila's Gift. Very few Telesā had walked the earth wielding this same kind of oneness with Fanua.

The afternoon sun bathed her in its glow, and for a moment Marc was blinded. He flinched as he peered through the stone bars of his cage. "What are you?"

"A daughter of Fanua," said Teuila. "Here to stop you."

Marc recovered quickly. "You can't stop me. No one can," he shouted at her, his voice a harsh, mangled version of itself as he spoke with Hunger. "You think you can face me? Don't you know who I am? What I am?"

He roared with indignant anger, and six tentacles made of Hunger ripped from his body, one for each of the stone columns that held him captive. He was distorted human and beast, as he tore through the stone barricade, blasting it to smithereens. Chunks of mortar and timber beams caved in on him as the roof gave way before his fury, but he batted it away easily. "You can't hold me," he laughed at Teuila. "See?"

Teuila strolled out onto the lawn, calm and unshaken as she stood in the midst of the ornate flower garden, watching Marc destroy a wing of his house.

"I see you," said Teuila. "I see a man consumed with greed and insane with power. I see a murderer, a killer who preys on the weak and delights in their suffering. And I see why Saumaeafe spurned you."

"She is nothing!" spat Marc. "This is the problem with you savages. You have resources, but you have no idea how to use them. That's why you'll always be stuck as a dirt-poor country."

Teuila raised an eyebrow. "Savages? Really?"

He continued as if she hadn't spoken. "When I am finished with you, I will hunt her and her sisters down one by one, and feast. I will burn down every forest on this island if necessary, until I find them. But first, Teuila, you must be taught a lesson. I made you an offer you can't refuse. You must be taught how to show your gratitude."

He advanced, exiting the shattered house, each step making the ground shake. He towered over her in his Hunger-fuelled transformation, but she did not falter. She carried the might and promise of Fanua within her, and knew how to stand tall in the face of any predator. She slipped her shoes off so she could better feel the earth beneath her feet, anchoring herself to that which was the source of all life. She sent out a call to Fanua, and felt her answer in the sunshine warm on her face, the breeze against her hair, and the prickling blades of grass between her toes. She smiled with the joy of it as Fanua enfolded her in a familiar embrace, and then she caught the whisper of a message – Fanua was angry with Marc.

We are both the creator and the destroyer. We give birth and take life in an endless cycle. That is as it should be. But when there is imbalance? It must be righted.

Teuila knew what she must do.

Before she or Marc could make a move, though, there was a shout from somewhere in the distance. "Teuila!"

They both turned as Keahi came into view, running at full speed.

Teuila gaped at the sight. Keahi was bare-chested, his scars and tattoos clearly visible in the afternoon sun. But it was his hands that captured her gaze. They were fists of flame. And his eyes burned with a red-jewelled fury that she recognised from many years ago.

"Keahi? You flamed? But how?" said Teuila in awed wonder. "I thought it was impossible."

"Sorry it took me a while to get here," said Keahi when he reached her. "I had to get through a few roadblocks on the way. Are you all right?"

Teuila nodded, bemused. "How did you get in? Past security? The wall?"

A wry grin. "About that ... I may have made a bit of a mess.

A couple of patrol cars, a few security guards, never mind." He scanned her up and down, searching for injuries. "I came as soon as I knew. I've got to get you out of here."

Marc interrupted then. He had a broad smile on his face — if you could call it a face, wreathed as it was in the Hunger mask. "How good of you to join us. I'm teaching Teuila a lesson. Showing her who's in charge. Making sure she knows what her life will be like as my eternal guest and Hunger feeder."

Keahi had no time to give in to the overwhelming relief he felt at seeing Teuila. He wanted to take her in his arms and reassure himself that she was all right. Standing there on the grass, with the wind in her hair and the valley in the backdrop, she'd never looked so beautiful to him. So precious. And so vulnerable. He did a quick assessment of the situation, his eyes taking it all in. The destruction to the building, the warped shape that used to be Marc, now a hulking monstrosity that towered several feet above him. He moved to position himself in the line of fire between Marc and Teuila, hands outstretched. "Get back, Teuila. I got this."

She was confused. "What are you doing?"

"I'm here to save you," Keahi didn't take his eyes off Marc as he firmly pushed against Teuila with his back, forcing her several feet away.

"Save me?" said Teuila. "I'm doing just fine …"

Marc roared like a berserker as he picked up a piece of fallen masonry. It must have weighed at least a ton, but he wielded it as easily as a matchstick. He threw it at Keahi with deadly accuracy and Teuila shouted a warning, even as the Hawaiian braced himself, arms of fire crossed against his chest. He met the missile with a half-smile on his face, fists of red fury demolishing the attack, shattering it into a spray of fragments. He laughed. "Is that all you've got, Marc?"

Teuila tried to get Keahi's attention. "Don't taunt him! You don't know what he can do."

Keahi ignored her warning, just motioned her to stay behind him. "Move away, Teuila. Get to where it's safe."

Keahi went on the offensive. It was his turn to launch missiles at Marc, balls of roiling flame that hissed and spat with steam in the humid air as they flew towards their target.

"Fire? Where did you get that from, huh?" said Marc idly. "Did you get a visit from the aitu bitches, too?" He laughed as his neck elongated with frightening speed, his jaw gaping, features morphing into those of a wild boar, but unlike any boar that Teuila had seen. Its mouth opened wide, so wide it was like staring into a chasm of darkness. And just like that, Marc gulped and swallowed the fire balls. Chomping down on them seemed to give him another boost of energy as the seamed veins all over his body burned even brighter, a fierce light that hurt Teuila's eyes. "Ah, that was delicious," he said. "An appetiser for my main course."

It wasn't the outcome Keahi was expecting but he quickly launched another attack, this time spinning a chain of fire around his head like a lasso before sending it to encircle his adversary in a layer of flame, binding his arms to his sides.

Dread grew inside Teuila as the battle unfurled. She wanted to tell Keahi her suspicions but there was no time. And she was certain that he wouldn't listen to her, anyway. "Arrogant ass!" she muttered under her breath as she watched her doubts come true.

Instead of stopping Marc in his tracks, Keahi's coils of fire only fuelled his Hunger. His smile was exultant as he absorbed the fire, as if he savoured it. As if he wanted more.

Teuila knew then that her worries were well-founded. She saw Keahi summon another two bolts of fire and tried to stop him, calling out, "Keahi, don't! Your fire only makes him stronger."

Too late.

It was Keahi's deadly mistake. Marc welcomed the fire, took it in and returned it tenfold, this time sending a cloud of Hunger pellets hurtling towards Keahi, so many he couldn't block them all. Some found their target, sections of his bare skin. Instantly they latched on like red-black leeches, gnawing and burrowing into Keahi's body, sucking his life force as they went. Keahi stumbled and cried out, more in surprise than pain. He tried to burn brighter and harder, and for a short while it seemed he would overcome, as some of the festering pockets of Hunger were incinerated in the blaze. But then Marc sent more hurtling towards him and they eagerly went to work on Keahi, consuming, growing as they dug into his body. If Keahi had been more practised, more experienced with his Gift, if he hadn't just unchained it for the first time in over ten years, perhaps he would have had a better chance of withstanding Marc's

Hunger attack. But as Teuila watched, she saw Keahi stagger and fall to his knees as he tried vainly to claw at his skin, trying to remove the hungry marauders.

"That's enough," she snapped.

With a flick of her hand, she threw up a shield of earth and stone that ran the length of the battlefield before her, a barricade ripped from the ground to shelter them from the storm of Hunger. In the reprieve, she ran to kneel beside Keahi. The heat that radiated from him was searing and she flinched instinctively, feeling the fire singe her eyebrows and bite at the skin on her face. She yanked water from the air and coated her hands in a shimmering glove, sending a silent prayer of thanks to Tangaloa-lagi that Samoa's air was thick with humidity. "Keahi, take my hand. My Gift can help you."

Keahi gave her a look of disbelief. "No. I'll burn you."

"Then turn Fanua Afi off," ordered Teuila. "I'm telling you, my Gift is enough to heal you. To get that stuff out of you."

Keahi shook his head with grim determination, even as his body was wracked with pain, fighting against the consuming Hunger inside him. "No. Without the fire, I can't beat him. I told you, get back! I'm here to save you."

"And I said, I don't need saving!" Teuila was exasperated. She tugged on earth's power with a mere thought and stripped a blanket of dirt and grass from beneath them. It wrapped itself tightly around Keahi like a mantle, and rolled him several times back and forth on the ground, effectively choking and then stilling the flames.

It happened so fast that he had no time to resist, his protests muffled by his face being rolled on the ground. As soon as she was sure the flames were out, Teuila yanked away the blanket and placed her hands on the razed flesh of Keahi's chest, where pellets of Hunger were visible in the gaping, open wounds, wriggling and pushing further into his body as they consumed him. She could hear Marc behind her, battering on the barrier, laughing as his armoured fists smashed holes in the rock. He was enjoying himself, taking his time, like a cat playing with a mouse.

Teuila took a deep breath and blocked out the maniacal laughter and the sounds of destruction, giving herself over to the earth. With the heart and mind of Fanua, she spoke to the Hunger burrowing inside Keahi, called it to come to her. And it answered. The Hunger came, eager and needy, obedient. The worm-like threads poured out of Keahi's wounds, coalescing into a single being. For a brief moment, it stabbed at her with vicious intensity, and she wavered as it sought to feed on her as it had on so many others. But then with a firm nudge of her Gift, she reminded the Hunger who she was and who they both served.

We are family. We are one.

That's all it took. The Hunger ceased its attack and melted away into the soil beneath her feet, returning to Fanua. Keahi was left bleeding and weak, but alive. With his fire out, the lacerations on his body could clearly be seen. His body looked as if he'd been strafed with machine-gun fire, leaving his torso a mangled, pulpy mess.

Teuila's breath caught in her throat at the sight. Rage consumed her and in that moment she lost her calm control. She stood up, ran to the opposite side of the barrier, drawing Marc's attention away from Keahi.

"You want more life, Marc? I'll give you more. I'll give you a feast you can't handle. Choke on this!"

Green vines sprang from the rubble beneath Marc's feet, pushing their way through soil and rock, glass and wood debris. Thick vines like rope wrapped around his legs with whip-like speed, hobbling him, jerking him off his feet so he fell backwards on the ground. Before he could regain his composure, more greenery enveloped him, so that he was bundled thick in swathes of creepers. The man laughed from his prone position. "You know what I do with this?" The Hunger glowed gold and red as it began to feed on the greenery, pulsing light, sparkling and beautiful. As fast as Teuila called more green ropes to wrap around him, the Hunger burned through them, feeding with furious delight and growing in power. Marc broke free and stood, a triumphant smile on his face as he held his arms out towards Teuila. "Thanks for the snack."

But Teuila wasn't finished. She was angry, and with a single high-pitched scream, hands raised up to the sky, she spoke to the wind and it answered. It came rushing through the distant forest, a sound like an approaching freight train or rather, a hundred freight trains. A crashing, roaring wind that swept across the open field and screamed its way towards the remains of the house. Straight at Marc. It swept him off his feet and threw him up into the air, churning him inside a whirlwind tempest of screeching wrath. Teuila smiled with grim delight, as she intensified the screeching winds, shaking him the way an angry dog shakes a helpless kitten in its jaws.

Her satisfaction was short-lived. Marc sent shoots of Hunger from his back and sides, pulsing chains of pure energy that clawed into the ground, raking deep into the soil to the stone below, effectively anchoring him against the whirlwind's pull. He broke free of the wind prison and lowered himself to the ground where he stood tall against the tempest.

"I don't know what you are, Teuila," shouted Marc, raising his voice over the scream of the wind. "But I've changed my mind. I'm not going to keep you, an honoured guest in my home."

Teuila raised her chin defiantly, her hands on her hips, daring him. "My invite is rescinded? I'm crushed."

"I'm going to kill you. I will feast on you until your blood runs dry and your bones turn to dust in the wind. Even if it takes me all day. And I will savour every minute of your suffering and the sweetness of every drop of your life." A sadistic smile. "Like I enjoyed draining Sione. Maybe when I'm done with you, I'll go and visit his wife and children. Can't have her pestering the police with her stories, can we?"

"Stay away from them!" Teuila walked towards her target, summoning boulders from the ornate rock garden at the side of the house, sending them hurtling towards Marc, cannonballs of fury.

He knocked them away and laughed. She wrenched at distant trees with her Gift, breaking them off at the root with a mighty snap and cracking sound in the afternoon sun. The massive trunks flew at her target and again he smashed them away with ease. Teuila was completely immersed in her Gift now, given over to Fanua and all her power. It emanated through her skin, appearing as raised tatau patterns of green and seamed gold, creating a kind of shield that encased her entire body. Her wiry, thick hair shone with a bold light, a halo of black and gold that framed her face. Bands of greenery adorned her body, coiled vines roped the length of her arms and legs. A warrior goddess of Fanua. Yet it seemed that with every missile she launched at Marc, he only grew stronger as he either deflected her attacks or absorbed them, which in turn made him morph even larger and even more triumphant.

Anger and frustration made her careless.

Keahi cried out weakly with a warning from where he lay propped up against the rock barrier. "Teuila! Look out!"

One minute Marc was swatting at tree missiles, the next he had jumped an impossible distance, landing right beside Teuila. The ground shook with the jolt, and she stumbled, off-balance. With a roar of glee, Marc drew one giant fist back, swung and hit her. If she hadn't been shielded by Fanua's energy, the blow would have killed her. Snapped her neck in an instant. As it was, her world fragmented in shards of pain. Darkness threatened. The impact sent her flying through the air towards the forest where she crashed into a clump of trees. Everything blurred. The air was knocked out of her and for a few frantic moments, she couldn't breathe, couldn't move – only lie there in agony. It felt as if every bone in her body was broken. From far away she heard Keahi scream her name. There was fear and panic and worry in his voice. Then Marc's wild shout of jubilation.

"You pitiful creatures! Don't you get it? Nothing can stop me."

Slowly the world stopped spinning and the pain subsided. Teuila tasted blood in her mouth. Warm. Red iron and salt. She groaned, spat, rolled slowly to her side, flinching at the hurt that movement caused. Her vision spun once more and then cleared. She could see. Marc was turning to Keahi.

"Your turn now, movie star," said Marc. He stomped towards the fallen man.

Keahi struggled to stand, one hand clasped to his mangled torso. Marc laughed at his efforts, then reached down and grabbed Keahi in a chokehold. He lifted him easily with one hand and began to squeeze, slowly. Keahi kicked and tried vainly to break Marc's grip on his throat. It was no use.

Teuila tried to shout. "No, let him go!" It came out as a strangled sound that only she could hear. She had to do something, and fast. With her Gift, she reached into the sky above and from the azure blue, she did the impossible. She yanked down a jagged line of lightning that struck Keahi in a crackling blast of light and sound. Marc fell back, releasing his victim. He roared in outrage and shock. And just as she had hoped, Keahi burst into flames, her lightning acting as the trigger for his Gift, just as it had done when they were teenagers. With the fire came renewed strength, and Keahi launched an attack on Marc, barrelling into him with fists and spinning kicks of inferno.

Teuila stood, still hurting, but resolute. She knew Keahi couldn't withstand Marc's fury for long. She called to Fanua for reinforcements. And the god of earth answered.

The ground beneath Marc rumbled and shook as a creature erupted forth. A conglomerate of rock, metal and earth, it flowed into a shape that was vaguely human. Arms like boulders and legs like tree stumps, it was evenly matched in size to Marc and his Hunger armour. Both Keahi and Marc paused in their battle, stunned at the sight of the behemoth.

Before either of them could react, the rock creature moved. It had surprising speed for something so large and unwieldy. It slammed into Marc head first, a cannonball several tons strong. Marc was knocked off his feet. He flew backwards, barrelling into the broken remnants of the house behind him. The stone giant wasn't finished. It ran to where Marc lay in a heap of debris, making thundering sounds with each juddering footstep. It raised both hands up above its head, clenched its joined fists and brought them down like a sledgehammer. The impact made the ground tremble. Marc roared in outraged protest as he lumbered to his feet, swinging wildly at the stone attacker. They met in a collision of juddering sound.

The two monoliths might have continued battling forever. They seemed evenly matched and Teuila could sense their life energies ricocheting off each other. But Fanua wasn't finished with answering her call for help.

First came a swarm of bees. They came from the mountains, an angry and foreboding army that descended upon Marc like a cloud covering the sun. Their buzzing filled his ears. They crawled inside his nose and mouth, finding a way inside his armour of Hunger, biting again and again. Marc staggered about, wildly waving at insects too small to smash with his large fists, momentarily blinded by their attack. Too bewildered and surprised to go on the offensive.

Fanua's snakes followed. Usually the Pacific Boa is reclusive and shy, a creature of the forested mountains and rarely encountered by humans. Unless called by Fanua, that is. They came from the trees, slithering through the long grass, a rustling, hissing flood of reptiles. Blinded by the bees, Marc was an unsuspecting target. Ancient large ones, moving slowly and with quiet intent, heavy with memory. Medium-length snakes, diamond patterns a brilliant beauty in the sunlight, faster moving. Hungry and determined. Small snakes, whip-fast and furious. Eager and joyous in their speedy race across the field. All intent on one thing. Marc Gold. They wrapped around his legs, coiled around his waist, furled down his arms, embraced his neck, rained bites on his face. Not venomous, but painful and profuse. Marc roared as his hands tugged snakes away from his face. His Hunger had no chance to consume and burn through the creatures because all the while, the stone giant battered him with relentless intent.

But Fanua still wasn't finished. A violent earth tremor toppled Marc to his knees and another sudden jerk forced him to the ground, still hitting at insects and kicking at reptiles. Manacles of rock burst through the soil, encasing Marc's arms and legs, pinning him to the earth. As fast as his Hunger tried to eat through the bonds, Fanua remade them. Only when he was bound did the stone giant grind to a halt beside the fallen man. In a heartbeat, the moving automaton collapsed and settled into a mound of stone. There was a sudden eerie quiet.

"Give up now!" Teuila called out to the fallen man. "Don't make us kill you."

She spoke toughly but inside she quailed. Teuila knew she didn't have it in her to end Marc's life. No matter what he'd done, or how many lives he had taken. But how could she allow him to go free, wreaking death and destruction on her people? She braced herself, took a deep breath, and summoned a weapon.

I require a blade. It has to be sharp, so sharp. It has to be strong.

Fanua heard her call. As in every time she fashioned a sculpture, the elements moved to her command, to her desire, melding into that which she imagined.

A speared blade of mingled stone and metal nearly as long as she was tall. At the centre point was a handle of intricate workmanship, embossed with whorls of greenery, flowers and leaves, mingled with butterflies and dragonflies. Because Teuila was an artist at heart even an instrument of death should be beautiful. There was a smooth space for her fingers, with slight indentations for a firm grip, so the blade would not slip when she administered the final blow. The handle tapered to shimmering steel that caught the light. A flash of silver fire, blinding all who looked upon it. Teuila gripped it firmly in one hand, holding it like a lance as she walked to where Marc lay prone on the ground, still writhing and battling against Fanua's manifestations. There was dread in every step. She knew what needed to be done, but every fibre of her being that revelled in the lifegiving force that was Fanua rebelled at the thought of taking a man's life.

Then a quiet, sure voice spoke. "I'll do it." It was Keahi, his fire stilled, standing with one hand bracing himself against the stone wall. He straightened, his face pale with the effort it took, but his voice did not shake. "Let me do this for you. For all of us. Please."

She saw his request for what it was. Not the posturing of an arrogant man, but the compassion and kindness of a friend who cared. They both knew she didn't want to do this.

They both knew he had killed before. Not once, but several times. Those deaths were a heavy weight on him that he would carry always. He did not want that for her.

And so Teuila nodded with relief and held out the spear. "Thank you."

But before Keahi could take the blade, everything changed.

Because she came. Saumaeafe.

Keahi saw her first. A woman who emerged from the distant forest and walked towards them. He knew instantly that she was aitu.

How could she be anything else? The very air around her seemed to shimmer and haze, as if the edges of her were uncertain. Leaving him with the lingering question, is she really real? And then as she drew nearer, that uncertainty fled and was replaced by a combination of cold dread and awed wonder. Awe because she was beautiful. Dread because she was an unmatched predator.

She wore only a simple ie tied at her waist, ivory siapo unmarked by any ink, a bone carving on a piece of sinnet around her neck. Her thick, long, brown hair fell in braided ropes to her waist, bare torso glistening faintly with coconut oil. The purple ti leaf knotted at her biceps and ankles accentuated the sheer strength of her. She was corded muscle and sinew, moving with a grace that seemed impossible for her size. But more powerful than her physical appearance was her mana. Spirit. Aura.

She was aitu.

You could meet this woman in complete darkness and still your every sense would scream a warning of power, fury, vengeance and absolute knowingness. She was the image you always suspected would stare back at you from an uncovered mirror in the night, appearing like a prescient being at your shoulder, just out of reach, causing every hair on the back of your neck to stand up. She was the malevolence that stalked the footsteps of drunken fools who disrespected the sanctity of the village spring, leaving as abruptly as she appeared from the shadows to punish and curse. She was the malicious slap on the face when a girl laughed too loud, dressed too brightly, provoked the aitu too confidently with her blood-red lipstick and taunting red sei. How dare a girl presume to a beauty and place that is not hers to claim? She was the slice of the bone blade across the throat. A stab to the gut, the spilling of entrails on black dirt. A smothered cry of pain, for help. Help that would never come. She was the swift end for men who forced themselves on the vulnerable. The hooded eyes of the lulu, razor claws of retribution. The fanged bite of the boa, peaceful and slumbering unless disturbed, until you trespassed. The slippery malice of the black eel that would stalk your footsteps to your dying day, no matter how far you ran, no matter how many villages you tried to take refuge in. The frenzied attack of the wild pig, tusks rending through flesh, sharp white teeth tearing, never sated until every last drop of blood had been eaten and your bones ground into the dirt of the forest floor.

Keahi and Teuila stared in wonder and fear as she approached them. Instinctively they moved closer to each other. Keahi reached for and found Teuila's hand. She clung to it gratefully. The entire time she had stood against Marc and his Hunger, she had not felt this kind of fear. She tried to quell the beating terror of her heart, reminding herself that Keahi needed her. She threw him a quick glance. His face was pale as he clutched his abdomen, still trying to staunch his wounds. She knew he would do all he could to protect her against whatever this aitu would throw at them, but he had been badly injured. Their safety would ultimately rest on her. She prayed she would be up to the task.

The woman drew nearer, and now Teuila could see she had a half-smile on her face. It only made her look more fearsome, though. Especially in contrast to the stone coldness in her eyes. Her gaze shifted from them to the struggle taking place behind them.

"First, that," she said. Cold finality. A snap of her fingers and it was as if a light switch in Marc had been flicked off. His body went limp, his eyes closed and the pulsing Hunger patterns dimmed. All the rage and power were gone. Just like that.

The ease with which she stilled the force they had been battling struck a cold stab of fear into Teuila. *If she can do that to Marc, what can she do to us? With only a snap of her fingers!* As if he could read her thoughts, Keahi squeezed her hand and gave her a fleeting smile. Reassurance. *I am with you. We stand together.* Teuila found comfort in that. Small comfort, but it was enough.

"You know who I am," Saumaeafe said. It was a statement, not a question. Regal and authoritative.

"Yes," said Keahi. "Saumaeafe." His voice came out strong and clear, but the tremor of his hand in Teuila's told her he was drawing on everything he had to remain standing, trying so hard not to show weakness in front of this being.

Saumaeafe ignored Keahi. She had eyes only for Teuila. "You are ... interesting. Like no other daughter of Fanua I have come across." An idle curiosity on her face now. "So much power and yet so little desire."

Teuila raised her chin, defiant. "I am Teuila. Why have you come?"

Saumaeafe made a grimace of annoyance. She was clearly not

interested in discussing her intentions. Yet. "Don't you want more?"

"What do you mean?" asked Teuila. Confused.

Saumaeafe waved her hand up and down. "You. All this. So much of Fanua's Gift in one person. It's quite ... surprising. And yet, you don't do anything with it."

Teuila was about to tell her that she was an artist, but Saumaeafe continued. "Oh, I know about your drawings and those things you make from rocks and wood and mud." A sneer of distaste. "Pretty trinkets. But what purpose do they serve?"

Teuila was stuck trying to come up with an answer.

Keahi jumped in. "They inspire you. Lift you up from the mundaneness of your daily struggles and remind you of the precious beauty and sacred gift of life, of the earth we live on."

Saumaeafe paused and seemed to be considering his words. She nodded. "I suppose there is some merit in that." Another frown for Teuila. "But still, it is such a waste that is all you have aspired to. Yet I see that Fanua is not displeased with your path." A shrug then. Teuila was merely an oddity to her, a puzzle for an ageless mind. "We all make our choice, after all. Some of us take a more proactive approach to our Gifts."

"Like what you did to Marc?" demanded Teuila.

Saumaeafe raised an eyebrow in question. "What do you imagine I did to him?"

"You cursed him. Turned him into a murderer. A destroyer."

"He was already those things," snapped Saumaeafe. "His hunger to own and control is an overwhelming one. The touch of Fanua does not make people do anything that they don't already want to do inside their hearts. The blood of every life taken is on his hands alone."

"You knew he was killing people?" said Teuila. "You saw him? But you didn't stop him?" She ignored the warning pressure of Keahi's hand on hers.

"We are not one of them. We are aitu. Why should we care what happens to them?" Saumaeafe walked to where Marc lay splayed on the ground. She looked down at the man she had once welcomed to her home. If she felt any hurt or regret, she kept it well-hidden. "Besides, he made his choice. His path is all his own doing. It's unfortunate for him that it has come to this. But not unexpected. My sisters and I, we foresaw it. Prepared for it." She knelt beside Marc, took her bone blade, and before either Teuila or Keahi could react, she slashed his throat. A single swift swipe.

"No!" exclaimed Teuila. She grimaced and turned her face away, unwilling to see the blood gush from his wound. Instead of a spurt of crimson though, it was the gold-black of Hunger. A living thing, it ran from the gaping wound, down Marc's chest and pooled on the ground beside him. There it waited.

"Teuila, look!" said Keahi urgently. She turned her head back reluctantly.

Saumaeafe cupped her hands and scooped up a handful of the golden, pulsing liquid. She muttered words they couldn't understand as she held it up to the sky, a smile on her face. Then she tossed it into the air where it scattered into a thousand droplets, catching the light in an exquisite shower before a gust of wind came from nowhere and took it away. The remainder sank into the grass.

Saumaeafe turned her attention back to Marc. She licked the bone blade and held it against the wound at his throat. The slash healed, the skin sealing at its touch, so that where there had been a fatal wound there was only the smoothness of unmarked flesh and a steady pulse. Marc's eyes fluttered open and he released a loud-rattling breath in the stillness.

"Stand!" ordered Saumaeafe.

Marc complied. He looked at Keahi and Teuila but there was no spark of recognition. He was alive and awake – but in some sort of trance, eyes unseeing.

Saumaeafe began walking back to the forest and Marc followed a few feet behind. Teuila couldn't let them go. Not like that. She slipped her hand from Keahi's and ran after Saumaeafe.

"Wait!" she called out. "Where are you taking him? What will you do with him?"

Saumaeafe paused, a small frown on her face as she regarded the younger woman. "What is it to you? He is a murderer. I have removed the touch of Fanua from him, but he still has the taste for blood. The hunger for power and domination. It's not safe to leave him here. My people will deal with him."

Her tone left no room for argument, and Teuila stepped back.

Saumaeafe was right. Marc had the blood of many on his hands. She would not stand in the way of justice.

Saumaeafe nodded over Teuila's shoulder to where Keahi stood waiting for her. "You must look out for that one."

"Who? Oh, Keahi? No, he's fine. He's my friend." Thinking of the stories about the way Saumaeafe and her sisters usually treated men, Teuila rushed to reassure her. "He's different. A good man."

Saumaeafe did not smile in return. "He is broken inside and sees salvation in you."

"What? You don't know him."

"I don't have to know him. I know you, Teuila, my sister in Fanua. You are a giver of life. Fanua is a spring within you. It's what drew Marc Gold to you, what he hoped to feed on eternally. Beware of giving your body and heart to this man."

Teuila felt a flash of anger at the aitu's words. "Keahi is nothing like Marc. And you don't know us."

Saumaeafe smiled now. It was a smile that chilled Teuila. "There are many ways that a man seeks to control and use a woman. Some call it love. They dress it up in the trappings of protection, safety and support." The curl of Saumaeafe's lip conveyed how she felt about each of those things. "When really they need you. To feed them and their brokenness. Be wary, sister. Of what he wants from you. What he will take from you. And if you ever change your mind about your path, come to find me. We will welcome you. Teach you our ways. Fanua is a gentle, loving mother, but she is also a destroyer who does what she must to protect what is hers."

With those final, enigmatic words, Saumaeafe walked away into the beckoning forest and took Marc Gold with her. No human would ever see him again.

CHAPTER EIGHTEEN

"I'm fine, Reuben," said Keahi. Abrupt and curt. "I said I can walk on my own."

Teuila stood back and watched the exchange, shaking her head at Keahi's stubbornness. He was the worst kind of patient. Rude, impatient and angry at everyone including himself. Even now – with bandages around his torso, face pale and drawn, markings on his arm where he'd pulled out his own IV when he demanded to be released from hospital – he was still behaving like master of the universe.

Teuila gave Reuben a sympathetic smile. When he had showed up at the compound with a full security team, it had felt like an action movie. Reuben's team had secured the site, put the fires out, neutralised Marc's remaining guards, given Keahi first aid and then stretchered him to a waiting van. Keahi hadn't wanted to go to hospital but Reuben had driven straight there anyway, ignoring Keahi's swearing from the back of the van. He had offered to have a member of the security detail drive Teuila back to her hotel, but she refused. She wasn't leaving Keahi's side.

There was usually a long wait at the National Hospital, but Reuben managed to get Keahi into a private room right away and tended to by no fewer than four doctors. Keahi had insisted the doctors examine Teuila first, but thanks to Fanua's healing energy, she was fine. She had then been a silent observer as they carried out tests and X-rays on their celebrity patient. The whole time, Reuben had men stationed outside the room and patrolling the entire block perimeter. It didn't matter that Keahi had told him the threat had been removed, that Marc and his Hunger were no more. Reuben didn't care. There had been an attack on his employer. As far as Reuben was concerned, they were in enemy territory and everyone was a potential threat.

Reuben had viewed Teuila with the same suspicion, until Keahi called him to his bedside and whispered urgently in his ear. A quick recap of the day's happenings. From the chair she had been sitting on in the corner, Teuila had the uncomfortable feeling that they were talking about her, but she was too tired to care. Reuben had given her an inscrutable look and then seemed to accept that she was friend and not foe. That had made the next few hours in the hospital much more bearable. It was as if she and Reuben were partners as they tried to wrangle Keahi into letting the doctors examine him. Once it was established that he had no broken bones or internal injuries, the doctors had ordered IV fluids and rest. The tension in Reuben had eased then. Everything was going to be all right.

Resting in hospital, though, was not something Keahi was willing to accept. He'd ripped out his IV, dragged himself out of bed and insisted they take him back to his island house immediately. So what if it was three o'clock in the morning? So what if the doctors wanted him under observation for twenty-four hours? "I've lived through worse, Reuben. You know I have. This is stupid. Get me out of here! Now."

Which is how they'd ended up here. Teuila had managed to hide her surprise when their destination became clear. The old tree house. It had been years since she and Keahi had taken refuge there, and she'd had her practice sessions with her Gift. She couldn't see much in the dim light, but it was obvious it had been renovated. It wasn't a crumbling, derelict shack any more. It was the same place she remembered — and yet so different. Where once only one ramshackle hut had clung to a majestic tree, three stunning structures now blended into the forest foliage, interlinked with walkways.

She had a hundred questions for Keahi. How long had he been staying here? Why the tree house? Who had carried out all the renovations? But she kept them to herself. This wasn't the time or the place. Especially not when Keahi was being an ass ...

"I got it!" snapped Keahi as he got out of the car, reaching to hold onto the window frame to steady himself. "Back off, Reuben."

Reuben had a stoic look on his face that told her he was well-accustomed to dealing with his fractious employer. He and Teuila watched silently as Keahi slowly made his way to the winding stairs that led up to the main tree house. Every movement looked painful and Teuila could see how tightly clenched his jaw was as he braced himself on the bannister and began to climb the stairs. When he tripped on a step and almost fell, muttering a curse word, Teuila had had enough of being the patient friend on the sidelines.

"Oh, for goodness sake, would you stop being a spoilt baby and let us help you?" she demanded, hands on her hips as she confronted Keahi. "The more you insist on doing things your way, the more risks you take and the bigger the nuisance you are to me and Reuben. So shut up and let Reuben get you inside. You need to lie down. Now."

Keahi opened his mouth to say something back to her, something rough no doubt, but then thought better of it when Teuila glared at him. He shrugged instead. "Whatever," he muttered. But he allowed Reuben to brace him with an arm and walk with him the rest of the way up the stairs.

Teuila caught the ghost of a grin on Reuben's face.

Inside the house, Reuben flicked a few switches, flooding the place with light, and Teuila's breath caught in her chest as she was able to look around. "Oh, wow!"

An open-plan living room greeted them, with a gleaming modern kitchen along one side. The floors were lacquered-black bamboo and teak inlay, the furnishings varying shades of green, here and there a hint of earthy brown. Orchids trailed their elegant white blossoms from the columns, and everywhere potted plants breathed a welcome. Somewhere a hidden fountain soothed the air with the murmuring sound of water rippling over what Teuila imagined to be black river rocks.

"It's beautiful," exclaimed Teuila. She didn't say it but the colour scheme was exactly what she would have chosen for her dream home. "Like living in a forest."

Keahi laughed. A weak cough of a laugh, but a laugh all the same. It gave Teuila hope that he really was okay. "We are in a forest," he said with his usual wry humour.

"You know what I mean," chided Teuila. "All this – the flowers, the plants, the bamboo and the water features? We're indoors but we aren't. This house is alive. I can feel it breathe."

"So you like it?" asked Keahi. He had a grin on his face, even as he leaned against Reuben for support. For the first time in this very long night, he looked happy.

"I love it, said Teuila. "It speaks to my soul."

Suddenly embarrassed by her reaction, she turned away and breathed in the fragrance of a bowl of freshly-picked frangipani. *What an idiot I am. Keahi's injured and here I am babbling about silly things like my soul. Ugh. Shut up, Teuila.* She adopted a no-nonsense tone. "Right, enough checking out the décor. Where shall we get you settled? Reuben could take you to your room so you can lie down."

In answer Keahi hobbled to the nearest couch, a massive cream divan that looked big enough to fit five people, where he collapsed with a grateful sigh. "This is fine. Y'all can go now." He gave his head of security a terse look. "Reuben, you need to make sure your team does a total wipe of that site. Security footage, prints, DNA, everything. I don't want there to be any evidence that Teuila was ever there."

Reuben nodded. "I understand, Sir. They're working on it now. We have a story prepared for the police. One that will cover you, and yes, Miss Teuila also."

"I mean it, Reuben. No one knows she was there. Pay them, silence them, whatever. Do it."

Teuila listened open-mouthed to the exchange. "Excuse me, I don't want anyone doing anything illegal on my behalf. I'm fine to talk to the police. I did nothing wrong today."

Keahi sighed, a sound of irritation. "Teuila, you punched holes through that man's house using stone breakers that you pulled through the ground using your mind. You summoned an earth giant that battered Marc Gold into the dirt. Oh, and let's not forget, you called on an army of snakes, bees and various assorted creatures as back-up crew. You really want the police to know all that? And how are you going to explain that nightmare shit Marc was doing, sucking the life out of people? Got a way to tell the police chief that?"

Teuila winced. "When you put it like that, I guess the answer is no."

"All right, then. So Reuben is gonna do what he does best. And you're going to trust me that I know how to deal with the aftermath of this. Agreed?"

It rankled her, but she knew he was right. She couldn't think of any other options. "Agreed." She turned to the burly security expert who stood there with an impassive face. "Thank you, Reuben. For all your help today. I don't know what I would have done if you hadn't showed up." For a moment, her composure almost slipped. All the tiredness, shock, grief and rage of the last twenty-four hours that she had locked up inside threatened to break free in a dam-burst of emotion. But she remembered who she was. Where she was. And she clenched her fists tightly, restoring her iron grip of control. She gave the two men a smile. "Let me know what the official story is and I'll back it up."

"You won't have to," said Keahi. "Reuben will make sure no one knows you were there."

Teuila hated lies. And she hated taking orders from anyone, especially from Keahi. So what if she suspected that she was in love with him? All the more reason not to trust herself and her emotions around him. Experience had shown her that love made you do dumb things and trust people who shouldn't be trusted.

"Reuben, I want you to take Teuila home on your way. Make sure she gets there safely," ordered Keahi.

"I'm not leaving," said Teuila.

Keahi raised an eyebrow at her from the regal throne of his couch. "Why not?"

"The doctor said you have a concussion. Someone needs to stay with you for the next twenty- four hours at least. Reuben's doing psycho-killer clean-up duty, so that leaves me as your babysitter-nurse," said Teuila. Arms crossed at her chest, showing she meant business.

Reuben had another half-smile on his face as he turned to go.

"I saw that," snapped Keahi at Reuben's receding back. "I don't want to hear a word from you about this at any time, y'hear me, Reuben?" He heaved an aggravated sigh with a petulant look on his face as he leaned back against the couch.

Neither he nor Teuila said anything until they heard the front door click shut and Reuben's footsteps go down the drive. The sound of the car confirmed he was gone. They were alone. Teuila felt an awkwardness, as if perhaps she shouldn't be there.

"So, what a day," she said. She walked into the kitchen, opening cupboards as she looked for glasses. "I'll get us a drink. Some water?"

"I'd prefer something stronger," said Keahi with the ghost of a smile.

She threw him a concerned look, one that asked how serious he was, and if he meant it, how she was going to stand in his way. "Really?"

He shook his head. "No. I'm fine. There's water and soda in the fridge. No alcohol in my houses anywhere. It helps."

Teuila poured them both a glass of the lemonade she found in the refrigerator. "Is it difficult for you?"

He knew she was asking about his addiction, and she could tell that he was debating for a moment how honest to be with her. "You don't have to tell me. I'm sorry for asking."

"No, don't be. I've got nothing to hide. I've always been open about it."

"Yeah, I read about it in that *Vanity Fair* article," confessed Teuila.

Keahi's face lit up in a triumphant smile. "Aha, so you were keeping tabs on me. I knew it."

Teuila flushed. "I was in a doctor's office and the magazine was right there with your picture on the cover. What else was I supposed to do? Of course I had to read it."

"Of course you did," said Keahi, a lazy drawl. Then he dropped the façade and, to Teuila, he looked almost shy. "It's nice to know you cared. I mean, I was watching your career from afar. It's nice to know you kept an eye out for me, too."

Only then did Keahi slump with tiredness, giving Teuila a mournful grin. "I'm sorry about before."

Teuila walked to sit across from him, a sigh of relief as she, too, melted into the comfort of being able to get off her feet. "For what? Being a jerkface or a chauvinistic ass?"

"Neither," said Keahi. "I'm sorry you're stuck here tonight. You must be exhausted."

"I am," she admitted. "It's been a crazy day."

For a moment they shared a look. Of relief, gratitude that they'd both made it through. Marc, the Hunger, using her powers, meeting Suamaeafe. All of it seemed like a different world from the real one they walked in now. A sudden thought occurred to her. "You flamed. Without a trigger. You spoke to Fanua Afi!"

Keahi shook his head slowly, as if just realising it himself. "Yeah, I did. I don't know how. But it happened."

A smile lit up Teuila's face as she grabbed onto this piece of happiness, something that didn't have her speaking of death and suffering and fear. "What did it feel like?"

"Amazing." A slow grin. Clearly he had relished every minute of it.

"I'm glad for you," said Teuila.

"Don't be. I don't deserve it," said Keahi. There was an unreadable look in his eyes, the lightness was gone. Anger and self-loathing made him spit out the words. "I screwed up today. I almost got you killed."

"What are you talking about?" said Teuila. "I'm fine. I was fine the whole way through."

"I came to save you. Protect you from that monster. But I only made things worse." Emotion choked him, made his voice harsh. "When I heard you went up there to see him, I came as fast as I could. The whole way up the mountain I kept seeing it in my mind. Imagining what he was doing to you. I couldn't bear it if anything happened to you."

The raw honesty of his admission stunned her. He really does care? She didn't know what to say, so she said nothing. After a heavy pause, Keahi continued. "You saved me out there. And my showing up only made it harder for you. I'm sorry. I didn't know you could do all that."

"Admittedly, I didn't know I could do all that, either. I mean, I know what Fanua is capable of, and the bond we share is pretty tight. So I knew I had enough power to take him down. I just don't ever get into situations where I need to use my Gift to attack people!" Seeing there was still anger in his eyes, she reached out to reassure him. A soft touch on his arm. "Thank you for coming to help me, though. Marc's hate got nasty-scary there for a bit. It was nice to have a friend by my side."

Her words didn't have the calming effect she had hoped for. "I didn't come there for a friend. That's not how I feel about you. That's not what I want from you."

"It isn't?" said Teuila, hating how stupid she sounded but struggling not to let disappointment show on her face.

It was a precipice moment. She could leap, and to hell with the consequences. Or turn away and never look back. Teuila chose to leap.

"So what do you want?" she asked into the quiet waiting.

"You. All of you." Keahi reached to clasp his fingers through hers. The barest of touches, and yet the feel of his skin against hers sent fire pulsing through her. She breathed in deeply, trying to soothe her pulse, trying to calm her racing heart.

'You, all of you.' What does that even mean? Like, you as in he wants to sleep with me? Or you as in he wants me to be his girlfriend, life partner, date to the Oscars? OMG, Teuila, that's so stupid. You're sounding like an idiotic groupie now. But I need to know. What does 'You, all of you' mean?

"This place, it's incredible," said Teuila, trying desperately to cut through the tension, to shut off the electric wires of emotion that connected them, to look anywhere except at his mouth. Because all she wanted to do in that moment was kiss him. Feel his lips on hers. She stood up. *Space is what I need. Distance. Move away from him.* She looked around the room. "Who are you leasing it from? They did an amazing job of the renovations."

You did not just say that? Why am I trying to strike up a conversation about architecture and interior design?!

He smiled at her as if he knew exactly what she was thinking and feeling. He no longer looked like a beaten-bruised man. No. He was a dangerously beautiful man whose crooked smile spoke of how much he wanted her. How well he knew her. *He's so arrogantly confident, screw him. And yet, I love that about him.*

"It's mine," said Keahi, interrupting her chaotic thoughts. "I bought it a few years back. Had an architect friend come up with the design, then hired a local company to do the work. It's my first time actually staying here, though."

"You bought it?" said Teuila. "Why?" The question sounded inane even to her ears.

"Nostalgia maybe?" said Keahi. And then a grin. "Also, I have an eye for real estate, now. I wanted a Samoan property and remembered my time camping out here. It had potential even then."

"Of course," said Teuila. Kicking herself for the pang of disappointment she felt at his matter-of-fact answer. *What were you* expecting? That he bought it because of rosy memories of the runaway brat he felt sorry for and looked out for sometimes?

He gave her a shrewd glance. Again Teuila had that hollow feeling that he knew more than he was letting on. As if he could see inside her and read all that she was trying so hard to hide from him.

She was painfully aware that she was alone with Keahi in the forest, miles from anything and anyone. When she had offered to stay the night with him, she had only meant in a friend-nurse 'watch so you don't go into a coma' capacity. Hadn't she? Not 'I want to have sex with you in every room of this house and on every surface'. Right? She hadn't meant that at all. She hadn't even been thinking she would be alone in his house with him. With his bedroom somewhere. Presumably with a bed in it. Where he slept. Skin on sheets. Body heat fogging the mirror ever so slightly when he shaved in the mornings. Soaping his body in the shower, rainbow bubbles catching the light as they swirled around his feet … Stop it, Teuila!

She would have taken the stand in a courtroom to swear that she'd only been worried about his possible concussion. Except now, it would be a lie. Except now, her eyes were being drawn to his chest. The ridges of his abdomen that peeked above the bandaging. The tattoos on his forearms that called to her, tempting her to come closer and get a better look. The scar that ran through his eyebrow, giving him a forever-rakish look. Hadn't she always wanted to trace that line with her fingers? Trail a line of kisses from it to his mouth?

"This was a mistake," muttered Teuila. "I should leave."

"Leave?" said Keahi idly. "But who will watch over me and my concussion?" He had that smile, now. The one that teased her and said he knew everything about her and more. The one that drove her crazy and made her alternately mad and weak with wanting.

"You'll be fine," said Teuila. Abrupt and serious. She put her hands behind her back so he wouldn't see how they were trembling.

He frowned. "I don't think so." Suddenly he grimaced, a hand to his head as if in pain. "Aargh!"

"Keahi, what is it?" Teuila leapt up and went to his side, worry clenching her chest in a vice.

He looked up at her, a smile on his face. "Nothing. I just wanted you near me. Come here. Sit with me. Please?"

"You jerk!" Relief made her laugh. It also made her shake her head at him as she carefully sat beside him. "That was cruel. If you weren't injured, I'd knee you in the face right now." Her smile told him she was only teasing. They shared laughter, a moment of perfect union and peace. It felt right. It felt like home.

"But my concussion!" protested Keahi. "It hurts for real now. Just thinking about your deadly kicks."

"I'm sorry," laughed Teuila.

"Sorry doesn't cut it," said Keahi, still mock-serious.

"Oh?" said Teuila. "What will help, then?"

"I dunno ... maybe a kiss will fix it?"

Their eyes met and Teuila's breath caught in her chest. Her heart was beating so fast and so loud that she was certain the sound filled the room. Every piece of her was on fire, high alert, straining, wanting to lean a little closer so she could feel his warmth. And every piece of her fought equally hard to stay away, to keep herself in check. Striving to keep it as light as he was, she flashed him what she hoped was a teasing grin. "Sure. One magic kiss coming up." She leaned forwards and placed the softest of kisses on his forehead. Quick and fleeting, before her body betrayed her. Somewhere the unseen water fountain increased its tempo, the tumble of water over rocks running a bit faster as if to catch up with her heartbeat.

Teuila shifted away from him immediately, creating a careful gap between them on the couch. A brisk no-nonsense tone was required. "There. Better?"

"A little," Keahi conceded. Another wince, this time with a hand to his jaw where purple bruising stained one side of his face. In answer to the question in her eyes he said, "Marc's security goons. A kick with steel cap boots."

She wanted to kill them. White-hot rage threatened to burst free as she imagined breaking every bone in their bodies.

Keahi laughed. A rich, golden sound. It brought her back to the present. "You want to kill them, don't you?"

"How can you tell?"

He nodded at the floor-to-ceiling windows that spanned the room. "Because of that. Out there. One minute it's calm, the next? That!"

She looked, and the swirling torrent of wind outside caught her by surprise. Floorboards creaked as the tree house shuddered. "Oh. Is that me? Sorry."

"Do you always have that effect on the environment when you're angry?"

She was bemused. "No. I usually have much better control than this."

She didn't like the dangerous look in his eyes. "What?" she demanded.

"Nothing. I guess I have that effect on women sometimes ..." His voice trailed off suggestively.

She groaned at his confidence. Keahi would always be arrogant. Even with his ribs bandaged and his face a mass of bruises. "Enough with the smug face. You're not that charming."

"Oh, so I only have that effect on you, then." A lazy drawl of self-satisfaction.

She'd walked right into that trap. She winced.

"So can I get any more of your magic attention?" he asked. He was grinning but his eyes spoke of hunger, need and molten want, all rolled into one. All she wanted to do was take him in her arms. It seemed an eternity since he had embraced her under a moonlit sky, since she had melded into him, seeking, wanting to feel every part of herself at one with him. She ached remembering the touch of his lips on hers, the way he had kissed her, as if nothing else in the world mattered. That's what she wanted right now. It was a physical longing so strong that it hurt. And she felt guilty about wanting him because he was injured and that meant he was vulnerable – didn't it? She snuck a glance at him on the sofa. Vulnerable was not a word that came to mind. He may have had bandages and bruises, but he still emanated the same dark magnetism and predatory confidence. His eyes spoke to her of mingled wrath and desire. He made no attempt to hide it from her. Keahi wanted her. They were alone in his house in the forest, and he was on fire for her.

Teuila stood up abruptly. Space. Air. Distance. Time. That's what I need!

"Can I go and wash up? Shower maybe?" she blurted out. "It's been a crazy long day and night. I'm filthy."

If Keahi was disappointed, he hid it well. "Of course. I should have offered earlier." He indicated a door further down the hall. "Guest bathroom. It should have everything you need."

Halfway to the door, Teuila turned back. Anxious. "You'll be okay while I'm gone, right? You won't try to do anything that could stress your injuries?"

He raised that familiar eyebrow at her. "Like what?"

Teuila felt foolish then. "I don't know. Like go for a night run. Do handstands. Or something. I don't want you collapsing and falling down the stairs or ripping your stitches."

He grinned. "I promise. No running. Or handstands. I will stay right here and wait for you."

Teuila escaped with relief, glad to put some distance between them. But also with a pang of regret that she hadn't taken up his invitation. That she wasn't in his arms right that minute.

Teuila felt much better after the shower. The blasting jets of hot water washed away more than just the sweat and dirt of the day. She stepped out feeling as if the strain and terror of her battle with Marc was a distant memory. Not only that, the shower had given her time to think and to decide. She knew what she wanted to do. No more running away from her feelings. No more trying to hide them. No more lying to herself about what she wanted. She wasn't fourteen any more. She was a grown woman and she was ready to act on the intensity of emotions Keahi sparked in her. She gave herself a pep talk in the mirror.

I don't need commitment or wedding bells. We have history. Friendship. Respect. And buckets of attraction. I can do casual with him. He doesn't need to know that I'm feeling a whole lot more for him than I should.

The pep talk was a failure, though. It didn't matter how hard she tried, Teuila knew that what she felt for Keahi could never be contained in the category #casual. Yes, she wanted him, but she would be honest with him first, go to him on her terms and see if he could meet them.

Keahi had left her a change of clothes outside the door while she was showering. The cotton shirt was huge and she had to roll up the sweat pants several times over so they didn't drag on the floor, but they were clean and that's what mattered.

She walked out still towel-drying her hair. "Thank you for the gear."

He was by the dining table. He'd showered and changed too, and he was shirtless, trying to rewrap the bandage around his torso. And making a mess of it.

"Let me do it," she said. She walked over and took the roll of bandaging off him. He opened his mouth to argue and she gave him a warning glare. "I got it."

He relented then. Stood there with arms half-raised as she expertly rewrapped and secured the bandage. Her hands were gentle on his skin. "There. All done."

"How did you know how to do that?" he asked. Still grouchy about being told what to do. He pulled his shirt back on.

"I watched the nurse when she did it. I have eyes. And I'm a fast learner." She frowned at him. "You sure you should be up and moving around?"

"You forget I'm a MMA fighter. I'm used to worse injuries than this. I'm feeling much better." He moved to the kitchen. "Hungry? Can I make you something?" He was friendly and casual, all traces of the fiery heat from before gone. It was as if he had decided to shift into being a good host and a polite friend. But Teuila wasn't deterred. She'd heard his question loud and clear, and she was ready now with an answer.

She shook her head. "I'm not hungry." A quick glance over at him and then a smile. She had a look in her eyes that he couldn't decipher. "Not for food, anyway."

She walked over to him and he went very, very still. He turned to face her as she came behind the countertop. Waiting. Poised. Hunger held on a very tight, very rigid leash. One touch and it would snap. One move is all it would take.

"Where did you say you needed my magic?" she asked.

The ever-present rustling of wind in the leaves outside seemed to still, holding its breath, as she stared up at him. For one long moment of suspense they held each other captive, poised on the clifftop edge of possibilities.

And then she raised her face to his, closer, closer still, so that they shared an indrawn breath. "Here?" she whispered, and brushed his lips with the very lightest of kisses.

Keahi was lost.

A growl from deep down low as he took her in his arms. Both of them breathless, hungry and honest. No more pretence concealed their desire. No more holding back. No more testing hopefulness. Only raw wanting and needing. He kissed her. She kissed him back with an equal fervour that surprised him. Delighted and thrilled him. Her hands slipped inside his shirt, nails raked his back. The scratch lines of pain lit up skeins of pleasure within him, and he gave a throaty sound of appreciation which changed to a hoarse exclamation as her hands dipped lower, seeking – and finding.

"Teuila, you're killing me."

An impish grin as she whispered against his ear, "I hope not. This is supposed to be helping ..."

It was her turn to cry out when he ripped her shirt open with one abrupt motion, buttons pitter-patter on the wood floor as he bent to take her in his mouth, kissing and teasing. There was a rushing, roaring noise. At first he thought it was inside his head, but then he realised it came from the forest outdoors. An almighty rustle and shake of branches and leaves against the tin roofing. He paused, straightened to give her a questioning look. "Is that telling me to stop?"

"Hell, no!" She grinned and in that moment – half-naked in his kitchen, surrounded by the tattered remnants of her shirt, cheeks flushed and a wild fire in her dark eyes – she'd never been more beautiful to him. "But before we go any further, there's something I have to tell you. I don't just want a one-night stand with you, Keahi. I want more. Or at least, I want us to try for more." She stood before him, tall and resolute in her declaration, but inwardly she was trembling, aghast at her forwardness, fretting over what his reaction would be.

He gazed down into her eyes, meeting their intensity with his own. His voice was ragged and raw as he whispered, "I told you, Teuila, I want you. All of you. You're mine." And then his mouth claimed hers again with a fierce hunger that made the world spin. She could have lost herself in him endlessly but pulled herself away one more time.

"Wait, you have to promise me that you'll take it easy. We shouldn't even be doing this right now. I'm worried about your injuries."

He took her warning as a personal challenge. There was a growl in his throat as he swept her off her feet, carrying her with ease as if she were made of feathers. There was no hint of pain as he strode towards the master bedroom.

"I promise you, Teuila. I will go very slowly. Taking my time, very carefully."

CHAPTER NINETEEN

Teuila woke to the soft blades of sunlight that feathered through the vine-covered window. Parts of her ached, but in a good way, and as she turned to look at the one who slept beside her, the memory of their night together, the reasons for the delicious weariness in her body, made her smile. For a moment she lay there, studying his sleeping form. In rest, with all his defences down, there was no knowing arrogance or daggered edge of violence to him. Only the gentle, generous lover that she now knew him to be. A rush of feeling enveloped her. Both frightening and fearless.

Love.

She loved him. With an unparalleled emotion that she'd never felt before. Not with Kennedy. And not even with the Keahi of ten years ago. She saw it now. That was a young girl's crush, a hero worship for the boy who had seen the darkness inside her and had not turned away. A boy who had helped her find the voice of Fanua within, and given her the strength to unleash it. She had imagined that was love, but she had been wrong, and she gave thanks that Keahi hadn't taken advantage of that.

No. Here, now – this was love. It both frightened and exhilarated her. She didn't know what a future with Keahi in it would look like, and even though that scared her, she wanted to find out. She wanted to love him, unchained by the fears of her past.

Right now, though – she was hungry!

She slipped from the bed, careful not to wake Keahi. A quick visit to the sumptuous bathroom adjoining the master suite where she marvelled at the beauty of the open-air shower. She was tempted to use it, but a growl from her stomach told her it could wait. She found her favourite cereal in the kitchen cupboard. Coco Pops! Munching on a bowl of the guilty pleasure with milk, she continued wandering through the epic tree house, idly exploring.

Several bedrooms, smaller than the one he'd taken her to the night before, but all with the same beautiful décor. Then she opened a door that led to a walkway platform across the forest and connected to a second structure in an adjacent giant tree. She paused to savour the golden sunshine filtering through the trees. The sounds of the forest embraced her, and for a moment she opened herself to the whispering of Fanua. The trill and chatter of birds, the resonant buzz of insects, and far beneath all of it, so deep and quiet that nobody else could hear it but her, the reassuring breathing of Fanua. If she had to describe it in words, Teuila would have said it was a humming sound, very low and very soft. Fanua had music if only you had ears to listen and a Gift to feel it. It always brought her peace and serenity when she heard it, when she felt its resonance within her chest, under the earth and all around in the air and forest. She stood there embraced by her earth god and smiled. Fanua felt Teuila's happiness and she was happy also.

Today was a good day.

Teuila continued to the next tree house and tried the door handle. Unlocked. She opened the door and stepped inside. She expected to see another beautifully decorated guest house, or perhaps a gym. Maybe a security centre where Reuben worked when he was on duty. Any of those would fit with the man to whom she had bared her body and soul the night before.

It was an art studio.

Not just any studio. An almost exact replica of the one she'd spent the last two years working in. It was as if she had stepped across the ocean and back into her studio in New York.

Initially established from a generous grant as part of the Tate award, her studio was a gem – a former warehouse on the top floor of a three-storey building. High ceilings, huge glass windows and doors that opened out to the city. This place had the same feel. Only here, the panelled glass accordion doors folded open to let the forest in. Everything else was the same. The colour scheme, the array of potted plants scattered throughout the room. The steel-topped workbench that ran the length of one wall, the trestle tables in the centre of the room, the massive kiln taking up an entire wall, and the floor-to-ceiling wooden shelves that held her supplies of paint, knives, brushes, paper and more. The rainforest-green comfy sofa in the corner, where she would often crash after an all-nighter of messy work, was here. Exactly the same. Even the mini-fridge in the corner where she kept her emergency Diet Coke for late nights was a bright purple. Just like back in New York. There was a stereo on the shelf, same brand and model as hers at home. Without thinking, Teuila reached out and pushed the 'play' button. It couldn't be, it wouldn't be, would it? It was. The familiar sound of Coldplay filled the room.

Teuila could have tried to call it a massive coincidence, some kind of paradoxical joke the universe was playing on her. Except for the music.

The bowl of cereal slipped from her fingers and fell to the floor. A splatter of milk and chocolate rice specks. The beginnings of a terrifying realisation, paralysing her as it grew, multiplied, took root. "No," she said aloud as she backed up. "No!"

"Teuila?"

She turned. It was him. Standing in the doorway, a pair of thin cotton pants hanging loose and low on his hips, a stark contrast to the intricately muscled tapestry of his upper body, the angry markings of ink. He was beautiful, even with the bandaging and scars.

He was a stranger.

Her voice shook as she pointed to the evidence around them. "What is this, Keahi?"

"I can explain. Come back to the house with me and we can talk. There are things I've been wanting to tell you." The soothing tone of his voice enraged her.

"No!" she shouted. "How did all this get here? Who did this? This studio is an exact replica of mine. But with more. Buckets of my favourite paints that I can't always afford, the DeWalt side strike wood chisel set I've been saving up for, it's all here." She took a deep breath and struggled for calm. "What's going on?"

"I did it. I mean – I had my architect include a studio in the plans."

"Yes," she interrupted, "but why? You're not an artist. Why would you have all this in your house?"

"You're an artist. My memories of this place have you in them. I wanted you to feel at home here."

"But we only just met again ... it's been years since you knew me. Why? How could you know what my studio looked like? All my favourite things, down to the music. How could you know? Tell me!" The last was a shout that echoed throughout the beautiful space.

He went to take her in his arms. Wrong move. She recoiled. "Get away from me!"

She was pale and breathing fast. "Have you been spying on me? Watching me?" A muffled sob as she covered her mouth. "Stalking me?"

His hands dropped to his sides as he fought to hold her gaze. "I can explain," he said softly.

"How long, Keahi?" she demanded. "How long have you been

watching me?" She shook her head, muttering almost to herself. "It all makes sense, now. You showing up to the auction, the documentary, all of it was a set-up from the start. You planned it. All of this." A wild wave at the tree house around them. "What was it? Some sick seduction ploy? An elaborate, no-expenses-spared strategy, to what? Get me in bed with you?" She clenched her fists at her sides, struggled not to break down. "No, that's not it. It was to make sure I'd fall in love with you, wasn't it? So you could own me completely. So there would be no doubt whatsoever that you would get what you wanted."

"No!" A single, agonised sound tore from him. "Teuila, please."

"How long?" she raged at him. "How long have you been watching me? Tell me."

"A long time," he said quietly. "But it's not what you're thinking."

Her mind raced, dredging through every moment they had spent together over the last two weeks, searching, analysing, seeking clues – and finding them. "Since art school!" she spat at him. "That's how you knew about Kennedy, about his family, and his father being a senator." A sick twist in her gut. "Did you spy on us together? Did you know everything about our relationship?"

The look in his eyes answered her question. "You sick creep!" she gasped. She looked around wildly, grabbed for the nearest missile she could reach – a vase of trailing white orchids – and threw it with vicious force. He ducked and it smashed on the wall behind him. "You let me spill my hurt out to you, give you the pitiful pieces of my past, when you already knew the whole sordid story. When you'd already witnessed it for yourself. What, did you have your security detail film it, too? Did you all sit around and laugh when Kennedy rejected me?"

"Of course not. They didn't film things like that," he answered. He was wary now.

"Oh well, thank you for not intruding on my privacy," she spat in disgust. "And thank you for not telling me you already knew my sexual and romantic history before you got what you wanted and had sex with me. Thanks for lying to me."

"Last night wasn't a lie. That was real, that was you and me with no barriers, no walls between us. I know you felt it, too." He took a deep breath. "Teuila, I love you. This isn't how I wanted to tell you how I feel, but I'm putting it all out there now."

She laughed. The panicked edge of hysteria. "Real? Love? How can there be love when there is no honesty, no truth? All of it's been a lie."

Her eyes widened as another thought sparked her awareness. Her rage simmered and calmed, replaced by something far more ominous. "I get it now. You didn't just watch me all these years, did you, Keahi?"

"What do you mean?"

But she didn't answer. Instead she stalked past him and out the door. He followed after her. "Wait! Where are you going?"

Silence.

Back in the main house, she grabbed her handbag from the room, shoved her clothes into it. Sharp, brisk, controlled movements that concealed the raging torrent of rage within. Then she went to the kitchen, searched, turned to him with her hand outstretched. "Keys."

He tried to take her hand in his and she pulled it away. Hissed. "Don't!"

"What are you doing? Where are you going?"

"Somewhere I can get answers," she replied. "Give me the keys to the car."

"I can answer your questions. Stay. We'll talk."

Her eyes flashed with the jagged edge of lightning, and from deep below their feet came a groaning, rending sound of rock as the earth shook. It was only a tremor, but it was enough. A telling sign that Teuila's hold on her emotions was very fragile. "You don't get it, do you? I can't trust you. Everything between us has been a lie. Every word, every feeling, every moment has had its foundation in your secrecy and your lies. If this were a psychological thriller movie, this would be the moment where you chain me up in the cellar and slowly flay pieces of my skin off while you tell me you adore me."

He flinched. "Don't be –"

She interrupted. "What? Don't be stupid? Paranoid? Don't exaggerate? A man I just spent the night with tells me he's had me under surveillance for at least six years, if not longer, stalking me – and you're telling me I should stay and chat?"

It made no sense. Every rational thought told her she should be afraid. Her skin should be crawling at the sight of him. And yet only a few short hours before, she had given her body, mind and soul to him and felt at home with him. Even now, as her stomach heaved and vomit choked in her throat, she longed for him to take her in his arms and hold her, breathe his reassurances against her hair. Lord help her, the man was a monster, and yet still she wanted him. Still she loved him. Still her soul sang at his touch, his kiss, his gaze. The contradiction rocked her, challenged everything she thought she was sure of. About herself. About love. About the world. And that made her angry. Sad. But most of all, she was confused and scared.

She could not trust him. She could not trust herself. And so she steeled her spine against his imploring words and the entreating appeal in his eyes. She took her vulnerability and her trust and her love for this stranger and she bound them into a box with fierce, steely resolve. Ever since childhood, she had been betrayed by people who said they loved her. She had believed he was different. In that moment she hated herself for the foolish weakness of trusting Keahi. Loving him.

A juddering groan tore from the giant tree as branches curved. A rushing wave of sound as greenery and vines unfurled, twisted and dug in through the roof, lancing it and peeling it back as easily as two giant hands, opening the tree house up to the sky. Corrugated iron and nails popped and tore with grating, screeching agony that violated the peace of the forest. Leaves rained down on them as the morning light streamed in. The skies darkened and lightning scissored in violent, silver streaks.

"Teuila!" Keahi said, darting apprehensive glances at the destruction all about them.

There was a burnt smell of cindered rage in the air as she raised her hand, palm outstretched. Blood dripped from her nose. "I said, Give. Me. The. Fucking. Keys."

More than the destruction of the house, more even than the swirling winds and lightning overhead – it was the curse word that convinced him to act. This wasn't the woman he knew. Carefully, he slid open a drawer and took out the keys, handed them over. The elements stilled. Teuila spun on her heel and left the building. Keahi went after her, then stood and watched as she started the truck and reversed with a screeching of tyres, then drove away.

"Sir, are you all right?" It was Reuben. Concern on his face as he ran from the guest house on the other side of the property. "Who's driving the truck?" He had a gun in his hand and the phone out, already dialling the number to alert the other agent at the end of the drive.

"Stand down, Reuben," instructed Keahi. "It's Teuila. I got this."

He raced to the garage to grab his bike, then he was roaring after the truck. Where she went, he would follow.

Always.

In the truck, Teuila finally allowed the tears. She was wracked by sobs of grief. It was a miracle she made it to the centre unscathed. Dimly she was aware of the bike roaring up to park beside the truck, but she ignored it. Ignored him.

He was there beside her. The touch of his arm on hers burned like fire.

"Teuila, please," he said.

It was all starting to fall into place. Pieces of a puzzle that she didn't want to see revealed. She shook his arm off. "Get away from me. I'm going to speak to Beth."

He let go and stepped back. Teuila rapped sharply on the director's door but didn't wait for an answer before throwing it open.

Beth was working at her desk and looked up in surprise, her face lighting up in a smile when she saw who it was, "Oh, Teuila, it's you. And you too, Keahi. Come and sit down. I'll call for some lemonade …"

She came forwards to greet them but Teuila stopped her. "No, thank you. No refreshments. I'm here to ask you a question. I need to know."

"Certainly, anything," said Beth. Her smile was a little strained as she picked up on the tension. "Is everything all right?"

Keahi leapt into the gap. "Teuila, you're wasting your time. Mrs Amani's got work to do. Come on, we can sort this out on our own."

"No!" snapped Teuila, and her tone brooked no argument. To the older woman she said, "Where did the money for my scholarship really come from?"

Whatever question she'd been expecting, this clearly wasn't it. Beth's involuntary flinch as her gaze shifted to Keahi and then back to Teuila told her all she needed. "I knew it," said Teuila with bitter triumph. "It was him, wasn't it?"

Beth took a deep breath. "That scholarship was from an anonymous donor, you know that. It was a condition of the donation. That their identity be kept secret. We have no idea who provided the funding."

"Don't lie to me, Beth. I trusted you. You've always been the person who didn't lie to me, didn't want something from me. You've always had my back. Please, don't lie to me now."

In that moment Keahi knew he had lost her. Because Beth had always been first and foremost an advocate for the children she worked for. She gave him an 'I told you so' look and then nodded simply. "Yes. The scholarship you won only covered the fees. Keahi provided the rest of the money for you to move to New York and take up the programme."

"But how did he know about it?" Accusation. "Did you tell him? Ask him to fund a charity case?"

Keahi wanted the director to shut up now. No more. Don't say any more!

"No," Beth answered. "After he left Samoa, Keahi would call regularly and ask about you. And about the centre. When he heard that you'd been admitted to the academy and we were fundraising for your expenses, he offered to help. On one condition. That his funding be anonymous. I saw no reason to refuse his offer."

"How could you do that? I thought it was some corporate company that funded the scholarship. How could you let him pay for my life?" Teuila's agitation was palpable. A ferocious animal contained in an angry space.

Beth's gentleness turned to steel. "You have an incredible gift. The beauty and power inside you should not be denied. I would have taken money from a drug lord to fund your art, Teuila."

Teuila flinched a little at her intensity but she couldn't deny the sincerity of Beth's words. "I always thought it was Leila who gave me the scholarship."

"She and Daniel were away in New Zealand then, remember? That was her final year of law school and the year Daniel was captain of Manu Samoa, and they went to the World Cup. Although her companies fund the centre, she was out of the loop with the day-to-day details. By the time Leila heard about the fundraising for your art school, Keahi had already taken care of it. Otherwise I'm sure she would have paid for it." A frown. "I'm sorry if that's the reason you did the art exhibition auction for the centre. Because you were under the assumption that Leila and the trust had paid for your schooling?"

"No, of course not. You saved me. This place saved me. That's why I did the art auction. I'm not angry with you, Beth. You're not responsible for this."

"Teuila, you should know that Keahi has been a key financial donor to the centre over the years. His sponsorship of you may have been personal but his commitment to the work here has never been in doubt." Mrs Amani gave each of them a shrewd glance. "Both of you have done immense things for this place. So many young people have been given a second chance here. There are many reasons people support the centre. Now, if you'll excuse me, I'll go and see about that lemonade. Let you two talk."

The door clicked shut and Keahi broke the tense silence first. "Teuila, I can explain."

She didn't answer. Just stood straight-backed and immovable. So he continued. "I know you're angry. You've got every right to be. I should have told you from the start. Come clean. But I didn't want to scare you off, not before I had a chance to …" He ground to a halt. To make you love me, is what he wanted to say. Is what every piece of him was burning to say. He reached out to place his hands on her shoulder, and gently turn her to face him. "Would it help if you hit me again?"

But what he saw stopped his attempt to get through to her with humour and cocky confidence. Teuila's cheeks were wet with tears, and the abject misery in her eyes shattered him. "You're crying?"

She brushed his hands away and pushed past him. "Don't you know how humiliating this is?"

"What do you mean?"

"All this time, I thought I'd made it on my own. I worked so hard at art school, and ever since then I've put my heart and soul into my career. Thinking that was me out there. When all the time, you paid for it all."

"Hey, you've got it wrong," Keahi argued. "I didn't buy you a place at that fancy school. You got that all on your own. Your work got you that scholarship. I just put in the cash to make up the difference so you could make it out there. That's it."

"And here I've been going on about being independent while the whole time you've known I didn't pay my own way. You did. What a fool I must have sounded. No wonder you've been laughing at me."

"That's garbage and you know it," Keahi exploded.

"I need to know. Everything. All of it." Her fury sparked and crackled in the air like a live thing. "What else did you do? What else did you pay for?"

He opened his mouth to answer her but she held up her hand. "No. Not from you. No more poison from your lips. From Reuben. He's your right hand. Am I right to assume he was in charge of it all? The surveillance, everything?"

Keahi's shoulders slumped. He nodded.

"Then I want to talk to him," Teuila snarled. "Alone. Now!" A ferocious wind howled outside and another stream of bright red stained her upper lip.

Instinctively he reached out to try and wipe it away, to soothe the pain he knew she must be feeling to cause such a bleed. But again she jerked away from him, an immediate look of revulsion. "Don't touch me."

He hated seeing her like this. He made a call. "Reuben? I need you here at the centre. Immediately."

He turned back to Teuila. "He's on his way." They were distracted by fearful cries from outside, as children crowded to the windows of their classrooms to gaze out at the raging wind that seemed to have come from nowhere.

"You're scaring them," he said in what he hoped was a soothing tone. In reality, he didn't care about a few frightened children. He wanted her to unleash the rawness inside her so that the pressure on her Gift would ease. So she wouldn't rupture too many blood vessels in one afternoon. No one knew better than he how much it pained her to use her Gift destructively. "You have to calm down."

She wiped away the blood with the sleeve of her shirt. "Don't tell me what to do."

She walked to the opposite end of the room, but he noticed the scream of the wind quieted a little and he breathed more easily. Reuben arrived quickly, and both of them turned to him with relief when he walked in.

"Teuila's going to ask you about your surveillance, about the last ten years," said Keahi. Reuben's eyes widened in understanding and his gaze shifted back and forth between them. "You are to answer every question. Honestly. Full disclosure. Are we clear?"

"Yes, Sir," Reuben replied.

Keahi had faced many opponents – both in the ring and out of it. His life had been in danger several times, including three narrow escapes and bungled special effects ops in his movies. But he had never been as afraid as he was in that moment.

Tell her you love her. Tell her you live and breathe for her. Tell her you're sorry. Tell her all you did, you did for love, for concern. Tell her you want to give her everything, anything, just to make her smile, make her happy, keep her safe. Tell her you want to protect her always. Tell her you will ensure no one ever hurts her again.

His soul cried out with so many unuttered words. But there was cold rage in her eyes when she looked at him. And a hint of fear. The two things he'd never wanted from her. Especially the fear. It shredded his soul to think that she could fear him.

And so he said nothing. Simply turned and walked out, shutting the door quietly behind him, leaving Teuila with Reuben.

Teuila asked. Reuben answered. He told her everything. As Keahi's director of security, he had been the one to oversee it all. Purchasing the apartment block she lived in, contracting the extensive renovations, sourcing a suitable Muay Thai instructor to run free classes in the apartment gym for all the tenants who wanted to participate, monitoring the security cameras in the building. Even running security checks on all her friends.

"All of them?" asked Teuila faintly.

Reuben nodded.

"Did he – did you – ever actively engage with any events or people in my life? Or were you just observers?" She paused, unsure how to phrase her question so it made sense.

"Very rarely," Reuben replied. His face was impassive as he

watched her pace the length of the room. "When Mr Meredith knew you were searching for studio space, he consulted a real estate agent and had us purchase and outfit a suitable building for your purposes. It was then handed over to a third party to offer it to you with the Tate award."

Teuila shut her eyes. Breathe! "So it wasn't the former studio of an artist who wanted to sell because she was moving to Florence?"

"No."

She swore. Kicked at the trash can. Reuben kept his cool.

"When else?" she demanded. "Any other times your team acted … interfered in my life? My final grades. The awards I won. What did he have to do with those?"

"Nothing."

"Are you sure?" Hands on her hips, she confronted him.

"Yes. We – Mr Meredith – had no input into your studies, academic results, project proposals or award applications." A hint of a sardonic smile. "Mr Meredith does not move in art circles so he has no contacts or influence on the awards you participated in. The only art he follows is yours."

Silence.

That answer gave her some small measure of comfort in the swirling abyss of disillusionment. She thought her heart would break if her art recognition had all been a fake. Purchased for her by an obsessed madman.

Reuben spoke. "Several times we provided routine security assistance. Without your knowledge."

"What do you mean?"

He looked thoughtful, as if searching his memory, wanting to make sure he got his facts right. "You were in the habit of working late in the New York studio. Walking back to your apartment alone." His frown conveyed his disapproval. "Twice the agent on duty removed an obvious threat. Random. A potential mugger. Or worse."

She shivered involuntarily at the thought of things she had not known at the time. Hesitated. "I suppose I should thank you for that."

"It was our job."

"Still, I appreciate it."

"You're welcome," he said.

"Was that it?" she asked. "No other times you actively got involved in my life?"

There was a flicker of something in his eyes. Hesitation. Uncertainty. "We didn't get involved any other times." She leapt on the emphasis on 'we'.

"You heard him, Reuben," she said sharply. "Full disclosure. If not you, then who?"

"Mr Meredith. He was provided with weekly reports, and there was no further feedback or interaction with the agents. Except for once. He requested further information. There was an incident in your personal life. An unpleasant confrontation between yourself and a flatmate – a Miss Chantelle. And a male friend of yours," he explained delicately. "The only reason we knew of it was because the argument spilled out into the hall of the building where the CCTV cameras are."

Teuila closed her eyes, mortified by the memory. "I know the day you mean." A deep breath. "So Keahi asked for more details. Then what?"

"He was on location in Australia at the time. Filming for *The Lost Sword*. He flew to New York the next day."

"What did he do?" demanded Teuila. Afraid she already knew the answer.

"He demanded the address of the man in question and paid him a visit. He didn't want any security with him. He wanted to go alone."

Teuila knew Reuben too well to believe it. "And did he? Go alone?"

There was inscrutable resolve in Reuben's eyes. "It's my job to ensure Mr Meredith's safety," he said stiffly. "Even when he's a danger to himself."

Silence.

"I followed Mr Meredith. Discreetly. He assaulted the man. Made it look like a random mugging gone wrong." Catching sight of Teuila's look of horror, he rushed to add, "Oh, he made sure there was no permanent physical damage. Beyond some scarring. Nothing a long hospital stay wouldn't fix. Don't forget Mr Meredith is a professional. Before the movies and the prettified version of his career, Mr Meredith was the very best in his field. He knows exactly how hard to push, how much to hurt someone before it's fatal."

"Is that meant to be comforting?" said Teuila drily. "Because it's not." She knew she should feel awful about what Keahi had done to Kennedy. Guilty. Upset on his behalf. But she didn't. She was a heartless monster. And she didn't care. "So Keahi beat up my ex, presumably because I caught him cheating on me. With my flatmate."

"Yes," Reuben replied. "And he pulled strings, got Ms Chantelle's modelling contract cancelled and her study visa revoked so she had to leave the US immediately."

Well, that answers a few questions.

"Thank you, Reuben, for your honesty," she said quietly.

The man turned to leave and hesitated at the door. "Miss Teuila?"

"Yes?"

"If it makes you feel any better, Mr Meredith funds the education of several other young women – all from the women's refuge centres that he supports with charitable donations, both the one here and three more in Hawaii. His commitment to eradicating violence against women isn't a publicity stunt. It's something he puts more than money into. He's established the Be Strong programme, and when he's not filming and he's back home in Hawaii, he personally volunteers as a self-defence instructor in the free classes that are offered to survivors of domestic violence. And he runs a trust that funds education, too. You're one of many in an extensive scholarship programme."

None of it surprised Teuila. As a former student of Keahi's martial arts training, she knew he was a dedicated teacher. But that wasn't the issue. "He doesn't have surveillance on all those scholarship students, does he, Reuben? He didn't have a rotating team of agents watching over them for years, did he?"

"No."

She turned away and heard the door click as Reuben left the room. And open again as someone entered.

"Teuila?"

It was Keahi. Was it just last night that she had been in his arms, beloved and complete? How was it possible that only a few short hours before, she had contemplated spending the rest of her life with him, and now the very sight of him lacerated her insides?

"Talking to Reuben was … illuminating," she said stiffly. "Thank you for allowing him to speak freely."

"Now it's my turn," said Keahi. He took a deep breath. "I'll start with the tree house. I know it freaked you out seeing the studio like that, and I apologise. But the reason I had it all set up is because I bought the house for you. Had the architect design the renovations with you in mind. The property is in your name. I wanted you to have a place in Samoa to work, create, make your art, feel safe, be happy. You haven't been back to Samoa in a long time and I thought maybe that was because you didn't feel safe here. I thought that if you had your own home to come back to, then you would visit. So I got you the tree house as a gift."

Teuila choked back her shock. "You bought me a house for a gift? Are you out of your mind?"

"I was supposed to give it to you on the night of the auction. Y'know, fly in, say hi and congratulations on your success, make a donation to the centre, and give you the keys. Then fly back out. But the night didn't go as planned." He grimaced.

Teuila didn't live in a world where people gave each other houses as presents and thought nothing of it. The fact that Keahi still believed there was nothing strange about what he had done was simply further evidence that she had been so very wrong about him.

"I was going to tell you. Everything. But it never seemed to be the right time. Jake, my therapist, has been on at me for months to go for full disclosure. I'm sorry you had to find out like this and I know it looks bad. Really bad," he amended. "But you gotta believe me, I didn't have some grand plan that would lead to us, to you, me, to last night. No. Paying for that scholarship was a bright idea I had when Beth told me you'd got into that art school and they were fundraising to pay for you to go. I'd just got paid for my first movie and I wanted to help an old friend. That's all. It felt good to do it. Then, when you moved to New York, I was worried about you. You'd never been out of Samoa before, and New York can be dangerous if you don't know what you're doing. You were only seventeen. I had Reuben and a few back-up guys by that point, so it wasn't a big deal to have a couple of them check on you regularly. I was being a friend, watching out for you."

"No, Keahi," she said coldly. "A friend would have picked up the phone and called me. Come to visit. Showed me around the city. That's what a friend would do."

"I couldn't."

"Why not?" she demanded.

His jaw tightened and there was darkness in his eyes. He didn't answer.

"Why not, Keahi?" She raised her voice. "Why couldn't you call? Stop by and visit on one of your many New York trips? You had time to drop everything and go beat up Kennedy." She caught the flinch in his composure and pushed harder. "Yeah, I know about that. So, why didn't you just call?"

"I couldn't. I was no good for you. I was no good for anybody. You deserved better."

"That's rubbish," snapped Teuila.

"You asked me why I left Samoa the way I did? Why I didn't tell you I was going?" There was raw appeal in his face. Keahi was a man laying down all his defences, and she could sense his fear. Keahi was afraid. Of what? It made her pause, hold back, be silent. He continued, only now he couldn't meet her eyes. "It was the day your mom's boyfriend tried to grab you from the centre. Remember that? And then you ran away, to the tree house?"

She nodded, memories rushing at her. "I attacked you. With trees."

"Yes. We talked and then I brought you back to Mrs Amani here at the centre," said Keahi.

"I know that," said Teuila. Impatient now.

"What you don't know is what came after. I went looking for him. For Toma. I found him at a bar. Drunk. Showing off to everyone about his newfound wealth, the money that Leila was going to pay your mother. When he left the bar, I followed him. It wasn't hard. He was driving drunk. I ran him off the road. His truck flipped and he was pinned underneath. He saw me. Called out to me for help. I lit a match and dropped it. The fuel tank had spilled. There was a fire. I watched him burn to death." Another deep breath. "I killed him."

Teuila reeled, took a step back, felt the seat of a chair press against the backs of her legs, and sank into it. "It was you. Toma died because of you?"

"Yes. Mrs Amani had called Leila and Daniel when she saw me leave after returning you to the centre. She asked them to look out for me. She had her suspicions, I guess, of the twisted, bitter teenager. But by the time they found me, it was too late. What was done was done. They convinced me I had to leave the island. Right away. In case there was an investigation and someone had seen me. They lent me the money for my plane ticket, drove me to the airport. I wanted to say goodbye, but I couldn't. If the police did suspect foul play, I didn't want to put you in a position where you might have to lie for me."

"It was ruled an accident," she said slowly, still in shock, still processing everything he had told her. "Drunk driving."

"Yes. Only three people knew the truth about what really happened. But that's why I stayed away from you. I'm a murderer,

Teuila. I killed a man your mother loved, a man who was important to your family. But I'm not sorry. And I would go back and do it all over again if I had to." A grim smile as he gave her a hopeless shrug. "I'm damaged. A mess. Always have been. Good at hurting people I care about. It was better for you that I stay far away. You'd worked hard, changed your life. You overcame the ugliness of your childhood, turned the darkness into something beautiful with your art. You didn't let the bitterness and evil sour you, make you hate. I watched that from afar and I was so proud of you. Your journey gave me hope. Your success, your art – all of it, that's what helped get me into therapy finally. Oh, I'd seen Jake a few times when it was court-ordered. But never voluntarily. Never stuck with it before."

There was a faraway light in his eyes, and Teuila was uncomfortably reminded of Saumaeafe's warning.

There are many ways that a man seeks to control and use a woman. Some call it love. They dress it up in the trappings of protection, safety, and support ...

But Keahi wasn't finished. "The truth is, I was afraid to tell you. Unsure whether you would hate me for killing him."

Teuila shook her head. "I don't hate you. Toma's death was the best thing that could have happened for me. That, and my mother leaving me alone. It helped me to be free. To live my life and make my own way. I suppose I should thank you for that. You, Leila and Daniel, and Beth. I wish you had told me a lot sooner. Come to me in New York when I was a student at the academy. Said hello at that art show. I could have used a friend. I still don't understand why you did ... all this. And why now? Why reach out to me now?"

"I wasn't planning on it. Feeling this way. Going this far with you. Being here like this. I was only supposed to see you, get you out of my system."

"Is that what last night was? Getting me out of your system?"

"No! The night I saw you at the auction, to be that close to you, it was like coming home. The next day, in the clearing, watching you with those trees, I couldn't breathe. I couldn't think straight. Being with you these last few weeks, you've broken down every wall I've ever put up, you're in my thoughts every minute of the day. I can't function without you. The last ten years apart? You're worried I was a stalker, obsessed with you?" A humourless laugh. "Not true. In the last two weeks, you've become my obsession. I think, breathe, move, eat, train – you. You're in everything I do. Everything. I don't know how to explain it, how to make you understand, how to get you to believe me." He bridged the space between them in one swift movement, took her in his arms. "I'm no poet. Screw words." And then he pulled her to him and kissed her.

Teuila stiffened in his arms and for a brief moment she was frozen in his embrace. She wanted to resist. Knew she should push him away. Knew her skin should revile at his touch. But instead she melted into him, supple and fluid, moulding her frame against his as she gave herself over to the delicious pleasure of his mouth. This was nothing like their first kiss. This time Keahi was a force that couldn't be denied. A rushing wave of desire, heat and electric-tipped edges. He kissed her with everything he had. In his kiss were a thousand floating, coconut candle lights, the breathless hint of a fiery dawn, a box of Coco Pops, the burning longing and unquenchable need of half a lifetime. He kissed her as if he loved her more than life itself. He kissed her as if he were drowning and she were his only lifeline, and for one tangled moment they were in perfect harmony, dancers in a flawless duet of give and take.

And then she turned her face away. "No."

Her voice was ragged and hoarse but Keahi pulled himself away all the same. His breathing sounded loud and hot in the confined space as he fought for control of the raging heat inside him. The wave that pulsed and pounded with Teuila's name. He backed away with clenched fists.

Teuila was flushed and just as out of breath. Her lips swollen, her eyes hazy with the fire that still burned in the space between them. She shut her eyes and took a deep breath before she spoke. "We can't do this."

Keahi agreed. "Yeah, this isn't the time or the place."

She shook her head and backed away. "No, we can't do this. I can't be with you. Trust is important to me and I can't trust you. Not after all you've done. From the day I first met you, you've been my self-appointed guardian."

He protested, "You were a kid with a shitty mom, having to put up with her even shittier boyfriends. You needed help."

"That's true. And I'm grateful for all the help, truly I am. The refuge this place provided, Beth treating me like I was her own daughter, and you, looking out for me. I needed that. I needed to be protected. But I'm not a kid with a shitty mum any more. And I don't need a guardian. Protection can become a prison, Keahi. You've got to let me go."

Keahi could feel her slipping away from him and he didn't know how he would ever get her back. "I love you," he said simply. "Tell me what you want me to do and I'll do it. Anything. Only please, let me love you."

"You've got to let me go." There was finality in her voice. She turned to leave.

"Wait!" he cried out harshly. "I can change. All the security, the surveillance – that's in the past. Back when I thought you needed it. But I see you don't need it any more. We can have a normal relationship."

"No, Keahi. We can't."

"Why not?" he demanded.

"The surveillance was never truly for my benefit. For me. It was for you." She came back to him, reached to touch the side of his face in gentle farewell. "I love you, Keahi. I've always loved you. Even when I was too young to know what love truly was." A wistful smile at the memory. "I think from the day I asked you to show me how to kill someone and you didn't even bat an eye, didn't freak out, didn't hesitate. You just said, 'Yes, show up here tomorrow'.

My vulnerability, my fears, my hate – they didn't repulse you or scare you. You accepted me as I was and then you took the time to teach me what I needed to know to feel safe. I loved you then. And I love you now." She kissed him. A slow, bittersweet, lingering kiss of farewell. "But I can't be part of your penance."

Keahi tightened his embrace, unwilling to let her go because he knew she wouldn't return. "What do you mean?"

"All the charity work, the funding for child-abuse organisations, the students you sponsor?" She shushed him before he could argue. "I'm proud of you and your commitment to helping abuse survivors but I can't help feeling there's something more to it than just an altruistic heart. I look in your eyes and I see emptiness. Guilt. You save us because you're trying to make up for the one you couldn't save. Is it guilt about your sister? Or is it more than that? What else are you hiding? You carry so much shame and anger. Why?"

He let her go then. Dropped his arms to his sides, tightly clenched fists and a determined set to his jaw. He was a man ready to attack. She waited but he had no answers for her.

"Fine. We all have our secrets. I respect that. But I can't be your project, Keahi. I can't be with you when I know every time you look at me, you see a victim. I'm more than that."

"I don't see a victim," argued Keahi.

"If I'm your pet project, the one who gives you light and makes you feel good about yourself, then how is that any different from Marc and what he wanted of me?" she accused.

He was outraged. "I'm nothing like Marc. He wanted to feed on your life force, use your Gift to replenish himself. I love you. I'm nothing like Marc."

"Are you sure about that?" she asked.

And then, she walked away. Out of the room and out of his life.

CHAPTER TWENTY

One year later

Teuila was packing for her trip to Samoa when the alert came up on her phone. The one she had set for any mention of Keahi Meredith. Her guilty pleasure. Yes, she still ached for news of him, any mention of his name, any pictures of him on social media. And for a movie star, there had been frustratingly little news of him for the past twelve months. He was taking a break from acting. For personal reasons, his agent had said in a carefully phrased press statement that Keahi didn't even appear on television to read himself. The speculating had been wild for a few weeks. 'Keahi Meredith is in rehab!' screamed one tabloid. 'Keahi joins a cult!' screamed another. But after weeks of nothing, not even grainy photographs of him buying Doritos in a grocery store or cavorting naked in a drunken orgy ... the interest had waned. Public attention is fickle and feeds on celebrities actually doing things. Mundane things, crazy things, wild things – it doesn't matter, so long as they do something. But Keahi Meredith simply dropped off the planet. He did exactly what the press statement said. He went on a break. And nobody heard anything about him, or saw him anywhere. Which meant that she didn't get to hear of him, see him, or read about him, either.

Oh, every so often, an article would mention one of his movies or revisit one of his old fights in the ring. And then Teuila's phone would ping and her heart would leap into her throat as she looked for news of the man she had walked away from. She'd long ago quit trying to lie to herself about how she felt for him. She'd known the day she left Keahi that she was in love with him. He was everything she'd ever hoped for and everything she knew she would never find with anyone else. Which was exactly why she had left. She didn't regret her decision. The sensible side of her knew she had done the right thing. And so she had thrown herself into her work, determined to 'get over' him. If indeed, such a thing were possible. But she did allow herself this. It always hurt to see any news of him, but she was glad of small mercies. Because his 'taking a break' had meant that she didn't need to see tabloid photos of him with a slew of beautiful, impossibly perfect, celebrity women. She knew he was probably holed up somewhere with that same slew of beautiful, impossibly perfect women, but she was thankful she didn't have to see it.

This alert was different, though. It wasn't a rehash of a recycled news item about Keahi. No, it was happening today. Happening right now? A press conference? In Hawaii? With her heart thudding in her chest, Teuila turned on the TV.

It was the opening of a new community clinic and crisis centre in Hawaii. A reporter was interviewing Keahi.

"So tell us, Mr Meredith, you personally funded this clinic. Why is this project so dear to you?"

He paused, and for a moment Teuila thought she knew what he was going to say. She'd heard him rattle off the PR-approved words before. About 'giving back' and helping the community, vague platitudes that made for good soundbites. He stared down at his clasped hands as if considering his words, weighing them up, and then he looked straight at the camera. Direct and unflinching.

"This clinic is dedicated to the memory of my twin sister Mailani who died when we were seven years old. Our mother died in the same fire which gave me the scars that I've carried ever since. Our mother struggled with drug addiction and was physically abusive and neglectful of her children. She also sold us for sex."

A stunned silence greeted his admission. Even an ocean away in New York, Teuila could feel the shock waves. The reporter gaped at Keahi and tried to think of an appropriate response. But Keahi wasn't done.

"Mailani and I were both sexually abused, and I have carried a weight of guilt, rage and shame for most of my life. I've long held myself responsible for Mailani's death because as her brother, I should have taken better care of her. I should have looked after her and protected her." Tears glistened in his eyes and his grief was a wound that all could see. Teuila wished she could take him in her arms right then and comfort him. Hold him close.

"This clinic will provide free medical care for those who cannot afford it," Keahi said. "The attached crisis centre will be a refuge for others who have endured what my twin and I went through. I want other children to know that they have the right to be safe, to have shelter with people who will advocate for them. For any of you who are watching today, who are living with abuse, living in fear, I want to share with you an important message that took me a long time to learn. Something that a person very dear to me – " his voice broke a little and his hands gripped the sides of the podium tightly. A steadying breath and then he continued " – what a special friend taught me. I didn't want to hear it at the time. But I know the truth of her message now. And that is, you may have been a victim of violence, but you are not broken. You are a survivor. You are strong and your courage and resilience have helped keep you alive. The abuse was not your fault. The shame and guilt is not yours to own, it belongs to the people who hurt you, those who enabled that abuse. It belongs to those who make excuses for abusers and fail to hold them accountable for their actions. I understand now what I didn't before. It's not my fault that Mailani died and that I couldn't save her. I wish I could have protected her. But I was only a little boy, a victim too. I've had to learn to forgive myself. I'm still working on it." A pause and a brief smile. "But I'm not that little boy any more. And today, we open this centre and announce our resolve to support as many other survivors as we possibly can. If Mailani were here today, I think she would be happy with this work and proud to have her name connected with this place."

Keahi went on to talk a little about his journey with therapy. As he explained to the stunned audience, "Mental health is just as important as our physical well-being, perhaps even more. Too often there is an added stigma for male survivors of child sexual abuse, and we stay silent and ashamed. We don't ask for help. We turn to violence, try to control everyone and everything around us. Many of us end up hurting the people we care about, those we love. That's why the crisis centre has a free twenty-four-hour helpline with trained professionals and counsellors available to talk with you."

Keahi then took the reporters on a tour of the centre during which one asked when the Oscar winner would be returning to Hollywood.

Keahi gave the camera an easy shrug and a slow smile, "Who knows? One day maybe. I work full-time here at the centre for now."

Long after the press conference had ended and the crowd had dispersed, Teuila sat beside her half-packed suitcase. The sun set and the shadows in the studio lengthened. She had a soft smile on her face as she thought of Keahi and his announcement. She was proud of him. It sounded as if he had found some measure of peace, at last, and she was happy for him.

Bree's buzz from downstairs interrupted her thoughts. She was bringing pizza over for their last dinner together before Teuila's early flight the next morning. And she wasn't happy.

She stalked into the apartment bearing pizza boxes in front of her like weapons, her purple stiletto heels click-clacking madly on the wooden floor. Her eyes scanned the room, quickly assessing Teuila's unfinished packing. She was triumphant. "I knew it. You don't really want to go. You don't want to do this." She set the boxes down on the table and confronted Teuila, a determined set to her face. It was a look that Teuila knew well. Bree used it on gallery owners and art critics whenever they needed prodding and pushing. For such a tiny woman, Bree could be fiercely imposing, and most people in the art scene either feared her or hated her. Or both. But Teuila knew her best friend well, and she was not worried. She gave her a quick peck on the cheek, hello, and went straight for the pizza.

"It smells so good! Thanks for picking it up for us." She gave Bree a wide-eyed smile as she moved around the kitchen, grabbing napkins, plates and glasses for the wine. "I'm starving. Let's eat."

"You haven't finished packing," said Bree.

"I have plenty of time," said Teuila with her mouth full of cheesy goodness. "Come. Sit."

But Bree was on a mission. Pizza would not get in her way. "I think you haven't finished packing because, deep down inside, you know it's a bad idea to do this. The wrong choice. And as your friend, I can't stand by and let you do it."

Teuila sighed and gave up on enjoying her barbecue chicken slice with extra cheese. "I appreciate your concern. But this is what I want to do. I'm sure of it. And since it's going to be a while until we see each other again, I would really like you to be okay with my decision."

"But why, Teuila?" A wail as Bree slumped into a chair. Dramatic as always. "Just tell me why you need to go there, for a whole year? Why now? To do what? And why can't you tell me where exactly you're going to be there?"

Teuila reached across the table to place a hand on Bree's. She had told her friend about meeting with Saumaeafe and her sisters – but described them only as 'family elders' and stayed deliberately vague about much else. Now she chose her words carefully, not wanting to lie to her friend, but also knowing full well that there was only so much Bree would be able to handle. "This is something I have to do. You know I had a bad childhood, pretty much raised in a shelter from the time I was thirteen. I never knew much about my family. Saumaeafe and her sisters have certain talents and Gifts, similar to mine. A rich heritage of traditional knowledge about how to use those Gifts. This is my chance to learn from them."

Bree shook her head. Disbelieving. "You're an international art legend. I don't think you need to learn from anyone, but especially not some old women living in the forest!"

"That's where you're wrong. I have learned a lot from Western teachers here in America and Europe. But I'm not a white American or European artist. I'm Samoan." Teuila stood and walked to the window to look out over the glittering city lights. "New York can be beautiful, and I have loved my time here. But this isn't my home."

She looked back at Bree. "Besides, this is about so much more than my art. It's about my connection to the land, to Fanua. I can't just take what Fanua gives me, use her inspiration to make art and make money. I have a responsibility to honour. My visit back to Samoa, seeing what Marc was trying to do, what others like him continue trying to do – to the forest, the ocean and the rivers – makes me angry. Saumaeafe and her sisters are guardians of Fanua. As are others …" For a moment she gave in to a pang of sadness at the memory of Sione. "Their Gifts call me home."

There were tears in Bree's eyes as she went to hug Teuila. "Okay. I get it now. It's just that, I'm going to miss you."

Teuila held the rest in her heart. Bree might be the closest friend she had in the world, but she couldn't tell her everything.

I'm going home to the forest. Where I will walk with the aitu and be taught the ways of Fanua. All her ways. Not just the gentle, peaceful, nurturing ways of Fanua. But her other face, too.

CHAPTER TWENTY-ONE

Another year later

Keahi got the invitation in the mail. He received a lot of invitations to charity fundraisers and society events. He chucked most of them in the trash unopened. He was about to do the same with this one but something stopped him. A tingling in his hands as his tattoos lit up with a hint of ruby red. A caress of fire. So he paused, gave the invitation a second glance. Opened the envelope. Read the words on the gilt-edged, cream card.

The University of Hawaii was proud to welcome their prestigious new Artist in Residence, the internationally acclaimed, ground-breaking sculptor and master carver, Teuila Mataloa. She would kick off the year-long residency with an exhibition of her new collection, Aitu. There would be an opening night cocktail event.

Teuila is here. In Hawaii. And she wants to see me?

Keahi was caught by something. Was it joy? Apprehension? Surprise? Or a mixture of all three? It had been two years since he'd last seen her, and yet the very mention of her name gave him butterflies. Butterflies … He smiled at the memories. He didn't know exactly what the invitation meant. But he knew that even stone giants couldn't keep him away.

Keahi found it hard to sit still in the limousine as it drew closer to the Arts Hall. He tugged at his collar. "This tux is choking me," he muttered under his breath.

"Sir?" Reuben glanced at him in the rear-view mirror. "Everything all right?"

"Yeah. Fine."

No, I'm not fine. I'm not sure about this at all. What am I doing? You don't even know if she sent you the invitation. What if she doesn't want you there? What if she's moved on? Married? With kids?

He gritted his teeth as he tried to calm down.

"I took the liberty of compiling a profile on all of the VIP guests in attendance tonight," said Reuben from the front seat. "Purely a precautionary measure, of course. I prepared some files for you to read before we arrive. On key guests. They're beside you on the seat, Sir."

Keahi was irritated. Why did Reuben think he cared about VIP profiles? The last thing he wanted to do was read resumés on every random somebody at this snobbish affair ... Unless, wait! He darted a look at Reuben, a question. But the man had his cardboard face on. The look that said nothing. Keahi picked up the pile of manila folders. The very first one was on Teuila. He saw her name and immediately felt a lightening in his chest. He wanted to smile then, but if Reuben could be a statue, so could he. Quickly he read through the single-page report. It was a brief bio of information you could get off Google, not a security clearance check or anything that had required digging into her privacy. But it told him exactly what he wanted to know. Teuila was still single. No husband, no partner, no children.

"Thank you, Reuben."

"You're most welcome, Sir. I hope it helps with this evening's festivities. And may I be so bold, Sir, as to ask that you convey my regards to Miss Teuila." Reuben was as formal and dry as always.

Keahi had a smile on his face when he exited the car. He patiently endured the screening checks at the entrance, the thermal scan and the pricking of his finger for the instant Covid test result now commonplace at all public gatherings. Once he was cleared, he moved quickly inside.

The first person he recognised upon entering was the Blond agent. Teuila's friend, Bree. Her face lit up when she saw him. "Mr Meredith, what a glorious surprise! How good of you to come." She slipped one arm through his and muttered so only he could hear, "Quick. Walk with me." She drew him to a corner behind a cluster of decorative plants. Once out of sight of the crowd, she dropped his arm as if it burned her and stepped back, arms folded across her chest, eyes narrowed. "So, what are your intentions?"

Keahi was bemused. "Umm, I don't have any."

It must have been a suitable answer because Bree relaxed, losing the aggressive stance. "Good, because last time you turned up to her art show, you dropped a million-dollar bomb. I hope you have something else in mind for tonight."

Bree still looked on edge, her eyes darting back and forth, as she scanned the room over his shoulder.

A sudden thought occurred to him. "Teuila didn't send me that invitation, did she?"

Bree clasped her hands together and stamped her stiletto heels twice. Shaking off nerves perhaps. "No. I did. She doesn't know you're here. I thought it was a good idea at the time, but now you show up looking dangerously delicious, and I'm not so sure that's a good thing."

Keahi raised an eyebrow at her, a low growl of a laugh. "Dangerously delicious? Excuse me? I'm not sure whether to feel offended or appreciated."

"Stop that!" snapped Bree. "Stop sounding all fiery sexy! I don't want you using that on Teuila tonight."

Keahi sighed and decided to stop teasing her. "What do you want from me, Bree? Why did you send me that invitation?"

"The thing is, Teuila's my best friend and you hurt her. Badly.

Inviting you here tonight could be my biggest betrayal of our friendship. Or my greatest act of what Teuila calls fiapoto meddling and she'll thank me forever for it. It's been two years. I did my research. You're not the same person you were when you broke her heart. At least, I don't think you are. And she's changed, too." A frown. "I'm still trying to figure her out. You know she went back to Samoa?"

Keahi shook his head. "No, I didn't know. She asked me to let her go and that meant stopping tracking her movements."

"She went. And not to stay with Mrs Amani. She went into the forest. By herself. No cell phone, no transport, no word from her. For a year. She says it was a family sabbatical. Claims she was with her 'sisters and aunties'. But you and I both know she has no sisters. She totally went off the grid for months, and then I finally get a message from her that she's coming home to New York and can I make sure the studio is ready because she wants to create? She's been back for three months and working like crazy in her studio the whole time. Many of the pieces tonight are from the last few months." A proud smile then. "Her best work so far. Truly powerful."

Keahi mulled over Bree's information dump. Unlike the agent, he knew where Teuila had gone. Or at least he thought he did. She must have taken Saumaeafe up on her offer. To visit them, walk among them and learn from them. What Teuila had done was dangerous. Who willingly went to the aitu? A slice of fear as he considered what might have happened if Saumaeafe had decided not to let Teuila go. "Where is she? I have to see her."

"There." Bree indicated across the hall. "I sent you the invitation, but you're on your own now, buddy. She may still be carrying a torch for you, but just in case it all goes bad tonight? We never spoke." And with that warning, Bree minced away, her heels doing a fast, clicking dance on the marble floor.

But Keahi wasn't paying attention any more. He only had eyes for Teuila.

She held court in the centre of the room, surrounded by admirers and art fans. The first thing he noticed was her hair. She wore it unbound and untamed so it fanned out around her face like a lion's mane, and trailed down her back. She wore a rust-red, off-the-shoulder evening gown that fitted her curves like a glove, and a thigh-high slit revealed she had got a malu tattoo sometime in the last two years. There was a complementary traditional tattoo on her right hand. A choker necklace of corded braid with a single black rock adorned her throat. A slash of red lipstick screamed of defiant beauty and restrained strength. She was fierce. She was beautiful.

Keahi was a man turned to stone at the sight of her. Stone that bled and wept and pulsed with fire. He looked at Teuila as if for the first time. He looked at her like a man long-starved. He looked at her as if he had been waiting for her all his life.

As if she could feel his gaze, sense his presence, Teuila stopped mid-conversation and turned to meet his eyes. There was a jolt of familiarity at the tableau they found themselves in, memories jogged of another night, another art exhibition, another crowd on another island far away. Only this time, instead of greeting him with shocked anger and apprehension, Teuila's face lit up in a smile. She looked happy to see him. It was a smile that unlocked Keahi's frozen state, and he walked towards her. The crowd parted and it seemed they were the only two in the room. They halted a few feet apart, unsure of how to greet each other.

Finally Keahi spoke first. "Welcome to Hawaii."

Teuila looked taken aback at the mundaneness of his greeting. Then, a grin. "Thanks. It's great to see you. You look ... good."

"You're the most beautiful woman I've ever seen," replied Keahi.

She smiled and blushed. "I didn't know you'd be here."

"I got an invitation," said Keahi. "And I remembered what an old friend once told me."

"Yes?"

"She told me that when someone you care about moves to a new place, you should go and see them," said Keahi. "Say hello. Welcome them. Offer to show them around. Ask how you can help them get settled into their new home." Not stalk them from afar like a psycho skin-flayer in the movies was what he didn't say. But he was sure they were both thinking it.

"Your friend sounds like a smart woman."

Keahi gave her a slow grin. "Oh, she is. Smart, funny, strong, a warrior – she can kick my ass, but kind when she wants to be, an amazing artist, and always absolutely stunning. So that's why I'm here, following her advice. Saying hello. Can I show you around, help you get settled in our beautiful Hawaii?"

It was the simplest of questions, yet layered with so much unspoken meaning. A question about new beginnings, fresh starts, and how much they believed in change. Keahi deserved an Oscar in that moment for projecting calm, casual friendliness. Inside, he hardly dared breathe, the ache of hope a gossamer-thin bridge that spanned a chasm of disappointment.

Teuila reached out and took his hand in hers. "I'd like that. Come, let me show you my new art pieces. I think you're going to find some of them familiar."

Teuila looked up at Keahi as they walked together through her exhibition. She didn't know what this was the beginning of, whether this was friendship or something more. She wasn't certain of her feelings around him or if trust could be rebuilt.

All she knew for sure was that her hand in his – felt like home.

The End

ABOUT THE AUTHOR

Lani is a Samoan and NZ Māori writer, editor, journalist and publisher. She was the 2018 ACP Pacific Laureate. When she's not writing, Lani bakes cookies, talks to cats, and is the #BadWatergirl to her Ironman husband. She has five fabulous children who are her creative inspiration and constant headache. You can find more of her writing at http://www.laniwendtyoung.com/

BOOKS BY LANI WENDT YOUNG

NOVELS:

Telesā:

> *The Covenant Keeper*
> *When Water Burns*
> *The Bone Bearer*

plus: *I am Daniel Tahi*

Telesā World:

> *Ocean's Kiss*
> *Fire's Caress*

SHORT STORY COLLECTIONS:

Afakasi Woman